SHADOWLIGHT

SHADOWLIGHT

A NOVEL OF THE KYNDRED

Lynn Viehl

AN ONYX BOOK

ONYX
Published by New American Library, a division of
Penguin Group (USA) Inc., 375 Hudson Street,
New York, New York 10014, USA
Penguin Group (Canada), 90 Eglinton Avenue East, Suite 700, Toronto,
Ontario M4P 2Y3, Canada (a division of Pearson Penguin Canada Inc.)
Penguin Books Ltd., 80 Strand, London WC2R 0RL, England
Penguin Ireland, 25 St. Stephen's Green, Dublin 2,
Ireland (a division of Penguin Books Ltd.)
Penguin Group (Australia), 250 Camberwell Road, Camberwell, Victoria 3124,
Australia (a division of Pearson Australia Group Pty. Ltd.)
Penguin Books India Pvt. Ltd., 11 Community Centre, Panchsheel Park,
New Delhi - 110 017, India
Penguin Group (NZ), 67 Apollo Drive, Rosedale, North Shore 0632,
New Zealand (a division of Pearson New Zealand Ltd.)
Penguin Books (South Africa) (Pty.) Ltd., 24 Sturdee Avenue,
Rosebank, Johannesburg 2196, South Africa

Penguin Books Ltd., Registered Offices:
80 Strand, London WC2R 0RL, England

ISBN-13: 978-1-61523-629-9

PUBLISHER'S NOTE
This is a work of fiction. Names, characters, places, and incidents either are the
product of the author's imagination or are used fictitiously, and any resemblance
to actual persons, living or dead, business establishments, events, or locales is
entirely coincidental.

The publisher does not have any control over and does not assume any
responsibility for author or third-party Web sites or their content.

For Amy Lee,
who sang me through this one

AUTHOR'S NOTE

Savannah, Georgia, is the most beautiful city in the South, a living museum that has existed almost as long as this country has. While I wouldn't change a thing about it, I have altered a few physical and historical details about it to serve the story.

trans·gen·ic (trāns-jĕn'ĭk, trānz-) adj.: Of, relating to, or being an organism whose genome has been altered by the transfer of a gene or genes from another species or breed.[1]

"Scientists will be able to create new transgenic organisms by manipulating genetic material in a totally isolated laboratory environment and then release the transgenic creatures into Earth's many ecosystems."

—Jeremy Rifkin, *The Biotech Century*

---

[1]The American Heritage® Dictionary of the English Language, Fourth Edition. Copyright © 2006 by Houghton Mifflin Company.

PART ONE
Lost

Antiquities Auction, New York
Lot 17—Collection of Olivia Kelly

Sealed Bronze Scroll Case, Carved as Figure of a Goddess, Roman Imperial, Augustan, Late First Century BCE/Early First Century CE, with Intact Papyrus Scroll, Height 7 in., 17.8 cm.

$600,000–900,000 USD

Outer Case Modeling:
The goddess Minerva standing with her weight on her left leg and her head turned to the right, her hands resting at her sides, wearing a chiton and peplos fastened on the right shoulder and falling in staggered folds down her left side, finely detailed face with thin nose, full lips, and narrow eyes with recessed pupils, her centrally parted straight hair woven into a crown of feathers and arrows.

Papyrus scroll, heavily inscribed in Latin, translation:

Gaius Maelius Tanicus to Nero Claudius Drusus, his friend and brother by the sword, many warm greetings.

Before all the gods I pray for your good health and safety, and send many salutations to your mother and her children and your family. Forgive the strange route by which I send this message, but I dare not place my trust in our couriers. Know that I arrived in camp in good health twenty-four days before the calends of October, and assumed my post as prefect.

I have discovered that the one in service to our enemies the Cherusci has been encamped here since the thaw, although at the time of writing this letter I have yet not confirmed his identity. The evidence of copied scrolls, diverted marches, and assassinations among the ranks persuade me to believe him to be one of the couriers sent up from Judea last winter. Several have left the camp since my arrival, some hastily, all traveling to the southern camps. Among them, I am convinced, hides the traitor.

Tomorrow I shall journey to the forests near the mountains, where the Cherusci have been in skirmish with our border legions. Many have been captured alive, and from them I will obtain his name. Whenever I find a trustworthy messenger I will write to you of my progress and, I pray soon, too, my success.

Remember me in your prayers, brother, as you are ever in mine.

(Seal of) Tanicus

September 29, 2008

Inside the cool, quiet offices at Finley's Auction House, the staff attended to the countless tasks involved with the acquisition, inspection, and sale of rare and costly antiquities from all over the world. Patrons compared the atmosphere to that found within the walls of a place of worship, where voices rarely rose above a murmur outside the spectacle of the services provided once each week. Others didn't care for the silence and shadows, or the dusty relics that arrived packed in straw and swaddling linens. The staff's reverence for their work was obvious, but some felt it excessive—as if the precious things they handled were sacrosanct symbols of some private, pagan religion.

"I'm sorry, sir," Harris Finley, the proprietor of the auction house, said over the phone as he reviewed the listing for the Minerva scroll case. "But bidding for that item is now closed." He listened. "No, sir, I don't have any information on the bidder. He purchased it through a third party and paid for the item with a certified bank check. May I ask—" He stopped, winced, and held the receiver away from his ear before he hung up the phone. "What an ass."

"Is there a problem, Mr. Finley?" Jean, his young assistant, asked.

"Late bidders inevitably have bad tempers, my dear, especially when they're very rich men unaccustomed to having their demands refused." He regarded the listing once more. "This time, however, he'll simply have to accept defeat gracefully."

Jean frowned. "Who do you mean, sir?"

"Mr. Genaro." Finley gave her a rueful glance. "It seems he never received a copy of last week's preview."

Now his assistant winced. "Oh, no. I thought I had e-mailed everyone."

"Not to worry. These things happen, my dear, even to the illustrious Mr. Genaro." Finley chuckled and patted her shoulder. "A two-thousand-year-old intact Roman scroll is a treasure worth having, certainly, but it isn't as if losing it to another bidder will destroy his life."

September 29, 1998

Minerva woke up early to watch the sunrise, and went out to sit on the front balcony of Sapphire House while the city's lights still glowed soft gold against the dark silk duvet night had pulled over Savannah. She often welcomed the day there, much to the annoyance of the neighbors, who believed that the only women who rose from their beds before noon did so simply to cook and clean for those who didn't.

Seeing the sunrise today was important to Min. She wanted the right beginning to this special day: the first day of her new job, the first step toward a secure future.

"I got it, Daddy," she said, lifting her coffee cup to toast the fountain in the square below. "I start today. Wish me luck."

Darien surely would have, if he'd still lived. Three months and six days ago, while sitting in the square and dozing in the sun, Min's father had gone home, his worn-out heart coming to a final, peaceful stop. She'd walked out to wake him for dinner and found him still and silent, his dark eyes closed and his white hair breeze-ruffled, a copy of *A Connecticut Yankee in King Arthur's Court* still in his hands. As if even Death himself couldn't part Darien from his beloved Twain.

For a long time afterward, the weight of Min's grief had flattened everything to gray facades of what had been. But gradually the terrible pain had eased a little, and she began to see Darien's death as more than her own loss. Her father had died as he had lived: quietly, with dignity, in a place he loved. Every time Min walked through the square now, she could almost feel him there, watching her and smiling a little.

It's all yours now, baby girl, he'd written in the letter that his lawyer had handed her after the funeral, along with Darien's entire estate. *Keep it safe and watch your back.*

That Min's father had left her one of the oldest and most historically important private homes in Savannah had outraged plenty but surprised few. Over the last forty years Darien had flatly rejected hundreds of generous offers to buy Sapphire House, and not even the richest of the museum people—the righteous snoots, he'd called them—could convince him to sell his home into their covetous hands.

"That girl's only twenty-three," the president of the Savannah Ladies Historic Society had mourned aloud after her fourth mimosa at their most recent monthly luncheon meeting. "I've got purses that are older."

"I don't know what Darien was thinking." Her vice president held a delicate lace hankie, with which she dabbed at the sweaty space between her large nostrils and thin upper lip. "She's never been one of us. She'll sell it to the first Yankee who comes along with a carpetbag full of cash and parking lot plans—I guarantee."

The ladies really couldn't be blamed for their assumptions. No one knew much about Min, except that Darien had kept her out of society and had sent her overseas to be educated. They had never bothered to get to know her, either, or they would have understood how much she loved Old Blue, and what she was prepared to do to take care of it.

She looked past the dew-beaded dark green iron leaves of the narrow balcony side railing to see the first rays of the sun gild the thick, bubbled glass panes in the third-story windows. The old oak shutters by the Rose Bedroom needed replacing; she'd have to talk to Thomas Gaudette about it the next time she saw him at church. He worked as a general handyman around the square, and had the know-how to find or make two new shutters to match the other forty-six—without charging her an arm and a leg in the process.

Her father's weathered face smiled at her from the shadows of her memory. *That's my girl.*

She blew a little steam off the top of her cup before sipping the sweet, milky coffee she'd brewed for herself. Geraldine's was better, but after her father had passed away the old cook had finally retired to live out her golden years on Tybee Island with her husband, six children, and twenty-seven grandchildren. Min was happy for her, but she missed her terribly.

Soon she'd have to go inside and start getting ready for work. She'd chosen what she planned to wear the night before—her favorite navy blue suit with a tailored snow-white blouse—but she wanted an hour to do her hair and makeup.

You can't run do everything, sugar, Geraldine had said whenever Min had complained about how long it took to brush and braid her long hair. *Young lady like you have to take her time, so she always look as cool and sweet as a peach.*

With time Min had tamed her impatience, and now carefully planned and prepared for everything. Last week she'd ruthlessly traded the long, girlish length of her hair for a more stylish, asymmetrical wedge cut. She still hadn't grown used to the weightless feel of it, but the more sophisticated look pleased her.

After a lengthy consultation at the salon where she'd had her hair cut, Min had also had her eyebrows shaped and her fingernails tipped with a classic, modest French manicure. She'd tested dozens of fragrances before deciding on a cool, subdued perfume that reminded her of the air after it rained. Her final splurge—and the most costly—had been a pair of decadently comfortable Italian leather pumps to match her suit.

Despite the care she took with them, Min had no illusions about her looks. A kind eye would call her black hair and full-lipped mouth striking, but her pallid skin had saddled her with the nickname Snowy as far back as grade school. Her narrow nose, angular cheekbones, and strong jawline kept her from being regarded as being pretty as a Disney princess, which she occasionally resented. Strangers regularly mistook her for a woman ten years older than she was, which she sometimes used to her advantage.

Her eyes were what annoyed her most. Beautiful eyes were a lifelong asset, and what girl didn't want big blue eyes? Hers were large and clear enough, but the blue of her irises was so light they looked more like clouds than sky. Because they were so light, looking into them seemed to unsettle most folks. At least her boyfriend didn't seem to mind them.

"You're probably part alien, sweetie," Tag would tease, and then kiss her frown away. "But I'm up for a close encounter with you anytime."

Min knew her differences could be useful. Among the many things she'd learned while going to school in Europe was that she should treasure her individuality and emphasize rather than attempt to disguise it. The French students at the academy had shown her the best colors and styles to wear to show off her tall figure and pale skin, while the Italian girls had infected her with their love of beautiful bags and shoes. Even the sullen, sultry Spanish girls had given her a crash course in how to project an image of cool, mysterious reserve.

"You want wealthy men to like you, you smile at them," Juanita, the daughter of a Madrid banker, had advised her. "You want them to *listen* to you, you don't."

Once the rim of the sun appeared above the treetops, Min finished her coffee and went inside to dress. Most of the jewelry her father had left to her was too old and ornate to wear, but on impulse she pinned to her lapel a fragile ivory-and-lapis cameo her father had sent to her for her last birthday at school.

This was my mother's favorite day brooch, Darien had written on the card. *Break it or lose it, and I'll put you back up for adoption.*

Twenty-one years ago the idea that old Darien, a middle-aged, confirmed bachelor, had had the nerve to adopt himself a baby girl had been the talk of the scandalmongers. At the time all of the still-single ladies in the city had been outraged at how neatly he had bypassed the usual way of getting children—marriage to one of them—while their parents had muttered darkly over his impropriety and disrespect by taking on some riffraff's unwanted brat. One needn't bring a no-named orphan home and install her in the house as if she were family; that was what children's charities were for. After the spectacle of Min's baptism at St. John's, when Darien had announced that he was not only giving Min his famous surname but making her his sole heir, his friends had publicly congratulated him, and privately mourned the end of one of the city's most historic bloodlines.

Darien never cared what anyone thought. "Having the mumps when I was a teenager left me sterile," he told his daughter once when she'd asked why he'd adopted her. "I think it was God's way of saving me from having to put up with some meddling woman in my house for the last thirty years."

"But I'm a woman," Min reminded him.

Darien's smile turned mysterious. "Oh, someday you'll be a lot more than that, honey." He laughed. "Besides, you were just a tiny little thing. First time I saw you at the orphanage I thought, 'Now, there's a girl I could teach to put up with my nonsense.' "

Min left the house at eight fifteen. She could walk from her home on Abercorn to the Oglethorpe Consolidated Investments building off Bay Street, one of the primary reasons she had taken the job as Boyd Whitemarsh's receptionist and personal assistant. The other, more personal reason had to do with her determination to preserve her legacy.

Sapphire House had been designed and built for the very first Darien, a cotton merchant and part-time smuggler who had made a very large fortune in the early eighteenth century, and who himself had often bragged that he ended up with more money than taste or brains. Happily, that Darien had hired an architect who had come to Savannah to see his sister married. William Jay's architecture would one day define the elegance and grace of the era, but at the time he met Darien he was just a cheerfully brash young man looking to make a name for himself in the New World.

With Darien's bottomless pockets and unconditional blessings, Jay designed a lavish four-story, Regency-style mansion, and over the next three years personally supervised the construction. As homage to his patron's magpie love of anything shiny, Jay had commissioned and installed an enormous lead crystal chandelier in every room, and ordered sparkling white sand brought over by the boatload from Tybee Island to be mixed in with the stucco and plaster.

There were stories told about the house almost from the day the first Darien had moved in. People had been observed entering through the back door but were never seen leaving, and then there were the mysterious deliveries made in the middle of the night by dour-faced men driving covered carts. When asked about the strange comings and goings, Darien would only smile and change the subject.

As both a historic landmark and a private residence, Sapphire House required an enormous amount of upkeep, and the financial burden had been a constant drain on Darien's modest fortune. But Min had been raised in the shadow of the Cathedral of Saint John the Baptist, and walked down streets paved with Savannah grey brick, the old building blocks of the city, that had once been river mud before it had been shaped by the hands of slaves. In every wrought-iron balcony railing and pocket doorway history stood, watching her with its sad eyes. She couldn't imagine turning over Old Blue to strangers who didn't care for anything but its prestigious address and resale value.

"I've spent more on Old Blue than likely I should have, and the way the economy's going, my accounts won't last more than a couple years," old Darien had told her. "If you're to hang on to the house after I'm gone, you'll need to catch yourself a rich husband."

Min had something better than a wealthy beau: her hunches. She'd started having them in her early teens, when she began having odd, random flashes of insight about things. She had no idea how it worked or why; at any given moment a feeling would come over her, suddenly and with no warning, and then she simply knew, as if she'd already experienced what hadn't yet happened.

It might have frightened her, had the hunches been about ominous things. Instead they always assured her of ordinary, happy events, like knowing that she'd ace a test before she took it or sensing that a present from Darien was about to come in the mail. Then at college she'd started following the stock exchange for an economics class assignment, and discovered that her hunches also allowed her to anticipate positive market trends with near-flawless accuracy.

She'd never told her father about her ability. Darien had been a strict, faithful Catholic, and believed such things were the work of the devil. But Min believed her hunches were a gift, and as long as she was discreet, they were going to allow her to marry whomever she wanted, live comfortably, and take proper care of Sapphire House.

All she really had needed was a job that would teach her everything else she didn't know about the market, which she'd already found. In a few hours she was going to start working as the receptionist/personal assistant for the vice president of one of the most successful commercial investment firms in the city. There she would gain the practical experience she needed in order to begin investing her own funds. And while her hunches weren't telling her anything about her new job, she knew she'd made the right choice.

Today would be the day that changed her life forever.

Diesel exhaust from the endless stream of trucks hauling cargo back and forth to the river hadn't yet overpowered the wet, earthy smell the river added to the chilly morning air. On her way to work Min saw a few tourists out walking, small Styrofoam cups of hotel room coffee in their hands as they stopped to admire and snap pictures of every other house around the square. One grand old lady in a purple cardigan pulled over a white lace blouse and pleated black skirt scooped up her tiny Maltese to carry him across Liberty Street, and responded to Min's good-morning with only an affronted glare.

The OCI building had five floors, but only the first two were occupied by the corporate offices, with the top three sublet to other satellite companies. Min had already been shown the way to Boyd Whitemarsh's office, and used one of her new keys to let herself in. As she closed the door behind her, she took a moment to inspect the receptionist's desk. Someone had cleared it off for her, but a large stack of reports and invoices sat in the filing bin, and what appeared to be a week of mail sat unopened in her in-box.

Min checked her watch; she had forty-five minutes before her new boss came in to get the office in some semblance of order. Fortunately Rebecca Morton, OCI's personnel director, who had hired Min, had warned her in advance that she would have a lot of cleanup work to do.

"The young lady who worked for Mr. Whitemarsh before you had some personal problems," Rebecca said, disapproval crimping her lips. "I gave her several warnings and three written reprimands, but she ignored them, and after an ugly scene we had to let her go." She looked at Min over the rim of her trifocals. "No doubt you'll hear every gruesome detail from the girls of the grapevine, Minerva. All I ask is that you don't encourage it; I think Boyd Whitemarsh has been through enough."

Min had sorted through most of the paperwork and had begun fielding calls by the time her new boss arrived in the office. Tall, silver-haired, and casually genial, Boyd Whitemarsh had the boyish smile and easy manner of a much younger man.

"Let me know if you need anything," he said after greeting her. "It'll be confusing at first, but you'll get into the swing of things by the end of the week."

"Thank you, Mr. Whitemarsh." Min turned to her computer screen and pulled up the virtual calendar. "I checked with the receptionist who has been filling in, and today you have a meeting scheduled at ten with the New York rep, lunch at noon with Mr. Kijorski at the Black Oak, and a two-o'clock sit-down with the Legacy Group in conference room four." She handed him a stack of envelopes. "These are all the letters from last week's mail that need a response. I can take dictation at your convenience."

Whitemarsh chuckled with appreciation. "Perhaps I spoke too soon."

As soon as her boss disappeared into his office, Min tackled the backlog of filing and in the process taught herself the filing system. Which, judging by the amount of misfiled items she discovered, her predecessor had ignored or had never bothered to learn. Whitemarsh's ten-o'clock appointment came and went while Min kept working. She ran out of tabs, but a thorough inspection of her desk drawers turned up only an enormous collection of empty, crumpled chip bags and candy wrappers, which she gingerly began transferring to the small trash can beside the printer station.

Ugh. Min excavated from the back of the hanging folder drawer a half-eaten, mold-encrusted cupcake that made her stomach turn. *Why was she eating all this junk?*

As she dropped the disgusting remnant in the trash, Min recalled that one of the girls at college had been addicted to the same type of snacks; she'd often gone from room to room asking if anyone had anything sweet or salty. The same girl had suffered a breakdown just before midterms, one so severe that her parents had had no choice but to take her out of school.

Once Min had cleared the last of the junk-food detritus out of the desk, she pressed the intercom. "Mr. Whitemarsh, I need to step away from my desk for a few minutes. Should I forward the phones to reception?"

"No, that's all right," her boss replied. "I'll cover them for you until you get back."

After taking the trash to the Dumpster behind the building, Min returned to the back entrance, where a young woman stood searching for something in a straw tote bag. The purple dress sagging over her thin frame had a badly wrinkled skirt, and the too-long brown bangs hanging over her eyes looked greasy. As she drew closer, Min smelled French fries and body odor.

"Must have left them in my desk," the woman muttered, her voice sounding unexpectedly high and childlike. She gave Min a vague look before she stepped out of the way. "Sorry."

Min eyed the OCI personnel badge clipped to the other girl's jacket lapel. Her name was Jennifer something. Min didn't know her, but it was her first day; she hardly knew anyone.

"Here, I've got mine." Min used her new key to unlock the door.

Without another word the girl reached past her for the handle and ducked inside.

"Hey." Min caught the door before it slammed shut in her face. "You're welcome," she called after her.

The girl didn't so much as glance back.

After Min returned to her office, the first thing she saw was a vase of delicate white roses sitting on her desk. She set down the trash can and picked up the vase. "Oh, how pretty."

"Cheap, too." Smiling dark eyes under an unruly mop of brown hair gleamed down at her as a tall, lanky man stepped out from behind the door and closed it. "Can I offer them as a bribe, goddess of mine?"

"It depends on what crimes you've committed." Min tucked the vase in one arm and used the other to give her boyfriend a hug. "What are you doing here?"

"I'm hungry, I'm poor, and I hate to eat alone." He kissed the end of her nose. "Buy me lunch, please."

Tag had been one of her strongest hunches. She'd known he would be coming around a corner on Bull Street a few moments before he'd bumped into her, but something had told her not to step out of the way. The moment his ink-stained hands had steadied her, she'd known that she would be the love of his life, the only woman he would ever love. That had enchanted her as much as his brilliant smile.

"Pretty good bribe." Min hefted the vase to inspect the roses, which had the faintest tinge of pink at the edges of the snowy petals. She'd seen roses like these before in only one place. "Tag. Please tell me you didn't steal these out of Mrs. Pardalia's garden."

"I swore I'd never lie to you, Minnie." Unrepentant, Tag dazzled her with his grin. "She'll never miss them."

"You don't know her. She probably counts every bud when she weeds in the afternoon." A series of odd, distant popping sounds distracted her briefly. "I really shouldn't take lunch, not on my first day. There's a ton of work to catch up on."

"Thirty minutes, then." He slid an arm around her waist. "Don't worry; it'll still be here when you get back."

"All right. Let me tell Mr. Whitemarsh, and then we'll—" Another burst of staccato sounds, closer now, interrupted her. "What is that?"

"Sounds like popcorn popping . . ." As the door behind Tag burst open, he frowned and turned.

A young, pale-faced man braced himself against the frame, one hand spread over a large red stain blooming on the front of his light blue shirt.

"Hide." He gurgled the word before he toppled over.

Not popping, Min thought as the vase fell from her hands. *Gunshots.*

Glass smashed as Tag grabbed the other man to keep him from hitting the floor and eased him down the rest of the way. He rolled him onto his back and pulled his limp hand from the massive bloodstain. A spattering of black powder encircled a large, dark hole.

Min knelt down beside them, but the hot tears filling her shocked eyes made everything blur. "Tag?"

"He's been shot." Her boyfriend put his trembling hand over the man's chest and applied pressure. Blood welled up between his fingers and streaked across the back of his hand. "Honey, call nine-one-one. Hurry."

As Min stumbled to her feet and groped blindly for her phone, more rapid popping sounds came from the hall, much louder than before, and she cringed as she heard men shouting and women screaming. At the same time, Whitemarsh came out of his office.

"Did something break?" His expression froze into a ghastly mask as he stared down at Tag and the wounded man. "God in heaven. What happened?"

"Someone shot him," Tag said. "Someone in the building."

The smell of French fries and body odor wafted through the doorway. *Jennifer*, Min thought as she stared at the woman in the purple dress as she strode into the office. She could see she was holding a large pistol in her hand, but she couldn't move or even think about that. *Jennifer something.*

"Jennifer." All the color had disappeared from White-marsh's face as he stumbled back, careening into the filing cabinet before he whipped up his hands. "Don't. Please. Wait."

"I waited," the woman told him in her shrill, little-girl voice. "Six weeks. You never came to get me. You said you would." She used the gun like a finger, jabbing it at him to punctuate every word. "You promised."

Whitemarsh's elegant hands moved as if he were conducting a symphony. "Please, Jenny, calm down. You don't know what you're saying. You're sick. You need help."

"I need *help*?" She let out a laugh like a shriek. "I love you. You love me. But you let them take me away to that place. That *hospital*. It wasn't for my eating problem. It was for crazy people. Why didn't you tell me that?"

The young lady who worked for Mr. Whitemarsh before

you had some personal problems, Rebecca Morton had said.

If only Min had known who Jennifer was, or what she meant to do, she would never have let the girl into the building. But her hunches were never about terror or tragedy; she saw only the happy or lucky things that were about to happen.

She didn't need a hunch to tell her how this was going to turn out.

Tag cleared his throat, and when she looked at him he deliberately looked from her face to the receiver in her hand. Slowly Min reached out her trembling hand and rested it over the buttons on the console. She didn't dare lift the receiver to her ear, but was able to push nine and then one twice without making it obvious. When the emergency operator answered, she covered the earpiece with her hand to block the sound.

"I didn't have anything to do with your being committed, Jennifer," Whitemarsh was saying to the woman. "It was someone else. Mrs. Morton called security that day, remember? I didn't even know about it."

"Mrs. Morton's dead. They're all dead." Her gaze grew unfocused. "I told them everything. Six months, you said. Six months and you'd divorce her. When we went on the trip to the sales conference, and you made me do it to you three times a night. You said we'd get married if I did what you wanted. They didn't believe me. They said I was making it up."

Min glanced at her new boss. He didn't respond to the accusations, but ducked his head. *What if she's telling the truth?*

"I gave you everything," Jennifer ranted. "*Everything*, and you left me there in that place. Like I was nothing to you." Rage turned her face a dark, ugly red. "Why didn't you stop them? Why didn't you tell them about us? Why?" When he still wouldn't answer, her voice rose to a shriek. *"Tell me why."*

"Jennifer, please," Whitemarsh said, matching her whine with his own. "This is all a terrible misunderstanding. I would never do anything to hurt you." His throat moved as he glanced at the gun in her hands. "You won't shoot me. You can't. Not if you really love me."

Jennifer looked down at the gun, too, as if she'd forgotten she was holding it. "I don't love you anymore." She raised the barrel.

Whitemarsh spun on his heel, running for his office, and then jerked and fell forward as Jennifer fired. Blood and some of his face spattered the carpet in front of him.

Bile rose up in Min's throat, gagging her.

"Jennifer?" Tag held his bloodied hands palms out and slowly rose to his feet. "It's over now. Let me have the gun."

"Why?" Jennifer frowned. "I don't know you."

Min couldn't move until the shots exploded and she saw Tag fall, and then she dropped the phone and stumbled to him, collapsing beside him. She cradled his head with her arm, and a stream of bright red blood poured from his mouth as he tried to speak.

"Goddess . . . sorry . . ."

"Tag, no." She shook her head as his eyes closed and his body went limp. "No, please don't leave me."

A shadow fell over them. "He's dead." The hot end of a gun barrel nudged Min's temple. "Get up." When she didn't move, Jennifer grabbed her by the hair and used it to yank her to her feet.

Min's scalp burned, and she couldn't take a deep breath, but a grotesque sort of calm settled over her. "How could you kill him?" she heard herself ask the woman. The expanding hollowness in her chest crept up her throat. "He didn't hurt you. You didn't even know him."

"Shut up," Jennifer screamed in her face.

Behind Jennifer two police officers with guns drawn appeared on either side of the doorway and began shouting at her to drop the weapon.

Min wrapped her hand around the pistol the girl jammed in between their bodies. The steel, hot from being fired, scalded her palm. "Put this down now or they'll shoot you."

"I don't care." Jennifer looked into Min's eyes, and her rage ebbed into an odd dullness. "Did he tell you that he loved you?"

Min's gaze shifted to Tag's still face. Of course she had been the great love of his life. She had been the *only* love of his life. "Yes."

"They lie," Jennifer whispered.

The sound of the next shot seemed muffled, but the white-hot spike that stabbed through Min's chest made no sound at all. Dimly she felt herself floating backward through the air, her body weightless, her vision clouding over as an enormous rose with a thousand thorns opened inside her heart.

A strange man's face appeared over her as her heartbeat slowed, and he shouted something, but she couldn't hear the words. The rose stretched out, impossibly huge now, and then contracted, tightening to smother her heart between its wet, dark petals.

She was dying, Min thought, startled by the knowledge but not particularly afraid. Tag was dead. She knew he would be waiting for her, as would Darien. She wouldn't be alone in the dark.

And then she was.

Chapter 1

"I don't understand," Ellen Farley said, gripping the arms of her chair. "I didn't pad my résumé. My references are genuine, and I have the experience required for the position. So why am I here?"

"Because if you had nothing to hide, you wouldn't care," Jessa Bellamy murmured as she watched the disgruntled young woman through an observation panel.

"North and Company retains Phoenix, Inc., to perform standard background checks on all their new employees, Ms. Farley." Caleb Douglas, the intake interviewer who sat with his back to Jessa, kept a perfect blend of sympathy and authority in his tone. "You're here because they'd like to hire you."

"Oh." She smiled, relaxing her shoulders. Her frosted pink fingernails, however, remained curled into the arm-rests. "Then I've got the job?"

"Almost. I'll let you get started on these"—he handed Ellen a clipboard with a number of blank forms on it—"while I grab some coffee. Would you like a cup?"

"No, thank you." She took a slim gold pen from her oversize blue leather bag and began filling out the top form. Absently she crossed her ankles, showing off her metallic silver pumps.

As soon as Caleb left the room, however, Ellen Farley put the clipboard on his desk, stood, and came over to the panel. Jessa knew that on Ellen's side of the wall, the panel appeared to be nothing more than a mirror with an ornate frame hanging behind Caleb's desk.

"Nicely handled," Jessa said as Caleb joined her at the panel and watched as Ellen fluffed and shook out her layered red hair. "What do you think?"

"Seems legit to me." The interviewer considered the preening woman. "She's not happy to be here, but North and Company gave her ten minutes' notice, so that's to be expected." He rubbed the end of his nose. "She smells like she was baptized with Chanel No. 5."

Jessa had already caught a whiff of the woman's French perfume, which seemed almost a cliché: *Expensive is as expensive does.* "Credentials?"

"Angela says they're sterling. Ellen Farley is the perfect candidate for comptroller." Caleb studied her expression. "Or not. What's setting off your bells, boss?"

"Her shoes. They're knockoffs."

Cal glanced down. "So?"

Jessa gestured at Ellen's tasteful floral sheath. "So you don't invest in a Michael Kors dress and a Balenciaga bag unless you can also afford five hundred bucks for the real Anya Hindmarch pumps."

The interviewer chuckled. "You should be a gay man."

"Maybe in my next life. Bring her to me after she finishes the busywork. And, Cal." Jessa nodded toward his empty hands. "Don't forget the coffee before you go back in."

Walking up the back stairs to her office gave Jessa time to think. She often used small, seemingly insignificant details like Ellen Farley's designer-clone shoes as rationale for further assessment of the applicants sent to them by their clients. By doing so she'd acquired a reputation for having a keen eye, and even Caleb, one of her most trusted employees, believed in it. Jessa had been very careful to cultivate that misconception.

Her ability to discover exactly what people hid from their employers had made Phoenix, Inc., one of the top personnel agencies in the South, but no one could ever know the truth of how she did it.

Angela Witt, her technical supervisor, intercepted her outside her office. Tall, rawboned, and a little awkward, Angela was barely out of her teens, and had originally come to the agency as a temp. Jessa had quickly discovered the very young secretary had a natural gift for computers, multitasking, and resource management, as well as a desperate need for permanence and a sense of purpose.

"Ms. Bellamy, Caleb said you flagged Ms. Farley." Angela sounded as stiff as she looked. "I checked every one of her refs, but they all came back a hundred percent. What did I miss?"

"Nothing," Jessa said. "Her shoes are wrong."

"A fashion mistake? Oh, good." Her shoulders drooped as her chin lifted. "I mean, it's not good, not at all, but at least I didn't . . ." She stopped herself and released a sigh. "Sorry."

"It's all right, Angela." Accustomed to her office manager's mild but perpetual paranoia, Jessa suppressed a smile. "I could be wrong about this one."

"No way, Ms. B." Her office manager shook her head, almost dislodging the stubby pencil holding her topknot of hair in place. "You're never wrong. It's like you have liar radar. I'll run her name again and see what I can find." She turned and hurried down the hall to the data center.

Jessa stepped into her office and closed the door. She'd personally designed her workspace to be quiet and uncluttered. Two clear Lucite columns supported the massive slab of polished black granite that served as her desk. Against one white wall, Asian black lacquer cabinets inlaid with delicate mother-of-pearl lotus flowers concealed her office equipment, and faced a four-by-five-foot print of Ansel Adams's *Birds on a Beach* over a modular black leather seating unit that surrounded a coffee table that was merely a smaller version of her desk. In the center of the table stood a crystal vase filled with fresh flowers. She'd had the back wall replaced with a single panel of glass, which provided a wide view of Peachtree Street and the Armstrong building.

For the floor, she'd commissioned and imported labradorite stone tiles from Sweden, which glowed with an ever-changing blue-green-amber light under the recessed incandescent fixtures in the white ceiling. At the corners of each tile were small, silver disks that to the naked eye appeared to be decorative touches. Each disk was hardwired to perform three different functions when activated by the remote: sealing the room, tripping the security alarms, and administering enough of an electrical charge to knock out whoever stood on them.

Her workspace appeared more like a room in a minimalist art gallery than an office, but it suited her tastes and kept anyone else who entered from getting too comfortable.

Jessa opened the doors to the cabinet nearest her desk to check her surveillance equipment. Six monitors showed six different-angled views of her office via the minicameras hidden all around the room. She picked up a small transceiver, switched it to take over her office line, and tucked it over her ear. She removed a slim remote sitting inside the cabinet and placed it in her jacket pocket.

A knock sounded, and Jessa went to stand behind her desk before she called for the person to come in.

Caleb entered with an unhappy Ellen Farley following him, but after performing introductions and handing Jessa a file, he excused himself and left.

"Please sit down, Ms. Farley." Jessa waited until she had before she did the same and opened the file. "I have a few more questions for you."

"More?" Ellen crossed her arms. "I filled out all of your forms. What else do you want to know?"

Unhappy and *defensive*, Jessa thought.

"You were born in 1974, an only child, is that correct?" She glanced up in time to catch Ellen's tight nod before returning to the file notes. "Very good education, majored in economics at Brown, graduated with honors. You were recruited to work for CitiCom, where you were promoted to assistant comptroller, paid very well, and then resigned a year later." She met Ellen's resentful gaze again. "Why leave a good job like that?"

"There was no possibility for advancement," Ellen said.

"Citi doesn't place women in the top executive positions. It's one big old-boys' network."

"You relocated from New York to Atlanta before you found a new position." Jessa pretended to skim through the rest of the forms, letting the other woman stew for a moment before she asked, "What brought you down here to look for work?"

"I've always liked the South." She moved her shoulders. "The weather is great and the country is beautiful, and the people are nice."

Jessa closed the file. "Established corporations like North and Company are somewhat more conservative than their New York counterparts. I believe our old-boys' network is in its fifth generation."

Ellen's lips thinned. "What are you implying?"

She was as suspicious as she was defensive, which might mean she was everything she claimed to be, or not. "Merely that your ambition may come up against yet another glass ceiling."

"I don't think any of this is your business, Ms. Bellamy," the other woman snapped.

"I am certifying for my client that you are who you say you are and therefore are also suitable for employment with them." Jessa offered her a cool smile. "At present, everything about you is my business."

"Yes, of course. I'm sorry." The faint lines around Ellen's mouth eased. "It was really a shock to find out I'm being investigated, or whatever you call it. Then they told me I had to come over here right away, or I wouldn't eligible for hire. It scared the heck out of me."

"No need to be afraid. It's all over now."

Ellen smiled. "Really? That's all I have to do?"

"That's it." Jessa stood. "I appreciate your taking the time to come in and fill out the paperwork." She held out her hand.

"Thank you." Ellen Farley's hand joined hers.

Shadowlight.

Jessa stood in the center of what appeared to be a cheap hotel room. The odors of cigarette smoke, sweat, and sex nearly choked her as she gazed down at the two bodies writhing together on the worn paisley carpeting. Neither had undressed completely, but the man's buttocks gleamed white beneath a low tan line, and shook as he thrust himself into Ellen Farley with eager, frantic movements.

She could feel their lust crawling inside her head, dragging with it everything they thought. While Ellen's mind focused on the need tightening in her pelvis, her lover Max's thoughts were at odds with his enthusiasm.

"We're going to be rich, baby," the man panted as he grabbed her bouncing breast through her damp silk blouse and dug his fingers into the mound. "So fucking rich. We'll never have to work another day of our lives."

Max Grodan was already rich, Jessa knew. Beyond rich. He could leave Ellen and never have to work another day for ten lifetimes—and he had worked very hard to keep Ellen from discovering that.

Ellen groaned. "What if I get caught? This time they'll know it was me. I'll go to prison, Max."

"Ellen Farley will go to prison, if they bother to dig her up out of the ground." Max nuzzled her neck. "Judy Tulliver is going to Rio with me and five-point-nine million bucks."

The image in Max's mind was of a shallow grave, but it was empty. At least until he shoved Ellen's limp body over the edge.

Sunlight.

Jessa released the other woman's hand, smiled, and watched her leave the office. As soon as the door closed, she dropped down into her chair and buried her face in her hands. She sat like that until the worst of the shakes from her vision stopped and she could think of something other than running after Ellen and pleading with her not to go anywhere near Max.

She couldn't do this. Not here, not now.

With a trembling hand she picked up her phone and dialed a two-digit extension. "Angela, check the U.S. interment database and see if you can find a listing for an Ellen Ann Farley, date of birth February nineteenth."

"What year, Ms. Bellamy?"

She flipped open the file and gazed at Ellen's date of birth. To use identity records belonging to another person, Ellen would have had to choose someone born prior to 1936—the year the United States began issuing Social Security numbers—with digits that could be easily doctored. The digit 1 could be easily changed to a 4—or a 7. "Try 1914."

"Searching." After a few moments, Angela took in a quick breath. "One hit. Holy Moses. Ellen Ann Farley, born 1914, died 1916. Interred in Mount Pleasant Cemetery, Albany County, New York."

"Good." Jessa put the phone on speaker so she could walk around the office and work out the last of the trembling weakness from being in the shadowlight. "Call the Office of Vital Statistics in New York, and have them fax a copy of Ellen Ann Farley's actual birth certificate to us. If the certificate numbers match, we'll move on to Social Security."

"Yes, ma'am." Angela hesitated before adding, "See what I mean? You're never wrong about people, Ms. Bellamy."

"No." Jessa looked down at the vase of white roses on the coffee table, and touched one of them. "This time I wasn't."

"Adele, standing there and breathing on it ain't gonna get that window clean," Maribeth Boden said as she finished rubbing the last streak from the glass in front of her.

Adele Watkins didn't reply, but swatted the air with her hand.

"Come on now." Maribeth walked over to help her friend, and studied the dusty inside of the pane. "We got three more offices to do before . . . we—" She stopped and gulped. "Sweet baby Jesus."

"Uh-huh," Adele murmured.

The man on the other side of the window stood in the shade the recessed arch over it provided. While Maribeth saw a lot of men during her rounds of the office buildings she cleaned every day, she couldn't recall ever noticing one put together like this one.

He was too dark to be white, and too light to be black. She would have pegged him as Hispanic or Indian, if not for his dark blond hair and light eyes, but that wasn't right either. If someone had asked her, she would have said his skin reminded her of her mama's homemade pralines, all hot and smooth as they cooled on waxed paper in the kitchen.

His pretty skin covered broad, heavy muscles, the kind she'd never seen on a white man, not even the ones at the gym around the corner. When he shifted position, they didn't ripple; they flowed.

"You think he's gonna put that jacket back on?" Adele murmured.

The white sleeveless shirt he wore clung to his chest and torso like body paint, and made it clear to Maribeth that everything it covered was just as fine as what it exposed. "God wouldn't be that hateful to me."

Adele sucked in a sharp breath as the man turned his head to look at the window. "He knows we're watching him."

"No, he don't," Maribeth chided. "It's privacy glass; the outside's like a mirror, 'member? He's just looking at himself." But he didn't do much of that before he went back to watching the street. "You think he works here?"

"If he does, we're blind." Adele pressed her dark hand to the dirty window. "Damn, Mari, but if he ain't the finest man I've seen in my whole life, I'll eat my mop."

Maribeth thought of her man, Darnell, who was still home in bed after a long night on the road. "Think I'm gonna go home for lunch today."

Adele sputtered a laugh. "I was thinking I'd take my coffee break in the back of my husband's cab."

"Morning, ladies." Carter Burleigh, one of the young attorneys who worked on the floor, walked up behind them. "Have either of you . . . found—" He stopped speaking, but his jaw remained in its dropped position.

Adele glanced back at him. "That your boyfriend, Mr. Burleigh?"

"God wouldn't be that kind to me, Adele." Carter

wedged himself between the two women to have a better look. "Damn."

"Amen," Maribeth said on her own sigh.

On the other side of the window, the man who had taken the name Gaven Matthias decided he'd concealed himself long enough to dispel casual suspicion, and moved out of the shade to cross the street. As he did, he heard the groans of the two women and the one man who had been watching him, and smiled a little as he kept his jacket slung over his arm.

On the other side of the street, he walked down the block, went to a meter, took out a handful of coins, and counted them. Everyone who walked past him paid little attention to what he did; he was simply a man avoiding a parking ticket.

They were not aware that he'd claimed the spot many hours before dawn, or that he had spent the time either watching the phone booth next to the parking space or feeding coins to it so he might eavesdrop on every woman who came to use the booth. Fortunately in this era of mobile phones few seemed to have need of it, and there had been only two since dawn.

The third came as he selected a quarter to add to the meter. He heard the click of her heels on the concrete sidewalk and smelled her scent as she passed. He didn't look directly at her, but from the corner of his eye he saw the gleaming twist of black hair at the back of her head and the smooth fit of her gray jacket over slim black trousers.

She dressed like a man but smelled like good clear water, crisp and cool. He closed his eyes briefly, taking her scent deep into his chest and letting it warm him. Few of his boyhood beliefs had withstood the passage of time and life, but he still kept faith in his senses. They whispered that she had come to him at last, the one he was meant to find. She smelled of tears and melting snow.

She smelled of rain.

Coins chimed as she fed them into the phone, and then her voice brushed against his ears, low and sweet, a taste of dark honey. She asked for an agent by name, waited, and said, "I have important information for you. Please listen carefully."

Matthias pressed a button on his watch to switch it to its timing function before he fed another quarter into the meter and listened. The woman spoke rapidly, offering names, dates, monetary amounts, and the electronic method used to commit the crime. She gave the address of a hotel and the room number where the criminals responsible could be found. She finished the call with a polite refusal—probably for a sizable reward—and hung up the receiver.

She walked away without looking back once.

He checked his watch. She had related everything in one minute and thirty-eight seconds. As he watched her turn the corner, he saw her remove first one black leather glove and then the other.

He took out his own phone and pressed the number two before bringing it to his ear. "Whom did she call?"

"FBI headquarters in New York City," Drew told him. "Did you get a clear shot?"

"There was no opportunity." Matthias went around and climbed into his rental car. As he pulled out and drove around the block, he repeated everything he had heard the woman say. "You can check what she reported to see if it is true?"

"Already on it." The sound of tapping keys came over the line. "Got a hit. The details she gave the FBI match an unsolved case that happened two years ago. Electronic embezzlement. The company lost close to a million dollars. No suspects."

"Soon there will be."

"No doubt," Drew agreed. "Why doesn't she report them to the local office? They're there in Atlanta."

He considered that. "Too close to where she lives."

"Then you were right. She lives in the city."

"Lives, or perhaps works." Matthias searched the faces of the pedestrians walking on either side of the street before he spotted the woman standing at a corner and holding her hand in the air. "She came by taxi."

"Smart lady. No car, no license plate we can use to trace her identity. Do you think she suspects that someone is looking for her?"

"She would not stay here if she did." Matthias kept one hand on the wheel and used the other to lift his camera to his face. He was able to snap three profile shots as the woman entered the taxi that had stopped for her. "Find out what you can. I will call you later."

"Good hunting, boss."

Matthias noted the number and license plate of the cab before he pressed the number 1 on his phone.

"Hit me," Rowan's cool young voice said.

He gave her the numbers along with the company name stenciled on the side of the taxi. "The driver took her from the street at one thirty-three."

"He picked her up at one thirty-three," she corrected him. "Kidnappers like us take people. Cabbies pick them up."

The subtle and sometimes maddening intricacies of American language still challenged him. "But he does not lift her. He takes her to her destination."

"To pick up can mean lifting a person, seducing a person, or giving them a ride in a vehicle."

"Seducing." He didn't know the woman yet, but the idea of her giving herself to anyone did not sit well with him. "You are certain of this?"

"It's my language, pal," Rowan reminded him. "Drew's faxing a bunch of police reports. You think she's the one who's been tipping off the feds?"

Her scent still lingered in his head and chest, a silent waterfall. "I know she is."

Rowan's tone changed. "Then you should take her as soon as possible."

Chapter 2

Jonah Genaro rolled away from the thin, damp body of his mistress, left the bed they had shared for the last hour, and pulled on his trousers.

Lorraine propped her head on her arm and watched him take a clean, pressed black shirt from the supply he kept in the closet. "I thought you were going to stay awhile."

"I have another appointment." He picked up his wallet and watch from her vanity table. Twenty years ago he would have left a handful of bills behind, but today he preferred the convenience of a rechargeable credit card. "The next few weeks will be busy for me. I won't have time to see you again until the end of November."

"You can't leave yet." Lorraine climbed out of bed, wrapping herself in a yellow silk robe before she shook out her hair. She'd stopped bleaching six months ago, at Genaro's request, and now had it dyed to match the dark roots as they grew out. "There's something we need to talk about."

Genaro knotted his tie. "I'll call you next week and then we'll talk."

"This can't wait that long." She came around to stand in front of him, holding her hands together like a remorseful schoolgirl. "Jonah, I've been to see my doctor. He did some tests, and, well, we're going to have a baby."

Genaro's hand went still for a second, and then slid the knot of his tie up under the edges of his collar. "You're telling me that you're pregnant?"

"I didn't realize at first." She released a pretty, helpless laugh. "I skip my periods all the time, and then I am on the pill, too, so it never occurred to me that I could be. I never miss them, but the doctor said sometimes in rare cases they don't work."

The schoolgirl quality of her confession didn't diminish the relief Genaro felt. Lorraine had been enthusiastic, and even occasionally entertaining, but his desire for her had begun to fade. This extortion attempt would allow him to get rid of her without the usual tears, recriminations, and final lump-sum payoff. "I presume you don't want to have an abortion."

"I couldn't do that, Jonah. I'm Catholic, remember?" She gave his arm a soft caress. "Besides, I love you. This is our *baby*."

"If your pregnancy is genuine," he told her as he removed her hand, "I'm not the father."

"Of course you are." The hopeful, beseeching quality of her expression faded into something harder. "I haven't been with anyone else."

As Genaro retrieved his jacket, he considered taking her to the lab to be tested. If she had become pregnant by another man, her fetus could still prove useful. But Lorraine had an active social life, and her father was a prominent Atlanta attorney who thought the sun rose and set on his only child. She would be missed.

"Well?" she demanded.

"My dear, you've miscalculated. Your baby—if one really exists—isn't mine." He adjusted his sleeves. "I'm sterile."

"You're—" She stopped and stared before she began to bluster. "What are you talking about? You never told me you couldn't have kids."

"You never asked." Genaro walked over to her. "Our arrangement is over. You have until the end of the month to pack your things and move out." As she opened her mouth, he shut her up by backhanding her. The blow proved hard enough to knock her to the ground, but not enough to inflict permanent damage. He bent over her, caught her chin, and made her look at him. "The next time you resort to blackmail, first do the appropriate research."

He left Lorraine on the floor and walked out of the apartment.

Genaro directed his driver to take him downtown before he picked up the phone and called his chief of security. "Void the credit balance left on Miss Lamar's account."

"Yes, Mr. Genaro." Delaporte, who had been with him for thirty years and had taken many such calls, didn't ask why. "The overseas shipment arrived about ten minutes ago."

A great deal of money had changed hands over this particular shipment: much more than Genaro had originally wanted to invest. But he had been unable to resist the rarity and high quality of the product. Even if he had to store it for some time, he suspected that in a year or two he'd be in a position to make an enormous profit.

"See that Dr. Kirchner attends to it," Genaro said.

He arrived on time for his two-o'clock appointment, and spent the next several hours going over the specs for the new lab with the architect and the foreman before he left to attend a charity dinner to benefit a local foundation for the prevention of neural-tube defects.

"Jonah, we're so happy you could make it." The hostess, a fortysomething, brassy-haired socialite whose younger, less fortunate brother had been born with spina bifida, took his hands in hers as she gave air kisses on each side of his face. "Where's Lorraine?"

"She couldn't make it." He scanned the crowded tables. "It looks like an excellent turnout this year, Jackie."

"We're very pleased, although—as usual—we have a last-minute glitch. Bad weather grounded our guest speaker's flight." Jackie sidled closer. "Can I do a terrible, presumptuous thing and impose on you to fill in?"

As much as he begrudged the time he wasted engaging in the practices of a prosperous, influential businessman, there was no other way to maintain the respectable facade. He agreed with a smile, and thirty minutes later stood before the dinner guests and spoke about the tragedy of genetic defects and the cures made possible by biotech research.

"Earlier this year researchers in Texas published their discovery of a link between variants in three genes that regulate glucose metabolism in children born with spina bifida," he told the guests. "Our geneticists are now working with that data in order to create a specific gene therapy that will correct these variants in utero. Once we have the cure, we can develop treatments for the other neural-tube defects, like anencephaly and encephalocele. No more children will have to spend their lives in wheelchairs. No more infants will be stillborn or doomed to die within a few hours after their birth. We will avert these tragedies long before they ever happen."

As he continued, Jonah noted that Jackie had hung several tasteful pictures of bravely smiling, wheelchair-bound children on the walls surrounding the dinner tables. Not one showed an image of a newborn with a severe NTD.

When Genaro left the dinner and returned to Gen-Hance, Delaporte met him in the lobby.

"Our man reported in this afternoon," he said as he followed Jonah onto the elevator. When the doors closed, he reached up and switched off the small security camera in one corner. "He's finally identified the woman who's been tipping off the feds. This is everything we have on her." He handed over an envelope. "She fits the profile."

Genaro took out and skimmed the report. "So she does. Have Lawson meet me in the lab."

A short time later Bradford Lawson stood for a moment under the UV unit before he placed his palm on the print scanner. As another public face of GenHance, he cultivated the image of geniality and prosperity, from the immaculate styling of his fair hair to the supple gleam of his hand-stitched leather shoes. Genaro didn't care for the color or the trendy cut of Lawson's cobalt blue suit, but the younger man carried it off as if he'd been born in a three-piece.

"Delaporte said we have an ID for the federal tipster who's been catching the uncatchable," Lawson said as he joined Genaro at the viewing panel. "Is this psychic informant anyone we know?"

"Not yet." Genaro handed him the photos and the report. "Clear your schedule. I want her verified and brought in by the end of the week."

"Yes, sir." Lawson read the top page. "I've heard of Phoenix. Small company, but they have an excellent reputation." He shook his head. "You'd think if she wanted to hide what she was, she would have done something else for a living."

Genaro didn't answer. He watched as two lab techs wheeled in a long, sheet-draped box on a gurney, followed by Elliot Kirchner, his chief geneticist. He switched on the intercom. "Dr. Kirchner, did you perform the initial microcellular tests?"

"As soon as it arrived." Kirchner, a tall, cranelike man with iron gray hair, glanced at the viewer. "Life support has sustained cellular integrity so far, but there is only negligible brain activity." He pulled the sheet away, revealing the body inside the glass coffin.

Genaro studied his investment. Bandages encased the head, but the rest of the specimen appeared to be in superb condition. "It looks better than it did in the photographs."

"It's close to physically perfect." The geneticist took some readings from the preservation unit's LED display. "BP and heart rate are strong. Once I've completed the physical and neurological exams, we can begin the preparation work."

"Cut off the bandages," Genaro said. "I want to see the head."

Kirchner nodded to one of the techs, who produced a pair of scissors and cut through the layers of gauze. He peeled them away, exposing a battered, unrecognizable face and a gaping, horrific head wound.

"Looks like someone blew away about a quarter of the skull," Lawson commented.

"Someone did." Genaro studied the wound. "You're sure the injury will affect only higher brain function, Doctor?"

"I'll verify it once I perform the necessary scans, but yes." Kirchner sounded confident. "For all intents and purposes, the body is mindless."

After he'd acquired a rare DNA sample from the bio-tech black market in Europe, it had taken Genaro another ten years to research and put into place the resources needed for GenHance's latest and most important phase of development. This final acquisition would initiate the last step toward his goal of creating, customizing, and selling the ultimate in human enhancement.

He turned to Lawson. "Where are we with the transerum?"

"The last series of human blood trials were quite promising," his director told him. "None of the primate test animals survived vaccination, of course, but you anticipated that." He glanced through the view panel at the shrouded body. "Once the subject is cleared by Dr. Kirchner, the lab is fully prepared to begin testing."

If the transerum developed by his microbiologists worked, it would bestow increased strength and enhanced senses, and make inviolate the immune system of the test subject. If it did not, and it killed humans as quickly as it did chimps and gorillas, they would still learn from it. The transerum had already undergone several hundred modifications; Genaro expected it would require many more before it was perfected enough to sell. Then nothing else would stop him from acquiring enough wealth and power to do whatever he pleased anywhere in the world.

Genaro noticed that Kirchner was bent over the body and studying the head wound closely. He switched on the intercom and asked, "What is it?"

"I thought I saw the eyelids moving," the geneticist said, and straightened. "My mistake."

Jessa checked in with Caleb before asking him to close the office for her. Normally she was the last one to leave, but after dealing with Ellen Farley, she needed time to think.

"Ange said to tell you that the certificate numbers were a match," Cal said. "That would make Ellen Farley a very well-preserved ninety-four-year-old, or an identity thief. Do you want me to call Linda McMann?" he asked, referring to North and Company's personnel director.

"Give her a heads-up so Farley doesn't get back into the building, but tell her we'll verify the information before we turn over our official report."

"Are you okay?" he asked. "You sound upset."

"Headache. I'll see you tomorrow." Jessa switched off her cell phone and leaned forward. "Would you drop me off here, at the corner?"

"Sure." The cabbie pulled over to the curb and accepted her fare before glancing out at the deserted park. "You meeting someone out here, lady?"

"My boyfriend," she lied, smiled, and got out.

No one except Jessa knew who had bought the four acres of prime Atlanta real estate and turned it into a public park, or that it had been modeled on a more famous square in the northern part of the state. Jessa had arranged it all through a local city beautification group, and donated the property to the city under the condition that it be given the name she had chosen for it, and that the land never be used for any other purpose than a park. It was her small piece of home away from home, and walking along the cobbled brick paths lined with magnolias and azaleas, she could almost imagine herself there again.

The fountain, a masterpiece of copper alloy sculpted to resemble a phoenix rising from the flames of the basin, was so new it still gleamed rosy red in the sunlight, but in time the weather and air would turn the bright metal green. As Jessa sat down on the bench before the fountain, she felt the weight of old grief and the sharp twist of new fear.

She couldn't keep doing this; she knew that. No matter how careful she was, eventually someone in authority would come looking for her. Then there would be the inevitable questions: *How did you know? Who told you? What evidence do you have?*

If she lied, they would know. If she told them the truth, they would have her committed.

Jessa knew she could stop reporting what she discovered when she went into the shadowlight. At most Ellen Farley would have been turned in as an identity thief to the police by North and Company. On that charge she probably could have made bail, left the city with her partner, Max, and started a new con somewhere else. In this era of electronic everything, high-tech grifters like Ellen and her boyfriend were becoming a common class of criminal. Corporations wrote off their losses and tightened their security measures. No one really got hurt by embezzlement, and often the crimes resulted in better business practices.

What no one but Max and now Jessa knew was that someone would die this time: Ellen.

Because Ellen had been having sex with Max when Jessa had looked into her soul through the shadowlight, the connection of their bodies had also allowed Jessa to see into his. As soon as Ellen finished this last job, her boyfriend planned to kill her, frame her for all the crimes they committed together, and then leave the country for the islands, just as he had seven times in the past. There he would transfer the stolen money into a fat numbered bank account, where he kept another $20 million from his past crimes before moving on to find and groom and teach the game to his next victim.

"I can stop doing it," Jessa told the fountain as if it were listening. "Step back and let my people do their jobs. They have the talent and the resources. They don't need me."

The water splashed, merrily indifferent to her quandary. But there was something else there, an unseen presence, like a lost soul hovering somewhere just out of sight.

Imagining he was there brought Jessa's emotions out of the tight, small place where she kept them secreted away. They were mirror twins, the desperate regret and yearning grief, born in agony, nurtured in silence. She protected them from the world, and in return they had grown to become her oldest friends, her closest companions.

Jessa felt tired of it, all of it. She'd done her best to save the Ellen Farleys of the world, and prevent the Max Grodans from hurting anyone else. If by now she hadn't paid for her mistakes, she never would. There would always be an endless supply of Ellens and Maxes in the world, and they would never stop, so maybe it was time she did.

"I'm not spending the rest of my life in this park. I don't

have the nightmares anymore. I was glad when they went away." She glanced down at her hands. "There has to be someone else. Someone I can touch. Someone you'd like. If I'd died that day, and you had lived, I know I'd want the same for you."

Talking to a man who wasn't there, who could never be there, made little sense. Jessa didn't believe in an afterlife. She knew he was gone forever. A therapist would have told her she was talking to herself, nothing more. But if by slim chance she was wrong, and the souls of the dead lingered around the living, she wanted him to know. He had always been the love of her life—and he would understand.

Her wireless chimed in her pocket, and she tasted something salty on her tongue. Jessa reached up to wipe away the tears that had trickled unnoticed down her cheeks before she checked the sender ID: *Aphrodite.*

The text, as always, was short and unsweetened: *You fucking off in the park again, Jez?*

Jessa popped out the tiny keyboard and thumbed a brief reply: *Not now, Di.*

Talk to me. The woman she knew only as Aphrodite sent a small graphic of a smiley face brandishing a bouquet of virtual roses between the lines she typed. *Or I'll start texting you about the last episode of* Grey's Anatomy. *Scene by scene.*

The joke threat tugged a smile out of her. *Oh, God, anything but that. Bad day here, but I won't whine. What's up?*

She forwarded an e-mail from Vulcan, tagged with the words, *Vulcan thinks he's found another Takyn. Wants to sched a group chat.*

The man they knew as Vulcan served as their chief scout. In the three years since Jessa, Aphrodite, and the other members had formed the Takyn, their very private online support group, he had been searching for others like them. Vulcan wouldn't kid about something like this; the unique problem they all shared was too dangerous.

I told you, Aphrodite wrote when Jessa didn't reply. *There are more out there. A LOT more. At least forty or fifty.*

I'll read the e-mail. That was as far as Jessa was willing to commit herself. *Don't get crazy about this.*

I've been crazy, Aphrodite wrote back. *Now it's starting to make sense.*

Jessa felt a pang of shame. Di had been through all seven levels of hell, and Jessa had no business spitting on her friend's hopes. *Your lips, God's ears. Got to go.*

Immel8tr.

Jessa ended the connection, switched off the power to her phone, and popped out the rechargeable battery pack and the SIM card. Vulcan had taught her to do that; anyone trying to trace their wireless communications would lose the signal.

Who would want to find us? she'd asked him once.

With what we can do? he wrote back. *Who wouldn't?*

In the very beginning, when Jessa had formed the private network with Aphrodite, the others they had found online had treated them and one another with guarded, suspicious reluctance. It had taken more than a year of cautious communications before they'd opened up to one another. That had been an enormous comfort to the entire group, but it had made them even more paranoid. To protect everyone, they'd agreed to remain anonymous to one another. No one used their real names, ages, addresses, or referred to any detail that might be used to identify them, even within the group.

To Aphrodite and the others, Jessa was the founder of the Takyn, a woman they knew only as Jezebel.

Vulcan wouldn't have made a mistake about this prospect; the criteria for joining the Takyn were too exact. The person would have to be between the ages of twenty-six and thirty-four, adopted from a specific list of placement agencies run by the Catholic church in only a handful of cities. There would be no records of the person's birth parents, and few official documents filed with state welfare agencies. The adoptive parents would have to be wealthy or well-to-do orthodox Catholics with no biological children of their own or other adopted children.

Finally, the person being considered would have had to

miraculously survive a fatal accident or illness, and come out of it with a very specific side effect, one they were subsequently compelled by necessity to hide from everyone in their life.

Aphrodite had been the first Takyn Jessa had ever encountered. They'd met on a discussion board for adult adoptees seeking their biological parents, and then had begun exchanging e-mails. What Di had told her had at first enraged Jessa, but then they had begun comparing personal histories and discovering just how alike they were.

Jessa had set up and named The Adopted Kids of Yesterday Network Web site, but it had been Aphrodite who dubbed their private group with the site's acronym.

We were taken from our real parents and families. We all remember bits and pieces of the rest in our nightmares. The doctors. The treatments. The pain. The goddamn tattoos. Whatever they did to us, they took away our chance of a normal life. Why not call us what we are?

Jessa knew her friend had every right to be bitter. Aphrodite had terrible memories of what had been done to her, and when a nearly fatal illness had caused her ability to manifest, she had been forced to leave home and live in hiding. Virtually the same thing had happened to her when a brush with death had transformed what had been a pleasant, helpful ability into something much darker, uncontrollable and ultimately inescapable. Still, Jessa refused to believe as Di did that they had been used as lab rats when they were children and then simply abandoned.

There had to be more reasons for what they were, and why they had been experimented on in the first place. If Vulcan was right and he had found another one like them, then the new member of the group might know more than they did. Every childhood memory, every ability, and even their individual theories illuminated another shadow of the past.

She would have sat there by the fountain until dark, but the park's sprinklers came on and the breeze rolled over the automatic sprayers, stealing some of the water and surrounding her in a fine mist. She stood and went to the edge of the basin, where she dug a penny out of her pocket and dropped it in. It sank and settled atop the hundreds of others at the bottom of the basin. A penny for her thoughts, which she paid every time she came to Price Park.

Her last thought before leaving was usually, *I miss you. I love you.* But tonight she was ready to say something else.

"It's time." Jessa looked around the beautiful place she'd created. "Good-bye, Allen."

She walked through the square to the small lot beside it where she had left her car. As the sweet perfume of the flowers grew distant, she breathed in and noticed another, almost familiar scent. She felt sure she'd smelled the same thing earlier today, downtown. As before it frustrated her; she couldn't identify it as anything except something very warm, nearly hot. It had been easy to dismiss it this afternoon as a trick played by the last of the summer heat, but now . . .

Jessa glanced over at the darkening horizon, and felt the coolness of twilight on her skin. The temperature had probably dropped fifteen degrees in the last hour.

Someone was here. Someone who had heard her.

She made a sharp turn and faced the park. It appeared as empty as when she'd arrived, but it didn't feel the same. Tiny nerves under her skin flared, sending confusing signals to the rest of her senses. She couldn't see or hear anyone, but someone was there. Someone who stood just out of sight.

Someone who had been watching her.

Running to the car and driving off would have been the safest option, but this was her place, her personal haven. Whoever had been eavesdropping on her had violated her most private moment.

She took out the illegal Taser she carried in her purse as anger propelled her forward toward the fountain and then around the base of every tree. She didn't find anyone, but wherever she picked up a trace of the scent, she stopped and scanned the area. The sprinklers had left the ground wet and soft, but she found no footprints or any signs that she'd been followed or observed.

If someone had come into the park after her, they'd left before she'd discovered the scent.

Slowly she put away the weapon and scanned the park one final time before she went to her car. She didn't make the mistake of going near it or unlocking it until she had checked the space beneath the undercarriage and looked into the windows to ensure that no one had broken in and hidden himself in the backseat.

Jessa glanced back at the park a final time, waited, and then disengaged the car alarm before getting in. She sat for another minute and watched the rearview mirror before she started the engine and backed out of the space.

She never took the same route home from the park twice, but now she drove in circles and made a half-dozen U-turns while she watched for a tail. No cars followed her, and after an hour of aimless driving she admitted to herself that she might have overreacted.

"No one cares who you are," she muttered as she took the final turn toward home. "They're all dead."

Chapter 3

Matthias stood looking down from his perch for some time after the woman had left the park and driven off into the night. He'd been right to assume that her senses were as acute as his, and after dealing with the only car parked in the immediate vicinity, he'd looked for cover. Concealing himself by climbing up into the twisted heavy branches and dense leaves of the oak tree across from the fountain was an old ambush tactic, but his vantage point had permitted him to watch her face nearly the entire time she had spent in the park.

Sorrow had brought her here, he guessed, as much as the need to change vehicles.

She took no joy from the solitude or the sound of spilling water, but sat like a new widow beside a fresh grave, alone and still. Listening to her whisper and watching her weep had made him restless. A part of him, the part that would never bow its head to the demands of his work, had wanted to go to her. No woman should have to bare her soul as she had, all alone in this lovely, quiet place. She needed to be shown that life had not forgotten her, that the emptiness could be filled again.

What Matthias first thought was sympathy for the sad beauty shifted inside him, impatient and demanding, growing hard and hot. His outcast state had left him cold to the feelings of others; he had drawn on that to make his way in this world. So had she. Of all the women who had come to him over the course of time, she would know what it was to be an exile. It was as if she had been fashioned for him, shaped and tempered to fit him, the lock only he could open, the armor only he could wear.

In another time and place he could have simply taken her for himself. Despite all her precautions, she had few true defenses. She would struggle like the wild thing she was, but in time he would gentle her. She would come to know him, and he would show her the truth of what they could be to each other.

There would be pleasure. She had a strong, young body and sensitive skin. Matthias's hands curled as he imagined stripping her down and laying her out. She would not be passive or accepting; she would demand as much as she gave. Her mouth would taste like her scent, as sweet as water from a hidden spring. He could feel his seed rising, eager to flood her hidden chambers and give her a child to put to her lovely breasts. He could see a small dark head resting on the graceful curve of her arm, the tiny mouth like a flower as the babe suckled. He could see himself holding them both and watching.

It bemused him when he realized that, in his mind, he already made her his bed partner and mother of his first-born. He, who had never given any woman more than a few sultry hours to ride out her pleasure on him before he deliberately spilled his seed on her belly. He'd never liked it, but unlike the other men he had served with, he had no intention of scattering a horde of fatherless children in the wake of his travels. He would not allow them to grow up as he had, unaware of what lay slumbering inside them.

Yet try as he might, he could not rid himself of the fancy—the woman at his side, naked and willing in his bed, his son at her breast.

He had not been able to read the messages she had received and sent on her wireless, but they had disturbed her, and destroyed his idyllic dreams. The change that had come over her expression had made him wish he could drop down, take the electronic device from her, and toss it into the fountain.

No matter how much he wanted to go to her, Matthias

knew that revealing himself now would be what Rowan called foolish and Drew counterproductive. Taking her too soon would jeopardize endless hours of surveillance and months of meticulous investigative work—and knowing that, still the temptation had come close to overwhelming him.

He climbed down and went to sit on the bench she had occupied. The wooden slats retained the warmth of her body heat, the air the faintest trace of her scent. He let both sink into him as he used his phone.

"Signal's strong, but I think she's suspicious," Drew told him. "She drives like she's trying to shake a tail." Before Matthias could ask what that meant, he added, "A tail is a car that is following hers. Shaking it means evading it."

"She cannot shake off our tail." The GPS transmitter Matthias had planted on her car would send a signal for the next two weeks before it drained its batteries. "Why does she come here, to this Price Park?"

"Maybe she likes to meditate. Let's see." Drew tapped on his keyboard. "It's a public park, built five years ago. Nothing really special about it, except the property and the landscaping. Both were paid for by a private party and then donated to the city."

He recalled the sadness on her face. "She did that."

"I can't find any records available other than some permits filed by a downtown beautification committee," Drew told him. "Considering what prime city real estate went for five years ago, I doubt it was her land. She could have made millions selling it to a developer."

"Not this woman." He glanced at the modest sign bearing the name of the park. "The name Price—see what you can learn from that."

"Sure, I have nothing to do for the next ten years. Why don't I look up Smith and Jones while I'm at it?"

"There was another name. Allen." Matthias glanced up at the sky. The moon had crossed the spangled celestial dome and peered back at him through a veil of charcoal clouds. "My receiver is in the car. Where is her vehicle now?"

"Signal says it's parked in a nice neighborhood three-point-three miles from your position." Drew gave him the street address. "City maps show that to be a pretty exclusive condominium complex. You'll need to find her specific apartment."

Three miles, so she could walk to this park, Matthias thought. "I will track her. You will monitor, and call me if she moves again."

"Rowan called me," Drew told him. "She's getting everything ready, but she's worried about you."

Rowan forever worried about him. Matthias found it alternately amusing and disconcerting. His mother had died in childbirth when he was a boy, and by that time his older sisters had married and gone off with their husbands. Growing up as he had, he was not accustomed to such attention.

Matthias left the park and drove to the address Drew had given him, a large network of buildings with several signs proclaiming them to be Falcon's Ridge Condominiums. An armed guard sitting in a shack before the gated entrance prevented him from accessing the complex. He didn't attempt to talk his way in, but scouted the boundaries of the entire property before parking his car beneath some trees in an empty adjacent lot and taking his pack from the trunk.

The seven-foot-high brick wall surrounding Falcon's Ridge appeared solid enough to discourage any trespassers, but the wide spacing of the street lamps allowed him to find a darkened area that would conceal his movements. Fortunately the decorative bird statuettes interspaced along the top of the wall had been cemented into place, and one held the loop of rope he tossed over it securely.

He climbed up the wall hand over hand, bracing his feet against the brick before removing the loop around the base of the stone falcon and dropping it over the side. He jumped down to a clear spot before rolling behind a row of hedges that had been trimmed into a neat rectangle.

After waiting for any sound warning that he had been seen, he coiled the rope and crawled twenty feet to a small grove of trees, where he stood and scanned the area. The two buildings before him appeared newly built and empty;

beyond them was a walk that followed the circular drive to the other buildings around the complex.

Each building had its own parking lot, and he was obliged to check five before he found the woman's car. From the vehicle he followed her scent, which led him up five flights of stairs to the very top floor of the building, which was occupied by four separate apartments.

The woman's scent ended at the door to the back right corner of the level, and when he stood in front of it he could hear music and water.

He went to the landing and studied the back of the building. No balconies or windows offered him a simple way in, but a sixth, narrow set of stairs led up to the roof. He climbed up and saw rows of dome-shaped transparent bubbles. He had to think for a moment before he remembered the word in English for it that Rowan had taught him.

Skylights.

Matthias eyed the domes, determined which had been placed over the woman's apartment, and took some tools from his pack. He took his time as he went to work on the bolts securing it, removing them one by one until he was able to lift the dome away.

Music drifted up to him, the clear notes soft and sweet, like lark song on a fair morning. They brought with them the woman's scent, and the need returned, so strong and impatient that he had to hold back for a moment and wrestle desire for control.

Below the skylight lay a bed draped with a shiny blue and green coverlet. Ribbons of dark violet wound through the fabric and gathered it in places. He saw only one pillow, clad in a violet cover and, on the wooden stand beside the bed, a cordless telephone unit and a small remote device. The rug beneath the bed, which covered the floor of the room, was a dark green, like thick grass. At the end of the bed lay draped an old, thick blue robe fashioned for a man.

The robe made his gut tighten, for he had not considered the possibility that she lived with a lover.

He slowly replaced the dome and sat, thinking.

Movement drew his eye to the skylight. The woman

walked naked to the bed, her head swaddled in a green towel, and picked up the robe. She pulled it over her body and belted it before walking out of sight.

Matthias rolled onto his back and stared up at the stars. Even through the distortion of the Plexiglas, he had seen the healthy gleam of her alabaster skin and the full globes of her naked breasts. Her limbs and torso had been all long, full curves, ripe and wanton, like a fertility goddess in the flesh. His hands shook slightly as he rubbed them over his face.

He had to stop this. She was a woman to be taken, and not in the manner his body craved.

The light showing through the bubble disappeared, and he heard the sounds of silk moving and the gentle give of a mattress. He turned over to look through the bubble, but the curved surface showed only a dark space.

Now that he knew exactly where she lived and could follow the vehicle she drove anywhere it went, the time had come for him to retreat and observe again from a prudent distance. He kept peering down until his eyes adjusted to the darkness inside the apartment and he could clearly see her form on the bed. She lay on her side, the coverlet pushed to the foot of the bed, her back toward him. Soundlessly he lifted the dome and set it to one side.

She had discarded the robe and wore nothing but a pair of light-colored panties that barely covered her bottom. The long line of her back showed the stretch of her spine and the nip of her trim waist. She had broad shoulders for a woman, but they curved from neck to arm in a beautiful shape, like the polished frame of an ivory harp. The subtle indentations of her ribs showed each time she took a breath, and while her eyes were closed, he sensed she remained awake.

For a time she remained still, and then she began shifting, first to one side and then the other. She took the lone pillow from beneath her head and put her arms around it, holding it against her torso. She pulled it over her face, and then flung it away.

Matthias had spent enough sleepless nights to know her

thoughts were not allowing her to leave this world for the river of dreams. Unless she found some peace within herself, she could not forge her way through the dark waters of the night.

The woman's left hand lifted from her side and came to her face, where she pressed three fingers against her lips. She used the tip of her tongue to lick at her fingertips, and then rubbed the pad of her third finger back and forth against her full bottom lip. The kissed hand curved down, over and under her chin, into the hollows of her throat. The stroking fingers lingered there, tracing the fine bones at the base of her neck as if she hesitated to do more.

Matthias's mouth dried as he watched, unable to breathe, unwilling to move.

She took a deeper breath, releasing it as she turned onto her back. If she opened her eyes now, she would see him looking down at her through the skylight. Matthias found he didn't care in the slightest. If she saw him, he would drop himself through and be on top of her before she could get out of the bed. The ache in his crotch began to beat like a drum.

Open your eyes, lovely one. Give me this reason to come down to you.

Her dark eyelashes remained where they were, but her fine brows drew together as her left hand glided down again. She traced the contours of one breast and then the other with light, unhurried touches, circling around each stiff nipple, pressing in and smoothing over the delicate flesh.

He watched her pinch and tug gently at the peaks, and smelled the change in her scent as her arousal swelled. She wanted a strong mouth there, kissing and suckling at her pretty breasts; he could tell from her manner of toying with them.

The fine edge of her teeth appeared, worrying at her bottom lip as the muscles in her legs stretched and her thighs clenched. Still she played, teasing herself until her breath quickened and tiny beads of sweat appeared on her brow.

Anticipating her, Matthias reached for the front of his

trousers, easing them open until he could work his hand inside. As her fingertips stroked the dent of her navel, he grasped his shaft. The stiff heat against his palm and fingers ached from the hidden tip to the tight cusp of his stones. When her legs parted for her questing hand, he tugged back his foreskin, letting the night air kiss the slick head.

The air rising from the apartment brought to him another gift: the damp scent of her sex, surely the loveliest aroma to ever fill his head. His chest swelled as he tightened his fist, and the steady, pounding surf of his need turned his shaft to inflexible iron and squeezed a single pearl from its blind, seeking eye.

She tended to her sweet place with loving gentleness, cupping and holding at first and then parting the folds beneath the triangle of dark curls to stroke her third finger in the silky moisture gathered between. The wet sounds made his teeth grind together; they called to him with wordless hunger, begging for him to bury himself in her snug little well and fill it over and over until she overflowed.

In she pressed her fingers, petting her pearl before reaching and penetrating herself as she mimicked a man's thrust. As her fingers danced, he stroked in time, his eyes hot and dry, the sight and smell and sound of her tangling inside his head. It had been too long for him since last he lay between a woman's legs; he knew he could not last as long as she could. As he pumped, he prayed he would.

She took in a startled breath and held it as her hips lifted high, and pressed her mound against the heel of her palm. Matthias bit back a groan as his own pleasure broke and he jerked his foreskin up, closing the end over the spurting head. The heat of his seed backwashed, bathing his shaft as he heard the wordless sounds she made, and he watched the change come over her damp face. She held nothing back, lips parted, neck arched, her breasts thrust up as if in a final offering. It took every ounce of control he possessed to watch her peak and do nothing more.

She turned over, slowly pulling the pillow to her face as her body became boneless with satisfaction. It gave Matthias time to cover himself and reach for the dome. He went still as he heard a wrenching sound, and glanced down to see the woman's fists tighten in the pillow as her shoulders trembled with the force of her sobs.

She gave herself pleasure, and then she wept after taking it? He had known women who shed tears in his arms, but they had been joyful—especially if the woman had never before known what a man and woman could give each other.

She has no man to take her in his arms and soothe her to sleep. She takes her pleasure in solitude, just as she weeps.

Matthias carefully replaced the dome. He could not offer her the comfort she needed; he had no place in her home or her bed. With what he had learned this night, he decided he would have to go slowly and carefully. He would have to consider how to initiate contact and cultivate an association. Friendship seemed unlikely; he might have to resort to a business relationship. His friends Rowan and Drew would have ideas on how best to do that without alarming her. When she accepted him—when she understood that she could trust him—he would have her. She would come to him openly and give herself to him.

Only then could he destroy her life.

Six hundred miles to the south of Jessa Bellamy's apartment, a tall brunette entered the penthouse suite of a beachfront building that served as her lover's home, business, and base of operations.

Samantha Brown shrugged out of her jacket and unfastened her shoulder holster, and sent a longing glance in the direction of the sinfully large master bath before booting up her computer terminal. As a Fort Lauderdale homicide detective she had spent most of her nights chasing after killers, and the paperwork involved with her cases never seemed to end. Not that she minded; she was a cop and that was part of the job. Nothing would change that, and nothing had. Not even when she had been fatally shot by a fellow officer who had been stalking her.

Lucan, a retired assassin and possibly the most lethal living thing on the earth, had killed her stalker and saved her life by changing her into what he was: a blood-dependent immortal who could heal instantly, possessed incredible strength, and yet who tried to coexist with humans peacefully.

Aside from the lousy diet, and the fact that she'd fallen in love with one of the deadliest men on the planet, Samantha really couldn't complain.

"You coldhearted bastard," Samantha muttered as she read the e-mail sent to her from a contact in the Atlanta FBI field office.

The reflection of a tall, long-limbed man appeared on her computer screen, and two large, lethal hands gloved in black velvet rested on her shoulders. "You called for me, my love?"

"Not this time." Sam rubbed her cheek absently against the back of Lucan's glove.

Ignoring a six-foot-five, two-hundred-and-thirty-pound vampire, especially one who looked like Lucan, was next to impossible. Even if Sam had been blind, she would have smelled him from a mile away. Tuned to the seductive scent of his immortal body, like dark fields of night-blooming jasmine, she'd known the moment he'd entered the suite. When he touched her, her own body responded with annoying immediacy.

But the information sent to her from Atlanta held her riveted.

Sam didn't sleep until dawn, and she usually spent the last hours of the night in her lover's arms. But when she had arrived home from work, Lucan had been busy downstairs clearing out and closing the club. She'd come up to the penthouse suite they shared to take a shower and catch up on some e-mail while she waited for him. She liked to stay busy when she was alone in the penthouse, the uppermost two floors of Lucan's building, which he had extensively remodeled before they'd met to serve as his private domain.

It wasn't that she felt uncomfortable in their suite. Anyone would appreciate the spectacular, three-hundred-and-sixty-degree views from the wraparound impact-glass windows recently installed; standing in the center of the great room, she could turn around and see the Atlantic Ocean, the Intracoastal Waterway, Port Everglades, and Fort Lauderdale's sleek modern skyline all at once. Comfortable lounges had been placed on the outer terraces so she could recline under the stars and watch the dark surge of the tide roll in over the pristine amber sands of their private beach. If she wanted anything, she just had to pick up a telephone and ask; no matter what it was, the serving staff, which worked three shifts around the clock, would deliver it within minutes.

All the splendor, elegance, and luxury of the suite had been designed to pamper the occupants. If she wanted to, she could sleep in either of the two master suites or any of three guest rooms, or take a long, hot shower in one of the four bathrooms. The library held close to five thousand books on every subject and in every genre, and had a wood-burning fireplace and armchairs made to nap in, while the media room offered every form of electronic entertainment, from the latest CDs and DVDs to the newest video gaming systems. There was even a workout room where she could use free weights, Nautilus, or run on a high-tech treadmill toward a screen that could be preprogrammed to show the view of a jogger running through parks and nature areas in the world, or sweat out her troubles in the adjoining wet/dry sauna.

None of that mattered to Sam in the slightest as she reread the report. "I can't believe it. They've nailed Max Grodan, this con artist who always killed his partners after framing them for his crimes. After all these years, they caught him."

"Marvelous news." Lucan's hands shifted to turn her computer chair around one hundred and eighty degrees. "Surely that brings a happy end to your police work for this night."

She glanced up at the indecently handsome face framed by a mane of corn-silk hair, and the glittering of chrome around the edges of his ghost-gray eyes. Lucan, the former assassin turned benevolent dictator, didn't like being ignored. He also remained mostly oblivious to the work she did, something that often annoyed her more than his looks. "You don't understand."

"Someone has been nailed. You are pleased. Justice doubtless has been served." He knelt before her and leaned in to nuzzle her throat. Against her ear he whispered, "Now, would you be so kind as to forget about being a cop until tomorrow night?"

"I can't." She linked her hands behind his neck and kissed his cheek. "Here's the thing: I have to fly up to Atlanta."

"Oh, no." Lucan pulled her into his arms and stood. "You are coming to bed with me."

"It would be much easier to have a conversation with you," she mentioned, "if you'd get your mind off hopping in the sack with me for, say, thirty seconds."

"Very well." He set her down on her feet and regarded her through narrowed eyes. "Twenty-nine. Twenty-eight."

"The feds in Atlanta busted a pair of grifters," she said quickly. "One of them turned out to be Max Grodan. He was the primary suspect in an old open murder case of mine."

"Twenty," he said, looking bored as he folded his arms. "Nineteen."

"He uses lonely young men and women to run his games," she continued. "He seduces them, trains them, and sends them in under fake or farmed identities. They take all the risk; he gets all the money. Then he frames them, kills them, and walks away. I know there were at least three others besides my victim."

"Thirteen. Twelve."

"God damn it," she said, suddenly furious with him. "You don't own me. This is my job. This is what I do."

The scent of jasmine grew thick and hot, and the empty wineglasses they had left by the window shattered.

"I don't give a bloody damn about your job. You belong to me." He backed her up against a wall. "I keep what is mine close. Here. Certainly *not* in another colony."

"We haven't been colonies for over two hundred years, and I'm going to Georgia only to extradite a prisoner." She threw out a hand. "You're acting as if I'm running off to Aruba with one of the boys in the garrison."

"You would not be that foolish." Popping sounds came from inside her computer, and the monitor screen went dark. "There is something you are not telling me about this. Why?"

"Stop." She pressed her hands against his chest, trying to push him away. She would have had better luck moving a brick wall. "Just stop. Have it your way. I'll let someone else go in my place."

"Samantha."

"He was the first one I ever saw with my talent," she shouted. "I put my hand down and accidentally touched the victim's blood and the vision hit me. One minute I was there looking at the body and the next I was watching the last hours of his life. I thought it was real, that somehow I'd been thrown back in time to be a witness. I saw every moment he suffered, Lucan. I watched that kid crying and pleading with him. Max beat him, and he sodomized him, and then he strangled him. He took his time. He fucking enjoyed it. It's his favorite part. Not even the money makes him feel that good. After he ran I had nightmares about Bobby. For years." She struck her fist into his chest. "Are you happy now? Satisfied?"

Lucan caught her hands and brought her scarred palm to his lips. "I did not realize." He kissed her hand, and then her brow, her eyelids, and the bridge of her nose before enfolding her in his strong arms. "Forgive me."

Sam held on to him, standing docile and quiet as he stroked her hair. He knew the old wounds she still carried from her human life were as deep and painful as his own. Because of the suffering they had both seen and experienced, Lucan understood her as no one else could. Sometimes when she was angry, she forgot just how well he understood.

"I'm a jerk," she said into his shirt.

"You are distraught." He lifted her face, urging her to look at him. "I will allow you to go, Samantha, but not alone."

"He can't do anything to me." She sounded so tired, even to her own ears. "He's only human."

"Fangs do not make the monster, my love." Lucan tucked her head under his chin. "But while I am your lord and master, which will be until eternity comes to an end, I will not let you face such nightmares alone. Now stop sniveling. You promised me no more weeping."

Sam knew she was supposed to adhere to the customs and laws of the Darkyn, which dated back to the Dark Ages. Which also meant she had to do what Lucan told her. But her lover gave her more leeway than another Kyn lord might, mainly because he did understand her calling. For six centuries he had done the same for the Darkyn, although none of the killers he had pursued and captured ever lived long enough to be tried for their crimes.

"How long will it take?" he asked her.

"Two days," she promised. "Three at the most, I swear."

She knew what she was asking of him. Aside from his possessiveness, there was a more pressing need for her to stay in Fort Lauderdale: their bond. Since Lucan had saved her life by changing her from human to Darkyn, they had never been apart from each other for more than eight hours. The bond between them, which had made them life companions, was enduring and demanding. Sam still wasn't sure she understood everything about being his sygkenis, but over time she had come to understand that they physically needed to be with each other in order to survive, as much as normal humans needed warmth and shelter and food.

Sam had also been warned by other Kyn women what would happen if she left Lucan. An extended separation would cause both of them to go through withdrawal, first spiritually and then physically. If they were kept apart too long, one or both of them would lose control and descend into madness. In that mindless state, they would kill anything that came near them.

"I'll be sure to make it back in two days," she said. "I swear."

"There is no need to make a vow." He went to the phone. "I will arrange it so that I can accompany you."

"Wait." She went after him. "You're the suzerain—the ruling lord here. You can't leave your territory."

One of his golden brows arched. "Do you imagine anyone could stop me?"

"No, but . . ." She paused, groping for an excuse. "It's not standard departmental procedure."

He offered her a thin smile. "Neither is your being Kyn. When do you plan to reveal that to your police commissioner?"

"You know what I mean—"

"I do." He stopped her from saying any more by resting a finger against her lips. "Rafael can see to the jardin while we are away, and as you say, it will be for only two days."

"You don't trust me," she muttered, and then the room flipped and she found herself on her back beneath his big frame, her arms stretched out on either side of the bed.

"On the contrary," Lucan said just before he lowered his head to kiss her. "I do not trust myself."

Chapter 4

In the morning Angela greeted Jessa as soon as she came through the office doors. Almost hopping with nerves, the young woman informed her that Ellen Farley had been arrested.

"Linda McMann called for you thirty seconds after Cal and I came in, and then when I said you weren't in yet she told me," Angela told her, so agitated that she tripped over her own feet and righted herself without pausing for breath. "She didn't have a lot of the details, but the detective who talked to her said Ellen and this guy she was with are wanted for running this scam and swindling a big New York corporation. Linda says her boss wants a sit-down so he can do a personal thank-you and all that." Out of breath, she gulped air. "I think she's sending you flowers, too."

Jessa saw Cal standing in the doorway of his office and watching them. He didn't look unhappy or disturbed, but something was wrong.

"Ms. B?"

She focused on Angela. "Everyone is innocent until they're proven guilty, so let's not jump to conclusions. Finish up the file and make sure all the reports are complete. Then whatever happens with the charges against Ms. Farley, she won't be able to sue North and Company for discriminatory hiring practices." She turned to Cal. "Got a minute?"

He nodded and followed her upstairs. Jessa stopped along the way at their small employee lounge to start the coffee, only to find it already made.

"Angela needed something to do besides squeal and bounce off the walls," Cal explained as he filled and handed her a cup. "I didn't supervise, so it's probably undrinkable."

"It's hot, which is all that matters at this hour." Jessa led him into her office and closed the door before skimming through the messages left on her desk. "You have something on your mind?"

"Ellen Farley, what else?" Cal took his coffee to the window to watch the downtown traffic streaming below them. "She didn't look like the con artist type."

"Good ones never do." She separated the callbacks she needed to make from the message slips. "The FBI will likely want copies of everything we have on her. Give them whatever they want, including the original forms she filled out if they ask."

"You didn't seem surprised to hear the news," Cal said, his tone casual.

"I've dug up a lot of dirty little secrets since I began this company," she reminded him. "I guess it's harder to shock me." She glanced over and found he was watching her intently. She set down the message slips. "Something else bothering you, Cal?"

"Ever since Linda called, I've been thinking about some things. For example"—he held up one finger—"you pegged Farley as a fake because she was wearing cheap shoes." He raised another. "You saw through her phony identity, which was good enough to fool North and Company and the rest of us."

"I notice little details, put things together." She shrugged. "It's mostly luck."

"There's one detail you forgot." He lifted a third finger. "You know that the FBI will be calling on us."

"Of course they will. They'll be investigating everything she's done recently—"

"Angela didn't say anything about the FBI being involved," he finished gently. "She said only that Farley had been arrested."

Jessa waited a beat too long before she said, "The

woman just moved from New York to Atlanta. It's only logical to assume that she was wanted by the FBI for out-of-state crimes."

"Nice comeback." He nodded his approval. "Only I'm not buying it this time. You knew about this yesterday." He gave her a measuring look. "You knew, and I'll bet you're the one who called and reported her to the feds."

No one knew what Jessa could do, and as much as she liked people who worked for her, neither could they.

"Sit down, Cal." She waited until he did. "I'm aware Angela and some of the younger staff believe that I'm some sort of psychic. It's flattering, I suppose, but I'm not and this has to stop now. I've built Phoenix on solid, ethical investigative work. If people spread rumors that I can see the future or the past or whatever, it will get around, and soon every quack in Atlanta will flood through our doors."

"Would it be so bad?" he asked. "To let people know just how good you are at spotting fakes?"

"If they think mystical mental powers are involved? Yes," she said. "It would be *very* bad for business. That kind of thing chases away the legitimate clients. Once the quacks find out that I can't actually tell them which stocks to buy or investments to make, they'll go, too. Things like this—Farley getting arrested the day after I flag her—are merely coincidences."

"Is that right." He stroked his jaw with his thumb and forefinger. "I wonder how many of the people Phoenix has investigated have—by coincidence—been arrested a short time after for crimes they thought they'd gotten away with."

He was too damn smart. Jessa had known that from the moment she'd met him. "I couldn't say. But you and Angela and the rest of the staff work for me. I can't have this kind of talk going around about me, Cal. Not even in fun."

"Then you'd better make some changes from here on out," he told her. "Delegate. Use me to initiate some of the searches. If you have to report something to the authorities, wait a week or two before you make the call."

He didn't believe her, and she was running out of lies and patience. "Maybe I should just fire you."

"You could," he agreed. "But I'm on your side, and I don't have to know everything. You're the best goddamn boss I've ever worked for, and that includes my father when he gave me a summer job teaching tennis to the nubile young rich things at the country club he managed."

"Caleb." She rested her cheek against her palm. "You're not helping."

"You know how we feel about you," he continued. "You hired me after I'd been blackballed by every decent company in this town. You persuaded the girls in accounting to leave that bookie they worked for only a week before he got busted."

She made a dismissive gesture. "A friend told me about them. I just gave them a chance to get legal jobs."

"Karen told me you cornered her in a grocery store and offered her a job she had no training for, and then you gave her an advance on her first paycheck. She said it's as if God knew she'd gone there to steal some food for her kids and sent you like a guardian angel to stop her. And then there's poor Angie." He leaned forward. "After her mom died, which roof was she planning to jump from downtown? Bank of America?"

She straightened. "Angela didn't tell you that."

"Someone made a joke about that gorgeous twenty-year-old supermodel who jumped in New York last year," he said. "Angie blew a fuse. Later I asked her about it, and she said no one can understand how miserable and desperate that girl must have been. Ange made it pretty obvious that she does know."

"I like to help people, especially when someone is in trouble," she said in her firmest tone. "That doesn't make me a psychic."

"Then why hire me? No one believed that female sales director who accused me of groping her was actually the one harassing me." He spread his hands. "No one but you."

"You're an attractive young man with good taste. She was a desperate older woman with bad teeth." She smiled a little. "Workplace sexual predators don't happen spontaneously. You had no history of harassing other women. She insisted on hiring only male assistants. I did the math, Cal."

"Einstein couldn't do this math," he assured her. "Jessa, if you asked, I think I'd set myself on fire for you. So would Angie and everyone else." He reached across the desk.

Jessa flinched, jerking out of reach before she could stop herself.

"Why does a warmhearted woman like you avoid being touched?" he asked.

Her temper wanted to answer him, because a month after hiring him she had accidentally touched him. A brush of her fingers against him when exchanging a form had pushed her into the shadowlight, where she'd discovered his secret lust for Angela. She'd seen into his most private fantasies, most of which revolved around scenarios where he seduced and dominated the girl into adoring submission. Caleb's secret bondage fetish was not the only shadow on his soul. When he had sex with other women, he always turned out the lights. His partners never knew it was so he could better pretend they were Angela.

"Shit. That's it, isn't it?" she heard him say. "Touching them. You always shake hands with the ones you don't trust."

The intercom light flashed, and with relief she answered it.

"Jessa, a Mr. Bradford Lawson from GenHance, Inc., is on line three for you," her switchboard operator said.

She had no idea who Bradford Lawson was, but she'd heard of his company. Everyone who did business in Atlanta had.

"Thanks, Karen, I'll take it." She looked at Caleb.

He smiled. "Am I fired now?"

"No." She'd come very close to revealing something she'd guarded for ten years, and while she thought she could trust Cal, she needed to regroup. "Let's talk about this again another time." As he rose to leave, she added, "Caleb, I do appreciate your concern."

"No, you don't. But you have it anyway." Still grinning, he left.

She let out the breath she'd been holding before she picked up the phone. "Good morning, this is Jessa Bellamy."

"Ms. Bellamy, Bradford Lawson from GenHance," a pleasant tenor voice said. "Tim Baker from Nolan, Hill, and Suskin referred me to your company."

"That was very kind of him." Jessa recalled the work she'd done for Tim Baker on three different paralegals he'd been interviewing for hire; one had turned out to be a plant from a rival law firm. "How can I help you, Mr. Lawson?"

"GenHance is expanding its research operations in the Southeast," he said. "That will create about forty new biotech-related jobs here in the city, and another two hundred support positions in our satellite operations over the next three months. The nature of our business has always required thorough background checks and credential verifications on all new hires, which until now was handled in-house. This new phase of our operations, however, is quite sensitive. To keep from having our research compromised, our CEO has decided to hire an independent firm like Phoenix, Inc., to screen our applicants."

"I'd be delighted to have the business, but I have to be realistic," Jessa advised him. "We're a small company, and two hundred and forty screenings can't be done overnight. My people will need at least two weeks, maybe three, depending on the availability of the applicants for interviews as well as the specific information you'd like verified."

"Your candor is appreciated," he said. "But what we're looking for is a more permanent arrangement. If we can agree on terms, GenHance will contract Phoenix to screen all of our new hires. I have the projected figures here. . . ." Paper rustled in the background. "About five thousand or so new positions over the next two years. Would you and your people be up to that kind of challenge?"

Jessa thought quickly. She would have to hire more investigators, at least ten, to handle that much work. But this was what she had been working toward, and with the right contract, GenHance's business would enable hers to grow exponentially. "I believe we are, Mr. Lawson."

"Excellent. I'd like to get together with you to discuss more of the details in person. What are you doing for lunch tomorrow?"

She glanced at her calendar, but the day remained blessedly free of midday appointments. "It looks like I'm meeting with you."

He chuckled. "How does one o'clock at Cecile's suit you?"

He'd picked the best French restaurant in the city, where reservations were usually required months in advance. "That's fine. I'll see you there tomorrow afternoon."

"I'm looking forward to it."

Rowan Dietrich took off her headset as soon as Jessa Bellamy ended her latest call, uttered the filthiest words she knew, and then dialed Drew's private number.

"Mom," he answered in a mocking, childish whine, "I told you not to call me at work anymore."

"Just wait till your father comes home," she said, keeping up the joke with her best stern-parent tone. "He's gonna kick your ass."

"Lovely." A brief crackle of static came over the line as Drew switched on his encryption unit. "We're clear, little mama. Is it her?"

She could have lied and said no, and Drew would have believed her. She wanted to. But the thing was out of her hands now. "Yeah, it's her. She's scheduled to be taken at Cecile's tomorrow afternoon. One o'clock."

"That soon?" He sucked in a breath. "Maybe we should reconsider this one."

"It isn't up for a vote, Andrew," she snapped. "They want her, we take her. It's what we do. It's what you do, when you're not jerking off."

His tone flattened. "Anything else for me?"

"Besides a spot right next to me when we burn in hell for this? Not really." She slammed down the phone.

She went upstairs, more to get away from the communications center than anything, and wandered through the dark corridors. On a good day she could spend hours going through the rooms, looking at all the beautiful old stuff in them, and imagining what it must have been like to live in the place. When Matthias was out of town, she sometimes dressed in one of the old gowns she'd found in the attic, and served herself tea in the Dove Room.

There, with the sunlight streaming through the blue, white, and green bits of stained glass framing the windows, she could forget who she was. There she played the lady, one who didn't know what it was to sleep on a park bench, or wash in the sink of a public restroom, or beg for handouts at the back door of a restaurant kitchen. No one looking at her could see the tats under the long, fragile satin sleeves, or the scars everywhere else. They'd never guess she was trash.

Rowan checked the windows and doors out of habit before walking out into the garage. She wasn't supposed to leave when she manned the fort by herself, but she couldn't stand the silence, and she knew she wouldn't sleep, not after making that call. She got into her Jeep and drove out onto the narrow back road behind the house. From there it was fifteen minutes to her favorite watering hole, Weeping William's, where she sat in the shadows and watched some tubby tourists shoot lousy pool.

The bartender, an old stretch of skinny bones and dark coffee-colored skin, brought her Cherry Coke and a small bowl of pretzels. He had a long, thin birthmark on his left cheek that looked as if he were crying black tears. "Where you been, girl?"

"Working." She took a sip of the soda to ease her dry throat before glancing over at the football game being shown on the small color TV above the bar. "How's the team look this year?"

"Falcons? Shit." He drew out the last word with much-relished disgust. "I can't even bring myself to bet against 'em, though I'd likely clean up nicely. Where's your man tonight?"

"Out of town." She felt a twinge of guilt. "You know he's my boss, not my man."

He leaned on his elbow. "Honey, I seen you looking at him. That's not the way my waitresses look at *me*."

She moved her shoulders. "They're just afraid of your wife."

"Baby, everyone is." He gave the framed picture of his wife, hung strategically over the cash register, a respectful nod. "That reminds me, Sally's been chewing my ear about having you over for supper again. She wants you to show her how to make that chocolate silk pie you brought for our Fourth of July barbecue."

Rowan loved visiting William and Sally. Their comfortable old house, set back on twenty-two acres of pine trees and marsh, was always filled with kids, grandkids, dogs, cats, and any other critter the boys could smuggle in. Sally would drag her into the kitchen the minute she arrived, and feed her bits of whatever she was cooking as they fiercely argued over every aspect of Southern versus Northern cooking.

"You might be a damn Yankee who doesn't know kale from collard greens," Sally said once, "but you the best natural cook I ever met. You should be seriously thinking about opening your own place, sugar."

The praise had embarrassed Rowan, but the pleasure of it had stayed with her for a long time. She did love to cook, and sometimes daydreamed about having a little café somewhere. But it would never happen, not in this lifetime. Reality had eaten up all the delicious dreams of her youth, and spit out only what it couldn't grind down and swallow: her spine, her hard head, and her battle-scarred heart.

"Hey, how 'bout you stay over this weekend and come fishing with me and the boys in the morning?" William was asking. "Found us a sweet little spot out by north side of the island. Coulda filled my cooler three times over by daybreak."

If everything went according to plan, Rowan wasn't

going anywhere until the end of October. "I've got to haul some stuff up north for my boss," she told him. "I'll be gone for a couple weeks. Maybe when I get back."

"Who you talking to, Willie?" One of the lousy pool players came over and peered at Rowan. "Your girlfriend?"

"Nah." William tossed his bar rag over his shoulder. "She my bouncer."

The pool player laughed. "This cute little thing?"

Rowan could tolerate being called a lot of things—even a whore, since she'd almost been one—but little? *Cute?* She might look as if she were still in high school, but she was damned if she'd be treated as if she were.

She slid off the barstool, startling the laughing man when he saw she stood a head taller than him. "You wanna play me a game?" She rolled up her sleeves, showing the twin black-and-red dragon tattoos scrolled around her forearms. "Fifty bucks."

The man glanced back at his friends before he inspected her, from her short, shaggy mop of brown curls to her scuffed sneakers. "Sure, kid." He eyed her small breasts and long torso, but it was her arm art that made him lick his lips. "I'll even let you break."

William glared at Rowan. "You ain't playing him, Ro."

"It's all right, old man," the player assured him. "I'll take it easy on her." He leered at Rowan. "Unless you like it rough, sweetie pie."

She dug her wallet out of her back pocket, pulled out two twenties and a ten, and slapped them on the bar, watching her opponent until he did the same.

William put an empty shot glass over the bills. "I can't watch this again." He retreated to the far end of the bar.

Rowan chose a cue from the wall case, racked the billiard balls at the end of the table, and chalked the tip of her cue. Her opponent and his friends gathered around behind her, and when she bent over she heard a low murmur and snickering sounds.

"If you're going to admire my fine ass, boys," she said as she set up the shot, "first you'd best get out the way of my stick."

The first ball she sank was an easy one; they actually cheered her on. The second she dropped with a bank shot quieted them down. They fell silent when the third and fourth balls knocked each other into opposing corner pockets. As she took each shot, the red eyes and scales of her dragon tats caught the light and gleamed beneath the fine sheen of sweat that formed on her skin. Beneath the ink covering her right arm, however, something else gave off a different glow, and when she saw the glimmer of blue through the black she jerked down her sleeve.

Five minutes later she had cleared the table and finished the job by tapping the eight ball so gently that it drifted into the side pocket.

"Good game." Rowan walked past the gaping men, replaced the cue, and went to the bar to collect her winnings. Her opponent reached her in time to grab her wrist and hold the folded bills in her fist between them.

"You ain't hustling me, jailbait," he said in a low, ugly voice. "You put the money back down and we'll do this two outta three. And I'll break this time."

Rowan stared down at his sweaty face. "The bet was one game, fifty bucks. I won. Let go."

"Boy, you pushing it," William called from the other end of the bar. "You turn her loose afore things get outta hand."

The loser gave him an impatient look. "What are you gonna do, old man? Jump on over here and kick my ass?"

"No." Rowan dropped the bills, which fluttered to the floor. When he looked down, she grabbed the back of his hair and rammed his face into the knee she lifted. "I am."

He toppled over, clutching his bleeding nose and uttering muffled, hoarse sounds. Rowan faced his friends, who did the wise thing and backed away. She bent down to check his injury and the amount of blood he was leaking onto the floor before she picked up the money.

"I haven't been jailbait for a good three years," she told him before she straightened and addressed his friends. "His nose is gonna be sore, but it's not broken. Wrap some ice in a washcloth and hold it on; that should keep the swelling down."

Before she left the bar, she handed William a twenty. "See you when I get back. Give Sally a kiss for me." She glanced back at the tourists. "Sorry about the blood."

"Uh-huh." He pocketed the tip. "Next time, you mopping it up."

Chapter 5

Bradford Lawson spent the morning with his personal trainer at the club, where he worked on his abs and obliques before swimming a hundred laps in the pool. Since he'd turned thirty he'd stopped taking his fitness for granted and spent a minimum of three hours each day improving it.

The results showed in the sleek pads of hard muscle all over his body, but he remained dissatisfied. Physical exercise helped burn off the extra calories from the gourmet food and rare wine he liked to consume, but it took too much time and effort. Fortunately his trainer also provided him with injections that maximized the benefits of his workouts.

"You're looking real good, Mr. Lawson," the trainer said as he drew out the needle and pressed a cotton ball over the dot of blood that appeared. "How are you feeling?"

"Tired and wet." Lawson closed his eyes and rested his head against the tile wall of the locker room as the booster streamed through him. The heavy, pleasant effect of the drugs faded after only a few seconds. "I need another one."

"I've been meaning to talk to you about that," the trainer said, closing his case. "You've been asking for a lot of doubles lately."

"What about it?"

"The mix I use is special, you know, best-quality stuff." The trainer's tone grew tentative. "Thing is, see, it's real easy to get hooked on it. I think we should scale back the shots for a couple weeks."

He opened one eye. "*You* think we should."

The other man shifted his weight from one foot to the other. "You hired me to look after you. That's all I'm doing."

Lawson chuckled. "In a couple of months I won't need you or your shit. But until then, you'll do what I tell you. Now give me another one, and do it fast."

The trainer shook his head. "Something happens to you, and word gets around, I could lose a lot more than my job."

Lawson got up from the bench and walked up until he was nose to nose with the trainer.

"Nothing is going to happen to me," he said very softly. "But if you don't shut your fucking mouth and give me another shot, I'll pop your head like a rotten grape."

"This is what I mean," the trainer said through white lips. "You can't keep boosting like this. You'll go off the deep end and kill someone."

"I think I know my limits, but all right. I'll cut back." He adjusted the collar of the trainer's polo shirt. "I've got to close a major deal today, though, and I'm not walking in there feeling like this. So you give me another one now, and tomorrow we'll drop it down to a half dose."

"Tomorrow. You mean it?"

Lawson nodded.

"Okay." The other man opened his case and took out a filled syringe. He extended Lawson's arm, tied a length of rubber tubing above the elbow, and tapped the inside bend until a vein rose up beneath the skin and he could administer the injection. "There you go." He removed the needle and turned to retrieve a cap.

Lawson brought his fist down on the base of the man's skull with enough force to drop him facedown on the slate floor. He picked up the case, checked the contents, and carried it over to his locker. As he dressed, the second injection refreshed and calmed him, so that when he went over to the stirring, groaning man he was smiling.

"You're fired. Find another place to work." Lawson carried the case out with him.

From the car he called ahead to Cecile's to confirm his reservation for lunch, and asked to speak to his usual waiter.

"Yes, Mr. Lawson."

"I'm meeting a lady for lunch at one," he told the waiter. "I'd like her to have the chef's special. Perhaps you could meet me on your break to discuss the presentation."

"Yes, sir. Will the lady need a ride home?"

"No." He glanced at the case on the passenger's seat beside him. "She'll be coming back to the office with me."

"She's to be taken today," Matthias repeated, to be sure he hadn't misheard Rowan.

"At one o'clock, at this French restaurant." She recited an address. "That gives you about three hours, unless you want to change your mind and back out."

He finished writing down the address before he replied, "Why is she to be taken so soon?"

"I don't know. Drew has nothing on paper. But for it to go down like this, the order had to come from Genaro himself." She hesitated, and then said, "You're not going to change your mind about doing this, are you? I don't think I can drive down there in time."

"You would take her yourself?" He didn't know whether to feel amused or dismayed. "She would know who you were and what you intended from the moment she touched you."

"Ms. Jessa Bellamy would never lay a finger on me." She sighed. "I don't like rushing this way, Matthias. It's happening too fast. None of us are ready for her."

He was, since the moment he'd entered the park last night. "We will make it do." He thought for a moment. "Rent two more cars for me. Attend to the doors and the harnesses and then have them delivered to the second and third drop points."

She took in a sharp breath. "You're going to drive her out yourself? Is that really wise?"

"There is no time to bring in the others." He started the engine of his car. "Do what you can to prepare for her there. I will contact you once I'm in position."

"Be careful."

Matthias drove downtown, stopping first at Jessa Bellamy's offices to check the lot for her car, which was parked in an end space. According to Rowan, she would meet Bradford Lawson at the restaurant, but he checked the signal of the GPS transmitter he'd planted to be sure it remained strong and steady. If she changed her mind about the meeting, or for some reason bolted at the restaurant, he might have to pursue her.

He found a space on the next block over that allowed him an unobstructed view of the lot beside Jessa's office where she kept her car, and parked there in order to pull up a map of the streets and businesses surrounding Cecile's. The large restaurant occupied a corner lot and offered valet but no public parking. Another concern was how he would remove Jessa from the premises. He called Drew and had him pull the building blueprints to check how many ways he might enter and leave the restaurant.

"On the plans I see two access doors and two emergency exits," Drew said. "You can go in through the front and walk straight through the kitchen out to the back. The alley has only one exit, though."

"I need two ways to leave so that if one is blocked, I can use the other." Matthias consulted the map. "I think I will take her from the front. I will need the car close."

"The valet isn't going to let you park anywhere in front of the place," Drew said. "Your best bet to get her out that way is to do a snatch and run: Pull up, leave the engine running, yell to the valet something about your wife being sick, go in, grab her, drug her, carry her back out, toss her in the car, and go."

He made it sound simple, when Matthias knew it would be anything but that.

"I haven't taken my lunch hour yet," Drew mentioned. "I could run over there, give you some backup."

Matthias grunted. "If you are seen, they will know."

"Yeah, that's why I avoid the fieldwork," he said, his tone wry. "But I don't think you can pull this off by yourself. It's too public. Too many things can go wrong."

"Place a call to Lawson at one fifteen," Matthias said finally. "That is when I will go in after her."

"Will do. Keep your gloves on," Drew said before he hung up.

Matthias watched the lot until he saw Jessa Bellamy emerge from the building and walk to her car. She wore another plain suit, this one a green so dark at first glance it looked black. Between her lapels a vee of emerald cloth and a flat length of golden chain gleamed. Another glint of gold at the back of her head came from the long, plain comb holding her jet-black hair in a smooth roll.

She looked serious and sedate and strikingly beautiful.

This time Matthias saw that she carried a briefcase instead of a purse, and when she slid on a pair of sunglasses he noted that she had once more donned her black gloves. She would not use her ability on her clients unless she had a reason to, he thought. That would prove helpful to him as well, for if she touched him with her bare hands, her ability might make her see that he had come to take her.

He reached for the pack he had left in the backseat, and set it in the space between the front seats. As Jessa Bellamy drove out of the lot, he rolled up his sleeves and strapped thin, flexible sheaths to his forearms before sliding his daggers into them and covering them again. Rowan had also packed a coin-size pressure dart that he could hold and hide in his hand, but after looking at it for a moment he placed it in his pocket. He would use it if he had to, but not unless things went wrong inside the restaurant.

His remote receiver showed Jessa's car to be a safe distance ahead now, so he pulled out of the parking space and followed her. She took the most direct route to Cecile's, which convinced him that she had no suspicions of what was planned for her. That would make things easier for him, but more difficult later, when the time came to tell her why she had been taken.

As he maneuvered through midday traffic, he put his

hand in his pocket and held the pressure dart between his fingers, turning it over and over.

Not long now, my lovely one.

Jessa surrendered her keys to the young valet parking attendant, who handed her a numbered stub and an admiring look.

"Enjoy your meal, ma'am," he said as he went around the back of her car.

She'd land the largest contract she'd ever been offered first, Jessa decided as she went into the restaurant. Then she'd enjoy the food.

She was met in a quiet foyer by a maître d' in an elegant day suit, who greeted her as if she were the first lady before asking for her name. When she gave it, he smiled and told her that her party had already been seated. She checked her watch before she followed him into the main dining room, but she wasn't late—in fact, she was five minutes early, as she'd planned to be.

Cecile's owners had made quite a splash when they had moved their four-star restaurant from Paris to Atlanta, for they had insisted on bringing the antique furnishings, kitchen equipment, and even the draperies from the original location with them. After some wrangling with OSHA over building codes and licensing requirements, they adapted their expectations to the demands of doing business in the States, and then proceeded to dominate the downtown fine-dining scene.

Jessa had never been to Paris, but Cecile's did the impossible by bringing the city to her. Deep, rich burgundy velvet had been gathered and draped to frame sheer panels of port wine organdy, embroidered with ivory and amber threads, covering the windows and gentling the afternoon glare of the sun. The carpeting, a series of old Turkish rugs, formed a graceful patchwork and disappeared under delicate floor-length ecru lace table linens. The cherry wood chairs, comfortably upholstered with champagne-and-pink tapestry cushions, gleamed with polish and years of loving handling.

The air brought a complex bouquet to her nose: the light florals from the vases of fresh flowers, fragrant beeswax from the tapers of the same in the old brass wall sconces, and the effervescent fruitiness of the champagne sparkling in dozens of flutes.

Couples and small groups occupied every table, talking and smiling over crackled porcelain plates as they politely devoured their meals. Jessa spotted red-brown game hens braised with wine and shallots, brilliant red lobster garnished with fanciful shapes in shimmering aspic, and delicate pastel soufflés that seemed to float on the fork. Not a wineglass stood empty—the owners were French, after all—and no patron had to summon his or her waiter, for they were attended as carefully as blue-blooded royalty. Some of them, she suspected as she noticed some famous faces, probably were the American equivalent.

Walking through this shrine to haute cuisine, Jessa thought of the tasteless microwave dinner she'd picked at last night and felt almost ashamed. She might not be as rich, powerful, or influential as the people who dined regularly at Cecile's, but she had been raised to appreciate well-prepared food. While living alone made cooking seem like an utter waste of time, she could certainly dust off her sauté pan and rice steamer once in a while and toss together something fresh.

The maître d' approached one of the tables set in a discreet corner, where a good-looking man sat reading a single-page menu card. She'd seen his Italian suit before, on a hip young movie star posing at the last big Hollywood red carpet event, but despite the overtly trendy cut, the dark brown jacket and camel trousers emphasized his even tan and professionally streaked hair. As he stood, the fit of his jacket changed enough to hint at a well-developed physique. She also noticed how short he had cut his nails; Angela did the same thing to avoid her lifelong habit of biting them.

Determined, up with the latest fashions, and something of a body peacock summed up her initial impression of Bradford Lawson.

He showed her the perfectly even teeth of a boyhood spent in braces. "Good afternoon, Ms. Bellamy."

"Hello, Mr. Lawson." Jessa returned his smile, relieved that he didn't also offer the traditional business handshake. She'd removed the gloves she always wore whenever she was out in public before arriving—September was cool, but not enough to justify wearing leather gloves throughout a meal.

Avoiding his touch was a business necessity. In the past she had considered using her ability on potential clients as well as the people they hired her to investigate, but she felt she had to draw the line somewhere. If she looked into the dark side of every soul, she knew someday she'd end up thinking about visiting the roof of the Bank of America building herself.

As she sat down, she saw he'd nearly finished a cocktail, and wondered if her watch battery had run down. "I hope you haven't been waiting long."

"Not at all. My previous meeting was canceled at the last minute, so I got here a little earlier than I expected." He motioned to a waiter, who trotted over to offer her a menu card. After he placed his order for one of the steak entrées, he turned to her. "What are you drinking?"

Jessa needed a clear head. "Water, please."

"They have an excellent cellar here, and as it happens, one of my favorite chardonnays," Lawson mentioned. "I think you'll enjoy it." He told the waiter to bring a bottle.

Jessa wasn't accustomed to being overruled, even as smoothly as Lawson had done it, but she'd met enough corporate alpha males to recognize a deliberate show of gender dominance. Lawson might want women to admire his body, but he liked ordering them around better.

"Just a small glass for me," she told the waiter, surprised to see his strained expression. Her gaze shifted to the rings of underarm sweat darkening his otherwise crisp white shirt. "I'll also have the shrimp St. Jacques with the endive salad and the lemon-caper vinaigrette."

"Very good, ma'am." The waiter hurried off.

"I hope he's not contagious," Lawson observed, watching the man disappear through the swinging doors to the kitchen before turning back to Jessa. ""I'm sorry. The service here is usually flawless."

She smiled. "Everyone has a bad day at work now and then."

"Not at GenHance. Jonah Genaro, our CEO, is very particular about whom we hire. He wants only the top people in their fields." He sat back. "Now let's talk about how Phoenix, Inc., can see to it that he actually gets them."

Matthias watched the dashboard clock as he drove through the streets around the French restaurant. At one fourteen, he took his pack, stowed it under his seat, and then turned the corner and moved into the right lane. He accelerated enough so that when he pulled in past the frowning valet and stopped, the car's tires squealed. He left the engine running as he shoved open the driver's-side door and got out, locking the door with his spare key's remote.

"Sir." The valet trotted over to him. "I'm sorry, but you can't park here."

"My employer came here to propose to his lady friend. I was to take the pictures, but traffic delayed me. If I do not go in right away, I will be fired." He handed over his business card. "It will take two minutes, I swear to you, and then I will go."

Thunder rumbled overhead, and dark clouds spread rapidly over them, casting heavy shadows as they blocked out the sun.

The younger man glanced up and scowled. "It was supposed to be sunny all day." He barely looked at Matthias's card before he handed it back to him. "I guess you can leave it there for a minute. Get back out here fast, though, buddy, or my boss'll call to have it towed."

"Thank you." Matthias strode into the restaurant.

He had decided to modify Drew's suggestion of the snatch-and-grab to something that would cause no disturbance. Rather than playing the part of a frantic husband coming to the aid of an injured wife, he was now a tardy photographer trying to keep his job. As soon as he saw the well-dressed man in the foyer, he took out another card.

"Mr. Bradford Lawson called for me," he told the man. "He wishes to have some photographs taken of him and Ms. Bellamy."

"I'm afraid we don't allow photographs to be taken in the dining rooms without making arrangements in advance," the man told him.

Outside the restaurant, the air flashed as lightning boomed nearby.

"The photographs I take will be of only Mr. Lawson and his companion, and they will appear in several of the city's newspapers," Matthias said. "Mr. Lawson is very fond of Cecile's, which of course will be mentioned prominently in the accompanying article."

The older man beamed. "Well, I think this once we can make an exception for Mr. Lawson. He and the lady are seated in the corner to your left."

Matthias thanked him and walked into the dining room. Several of the patrons frowned at him as soon as they saw the camera hanging from the strap around his neck, but Matthias ignored them as he spotted his target.

Lawson had moved his chair out of place so that he could sit closer to Jessa, who was listening to him talk. Her expression seemed odd, almost slack, and her eyelids hung low over her eyes. Lawson put his arm around her shoulders and leaned close, speaking in a lower voice.

Matthias stopped in front of their table and lifted his camera. "Would you care for a picture of you and your lady?"

Lawson glared up at him, and then muttered an obscenity as Jessa's head drooped and she slumped against his shoulder. "No, my friend isn't feeling well. Too much wine, I think."

A rushing sound distracted the patrons around Matthias, who looked at the rain drumming on the outside windows at the front of the restaurant.

A waiter standing nearby hurried forward. "Do you need help escorting the lady out, Mr. Lawson?" He bent over, his arms outstretched.

"No—"

That was the only word Lawson uttered before Jessa flung the steaming plate of seafood in front of her into his face. As he fell back, she produced a slim case and swung it, ramming one end into the waiter's midsection. He doubled over, his head bouncing as it hit the edge of the table before it drove him to his knees.

Lawson swore and grabbed at Jessa, grasping the sleeve and yoke of her jacket, holding her down. Lightning struck so close to the restaurant that the wineglasses and porcelain dishes on the tables rattled. Several women and a few men uttered startled, fearful cries.

Matthias dragged the table out of the way and shoved Lawson off his chair. As he went down, GenHance's director flung the wine in his hand, glass and all, into Matthias's face. He turned his head at the last moment, and the glass burst against the side of his skull, dousing him with the chilled liquid.

As he shook the fragments of crystal from his face, Jessa stepped around the waiter to face him. Her eyes, like tide pools in moonlight, were wide and clear. She had been playacting.

"Go through the front," he told her.

She didn't move. "Who are you?"

"Run." He gave her a push as Lawson got to his feet, a gun in his hand. Matthias stepped on the waiter, palming his second blade as he blocked her with his body.

"Fucking bitch," Lawson swore as he changed his aim from her back to Matthias's face.

Before he could fire, Matthias slashed his wrist with one dagger and hamstrung him with the other, the honed steel cutting so deep that Lawson screamed.

He turned and ran after Jessa, catching up with her just outside. She looked from one end of the street to the other, her eyes wild. The heavy downpour became furious, flattening her hair and saturating her clothes in the time it took for her to turn her head to see him.

He didn't make the mistake of touching her, but he stepped close so she could hear his voice over the rain.

"Come with me," he told her, and held out his hand, "or you will die."

PART TWO
Found

RomanRelics.com
The Official Web Site of Roman Relics Magazine

September 2008

Special Report:

**Controversial Imperial Scroll Raises New
Questions about Roman General's Death
by Alphonso York**

One of the more intriguing artifacts found among
the hundreds recently unearthed at a parking lot
construction site in Rome is the so-called "Germanicus
Scroll," a personal communication that may have
been sent by the Roman army proconsul of the same
name to his grandfather, Emperor Augustus, in the
year 14 CE.

Inked on well-cured leather and preserved by
not one but three different resin-sealed casings, the
scroll offers a poignant account of Germanicus's
ceremonial visit to Kalkriese in Lower Saxony, where
ten years past thousands of Roman soldiers were
ambushed and massacred by a rebellious German
chieftain and his army of Cherusci warriors. Dated
in the year 14 CE, the scroll when authenticated may
serve as proof that the Roman general visited the

site a full year earlier than historians have always claimed.

The scroll itself consists of one hundred two lines of script, divided into two columns. The text is written in the first person, apparently by the general's own hand, and contains references to several personages of the time, including a popular senator who was also a protégé of the emperor's wife.

Written only a matter of weeks before Augustus died, the scroll offers a fascinating glimpse into the mind of the great Roman general as he recovered the remains of his fallen comrades from the battlefield. Even more tantalizing, however, are the hints regarding the mysterious fate of Germanicus's childhood friend, Tanicus, whom historians have always included among the casualties at Kalkriese.

Roman Relics has obtained for our readers a complete translation of the text, provided by Professor Angelo Calabrese of the University of Rome:

Nero Claudius Drusus, named Germanicus, to most beloved and glorious Augustus Caesar, divine son of Julius and protector of the Republic, many fond greetings and continuing prayers for your health.

You write to me, Grandfather, of your displeasure that I do not report more of my travels and deeds. Since you demand it of me, under your compulsion I shall relate what I would have happily concealed until I might return to Rome and advise you in my own voice.

I have brought the legions north, as you commanded, and three days past we came upon Kalkriese. I came so the men would see it and know what it is to be a soldier of Rome, and so that I might in your name offer prayers and pay homage. My second task was to search for the remains of Varus, as asked of me by his wife and daughters when last I visited them.

We followed that pathway though the wood between the great bog and the high hill. Remnants of the rampart in the turf at the base of the hill can yet be seen, and it chilled my heart to think that Arminius and his horde concealed themselves there to await the first column. A hundred paces across from it, one can still pluck from the ground the broken shafts of the spears they threw in vain, but they were close and there are not many.

Two days we rode on through the open country and reached that place where the final three legions sought refuge so they might stand the last against the horde. As we made our way there we saw signs of how they pushed through, ever under attack. The bodies of those who fell from the outside ranks marked the way for us, and my horse could go no more than a hundred paces before I saw another of our dead, slain and left to rot.

You cannot know what it is to see fourteen thousand dead. In your darkest imaginings there is no equal. Weather-bleached bones cover the open ground, scant few where men fleeing the ambush were brought down by their pursuers, but here and there again piled where the ranks stood their ground back-to-back.

As we entered the woods, we saw skulls pegged to the trunks of every tree within our sight, a thousand and more, their hollow eye sockets staring at us in empty reproach. Others who had come here before me claimed that Arminius hanged them as a warning to us, that Rome may never again invade Germania. It proves useless on me; I can feel only rage that Romans were used for such a thing, and that no one thought to remove them and consign them to the flames.

My aide worried me with how we might know which belonged to Varus, and then the scout returned and called us to follow into the groves ahead. So we rode on, and now I must tell you: the years I have spent on the frontier have accustomed my eyes to sights of such barbarism that I should not have blinked. But who among us could have expected to see still standing the altars where the captives were made sacrifice?

The tribesman fashioned the altars from the armor hacked from the remains of the fallen. They did not concern themselves with removing the arms and legs and chests still within; they stacked and bound them together as they were taken, and used whole bodies roped together to serve as platforms. The flesh of these poor brothers has long gone, but their bones remain to give testimony. Upon these obscene mounds of flesh and iron, Arminius and his wretches laid out the finest soldiers ever to serve the Republic, and butchered them in more ways than I may tell you, and so they piled others atop them, again and again, until no more could fit, and another altar was made to be built.

I felt no peace, Grandfather, until we discovered in a hollow well hidden from the groves the untouched bodies of Varus and his staff. The reports brought out of Germania by those few who escaped were true. In the end the sons of Rome came together as brothers, united by their determination to die as they had lived, with courage and honor. The bones of their hands still clasp the hilt of each sword; their bodies still cradle the blade upon which each ended his life. Glad I am that they did not fall to the Cherusci, but had the heart and spine to do what every man dreads.

In shame I wept as I sent my men to collect the bones of our valiant fellows. We give them a funeral pyre this night, and I have sworn to return after the campaign to recover and send all of our dead to their rest. For now my priests consecrate the ground and entreat the gods to richly reward our noble dead. It pains me that I cannot remain here long enough to attend properly to all of them.

My only other regret is that I have found no proof of Septus Janus Genarius's claim that my friend and blade brother Tanicus accompanied Varus or died with him here. I know it possible that he was taken prisoner with the thousand sold into slavery, but my heart insists that, like Varus, he would have fallen on his blade before accepting the yoke. I never believed the tale that he remained in Germania in secret so that he might spy upon the barbarians, not for thirteen years with no word to us or his family. I will have council when I return from the frontier, and perhaps then the senator may be persuaded to speak more on the matter. He has always claimed that he himself escaped the barbarians when they killed Varus and his commanders. Now that we have proof that they took the only honorable course, the senator must explain why he did not do the same.

If we are to erase the memory of what was done here, we must push on beyond the boundaries of the great river. These rebels must be shown what Rome is. I implore you in the names of Mars and Varus to speak to the senate and make this clear to them, especially Genarius, who continues to press you to recall our legions marching north so that Rome might not anger the tribes.

We cannot allow this massacre to go unanswered, Grandfather. If we do, then Rome will fall.

(Seal of) Germanicus

Dr. Calabrese strongly believes that the scroll may never have been delivered to the emperor, as it was found with its original seals intact. The professor is currently attempting to locate the construction site on available maps of the ancient city in order to determine ownership and possibly identify who buried it.

For more on this two-thousand-year-old mystery, pick up the latest issue of *Roman Relics* magazine, available at fine bookstores and newsstands near you.

STORY UPDATE:

Controversial Imperial Scroll Proven to Be Forgery
by Alphonso York

The so-called "Germanicus Scroll," an intact first-century imperial scroll believed to be recovered from a parking lot construction site in Rome, has been proven to be a forgery by American experts who were given permission to examine it. After a second examination, a team of Italian experts has agreed.

"The forgery was very well-done, but upon closer inspection we found we were able to confirm the Americans' findings," Geno Zanella, the leader of the Italian team, told reporters. "This scroll was made in the last few weeks, not two thousand years ago."

The American experts, whose trip to Rome was underwritten by a grant from biotech corporation GenHance, Inc., made no comment about their scandalous revelations, and released their findings and test results before they left Italy to return to the States.

RomanRelics.com attempted to reach Professor Angelo Calabrese at the University of Rome for his comments, only to be told by university officials that the professor has been missing since the forgery was exposed. The president of the university about

Calabrese's abrupt disappearance: "Angelo was the most honest of men. If he said the scroll was genuine, it was. You can be sure he will explain everything as soon as he returns."

Another colleague, who wished to remain anonymous, had this to say about the scandal: "I think those Americans tampered with the find. They might even have switched the scroll with a counterfeit in order to steal it from us." When asked why Professor Calabrese vanished on the day the forgery was made public, the anonymous colleague said, "He was the only one who had worked with the scroll. I think they had him killed to cover up the theft."

At the time of this update, police in Rome were still investigating the matter.

Chapter 6

The violent storm confused Jessa as much as what had happened in the restaurant. There hadn't been a cloud in the sky when she'd left the office—and not the slightest hint that Bradford Lawson had intended to drug her and abduct her. Now this strange man had come after her and uttered some nonsense about her dying.

"What?" Jessa stared into beautiful, angry eyes the color of old jade. "What did you say?"

"GenHance," the man told her. Tall and powerfully built, he stood like a prizefighter ready to throw a punch, his chin down, his arms bent, his hands fists. "They brought you here to take you. To kill you."

"You're crazy." Jessa backed away from him. "Get away from me." She turned toward the valet. "Call the police—"

The man bent over, shoving his shoulder into her belly almost as hard as she'd hit the waiter with her case. Before she could recover or fight him off he upended her over his shoulder and ran with her twisting, kicking body to the car. Screaming for help, she struggled frantically, but he simply pulled her off him as if she were no more than a rag doll and flung her inside.

She landed on her side in the passenger's seat. Before she could push herself upright he clamped his right arm across her heaving form, slammed shut the driver's door, and drove out into traffic.

"Let me out of here!" She tried to free herself, clawing

and pushing at his arm before grabbing at the door handle, which wouldn't move. "What are you doing?"

"I'm taking you to safety," he said, weaving in and out of the traffic lanes with terrifying speed. "I'm saving your life."

The back of the car skidded on the wet road, fishtailing for a second before the man quickly righted it.

"You can't drive like this." She pushed at his arm. "The rain is flooding the roads. We'll crash."

He checked the rearview mirror. "Better to crash, then."

She forced herself to calm down, catching her breath as she looked at the interior of the car. The lock on the door had also been removed, and the windows of the car had been tinted almost black.

"You cannot get out," he told her, shifting his arm and reaching for something on her other side. "There is nothing you can use as a weapon. I will not harm you." As the traffic on the road ahead of them thinned, he leaned over her and pulled a funny-looking seat belt over her, clipping it into place.

She glanced down and saw the dark stains on his dripping sleeves. She almost asked him if he'd been shot before she recalled the flash of steel she'd seen in his hand. "Did you stab Lawson?"

He nodded. "Twice."

The matter-of-fact tone he used made her stomach roll. "Why?"

"He pointed his weapon at my face." He glanced at her. "He would have shot me. He would have done the same to anyone else who came between him and you. Then he would have shot you."

"You're wrong. Bradford Lawson is a businessman." She pushed the wet tangle of her hair back from her eyes. "He works for one of the largest biotech firms in the country."

"He does."

He wasn't asking her; he was agreeing. Maybe she could talk him out of whatever he had planned. "Then you must know he has no reason to shoot me."

"I know he has many reasons. He was sent to take you,"

he told her. "They need you, but not alive. The drugs were the usual measure, but shooting you would have stopped you and made you easier to transport."

He sounded delusional, but she realized something else—he wasn't American. She couldn't place his accent, but his careful English and the words he used made it clear that he wasn't speaking his native language. He might come from a country where violent confrontations were normal events.

"You're mistaken," she said, as gently as she could. "A lot of Americans carry guns for protection. He probably took it out as soon as he saw you with your knife."

"Knives," he corrected. "I had two."

She swallowed. "Then you can understand how that might have frightened him."

"He took out the gun after you put your food in his face." He paused as he made a quick, tight right turn. "I drew my blades only when I saw the weapon in his hand."

She was reasoning with a seriously disturbed man, and that required another deep breath. "With everything happening all at once, maybe it seemed that way to you, but I'm sure it was the other way around."

"You know it was not," he countered. "You knew he meant to take you before I came to you."

"I don't know—"

"When I first saw you, you were making a pretense of being drugged," he reminded her. "You knew what he had planned before I reached you. You used my interruption as an opportunity to escape him."

"I don't know anything about his plans." Her fingers hurt, and she looked down to see she had them laced so tightly together that all the joints had turned white. She forced herself to relax her hands. "I knew only that the waiter drugged the wine."

His mouth hitched. "How did you know this? Did he whisper it to you? Did he pass you a note?"

He couldn't know, but he sounded as if he did. "I tasted it when I took a sip," she lied.

"That was a remarkable feat," he said, "as the drugs Lawson uses have no taste."

He *was* toying with her. "Look, mister—"

"My name is Gaven Matthias."

Why was he telling her his name? "Gaven, I'm Jessa." Maybe he was some sort of deranged Good Samaritan who would respond better to some assurances—not that she planned to keep them. "I appreciate what you did back there. It was very heroic of you to risk your life for me. But you have to pull over and let me out now. I won't report you to the police, I promise." At least that much was true.

"Lying to me and yourself will not change what has happened. Lawson was sent to take you, and you know it." He gave her a quick sidelong look. "Now that he has failed, others will be sent. Professionals this time. They will go to your office and your home. They will watch your employees and your friends."

Her throat tightened. "I'll call the police—"

"By now Lawson has reported you to them," he said, startling her again. "He will say that you arranged to have me attack him. That you are with me now. That we are armed, dangerous. The police will begin to search for us. They will block roads. They will issue warnings to the people. They will use the television."

She went rigid. "If you know he'll do that, then you had to be in on it."

He stopped at a red light and turned to face her. "You are not the first to be taken. Nor will you be the last."

Now he was going to tell her how many women he'd murdered, and how he planned to kill her. "You've done this before?"

"GenHance has. Many times." He saw the light turn green and returned his attention to the road.

Every book she'd ever read featuring a serial killer had a scene like this, Jessa thought. The newly abducted victim, bound and helpless, begged for her freedom. The satisfied killer ignored her pleas or mocked her. So far Matthias had ignored every request she'd made, and his cryptic statements could easily double as taunts. Even his assurance that he was taking her to safety didn't make her feel any better.

The safety might be for him rather than her.

The seat belt he'd pulled over her had three straps instead of two, which crisscrossed tightly over her from shoulder to waist. When she tried to loosen them, she discovered they had no give, and the belt clip on her left had no release button.

She was trapped, as surely as she had been in the restaurant. "If you really want to help me, Gaven, then please take this belt off me. It's too tight and I can't breathe."

He didn't look at her as he drove onto the ramp leading to the expressway. "If that were so, you would be unconscious by now."

He was the last man on earth Jessa wanted to touch, but if she knew what he had done in the past, she could be ready for what he intended to do to her. Working an arm out from under the restraining straps, she reached over and clamped her hand over his.

Shadowlight.

A cutting wind scoured her face with tiny, stinging ice crystals, and she had to squint against the blinding intensity of white light. Taking a breath was the same thing as being stabbed in the lungs. Buried to midcalf in fresh, powdery snow, she felt her feet go numb.

The blizzard didn't allow her to see much of her surroundings, but she was outside, alone, and so cold her body shivered with the helplessness of someone having a seizure. If Matthias were here, she couldn't see him, but she slogged forward, wrenching her legs up and down, pitching forward as the snowdrifts collapsed under her weight. She landed on her hands and knees, and then she saw the vague shape of a man fighting through the snow ahead of her.

He struggled to stay upright against the wind. Under his arm he carried something, a snowy bundle too small to be a body but too large to be his laundry. The ice-encrusted scarf wrapped around his head covered all but his eyes, but it was Gaven Matthias. She could feel him as surely as she felt the wind and cold.

She couldn't read his thoughts, however. His mind seemed wiped clean of everything but staying on his feet and taking the next step.

Jessa heard thunder, and what sounded like a low-flying jet over her head, and looked up. That was when the bomb went off, exploding with enough force to scatter the violent wind and create a momentary window of visibility. She could see the top of a ridge with an enormous shelf of snow that seemed to be rising higher.

It wasn't until several smaller bombs went off and a cloud of white billowed at the base of the ridge that she realized the mountain was not rising but that the shelf of snow was sliding down, all of it at once—on top of her.

Jessa flung up an arm as the first chunks of snow crust pelted her, as hard as thrown rocks, and then a white ocean roared over her, lifting and rolling her, flinging her against tree trunks and bouncing her off boulders before it swallowed her whole.

As a crushing weight settled over her, her thoughts became a jumble of disbelief: *Snow? Mountains? Not Atlanta. Where? Where is he? What did he do?*

Her fingers slipped away from the disembodied hand she held, and she was glad. She didn't want to see the airless void of white anymore. But the cold that bit into her aching body didn't retreat, and the grinding weight pressing over her didn't ease.

The sunlight never came.

After speaking to Cecile's owners about the incident involving Lawson and his latest acquisition, and assuring them he would pay for all the damages they had incurred, Jonah Genaro called for his car. Before he left the office, he confirmed that Delaporte was dealing with the witnesses and the evidence left at the scene. Fortunately the waiter and Lawson had been removed by Lawson's driver and taken for medical treatment to a private hospital owned by one of his subsidiaries, or he doubted he could have kept the police from becoming involved.

"I took the liberty of posting retrieval teams at Bellamy's office and home," Delaporte added. "She hasn't surfaced yet."

"Tap every phone line and have Riordan run a sweep

for her mobile," Genaro said. "Monitor her personal and business bank accounts and credit card activity. She'll need money to flee the state. Have you identified the male accomplice at the restaurant?"

"Not yet, sir, but we're still interviewing the witnesses. Descriptions indicate he's a white male, early to mid-thirties, casually dressed and carrying a camera. The valet said he identified himself as a photographer Mr. Lawson called to the restaurant to take photos of him and Bellamy."

Had Bradford Lawson staged this entire incident in order to blackmail him, or grab Bellamy for himself? Genaro felt his temper rise. "I'll speak to Bradford. Send additional men out to keep Bellamy's employees under surveillance. Use whatever means are necessary. I want her brought in before morning."

At the hospital emergency room, a nervous charge nurse led him back to the treatment room, where two physicians were attending to Lawson, who was fighting restraints and raving.

Genaro's suspicions that his director had staged the incident for his own purposes or profit faded. From the amount of blood spattering the gurney, Lawson, the two physicians, and the floor, whoever had attacked Lawson had not been playacting.

"What's wrong with him?" he asked the senior physician.

"He has two knife wounds, one serious," the doctor replied. "The rage seems to be chemically induced, possibly from cocaine and steroid abuse. We're running a tox screen to confirm. He won't allow us to bandage him."

"Leave us," he told the doctors, who reluctantly withdrew. When the door closed, he approached the gurney and stood over Lawson. "Bradford. What happened today?"

"What the fuck do you think happened?" Lawson snarled back, jerking at the straps holding him down. "That sorry bitch knew, Jonah. She knew before she got there. She brought protection with her and the fucker cut me."

"Control yourself." When he didn't, Genaro wrapped his hand over Lawson's wrist wound and tightened his fist until the younger man howled. "Do I have your attention now, Bradford?"

He groaned a yes.

"Good." He eased back on his hold. "Pull yourself together and tell me everything that happened this afternoon at Cecile's."

As Lawson sullenly related the details of his meeting with Jessa Bellamy and how it had suddenly and inexplicably gone wrong, Genaro silently studied both of his wounds. The photographer who had attacked his employee had great skill with a blade; he had effectively crippled Lawson with two meticulously placed slashes but had not bothered to follow either with a jab to the heart or a major artery. Given the circumstances, the man who had come to Jessa Bellamy's rescue had intended to disarm and disable, not kill.

That made it almost certain that he was not a photographer.

"Did the man have a military haircut, or use government-issued blades?" he asked Lawson when he had finished his tale.

"He wasn't military. The bastard's knives were strange. Old-looking." He shifted his leg. "Fuck. Maybe handmade."

"What about an accent? German? South African?"

"I don't know. Not American. Maybe Dutch. He went right for my gun and my fucking leg, the cocksucker." He squinted up at Genaro. "He had a tat on the left side of his neck. Black, maybe a snake."

He went still. "What shape was the snake?"

"I don't know. Like a number eight, maybe. But sideways."

After grilling Lawson for another ten minutes, taking care to get a full description of the photographer, he released his wrist and went to the sink in the corner to wash the blood from his hand.

"When you find her, I want her first," Lawson demanded. "All I need is a room, some cuffs, and eight hours."

"Bradford, you're not in any condition to deal with Ms.

Bellamy." He reached for some paper towels and carefully dried his hands before turning back to him. "Let the doctors finish working on you and get some rest."

"You can't leave me here like this," Lawson raged. "Not after what she did. She planned this, Jonah. She knew I was coming for her. Someone warned her. Just have them sew me up and let me out of here, and I'll find that fucking cunt myself."

Genaro found it interesting that Lawson's rage centered on Jessa and not the man who had attacked him. He knew about the younger man's predilection for intimidating and sometimes battering his sex partners; on more than one occasion he'd exploited Lawson's weakness to deal with female subjects who subsequently proved much more cooperative.

A pity, he thought, that his director's present physical and mental condition rendered him useless, possibly in the permanent sense of the word. He'd decide the younger man's fate as soon as the physicians reported back to him on the prognosis.

From the hospital Genaro had his driver take him to his private estate outside the city. Genaro rarely visited his personal residence during the week, as the guest suites at the GenHance building were more convenient, but tonight he needed a few hours alone to think.

His butler, who had once served in the households of British royalty, met him at the door. "Good evening, Mr. Genaro." He took his coat and briefcase. "Will you be dining at home tonight?"

"I'll have coffee and sandwiches, James. Bring it down to the armory." He walked to the elevator and took it down to the third sublevel of the house, where he stepped out, closed his eyes, and waited as jets of cool air blew down from the ceiling grid and a beam of UV light passed over him. A soft chime indicated the end of the decontamination cycle, and he went up to the wall scanner beside two massive steel doors and leveled his left eye with the lens.

The automated security system scanned his retina, identified him, and produced a small keypad from a concealed slot. Genaro entered his master code and stepped through as the doors slid silently apart.

He'd originally built the armory to serve as his personal vault and a lockdown safe room where he could retreat if the house security was compromised. The room had independent power, ventilation, and water supply systems as well as enough nonperishable foods to keep a single occupant alive for as long as eighteen months. One wall contained security camera screens that continually monitored the interior of the house and sublevels as well as the grounds of the estate; the other had been outfitted with televisions that received their signals from three different satellites, an Internet server and access terminal, a powerful radio array, and direct voice lines to trusted allies in half a dozen countries.

An adjoining room served as a personal living space, with a comfortable bed, a large bath, and movie screens modeled as faux windows that displayed realistic outdoor views of the country and were timed to lighten or darken depending on the actual hour of the day.

When Genaro had left Italy to come to America in the nineties, he brought with him a small but unique collection of antiquities, which at first he displayed in the house and then moved to the vault room after some of the more fragile relics began to show signs of deterioration. The filtered air and climate-control units helped to preserve his collection, but there was another, more immediate benefit: securing them away from all other eyes. Genaro had spent most of his life acquiring the antiquities, and felt very possessive about them. He found he enjoyed storing them in the one place where they were safe and only he could enjoy them.

That was something taught to him by the practices of the one man he thought might have understood him, his noble ancestor Septus Janus Genarius of Rome.

The twelve hundred and forty-two artifacts ranged from marble statues liberated from his ancestor's ancient Tuscan villa to dozens of bronze and terra-cotta figurines that had been purchased from collectors or the various Middle East black markets for antiquities. All depicted the head, bust, or form of Genarius in the flowing toga of a Roman senator or clad in the ornate armor of a legion commander.

Several ensembles of armor, exact reproductions of what Genarius would have worn during his years serving in the legion, were displayed on mannequins Jonah had commissioned to be made in the image of his ancestor's many busts and statues. He would have preferred to have the originals, but they had been lost to the sands of time.

Genarius had been one of the wealthiest men of his time, and his possessions reflected that privileged life: costly bronze mirrors, cast vessels, hand-fashioned goblets, and extravagant lamps had been recovered from his country home, as well as a few of the only blown-glass ornaments and finger rings of the era known to still exist. The cautious senator had also hidden beneath his villa sacks of coins, some so rare that they had yet to be cataloged by anyone in the world except Genaro.

Records and carbon dating indicated that all of his possessions had been removed from the house and hidden in an underground bunker by Genarius a short time before he had died. Perhaps he had been warned about the epidemic and tried to secure his wealth before the sickness reached his household; Genaro would never know for certain. In any case, before he had died the senator had moved most of his wealth to secret caches and vaults, where it had lain undisturbed for two millennia.

It had taken longer to find the scrolls Genarius had written, sealed, and secreted away in the tunnels beneath his city compound, but eventually Genaro had also discovered and opened that vault. There were books, letters, and manuscripts written about Genarius or mentioning him in some significant manner that dated back to the tenth century, many telling the tale of the common foot soldier whose courage had brought him up through the ranks until he had commanded his own armies.

The prize of Genaro's collection was the original proclamation issued by Augustus appointing Genarius to the

Roman senate; that had been preserved and passed down through countless generations of the Genaro family as proof of their ancestor's nobility.

Genarius had been an important man, serving three grateful emperors and building much of the Roman Empire. Aside from the Caesars, few Roman noblemen had ever been depicted in stone, which emphasized Genarius's standing among the elite of the empire.

His ancestor had also left behind evidence of a devoted but puzzling interest in the career of a distinguished *praefectus castrorum*, Tanicus. Like Genarius, Tanicus had risen through the ranks from foot soldier to centurion to *primus pilus*, and then had been named third in command of his legion. At first Genaro had assumed his ancestor had used his influence to help promote the man, until the translations of Genarius's many letters and records made it obvious that Tanicus had been made *prefect* while Genaro's ancestor still served as a centurion. From the intense interest Genarius had shown in following the commander's career, he assumed the man had been one of his ancestor's mentors or patrons.

Tanicus had been listed as one of the casualties of Kalkriese, but for years after the tragedy, Genarius continued to search for the commander. Apparently worried that his friend had been sold into slavery by Arminius, he had written to every known survivor of Kalkriese, begging for news of what had happened that day. He had a statue carved of the commander, which he kept in his house and, according to the dates on the scrolls, had continued looking for him until the last day of his life.

All that historians knew about Tanicus was that he was the childhood friend of Germanicus, the emperor's favorite grandson, and the most trusted of his commanders. He was also rumored to have been a member of a small, elite group of *triarii*. Little was known about the band of veteran soldiers, except that each member had been awarded the *corona muralis*, the simple crown of laurel leaves given to soldiers who had risked their lives to save another's. That highly prized award had prompted scholars to refer to the unit as the Laurels, and some estimated that the group might have been established as far back as the foundation of Rome itself, some seven hundred years before Tanicus had been born, and continued until the final collapse of the empire some five hundred years later.

Only Genaro knew that Tanicus had indeed belonged to the Laurels, and like the other members had tattooed himself with their distinctive mark. His ancestor had referred to the mark over and over in his descriptions of the commander, and had gone so far as to have it carved into the statue of Tanicus that he had commissioned.

Genaro went to the statue recovered from his ancestor's villa, the only known image of Tanicus. Oddly the sculptor had not attempted to idealize the commander's features, but portrayed him as an ordinary man with an austere face and dressed in the unadorned garments of the freeborn.

He seldom looked at the statue, for it had no value to him except as one of Genarius's personal possessions, but now he went to it and removed the protective cover draping it. Across two thousand years, the grim-faced commander stared at him through his blank marble eyes, his arms at his sides, his body poised as if he were preparing to take a step toward him. Genaro reached out and touched the mark chiseled on the side of the statue's neck, the tattoo of the Laurels, a mark that would have been covered by his armor or easily concealed by the collar of a cloak.

Only Genaro knew that the mark of the Laurels was an ancient pagan symbol that had been found etched into the walls of caves in Tibet and on the trunks of enormous trees worshiped by forest pagans. No one knew the true origins of the mark, but the Romans had called it the *lemniscus*—the ribbon—and the Greeks sometimes called it the *Ουροβόρος*, the tail-devouring snake.

The Greeks had named it correctly, Genaro thought as he traced the mark with his fingers. It did resemble a snake that had twisted itself in half as it ate its own tail.

It also looked exactly like the number eight, tipped over on its side.

Chapter 7

Matthias left the freeway and drove to a busy twenty-four-hour rest-stop complex, where he parked his car out of sight in a back lot next to the second vehicle Rowan had arranged for him. A magnetic cache hidden in the second car's rear wheel well also contained a tight roll of currency, a new disposable mobile phone, and a note from Rowan.

They're after you now. Keep her out of sight and call in when you switch cars.

He transferred his pack and wiped down the surfaces he had touched before lifting Jessa out of the passenger seat of the first car. As he straightened and nudged the door shut with his knee, Matthias noticed a couple with four young children walking from the restrooms into the back lot. Quickly he turned around and went to one of the metal benches beyond the curb and sat down, holding her upright against him on his lap. He placed her hands inside his shirt and tucked her face against his neck as he lowered his head and put his mouth against her cheek.

"What's that man doing, Mommy?" he heard one of the children ask as the family passed him.

"He's taking a rest with his wife, Justin." The frowning mother quickly herded her children along at a faster pace while her husband slowed his step to take a longer look. "Peter, please."

"Okay, honey." The husband gave Matthias a grin and a wink before trotting to catch up.

Matthias didn't want to move Jessa until the family departed, so he held her and waited as the couple helped their children into the backseats of their van. He would have been concerned with handling her as much as he had, for it surely would have roused another woman, but some indefinable sense of her told him that she had retreated into herself and would not wake for some time yet.

This brief delay gave him the time to look at her as much as he wished, and he mapped every inch of her face, from the off-center peak of fine black hair above her left brow, down the gentle slope of her nose, and over her pretty lips to the strong line of her jaw. Awake she likely kept her features composed, giving away only as much as she was willing to allow others to see. Now she seemed softer, younger, untouched by the suffering she had endured.

He could only guess what her life had been like since her ability had come over her. Knowing that with a single touch she could see into the darkest corners of the soul could not have been a temptation; it must have seemed like a curse. He thought of all the people he had contact with in the course of a single day. He disliked touching strangers, but some contact was unavoidable when exchanging money, accepting goods, or walking through crowded areas. She could not wear gloves year-round and have it go unnoticed; she could not lock herself in her office to avoid the people who worked for her or the clients who sought her services.

"How do you manage it?" he murmured to her. "Do you surround yourself with the innocent, or do you make them think you are cold and distant?"

A strand of her hair had caught in the corner of her mouth; he used a fingertip to brush it away. Even that small touch caused his hand to come alive with tingling nerves, just as it had when she had put her hand over his.

The brush of the tiny, invisible hairs on her thin skin reminded him of a delicate veil over silk. The paleness of her flesh still astonished him; he had grown accustomed to the uniform glowing tans of American women. Such ivory beauty should have been too fragile to bear anything more than a whisper or a breath without bruising.

Matthias saw a flash of red brake lights as the van drove out of the lot, and knew it was time to move her. As he put his hand under her knees, her head slipped back against his arm, lifting her face to his. He held her for another moment so that he might feel her breath warming his mouth. He had never been so close to a woman and not had her pinned beneath him, opening herself to welcome the thrust of his shaft. With her ability, Jessa would not even have that much. Her loneliness was not by choice, he realized. To take a lover, she had to touch—but he had seen it with his own eyes: The only touch she permitted herself was her own.

"I understand now." He lifted her against his chest as he stood and carried her to the second car.

Lowering the seat, he eased her back until she couldn't be seen through the car's windows. As he made her comfortable, she remained limp, but the strength and steadiness of her heartbeat and breathing assured him she was not in a dangerously deep sleep.

He couldn't know what she had seen when she'd touched him, but he could guess. He had relived the moment a thousand times in his own memory, cursing the desperation that had driven him that day. He had been an arrogant fool, so intent on seeking justice that it had blinded him as surely as the storm.

But had she seen everything? Would she understand?

After he returned to the highway, Matthias called Rowan to tell her he had made the first transfer, and to send one of their helpers to pick up the vehicle he had left behind.

"Who is after me?" he asked.

"Try everyone with a badge in Atlanta," she said. "You and Ms. Know-it-all also made the six-o'clock news. They don't have any shots of you, but by eleven her face will be plastered on every major channel in the nation. All they're saying is that you're both wanted for questioning as a person of interest in an attempted murder of a prominent businessman. You know how fast Genaro moves when he's motivated."

"Indeed." He had hoped for a little more time, but that was not to be. "What more?"

"Drew stole a copy of the GenHance file on her," Rowan said. "Records only go back ten years, and then she doesn't exist, so Jessa Bellamy and her background are definitely bogus. She would know how to do that the right way, of course. He had more luck with the name you gave him. By the way, how come she's not making any noise? Did you gag her?"

"She sleeps." He flexed his right hand, trying to dispel the lingering sensations from touching her face. "She used her ability on me."

"Bad move, boss." She sighed. "What are you going to tell her when she wakes up?"

"She may already know." Matthias glanced at Jessa. Now when he looked at her face, he wished she would wake. It would make moving her more difficult, of course, but he wanted to see her eyes again. He had never known a woman with rain-colored eyes. "Tell me about this luck with the other name."

"I'm still downloading everything he stole from Genaro; give me a sec." After a short pause, she said, "I've got it. Okay. An Allen Taggart Price died during a workplace shooting in Savannah back in 'ninety-eight. Seven other people at this investment brokerage were also shot and killed by a mentally ill former employee, one Jennifer Johnson. The only unconfirmed survivor was Minerva Jessamine Starret, twenty-two years old." Rowan paused and then added, "It was her first day at work, poor kid."

He hardly heard her over the rush of blood to his head. "Minerva."

"It's not that bad. I knew a kid in middle school named Jesus Supreme Lord Loomis. We called him Loomy Tunes." She flipped a paper. "No birth records but a child welfare report, estimated born 1976 in Chicago, abandoned at birth, placed as an infant in a Catholic group home for unwanted children—big surprise there—adopted in 1981 by Darien Thomas Starret of Savannah, no wife, so no mother for her. Enrolled same year in very expensive private Swiss school, stayed there until she graduated and attended college in France, returned to the U.S. in 'ninety-seven, resided with father until his death by natural causes in 'ninety-eight. Couple of months before she was shot."

"You said Minerva was the unconfirmed survivor," he said. "What does that mean?"

"It means they're not sure she lived. Minerva took a slug to the chest, point-blank range, was admitted to Savannah General and listed in critical condition for three days. Intake report notes indicate extensive lung and cardiac damage from the GSW. She wasn't expected to live more than an hour or two, so they didn't operate." Rowan flipped more pages. "Okay, and now it gets really interesting. Minerva left the hospital three days later."

"After being shot in the chest."

"Ten witnesses swear they saw her walk out of the building. That was the last time she was seen alive. Officially reported as missing and declared dead by the state in 2005 so they could auction off her inheritance and drop the proceeds in the treasury." She made an amused sound. "I'll give you three guesses what comprised the bulk of her estate."

He already knew. "Sapphire House."

"Uh-huh. Now, would you mind telling me—"

"Yes," he said. "I would mind. Are there any photographs of Minerva Starret?"

"Driver's license from DOT." Rowan's friendly voice became distant. "Transmitting a JPEG. Should be on your screen now."

Matthias looked at the small image that appeared on the viewscreen of his mobile. The identification picture showed a young, smiling girl with short-cropped black hair. The poor camera and indifferent lighting had washed most of her vivid coloring and muted the gleam of her black hair, but it could not erase the blaze of energy and determination in her eyes.

"Well?" Rowan asked, her voice oddly strained. "Is this little princess our girl?"

"Jessa is more queen than princess." Matthias pulled off the highway onto the shoulder, parked, and shut off the engine before he held the phone next to her face. The lines and shape of the nose, mouth, and jaw of the image were very similar to Jessa Bellamy's. "There is a strong resemblance. Do the hospital records say if Minerva had any marks or scars on her body?"

"Besides the great hole in her chest ..." Rowan fell silent for a time. "How about that. Minerva had a small tat on the inside of her left wrist. A gold and black owl."

Matthias took Jessa's left hand and turned it up so that he could inspect her wrist, but saw no tattoo of any kind. "Jessa does not have a mark."

"Maybe she was the shooter."

"No." Matthias took a piece of her hair and idly wound it between his fingertips. "She could not kill."

"You're basing this assumption on what? Listening to her snore for an hour?" Rowan made a rude sound. "Gaven, I know you like her, and I'm sure she's gorgeous and troubled and helpless and all that shit. But if this is going to work, you can't get involved with her. None of us can."

He let the strands of dark hair slide out of his fingers. "She doesn't snore."

"Excuse me?"

"Nothing." He sat back and closed his eyes. "Is everything prepared?"

"Room's ready, fortress is secure, and Drew is starting the paperwork. We should be able to relocate in a week."

Seven days, that was all he had, and then he would never see her again. "Very well. Go to bed; sleep. Tomorrow will be the worst."

"Wake me up when you get in."

Matthias switched off the mobile and reached for the locking security harness installed in place of the passenger seat belt. He disliked restraining her, but if she were to wake during the last leg of the journey, she would likely try to escape him. He shifted her so that she would be as comfortable as possible under the harness, and tucked her hands beneath the straps. As he did, his thumb brushed across the thin skin of her left wrist, and he felt something. He reached up, turned on the interior overhead dome, and brought her wrist under it.

A series of pale lines marked the inside of her wrist, almost too light to be seen. As he turned her arm, unlike the rest of her skin, they caught the light and reflected it. The shape they formed was that of a small, round-headed bird.

Exactly, in fact, like the outline of an owl.

Lucan noticed three things about the state of Georgia: The land was beautiful, the natives' dialect made them almost as incomprehensible as the Cubans of south Florida, and the men in authority here did not care for females having the same.

"That there's the problem, miss," the fat desk sergeant said as he settled his bulk on one elbow so he could get a better view of Samantha's neckline. "Y'all come here without an invite to pick up a prisoner after hours. I don't know how y'all run your department down there, but that's not how it works in Atlanta."

Much to Lucan's disappointment, Samantha did not leap across the scarred surface of the reception desk or rip out the offensive mortal's throat. She, the soul of patience, merely smiled.

"The prisoner has considerable financial resources at his command and is a serious flight risk," she told the insolent mortal. "The last time he made bail on capital murder charges, he fled the state. The district attorney wants only to assure that he stands trial in Fort Lauderdale."

"Lady, my captain don't care if he has to go before a judge in the North Pole." He chuckled at his own joke. "We got our way of doing things, and this ain't it."

"Obviously." Lucan took her elbow and pulled her to one side. "This is a waste of time. I will go and retrieve the bag of scum."

"Scumbag," she corrected. "We had an agreement. We're here to extradite Max Grodan, not terrorize and destroy half the city." Before he could reply, she added, "Behave yourself, suzerain, or I'll make you fill out the paperwork."

He eyed the stack of forms the desk sergeant had produced. "You would not be so heartless."

"Keep pushing and find out." She went back to the desk,

collected the forms, and made an appointment to see the chief of homicide the following afternoon. "Would it be possible to obtain a copy of the arrest reports?" When the man scowled, she added, "I have to call the district attorney tonight, and I'm sure he'd be interested in how cooperative your department has been."

The sergeant released a long-suffering sigh before he trudged into a back office and returned a few minutes later. "Here's copies of what all the feds sent over with him."

"Thank you." Sam took the folder and glanced at Lucan. "We'll need a hotel room."

"Five of my favorite words." He clasped her hand in his. "But I've already arranged suitable accommodations."

She didn't seem to hear him, engrossed as she was in the contents of the file.

In the car, she finished reading and closed the folder. "That's odd. I thought they caught him in the act, but they didn't even know he was in the city. Stop driving so fast."

"This is a Ferrari," he reminded her. "It does not allow itself to be driven slowly. What act?"

"Setting up another con," Samantha said. "The guy uses his partners for everything—making hotel reservations, renting cars, buying whatever he needs—all under their names. That way there's never any evidence implicating him. He never leaves a trail. I figured his new partner tipped off the Bureau. Instead, they get an anonymous phone call reporting him and the partner."

Lucan shrugged. "So a good citizen did their duty."

"Someone knew everything—where he was, who he was with, what they'd already done in New York, and what they planned to do here. Max is a ghost. He just doesn't exist." She frowned, thinking. "Maybe one of his old partners got away from him. But how would she know where he was, and what he was doing?" She looked up through the windshield. "Where are we?"

"Our hotel room, so to speak." He parked at the curb in front of the Armstrong building. "I spoke to Scarlet. He was kind enough to extend to us the use of his city stronghold."

She didn't look happy as she got out of the car. "All right, I suppose it's okay. Which floor is it?"

"All of them."

She stared at him. "You borrowed the entire *building*?"

"Of course. I am a visiting suzerain." He put an arm around her waist. "What would you have me do, Samantha? Take rooms for us at the Motel 6?"

"Oh, shut up." She walked with him to the entrance, where a human male dressed in a dark brown suit met them at the doors.

"Suzerain Lucan." The mortal bowed. "I'm Charles Kendrick, the building manager. Suzerain Scarlet sends his regrets that he could not personally attend you, as he is still overseeing the repair work at Rosethorn. We've prepared a suite for you on the fourth floor. If you require anything during your stay, please notify the staff by pressing zero on any phone."

Lucan noted the small black cameos glinting in the mortal's cuffs, indicating the mortal was a *tresora*, a trusted human who had been trained from birth to serve the Kyn. "Thank you. We should not be here for long."

Lucan could feel Samantha's tension building as they took the lift to the fourth floor, where it opened as an entrance to the massive guest suite.

She glanced around the walls covered with peach silk hand-painted with trompe l'oeil trellises and dark green ivy, the light oak English country furnishings, and the crisp white and sky blue draperies. "Jesus. I feel like I just stepped into a dinner mint."

"I could inquire to see if they have something more in line with a Skittles theme," he said, bending to place a kiss on her shoulder, and then frowning as she moved to avoid his touch. "Perhaps the bedchamber will be more to your liking."

She ignored him and wandered around the sitting room, almost but not quite touching several of the room's treasures. "You only see stuff like this in high-end house porn magazines." She looked up at the room's rock-crystal chandelier, from which a small bluebird hung in perpetual flight.

She pushed her hands into the pockets of her trousers, but not before he saw that they were shaking. "How far away is Motel 6 again?"

Lucan realized his *sygkenis* had little exposure to the sort of luxuries the centuries had allowed the Kyn to acquire, but she was hiding something else behind her sarcasm. "We can leave and go anywhere you wish. You have but to say."

"No, I can do this." She sat down gingerly on a French chaise and hunched her shoulders as she rubbed the side of her forehead. "Sorry. I'm just a little tired."

As he went to her, her scent wrapped around him. It had a deeper, more pervasive note than usual, one that betrayed her real state. "You lied to me."

She glanced up. "Huh?"

"You said that you would attend to your needs before we departed Fort Lauderdale." He cupped her cold cheek. "If you had, your body would be warm, and your hands would not be trembling."

"It slipped my mind." She rose and tried to go around him, but when he countered the move she came up short. "I'll give myself an injection later."

"Why not now?"

"I forgot to pack my syringes, all right?" Her pupils shrank to thin black crescents as her hazel eyes turned pure gold. "I'd order some more from the local pharmacy, but I doubt they carry the copper-tipped, blood-filled brand."

Knowing that her temper could easily incite his own, he forced his own thoughts to remain calm. "You cannot keep depending on the needles. Before you shout at me again, remember that our bond and your distress rouse my talent, and you are standing directly beneath a crystal chandelier."

"I'm sorry." She exhaled slowly. "Alex told me she uses only injections. She said it's better this way. Easier to live with—like being a diabetic."

"Alexandra heals humans," he reminded her. "You hunt their killers. Your personalities are different, and so are your instincts. The needles have not been satisfying you for some time now, have they? Why have you concealed this from me?"

"It's my problem," she snapped. "I don't need blood all the time. I can go a couple of days without it."

"But tonight you want it. Very badly, I think." He studied her stubborn expression. "Who tempted you? Rob's *tresora* downstairs? Or that annoying mortal at the police department?"

"I didn't do anything." She wrapped her arms around her waist. "I'm still in control."

"Are you?" She didn't seem to realize that her *dents acérées* were fully extended, or that she was shedding enough scent to seduce a small army. "There is no reason to deny yourself any longer." He took hold of her arms and tugged her closer. "I will hunt with you."

"Honey." Now she bared her fangs. "You're not helping."

"You would not blame a starving mortal for feeling hunger," he told her gently. "Yet you condemn yourself for this."

"When I look at someone and all I can think of is sinking my teeth into his throat, being happy is a little hard to swing." She turned her head. "They must have some bagged blood in here somewhere."

"You cannot hunt a plastic bag."

Her fiery golden eyes flashed up. "I don't *hunt* anything."

"I disagree, Detective." He pulled her closer, ignoring the stiffness of her limbs as he pressed her face to his chest. "Do you trust me?"

"No," she said into his shirt, and then, reluctantly, "Yes."

In that moment, his love for her almost overwhelmed him. "We are hunters, Samantha. Our needs cannot be ignored or forgotten, or we risk losing control. When that happens, we do not merely feed. We kill. You *will* kill."

"You've seen it happen before, haven't you?" When he nodded, she uttered a wretched sound. "You should have let me die, Lucan."

He smiled. "You should never have given me a reason to live." He shifted around her, curling an arm around her waist. "Come. There is a club in the hotel at the end of the block. It should offer some variety."

"Stop talking about people like they're entrées," she said as she walked to the lift with him.

Lucan stopped on their way out to have a discreet word with Kendrick before escorting his *sygkenis* to the Bar with a View. Samantha remained mute as he led her to a table and ordered wine, and didn't object when he left her to walk among the mortals to select a likely candidate. He found an attractive, healthy young thing, took a moment to compel and instruct her, and then returned to the table. Samantha looked rigid and miserable as she stared into her wineglass.

"Always choose someone young and of a healthy weight," he said, startling her. "Take in their scent; it will tell you much about them. Inebriated or drugged humans give off an unpleasant, acrid odor. Those with diseases smell of strong chemicals or rot."

"I am *not* going to sniff anyone."

"You do not have to." He looked up as the fetching young black female he had chosen for Samantha approached them. "They will bring their scent to you."

"Hey, there." The girl, barely out of her teens, flashed her pearly teeth at Lucan before turning to Samantha. "I saw you walk in, and I had to come over and say hi." She sat down in the chair beside his *sygkenis*. "I'm Abby."

"I'm leaving." Samantha made it halfway to her feet before Lucan caught her. "No. She's just a kid."

"She is an adult," he assured her. "Adolescents have a simpler scent. It does not attract us."

"I'm twenty-four," Abby said at the same time Samantha said, "I'm not attracted to her."

"I am not suggesting you take her to bed, my love." Lucan reached over and took Abby's hand, bringing it close to his *sygkenis*'s face. "Breathe her in. That's it. Can you feel her pulse in the air?"

Samantha closed her eyes, swallowed, and nodded.

He turned to the mortal female. "Abigail, would you be kind enough to show my lady to the powder room, please?"

"Sure. It's right around the corner." Abby took Samantha's hand in hers. "Come on."

Lucan watched them cross the crowded floor of the club before he followed. He stopped outside the women's restroom, moving aside as several smiling females streamed out before he entered.

Inside he found Samantha holding off the young female, who was trying in vain to embrace her.

"You're so beautiful," Abby was saying, her expression dazed. "I'll do anything you want."

Samantha turned her head and saw him. "Get her off me."

Lucan reached back and flipped the bolt on the door. "She is under your influence now. Command her."

"Stand still," Samantha told the girl, who immediately dropped her arms and stood quiescent. She began to reach for Abby but suddenly jerked her hands away. "I can't do this. Lucan, please, get her out of here."

"You must trust yourself."

"I don't." She gave him a wild look. "For God's sake, help me out here."

"You know you will not harm her." Lucan went to stand behind the girl and rested his hands on her shoulders, urging her closer to his *sygkenis*. "You will be gentle. You will take only what you need from her."

"Please," Abby whispered.

Samantha took hold of her wrist and brought it to her lips. She hesitated again, but this time the call of the girl's blood proved to be too much for her, and she struck. As she drove her fangs into the mortal's flesh, Abby shuddered and groaned her pleasure.

Lucan supported her as he watched Samantha feed, stroking the girl's arms with soothing hands. He did not have to tell his lady when it was time to stop; Samantha wrenched her mouth away and pushed at the girl.

"That's enough," she panted.

"You must see to them when you are through," he told her, taking a handkerchief from his jacket and pressing it over the puncture marks in the girl's wrist. "Most will stop bleeding at once, but should it continue, you must tend to her. A small amount of your own blood will seal the wounds." Fortunately the girl responded well and her blood clotted immediately. "When you know she is well, you must remove the memory of this." He turned Abby toward him. "You will forget us and return to your home now. Go to bed and sleep the rest of the night."

"Forget. Home. Sleep." Abby nodded and left the restroom as soon as he unlocked the door.

Lucan turned back to find Samantha sitting on the floor, her flushed face buried in her hands. He crouched down beside her. "It was not so bad, was it?"

"No. It was horrible. I wanted to ..." She pressed her hand over her mouth for a moment. "I felt something when I was ... I could feel everything she felt. I knew. I knew she would have done anything I told her to."

"*L'attrait* is very powerful. Most humans cannot resist it." He brushed the dark hair back from her face and lifted her to her feet. "The more you deny yourself blood, the more you will need. If you take too much, you will enrapture the mortal and become enthralled. You will drain all the blood from the body and fall unconscious for many days. The human will die beside you."

"This happens every time you use humans for blood." She spoke as if to herself rather than him. "You can see inside them. Feel what they're feeling. The pleasure. The lust."

Lucan couldn't understand why she sounded so disgusted. "We are designed to be attractive to mortals. It is what brings them to us."

"No, I saw what you did. You went and picked her out for me. You made her come to me." She shook her head and laughed bitterly. "Like I couldn't get my own."

"You will not allow yourself to hunt," he pointed out. "I had to do something."

Furious eyes met his. "Why her?"

"She seemed adequate—" Her fist stopped him, and he staggered backward. Over the sinks, the mirrors began to crack. "What the devil is wrong with you?"

"Do you feed only on men?" she shouted.

He used his hand to wipe the blood from his mouth. "Not unless there are no healthy females for me to use, and what the bloody hell does it matter?"

She shoved him back. "Do you have sex with them? These women?"

"Why would I, when I have you for that?" He caught her by the wrists before she could punch him again. "You are not always as obliging as the bespelled, of course, but I am learning to be patient." One of the sinks behind her split in half and crashed to the floor. "Is that it, my darling? Are you jealous?"

She leaned in close. "Why didn't you bring me a man?"

"There is no difference in the blood."

"Then go and get me a man," she snarled. "A cute one with a nice body. I'll do him right here on the fucking floor."

The window in the opposite wall shattered. "I think you've had enough for one night."

"You were going to do me that first night I met you in the club." She wiped her mouth with the back of her hand and stared at the light smear of red it left on her skin. "This is why you got so pissed when you couldn't put me under. Because I resisted you. I wouldn't spread my legs for you."

Another sink exploded. "In the end, darling, it was your choice to come to my bed."

"If I was like that girl, if I was that fucked-up, how the hell could I choose anything?" She didn't wait for him to answer, but quickly strode out.

Chapter 8

Jessa hadn't slept through the night in years, not since the moment she'd woken up in an intensive care unit, breathing through a tube and hearing the slow beeps of monitoring equipment. The fact that she knew she was unconscious, and not by choice, initially alarmed her, because she didn't want to wake up in a hospital bed again. But on some level deeper than consciousness or awareness, she knew she wasn't injured, sick, or even in danger. The frightening sensory overload from the shadowlight had knocked her out, and her mind needed time to absorb the impact and recover.

She didn't dream, but she didn't lose her sense of herself in oblivion, either. That, she was sure, was because of the man. She could feel him there, on the other side of the darkness, waiting for her. He had caused this, but he was also watching over her. There were moments when she could almost feel him all around her, on her face, against her body. For all she knew he could be doing anything to her, but she didn't feel helpless or vulnerable, or even frightened.

She couldn't understand it—not after the memories of being swept away and buried alive in the suffocating cold slowly emerged. If he did that to her—and she knew touching him had caused it—why did he feel so warm and safe?

Gradually the darkness thinned around her, and her senses began to work again. She felt a pleasant texture against her cheek and smelled lilacs close by. Something covered most of her body, something light and soft and luxurious. She heard the tick of a clock and the trickle of water. The only discomfort she felt was from the dryness of her mouth and a vague soreness in her right arm.

Her senses also told her that she was not home, or at the office, or anyplace she recognized. She waited, listening for the sound of voices or the movements of bodies, and when she felt sure she was alone she opened her eyes a fraction.

Someone had switched on two lamps with brown and amber stained-glass shades. She saw books, shelves, small tables, and many armchairs. To her right sat an old desk; her cheek pressed into a new pillow. She felt the edge of carved wood under her palm. None of it was familiar.

Turning her head slowly, she saw that she lay under a heavily embroidered velvet crazy quilt on the comfortably pillowy cushions of an oversize love seat or daybed. Her feet were bare, and someone had also removed her jacket, but otherwise she was still dressed. Some of her hair fell around her face as she levered herself onto one elbow.

A door opened, and before Jessa could think better of it she looked toward the sound. A very tall teenager wearing a ragged gray sweatshirt and worn, stained jeans walked toward her, a wooden tray in her hands.

"Too late to fake it," she said as Jessa dropped back down and closed her eyes. "I already saw the baby blues. Hopefully you like grilled cheese and tomato soup."

Jessa stayed where she was and watched as the girl placed the tray on a table by the daybed. "Where am I?"

"Safe. Welcome to the Freak Protection Program." She straightened and tugged her sleeves down, covering the black swirls of the tattoos on her forearms. "Eat something."

Jessa checked the tray, but the only utensil on it was a plastic spoon. The sandwich had been put on a paper plate, and the bottle of iced tea was also plastic.

Nothing I can use as a weapon. "I want to talk to the man who brought me here." She had to concentrate for a moment to recall his name. "Matthias."

"Do you." The girl smiled, a vicious show of dazzling white teeth. "Well, Queenie, I'm not your fucking gofer." She walked out.

Jessa rolled off the daybed and went after her, expecting to find the door locked. It wasn't. She looked down at her bare feet; if she had to run, she needed shoes. Luckily she spotted her pumps sitting under the table by the daybed, and put them on before she slipped out.

Outside the room she saw no sign of the girl. Two long walls of old, cracked, whitewashed concrete interspersed by closed wooden doors formed a long, windowless corridor. The low, rounded ceiling, heavy-duty shop lights wired above the doors, and old bricked floor made her realize she was not standing in a hallway but some sort of underground tunnel.

Underground where?

Jessa had worked with enough people from New York City to recognize the girl's Brooklyn accent, and considered the odds of that being where she was. It would take most of a day to drive to New York, but the clock in the library room had shown the time to be seven fourteen. At the same time, she didn't know if that was the morning or evening hour. Had Matthias drugged her? How long had she been unconscious?

She walked past the doors to one end of the corridor, keeping her footsteps as quiet as she could, only to discover it turned off into another pair of tunnels. She took the right, which stretched out for two hundred feet before it split in two. There she went left, and then right again, until she stopped. Wherever she was, the place was a labyrinth, with no exit signs or any indication of what lay behind the twenty-two doors she'd already passed.

Jessa walked up to the nearest door, braced herself, opened it, and stared into a shallow closet filled with small, brand-new kitchen appliances. The top shelf was packed with can openers, the next a row of coffeemakers, and the third an assortment of blenders. All of them were neatly arranged, still in their boxes, but they didn't make sense. Who needed eleven can openers, or nine coffeemakers?

She moved down to the next door, but it proved to be another closet, this one packed with long bolts of designer drapery fabric standing on end and arranged by color.

There was enough material to dress the windows of a dozen houses.

She looked up and saw at least fifty spools of satin cord and clear plastic bags filled with a variety of hanging tassels.

Confusion piled on top of her anxiety. She'd expected to see guns, men huddled together around a phone, or at least some scowling guard to grab her and march her at gunpoint back to the library room—not Martha Stewart's spring window-treatment collection.

The sound of stone scraping against stone came from the end of the hall where she stood, drawing her attention. She closed the closet and followed the noise to the last door before the next intersection. This one stood partially open, and she pressed herself against the wall beside it before she glanced around the corner.

From where she stood she could see almost half of the room. Candlelight and a working fireplace filled the interior with a warm, shifting amber glow, and cast shadows over what appeared to be neatly stacked short columns of smooth stone disks. She would have thought them to be garden pavers or stepping-stones, except they each had a notched hole in the center, through which stood a four-foot wooden pole. Bundles of wide leather straps sat on top of some of the stacked disks, along with long lengths that resembled belts with odd hanging loops. The floors and wall were empty except for a layer of fine white sand.

She listened but heard only the scraping sound, and carefully eased the door in another inch.

A barefoot man dressed in a pair of old, loose khakis stood to one side of the room, his back facing her, his arms outstretched. Around each hand he had looped one of the wider straps, from which dangled two of the stone disks. Slowly he brought his hands up over his head, causing the stones to scrape against each other with the movement. He lowered them again, just as slowly, but this time in a diagonal direction, forming a vee with his arms. After several similar movements it became clear that he was working out with the stones as if they were weights.

It wasn't the first time he'd used them, either, Jessa guessed, mesmerized by the powerful lines of his upper body. She'd seen a lot of men who worked out, but never one like this. He seemed built out of pure, perfect muscle, not simply developed but brutally beautiful, thick and smooth, with every contour in absolute balance.

Unwelcome heat crept up her neck, tightening in her throat and sharpening her field of vision. Her body reacted to the sight of all that masculine beauty like a brainless bimbo's would, all shivering nerves and surging blood. Intellectually she knew she couldn't touch him, not after what had happened to her in the car, but her senses didn't seem to care. They were in full-blown lust now, eyeing and measuring him, speculating on how it would feel to be held in those magnificent arms and petted by those strong hands. He'd be a hard lover, thorough and demanding, the sort of man who had sex the way soldiers went into battle: Breach the defenses, break through the lines, and claim whatever was on the other side.

She'd never had a lover like that. Would never, she reminded herself.

The uncertain light reflected off the gleaming sweat on his skin, added the intense aura of primal male, but it also revealed here and there the corded scars of old wounds. Too many to have been inflicted all at once and for him to survive. However he had been hurt, the man showed no physical sign of impairment.

Jessa knew what the scar of a gunshot wound looked like and how difficult they were to remove, even with dermal laser treatments. The scars this man carried were straight and jagged, and of varying lengths, and seemed to be from the sort of injuries a wide, heavy blade would inflict. If he had been stabbed that many times . . .

He can't be one of the Takyn, she thought, drawing back a little.

"Do you mean to stand there for the rest of the night?" he asked without looking at her.

She knew that voice, but stayed where she was. "You're Matthias."

"I am." He finished his lift before lowering his arms and moving toward one wall, where he hung the straps on two pegs. He took a towel from a third and rubbed it over his face before he turned around. "How do you feel?"

She decided to be blunt. "I feel kidnapped."

He tossed the towel over his shoulder and went to a wrought-iron stand that held a large, shallow porcelain bowl filled with water. He splashed his face with the water several times before using the towel again.

The fact that he wasn't running after her nor did he even seem worried that she would escape gave Jessa enough confidence to step into the room.

"Where am I? Why did you bring me here?"

"GenHance lured you to the restaurant in order to take you." He took a shirt hanging from the basin stand and pulled it on. "I can protect you better here."

"Why would they do that?"

"GenHance wants your ability." He walked toward her. "To have it, they must harvest it from your body. That would kill you."

She had thought from the way he spoke in the car that he was disturbed, possibly temporarily unbalanced by the attack in the restaurant. Now she was convinced he was permanently delusional. "So you brought me here to keep GenHance from killing me."

He stopped and looked down at her. "I did."

"Are you going to keep me here so they don't try to kill me again?" she asked, very carefully.

"I will protect you, Jessa Bellamy." He reached out to her, and frowned as she avoided his hand. "I told you in the car, I will not harm you."

"I remember you telling me that after you threw me in that car and restrained me."

"There was no time to explain," he said. "I had to move quickly or they would have taken both of us."

The way he kept saying "*taken*" bothered her. "There's time now. Why don't we go to the police together? You can tell them what you know, and they can arrest Lawson and whoever else was trying to hurt me."

He began buttoning his shirt. "Will you tell them what you saw when you touched the waiter's hand?"

She forced out a sigh. "I told you in the car, I didn't see anything. I tasted the drugs in the wine."

"We know what you can do, Jessa. So do they." He walked past her and left her there.

She should start looking for a way out, but something told her it would take hours, and even if she did find an exit, it would probably be locked. She had no money, no identification, and no idea where she was. She might still be in Atlanta. She could be in New York—or New Zealand.

All she knew for certain was that Matthias had brought her here, and since he knew the way in, he had to know the way out.

Matthias had already disappeared around a corner by the time she moved to follow him, but he didn't vanish like the girl who had brought her food. She caught up with him in the next tunnel, and kept her distance while sorting out how she might convince him that she didn't need protection and to let her leave.

He made two more turns, entering a third, darker passage with no doors, and stopped at a narrow, rusting hatchlike door. There he waited until she came as close as she thought was safe.

"This is the way out. Go through, climb the stairs to the top, and you will be outside." He watched her face. "The nearest police station is three streets to the south."

She didn't believe him. "You're not just going to let me walk out of here."

"I am not Lawson," he said. "You are a free woman. Go."

He didn't move, and to get to the hatch she would have to stand within inches of him. "This is a trick."

He held out his hand. "Touch me. If I am lying to you, you will know."

"It doesn't work like—" She stopped, appalled at how she had nearly given herself away. "All right. Thank you for . . . helping me." She went to the hatch.

He made no move to stop her. "Do not return to Atlanta or contact those you know there. They are waiting for you to do that. When GenHance finds you, they will not attempt to take you alive. They have some of the police in their employ. If you are detained, they will see to it that you die in your cell, and then arrange to claim your body."

It sounded like the plot for a bad techno-thriller movie. "How can you know that?"

"You are not the first they have tried to take."

The cold, rusted steel of the hatch wheel bit into her palms as she gripped it. "You're wrong. GenHance is a research-and-development firm. They're working on cures for birth defects and genetic diseases. They have no reason to kill me." She met his narrowed gaze. "I'm just a businesswoman."

"You are Kyndred. Made from birth to be unique among humans. Your ability is genetic, Jessa. It was encoded in your cells deliberately. GenHance knows this, and that it can be taken from you and given to another." He paused, and then said, "That is why it does not matter whether you are alive or dead. They need your cells, some of which they cannot retrieve without killing you. Your life is not important to them."

The thought of deliberately cursing someone else with her ability made bile well up in her throat. "If I did have this ability, which I don't, it wouldn't be worth it."

"You think not? With a single touch you can know the darkest secrets any man possesses. Knowledge is power. You use it to bring justice to those who have eluded the law. Another would take those secrets and wield them like a weapon. No one in power anywhere would be safe."

She was letting him talk her into believing his delusions. "Then I'll have to be careful."

"You were careful when you called the FBI," he said. "You used different pay phones away from where you live and work. You kept the calls short, and gave them nothing they could use to identify you. Still I was able to find you. So did GenHance."

He knew.

She released the hatch wheel and looked at the flecks

of rust on her hands. "I was going to stop calling them. I promised myself this was the last time."

"They would have found another way to identify you. The business you do. The people you expose. In time it would have led them to you." His tone changed. "They will attack your resources, and they will not stop until you are penniless. Tomorrow they will file a lawsuit against your company and use it to close the business. Your bank accounts will be emptied and your credit cards canceled. Your loans will be terminated and your home will be repossessed."

He was talking about everything she'd worked for, everything that mattered to her. Jessa wanted to hit him. "They can't do that."

"It has already begun." He gestured toward the corridor. "Come and I will show you."

Rowan switched off the tunnel monitor as soon as she saw Matthias escorting Jessa Bellamy into the security center. "No problems so far," she told Drew on the phone. "He's already got Queenie following him around like a groupie."

"Queenie?"

"The boss thinks she looks like a queen." That still rankled on more than one level. "I expect they'll be tied up for a couple hours while he shows her the stuff and she has another why-me meltdown. You want to drive up and grab a couple of beers?"

Drew chuckled. "Sure. Right after I quit my job and set fire to my house."

She let her voice drop a sultry octave. "After all this time talking to me on the phone but never once meeting in person, you know you want to see what I really look like. And, baby? I'm even better than I sound."

"Uh-huh." He didn't seem impressed. "More like you want to check *me* out."

"You give great phone," she admitted. "I've got you figured for a six-five, two-twenty, blond ex-surfer dude."

He choked on whatever he was drinking. "Try a five-nine, skinny, red-haired, pale-faced geek," he said after he finished coughing.

"Shit." She laughed. "That makes me a head taller."

"See?" He sighed. "Better we stay phone buddies. With my delicate ego, I could never handle facing the real Rowan."

Her smile faded. "Honey, no one can."

After she finished the call, Rowan went to retrieve the tray from the library. Queenie hadn't touched a crumb, so she picked up the cold grilled cheese and ate it on the way to the kitchen. There she reheated the soup and sipped it from a mug as she prepared dinner. Matthias wouldn't care, but she could never bring herself to throw away perfectly good food.

Especially not sandwiches.

Rowan knew what it was to be hungry; she'd lived on the street for almost three years. Back in the day she'd gotten used to the cold, the wet, the filth, and the dark. She'd found the places where she could hide and rest, in the parks and the alleys and the doorways. In time she'd learned how to make a shelter out of a couple of crates or a cardboard box. During the winter she'd discovered which abandoned buildings were the warmest and safest, and how to barricade herself in a musty old closet for a blissful eight hours of uninterrupted sleep.

It was hunger that she feared. That grinning death-headed motherfucker had taken a liking to her, thanks to her screwed-up metabolism that kept her perpetually skinny, and once she'd run away from her last foster home he'd stalked her every day. Even after she'd quieted her belly with a handout or a church meal, he'd waited and watched just out of sight, knowing he'd soon get another chance to sink his dull tombstone teeth into her again.

Living on the street, Rowan discovered she could do a lot of repulsive things, like go two weeks without bathing, wear clothes that were little more than bundles of rags, or bat away a rat with her bare hand. She'd grown wise and tough and strong during those years, fighting to survive. But she'd never been able to shake her obsession with food. When she wasn't spare-changing or standing in a line outside a soup kitchen, she'd haunt hot-dog stands and pizza joints and burger palaces so she could breathe in the delicious scents. A walk through an open-air food market was for her like cruising through Tiffany & Co. had been for Holly Golightly. She couldn't even pass a Coke or gumball machine without checking the slot to see if someone had left something behind.

On the bad days when she couldn't stop herself, she'd take the subway to Manhattan and walk the rows of restaurants there. She'd pace back and forth in front of the windows, stopping occasionally to look in at the rich people stuffing their faces. She didn't care about the people; they were no better than her, but the food they ate was so beautiful and elegant that it sometimes brought tears to her eyes. Usually a waiter or busboy would be sent out by the manager to chase her off, but that hadn't been the worst.

People coming out of the restaurant would sometimes notice her there, and come over to offer her their take-home containers and doggie bags.

Then she'd feel the shame of it, of what she was, crawling over her dirty skin, and she'd cringe inside her ragged clothes and stumble away. But first she'd snatch the doggie bag of scraps or the plastic bowl of leftover soup. Because as much as every mouthful shredded her dignity, it held off the specter of hunger for another day.

Rowan hadn't wanted to live like a stray dog. She'd tried to get work, even going to stand with the illegals on certain corners where they were picked up every morning and were paid twenty bucks for ten hours of backbreaking labor unloading trucks or clearing out debris from demolition sites. The labor bosses never picked her to join their crews, even when they thought she was a boy—she was too skinny and pale. One told her that he didn't hire junkies.

Unwilling to become a thief or a whore, Rowan had tried collecting discarded cans and bottles out of the trash, but it took hours and she burned up too much energy hunting for them. Then she could take only as much as she could carry to turn in at the recycling center, and that amounted to only a dollar here and there. She remembered with perfect clarity the first time she'd been desperate enough to eat a piece of half-eaten fried chicken she'd taken out of a garbage can, and being so sickened by the spoiled meat that minutes later she'd puked until she dry-heaved.

To this day she couldn't stand the smell of fried chicken.

During her last year as a homeless kid she began to think of nothing but food, daydreaming about it, planning elaborate meals she would make someday when things were better. If she saw a TV in an electronics store window tuned to a cooking show, she'd stop and watch it through to the end. She'd go into the public library to get warm on a cold day, and end up spending the afternoon reading cookbooks.

The fear of starvation followed her into her sleep, swallowing her up in nightmares where she watched her body shrink down to skin over a skeleton in a matter of seconds. When she woke, she would huddle, touching herself with her hands to make sure it hadn't happened while she'd slept and there was still a little flesh under her cold, clammy skin.

If it hadn't been for the sisters, Rowan might have ended up that way.

She met them when she'd gone to a church to get in line for the free dinner on Thanksgiving Day. It had been crowded, and then the food had run out just as she'd gotten to the front of the serving line. One of the old ladies who was handing out cards with directions to another soup kitchen touched her hand, and without thinking Rowan held on to her.

The lady stared at Rowan's face without blinking, and then abruptly asked her to come into the back to help her with the dishes. Having nothing better to do, Rowan followed her.

"Here." Instead of handing her a dish towel, the lady offered a white box. "It's a box lunch. They give them to us for serving today."

"I can't take this." Instantly ashamed, Rowan tried to give it back to her. "You're supposed to eat it."

"I don't particularly like turkey sandwiches. Too dry." The thin lips crimped. "If you don't take it, I'll throw it away."

That was enough to convince her, and she started to go, but the old lady asked her to sit down at the table. Then she did the same, and started talking to her about living in New York since the forties, and how hard it was for older women on their own to feel safe.

Rowan wolfed down the skimpy turkey sandwich and celery sticks before she saw the last item in the lunch box: a slice of apple pie in a neat triangular cardboard container. It was the kind they sold frozen by the slice in the supermarket, and was more crust than anything. But her favorite dessert had always been apple pie, and she hadn't tasted it in more than a year. Seeing it made her throat hurt.

"My name is Deborah," the lady told her. "I have a house in the Bronx that I share with my sister, Annette. She's a widow and I never married, so living together saves us a little money. Where are you living, my dear?"

"What do you care?" Rowan tried to look defiant, but she knew she wasn't impressing the old gal, not with a week of dirt on her face. In a smaller voice she said, "I don't have anyplace. I'm homeless."

"Do you use drugs?" When she glared at her, Deborah smiled. "I didn't think so. Your eyes are too clear. Are you in any trouble with the police?"

"Not unless they catch me. Next year I'll be too old for them to put me back in foster care." Angry with herself for saying too much, Rowan placed the slice of pie in front of the old lady. "Thanks for letting me have your lunch. It was really decent of you. I gotta go."

Deborah's fine silver eyebrows arched. "To where? You said you have no place to live."

"You shouldn't do stuff like this," Rowan told her. "Chatting up people like me . . . it's dangerous. You don't know who I am. I could beat you up or mug you."

"I won't have any money until my check comes in on the first," the old lady told her. "But I have a nice little house, and a spare room, and no daughters or sons to look after me and Annette. How would you like to come and see it?"

"Why?"

"You came to help me even though the food was gone."

When Rowan would have replied, she waved one of her hands. "You'd be doing me a favor. I have to take the bus, you see, and I hate to ride it alone. The young men who sit in the backseats are always watching me."

Rowan had gone with her, scrounging enough change from her pockets to pay the bus fare. The little house turned out to be just that, a small but tidy place in the Bronx with geraniums in the window boxes and lace curtains in the windows. Deborah's sister, a slightly older woman with the twisted fingers of advanced arthritis, had welcomed her in like a visiting niece and fussed over her, offering her tea and cookies and then asking her to help with dinner, which Rowan then had to stay and help them eat. As Rowan washed the dishes, Annette began nagging her sister to make her stay with them for the night because the buses had stopped running.

Rowan wanted to leave, but neither of the old gals would hear of it. Deborah persuaded her to use their tiny bathroom and shower, and when Rowan stepped out of the shower she found a pile of clean, folded old clothes waiting for her on the bathroom counter. Her clothes had been taken away, and later she would find out that Deborah had immediately tossed them out in the trash.

As elderly and frail as they were, the sisters were amazing bullies, and refused to listen to a word Rowan said. Shortly after nine, Rowan found herself sitting on the bed in the spare room, looking around the neat little room in disbelief as Deborah called out a good-night and that they would see her in the morning.

She had stayed with the sisters that night, and settled down in that real bed. The clean sheets and fluffy pillows had felt so good and soft against her scrubbed skin that she'd wallowed for a while, but in the end the soft mattress had felt too alien, and she'd tossed the top sheet on the floor and settled down there.

In the morning Deborah gently shook her shoulder to wake her. She didn't say anything about finding Rowan on the floor, but asked her to join them for breakfast. Over homemade waffles, sausage links, and the best coffee Rowan had ever tasted in her life, the sisters offered her a job as their housekeeper and companion.

"We'd pay you if we had the money," Annette said, her kind eyes worried, "but between the two of us we barely have enough to cover our prescriptions and living expenses. That's why we can only offer you room and board."

Rowan didn't understand. "Why me?"

"You don't have a job or family," Deborah said. "Annette and I are getting on now, and we need a young person around the house to help us. You need a home. It's a perfect match."

"But you don't know anything about me," Rowan protested. "I could be a thief or a killer. I could take advantage of you, clean out this place while you're sleeping and take off."

"Nonsense," Deborah said, her expression stern. "You're a good-hearted girl; anyone can see that. Besides, by not offering you a salary we're taking advantage of *you*." She stood up. "Your first job is to help me with these dishes. Annette keeps dropping and breaking things."

Her sister nodded. "My arthritis makes me clumsier than a Republican at a gay bar."

Rowan knew what waited for her outside that little house, and the last three years had taught her never to question an act of kindness. So she moved into the spare room, and became the sisters' housekeeper and companion, and repaid their kindness by keeping the little house spotless and whipping up the most delicious meals she could manage from the food they could afford. The two sisters only just scraped by on their Social Security checks, so Rowan became a champion at clipping coupons and finding the best prices at the local markets.

Every weekend she worked with Deborah cooking for the homeless at the church, and through her work there was offered a part-time job supplying muffins and cookies to the owner of a convenience mart. At the end of the first year she'd lived with the sisters, she was bringing in enough to cover her room and board and improve their living conditions considerably.

Deborah refused to accept any rent money from her, but Rowan used her earnings to see to it that her ladies never wanted for or needed anything. She would have happily lived with the sisters forever, but one morning Annette didn't wake up. After her sister's funeral Deborah seemed to grow old overnight.

"I've never wanted to pry, Rowan, but I must if we are to talk about your future," the old lady had said to her one night over dinner. "I can't go to be with Annette unless I'm sure you'll be all right."

"You're not going anywhere," Rowan assured her.

"I'm eighty-seven years old, my dear," the old lady said. "We both know I'm not long for this world. I want to leave you the house and everything we have, but our lawyer tells me to do that I must give him your full name and Social Security number." She studied Rowan's face. "If we do that, they'll find you, won't they?"

Rowan started to deny it, and then sighed. "Yeah, they would. I'd explain but you wouldn't believe me."

"I already know," Deborah said, looking a little ashamed now. "You talk in your sleep. The first couple of weeks you were with us, Annette and I would take turns listening."

"You know everything?"

Deborah nodded. "I won't allow you to be in danger again, so I must sell the house before I go. We'll put the money in traveler's checks."

Rowan shook her head. "Even if you did that—and I wouldn't let you—I couldn't cash them. She touched the old lady's frail hand. "Leave everything to the church, the way you and Annette planned to. I'm working now, and when the time comes I'll find a place. I'll be all right."

"What about your past?"

"It's dead and buried." Rowan plucked at the edge of her sleeve, tugging it down over the new black dragon tattoo she'd just gotten to cover the other mark. There was one question that remained unanswered, and it was one she had to ask. She glanced up at Deborah. "Why did you take me in?"

The old lady looked uncomfortable. "You know why. We needed a housekeeper. You needed a home."

"That's nice, but I know what I did to you the day we met." Rowan took a deep breath. "What was her name? The girl you loved?"

Deborah put a hand to her throat, and then her face crumpled like an old tissue. "Mary Margaret O'Brien. She never . . . I never told her." Regret dulled her eyes. "She wasn't like me, so there was no point. She married very young, and died in childbirth. It broke my heart."

"I didn't mean to do it," Rowan told her. "I was just so hungry. I didn't even realize what I had done until later, and I should have gone. But you and Annette were so nice, and I was lonely and afraid. . . ." It was her turn to be swamped by shame. "I'm so sorry."

"Don't be." She gave her a wistful smile. "It was a lovely moment for me, to see her face again. I didn't understand what had happened until Annette and I began to eavesdrop on your sleep. Rowan, can you . . . do that . . . for everyone?"

"No. Only for men." She grimaced. "I mean, only for someone who's been in love with a woman. I can only be a woman."

Deborah held out her hand. "Then would you do an old lady one last favor?"

Rowan slowly gripped her hand and closed her eyes. She had never used her ability in front of another person who knew about it; not even when she had been screamed at, threatened, and then beaten. She held her breath as she felt the skin on her face stretch and shift as the shape of it gradually changed. Her short, dark hair became a cap of thick ginger curls, and when she opened her eyes and looked at Deborah, she did so through the grass green eyes of Mary Margaret O'Brien—just as she had for a moment when she'd first met Deborah at the shelter.

"Just as I remember her," the old lady said, and lifted Rowan's hand to press a gentle kiss on the back. "Thank you, my dear."

Deborah contracted pneumonia that winter, and never really recovered. A few months later she died as her sister had: peacefully, in her sleep. When Rowan came back to the house after the funeral to pack up her things, she found an envelope tucked away in her bureau, and in it a note from Deborah along with enough cash to pay the rent on a small apartment for a year.

The church didn't need our old jewelry, Deborah had written. *Thank you for being so good to us, and remember us in your prayers. We love you, Rowan.*

At least someone had loved her once in her life, Rowan thought as she went to the fridge and surveyed the contents. At least she'd had that much.

Queenie's dossier didn't specify her eating habits, but since Rowan went along with Matthias's vegetarian diet, they didn't keep any meat on hand. Italian would just have to do, she decided as she took out a basket of plum tomatoes and a couple of sweet yellow onions. Her hands flew as she took out her frustrations on the ingredients; ten minutes later she had a pot of marinara sauce bubbling on the stove and went to work on hand-making the pasta.

She didn't have to go to all this trouble—she'd personally seen to it that the pantry was stocked with enough nonperishable supplies to see them through an ice age—but she'd bet good money that Queenie couldn't boil an egg. Maybe if she reminded Matthias more often that she could do a lot more than simply clean up and whip his ass at pool, he'd start realizing how important she was to him. Maybe he'd finally figure out why she'd followed him around like a goddamn groupie ever since she'd first laid eyes on him.

Yeah, and if he ever does, he'll just pat me on the head and tell me I'm sweet and he's too old for me and I'll grow out of it someday. Then I will take a pool cue to the blind son of a bitch's thick skull.

"Rowan."

She whirled, her dough knife in her hand. "What? Fuck." She drove the tip of the knife into her cutting board and kept her back toward Matthias until she could compose herself. "Sorry. You scared me." She looked around him. "Where's Dazed and Confused?"

"Jessa is using the computer."

"We're giving her access to our hardware?" She leaned

back against the counter. "Want me to write down the main number for GenHance for her? Might help speed things up."

"Jessa must know what Genaro has done to her. The computer will tell her everything." He went over to the stove and lifted the cover on the sauce pot. "This smells very good."

"It needs fifteen more minutes." She took the cover from him and replaced it. "You want this on a tray, or will Her Highness be dining in?"

"We will eat here, as always." He frowned. "Why are you angry with me?"

"I don't know. I should go grab a couple of hot prospects, bring them down here, and give them the run of the place. Would liven up things considerably." His blank expression made her hands curl into fists. "You left her alone, on a computer, an hour after she wakes up—and you don't see anything wrong with that?"

"Jessa adjusts quickly. She will accept us as her friends."

"In case you forgot, we don't know Jessa. Jesus Christ, Matt." She threw out her arms. "You have no fucking clue what's going on inside her head right now. She could totally freak out, wreck the equipment, start running around and screaming for help—"

"I believe she is checking the balance in her bank accounts through the encrypted server," he said mildly. "After that she plans to review the information we have on Genaro, and she will likely send a warning to her friends."

"Sure. Okay. Terrific." She went over to the counter, picked up the linguine she'd hand-rolled and cut, and threw it into the boiling water. "Dinner will ready in thirty minutes." She stiffened as his hand rested on her shoulder. "Don't."

"I have not disabled the security measures, so she cannot leave," he assured her. "But if we are to gain her trust, she must believe that she can."

Rowan exhaled. "She's not stupid. She'll try to go anyway."

"I do not think so," he said. "Not after she learns what

Genaro has done. She is a good woman, Rowan. We will persuade her to help us." He gave her shoulder a fond squeeze before he left the kitchen.

A good woman. One who could be trusted. Of course she was.

Steam from the pot heated Rowan's face but she didn't move. A year ago she had gone into Matthias's bedroom one night, a small mirror in her hand, and she'd sat by his bedside and held it, watching as she touched him and let herself change. Her ability allowed her to assume the image of any man's ideal woman, the woman he would ultimately fall in love with. She'd desperately wanted to know whom Matthias could love, but she hadn't recognized the beautiful, regal face in the mirror. All she found out was that his ideal woman looked nothing like her.

Later she saw that face two more times: first when she had uploaded the driver's license photo of Minerva Starret, and then when she had seen Jessa Bellamy's face.

His dream girl had arrived, and nothing would keep them apart now. Not even her love for him.

As Rowan watched the long strips of pasta dance around the bubbles, she let the tears slip down her cheeks and drip, one by one, into the boiling water.

Chapter 9

Lawson didn't remember much after Genaro left. The doctors came back and he shouted at them to leave him alone, until one of them stuck a needle into his IV tube. From the way things got fuzzy after that it must have been a tranq. He was too doped to fight them when they dragged him over to another gurney, and when they rolled him onto a bed, he passed out. Sometime later he woke up in the dark, fiery pain shooting up into his hip, and howled until someone came. A fat-faced nurse blabbed at him to be quiet as she stabbed what felt like an ice pick into his hip. He would have taken a swing at her, but she split into three and then danced around the room.

Morning came like a rancid bitch with a rolling pin, pounding on his head and shrieking in his ears. He groped until he found the call button and thumbed it over and over. Another hatchet-faced twat in whites appeared, but this one wouldn't give him the stuff. She told him he'd have to wait until the doctor made rounds.

He told her what he thought of her until she left, and then he waited. He hit the call button. The lazy slut of a nurse didn't come, but spoke over an intercom in the wall. She said the doctor wasn't in yet. They did that three more times, and then the stupid whore stopped answering the call signal. Like he was nothing—he was nobody.

Lawson saw an empty wheelchair sitting at the end of the bed, but when he tried to sit up his thigh stretched and the pain became a thousand snakes, crawling and biting their way up his chest. His heart thundering in his ears, he eased back on the pillows and tore two holes in the sheets with his clenched fists.

"What kind of hospital are you running here?" Bradford said as soon as the doctor came in. "I've been waiting on you for hours."

"You've been waiting for thirty minutes, Mr. Lawson." He picked up the chart hanging from the end of the bed and read the top page.

"Where's the needle?" When the doctor didn't answer, he added, "The nurse wouldn't give me anything for the pain. She said you would. Where is it?"

"The amount of drugs still in your system makes it unwise to continue to administer IV morphine, and oral analgesics will only promote more bleeding." The man barely glanced at him. "You'll have to tough this one out for now, but in a few days the pain should begin to ease."

He was in agony, and the shithead wasn't going to give him anything at all. He'd have to get to his stash. "Just sew me back together and discharge me."

"I'm afraid I can't do that, either," the doctor said. "The man who attacked you completely severed your semimembranosus, semitendinosus, and biceps femoris muscles. We'll schedule the first surgery as soon as your condition stabilizes, but you will be hospitalized for several weeks, and then you'll require extensive physical therapy to restore some function to your leg."

His condition. Extensive therapy. Some function. Lawson's gut knotted, but he wouldn't give in to fear. Not when he had work to do. "Give me whatever papers I have to sign to get the fuck out of here."

The doctor met his gaze. "Mr. Lawson, listen to me very carefully. The muscles that your attacker cut through are what allow you to bend your knee and extend your hip. If you leave this facility without proper treatment, and they heal as they are, you will never walk normally again, and it will be impossible for you to run, jump, or climb."

"I'll take care of it later."

The doctor's cold eyes remained pitiless. "Continuing

to inject steroids and cocaine won't help you, either. Aside from inducing the unacceptable levels of aggression and anger you've been displaying since you were admitted, your addiction has inflicted a considerable amount of damage to your liver and spleen."

He slammed his arm into the aluminum bed railing. "I'm not a fucking addict."

"I have the test results from the lab here in your chart. I understand you run a lab for Mr. Genaro." The surgeon tossed the folder on the bed. "Read them for yourself." He turned and left the room.

Lawson picked up the chart and threw it at the door, shouting after the doctor until his voice gave out, and then collapsed and covered his face with his shaking hands. They wouldn't give him anything to help him cope, and now they were giving him this runaround about fixing his leg. But he didn't blame the doctor. He might be as much a prick as Genaro, but he was just another workingman, trying to clean up after all the stupid fucking bitches of the world.

Like Jessa Bellamy, the cunt from hell who had done this to him.

Somehow she'd known the worst thing she could do to him was to have her asshole boyfriend cut him up and cripple him. And there was no way in the world Bradford Lawson was spending the rest of his life on crutches or in a wheelchair while that snotty little tramp danced off laughing at him. She was going to be sorry she'd ever thought of fucking with him.

Lawson had to get out of here, now.

His head felt as if it were going to split open, but he forced himself to calm down. He couldn't risk any more injections; the doctor was probably right about the liver damage. Besides that, the steroids wouldn't do anything to fix the problem with his leg. But Lawson needed something; he couldn't stay here and let them fumble around with him, not when every minute he spent on his back was one that Jessa Bellamy didn't deserve to breathe.

Genaro thought he was too messed up to go after the bitch, but Lawson knew better. He'd limp into hell if it meant he could drag that conniving slut back out and show her exactly how much damage a blade could do. He could call Genaro and find out if they had her yet, and demand he have the extreme pleasure of putting her down, but the old man wouldn't keep her alive one second longer than he had to, not now.

All Lawson needed was a good leg, and something to knock back the pain. He could steal the morphine from the lab, but the leg ...

He sat up, swearing as the sudden movement jolted his leg, and then panting out a laugh. He didn't need to steal morphine, or anything. The answer to all his problems was back at the lab, locked up in secure storage and guarded around the clock.

A secure storage to which Lawson had the key code. Guarded by techs and security who worked for him.

He eyed the wheelchair, which had a metal frame, and then groped for the phone beside the bed. After getting the dumb twat at the switchboard to give him an outside call line, he phoned a car service he used for special appointments, and issued terse instructions for a car, a gun, and a driver who could keep his mouth shut.

Getting out of the hospital bed took the last of his strength, but every time his vision grayed Lawson imagined the Bellamy woman standing just out of reach and smiling. He managed to drag the wheelchair around the bed and hoist himself into it before he sagged over, trembling and covered in sweat.

The driver slipped into the room a half hour later and, after giving Lawson's bloodstained bandages a troubled look, silently offered him a Glock, which he tucked out of sight by his hip. The driver then wheeled him out into the hall.

No one stopped them on the way out, but Lawson would have shot anyone who tried. The driver had to lift him from the chair into the back of the car, which nearly made him pass out again, and then drove him from the hospital to GenHance's downtown headquarters.

Lawson sent the driver away as soon as he was back in

the wheelchair outside the main entrance. Delaporte came out personally to open the doors for him.

"Mr. Lawson." The chief of security wheeled him inside, taking him around the metal detector every employee had to pass through, just as Lawson had hoped. "Mr. Genaro will be out until morning." His eyes dropped to the red-soaked bandage wrapped around Lawson's thigh. "Shouldn't you be back in the hospital?"

"One of my sources called me about Bellamy's medical history," he lied. "I have to pass the information along to Kirchner so he can avoid the same problems with the new acquisition."

"If you'll tell me, I can—"

"Jonah already thinks I'm washed-up, Don," Lawson said, keeping his voice low and humble. "Please, let me do this much. It'll prove to him that I can still be useful."

Delaporte's expression didn't change, but his tone did. "All right. But once you're through with Kirchner, you'll let my guys take you back to the hospital."

Lawson nodded. "Absolutely." He reached for the wheels and propelled himself to the elevators, gritting his teeth against the fresh burst of pain that erupted from his thigh. Once inside the elevator, he wrapped his hand around the gun, but Delaporte didn't follow him inside.

On the top floor, Lawson wheeled out, checked the hall, and then rolled down toward the main lab. He knew Kirchner spent every waking hour working on the new acquisition, so he didn't worry about being discovered.

Only one tech remained on duty at night, and he opened the door for Lawson as soon as he saw him through the window.

"Sir, we just heard this evening what happened to you." Carl Linder's eyes widened as he took in Lawson's appearance. "Jesus, I mean, sir—are you okay?"

"It looks worse than it is. Close the door, Carl." While the tech did that, Lawson shifted the Glock and tucked it under a front fold of his patient's gown. "Would you take me back to the storage area? The old man wants a quick count on the transerum."

"Sure." Carl pushed his wheelchair back through the lab and stopped by the keypad, where Lawson input the code. It didn't release the locking mechanism. "Here, let me—they just changed all the codes today."

If Genaro had changed the codes, it meant someone with access to the lab had fucked up royally and was due for termination—and there was no one else as fucked-up as Bradford Lawson.

His rage swelled as he thought of how the old man had looked at him in the hospital. What he'd read as pity had been contempt.

Lawson waited until the tech input the correct code and opened the massive reinforced steel door before he wheeled himself inside. The chilly interior of the storage unit smelled sharply of the alcohol and formalin used to preserve the various tissue and bone samples collected from previous subjects. But Lawson had eyes for only one case containing four shelves of glass vials, each filled with colorless liquid.

"Do you want me to get you an inventory form, Mr. Lawson?" Carl asked.

"Who put this in the case?" Lawson demanded, pointing at the middle shelf.

Carl wandered over and peered in. "I don't see what—" He stopped as he felt the muzzle of the Glock touch his ear. "Mr. Lawson, don't kill me, please. I'll do whatever you want."

"Take this." Lawson shoved a syringe into Carl's hand. "Fill it with the transerum."

Carl fumbled a little, but after a moment he had the needle ready. "Now what?"

"Inject me in the left thigh." Lawson kept the pistol against the younger man's head, and when he didn't move, he shouted, "Now."

"You can't take this stuff," Carl pleaded. "We haven't tested it on the brain-dead guy's wound yet. You don't know what it'll do to you."

"Inject me," Lawson said calmly as he pulled back the

edge of the gown to expose the bandaged surface of his leg, "or I'm going to make you his twin brother."

Carl's hand shook, but he managed to plant the needle in the muscle, and slowly depressed the plunger. The transerum felt hot as it poured into Lawson's tissues and spread out with a beautiful glow.

"Yeah," he breathed as the pain diminished. "That's it. That's what I need." The heat grew more intense as it wrapped around his leg. "Fuck, that burns."

"Let me call Dr. Kirchner," Carl suggested. "He'll know what to do. He can give you something, you know, to make you more comfortable."

"Comfortable." Lawson looked at him through half-closed eyes, smiling a little. "Do you know what this will do to me? What this will make me?" He laughed as the burning sensations tightened around the huge stitched gash in his flesh. "I'm gonna be like a god. They'll all crawl to me now. Every one of those sluts."

"Sure, Mr. Lawson." Carl began backing toward the door. "I'll get some clothes for you, huh?" He turned, and then crumpled forward as Lawson shot him three times in the back.

The heat became the world for a time as the transerum worked quickly up through his torso and down his arm. But Lawson endured the burning sensations, knowing that this was his trial by fire, and that with each passing moment every weakness, every flaw in his body was being systematically destroyed. He could feel the residual glow the transerum left behind, swelling in his muscles as they regained their perfection, knitting together every fiber and sinew that had been damaged. The center of his chest blazed, and he laughed helplessly as he realized that even his damaged liver was being regenerated.

Finally the blaze inside died, and his senses expanded, bringing the world to him in infinitely minute detail. The rush of the air through the ceiling vent, the faint whir of the centrifuge in the next room, the dripping of the blood still oozing from Carl's wounds—his hearing had become so sensitive he could probably hear a pin drop from a mile away now.

Slowly Lawson got up from the wheelchair and felt the bloody bandage stretch across his newly healed muscles. He reached down and ripped it away, running his palm over the unmarked surface on the back of his thigh.

"Better than new," he murmured, and did the same to the bandage on his wrist. The transerum had erased everything, leaving nothing behind, not even a scar. When he took a step, power spread through his limbs, eager and limitless, as if every muscle in his body had been changed into coiled steel. On a whim he jumped over Carl's body and landed on the other side of the door.

Lawson retrieved the other item he needed before he took stock of his appearance. He couldn't leave in the stupid open-backed patient's gown he was wearing, but fortunately Carl was about the same size. He tore the sleeve of the dead man's shirt as he pulled it from his torso, and chuckled.

He'd have to be careful now that he was a god, or he'd tear the world apart.

He dressed, and then pulled a lab coat from a rack in the lab. It covered the bloodstained holes in the back of Carl's shirt, although he didn't expect to encounter any opposition when he left the building. Anyone who saw him—even Delaporte—would know he had transcended into a new being. They wouldn't meddle with the god he had become.

Lawson walked down the hall, but instead of taking the elevator he went to the stairwell. After the first flight of stairs he stopped being careful and started jumping from landing to landing. His body sang with strength and ached with agility; by the time he reached the first floor he was laughing again.

As much as he would have liked to jog back to the city on foot, it would take too much time, so as soon as he left the building Lawson went to where he had left his Lexus.

The parking spot was empty, which puzzled him; he never lent his car to anyone. The old man must have had it moved to a better spot. He saw that Kirchner had locked his keys in his SUV again—the doctor was incredibly absentminded—and punched a fist through the driver's-side window. After he brushed the glass off the seat, he got in and drove down to the main gate.

The security guard, a beefy ex-SEAL named Ted Evans, lowered the gate and stepped out of the shack. "Mr. Lawson, Mr. Delaporte just called down. He'd like you to get out of the vehicle and wait here, please."

Lawson frowned. Ted Evans had played racquetball with him a few times in the company gym; he seemed like a nice guy. It was a real pity he didn't understand what had happened to Lawson.

"Ted, I need you to give Don a message for me." He climbed out, grabbed the guard by the throat, and threw him into the side of the shack. Before Ted could fall Lawson pinned him there, shoved the Glock into his belly, and emptied the clip into him. The guard left a wide swath of blood on the decorative brick as he slid down to the ground.

Lawson grabbed Ted's hair and jerked on it in order to check his eyes and make sure he was done. He heard a quick, liquid tearing sound and straightened, still holding the guard's dripping, decapitated head. "Sorry," he murmured, dropping Ted's head into his lap before he grinned. "Guess I don't know my own strength."

Lawson took the guard's .32 from his holster, dropped the empty Glock onto the ground, and got back into the SUV. He drove through the lowered wooden arm, splintering it, and then turned off on the road toward the city.

He'd start at Jessa Bellamy's house, he decided as he enjoyed the cool breeze coming in from the open window. She'd probably called one of her neighbors by now; women were always worried about silly shit like watering their plants and collecting their mail. He'd talk to each and every one of them until he found out where she was hiding. And then Jessa Bellamy was going to spend some time with him.

Extensive, quality time.

TalkBoard.com
Forums > Private > TAKYN Group > Lights Out

October Discussions
Topic: Miles to Go Before I Sleep
From: J
To: All members

I've had to relocate due to problems at home and
will not be online until I've found a new place. I'm
sorry for the short notice but circumstances beyond
my control, etc.

A and V will take over as moderators for the site
until I'm reconnected. If you don't hear from me in a
week it's because I don't have access anymore where
I am.

Keep safe. If you have to move on, remember to
turn the lights out before you go.

J

Jessa posted the message to the board before she logged
off from the anonymous browser. She used the terminal's
erase function to remove the URL from the cookies list,
but even if the computer was caching her session, no one
would be able to track who accessed the discussion board
and read the message.

Early on, the Takyn had established a private code and
found random public-access sites where they could use it
to leave messages for one another; it was one of the many
security measures they'd put in place to protect the group.
She logged off from the public library's ISP she'd used to
get to the board and returned to the files Matthias had
opened for her.

The documentation he'd scanned was extensive and
looked quite genuine, even down to the GenHance masthead and the highly technical content that each memo,
report, and case file contained. It supported everything he
had told her—that Jonah Genaro was using his corporation
as a front, and the philanthropic work he publicly carried
out to cure genetic birth defects was merely a smoke screen
for a far darker purpose.

Jessa couldn't decipher the laboratory test slips, but the doctor's reports were written in layman's terms. Ten years ago GenHance had obtained a sample of human cells that had contained what was referred to as an unidentified genetic anomaly. At first research carried out on the sample showed it to be infectious and lethal until a portion of the anomaly was eventually successfully removed from the cells via a complicated process of genetic splicing and cloning. More samples were obtained, and the entire process was repeated.

It had taken more than a decade to complete the experiment, but according to the final report—signed by Bradford Lawson himself—the resulting transerum contained aggressive blood, tissue, and bone cells that would infect the body like cancer, and then genetically alter the existing cells in order to provide very specific physical and mental enhancements—all without killing them in the process.

She read over three times Lawson's predictions of what benefits the transerum would provide before she let it sink in. The transerum had been created in order to change normal people into superhumans, strengthening their immune systems to be almost inviolate at the same time it increased their physical strength tenfold. Then there were the notations on the specific endowments outside the realm of human ability: sensory acuteness, telekinesis, and precognition. There was also a list of abilities that sounded like something out of a science fiction novel: memory manipulation, sonic disruption, and body alteration.

Lawson seemed to believe that any human given the transerum would undergo a massive genetic change that would allow him or her to acquire these unnatural abilities; the only good thing in the report was that every nonhuman specimen they had tested the transerum on had died within minutes of being injected.

Jessa closed the file and sat back in the chair, rubbing her eyes. Over time the Takyn had discussed what they believed had changed them: genetic experiments performed on them when they were infants, possibly when they were in utero. What had been done to them was the worst sort of violation, but at least they had had the comfort of knowing from the few details they could put together that the experiments had stopped sometime in the eighties.

Judith, the youngest member of the group, had offered the most information on that; she had survived the destruction of one of the facilities where the Takyn had been kept as children, and her immediate escape had allowed her memory of the event to remain intact. Paracelsus, whose ability allowed him to see the past while handling physical objects, had traveled to other abandoned facilities around the country while searching for other Takyn. All he had discovered with his ability, however, was an orchestrated effort to shut down the program and disperse the test subjects into the general population.

Now GenHance intended to restart the experiment, and Matthias and his people were somehow involved.

If Matthias had created all this as part of some elaborate hoax in order to gain her trust, it was doomed to failure. Although the first time she had touched him hadn't shown her anything useful, that had been under extreme circumstances with her life in danger, and fear must have affected her ability. Now that things were calm and there was no immediate threat, all she had to do was touch him and she felt sure that, as with everyone else, she would see the truth.

Her first instinct—always to run away from what she was—faded as she thought of what he had said in the car: *You are not the first to be taken.* If Matthias had found her, he might have identified some or all of the other Takyn. She couldn't leave here until she discovered just how much he knew about them; to do otherwise would put her, the Takyn, and all the other children who had been part of the experiments at risk.

She would have to convince him that she was willing to go along with whatever he had planned. Gaining his trust was essential, but she'd have to go carefully. She couldn't pretend to be cooperative too fast; he'd never believe her.

"Jessa," Matthias said from behind her, making her jump. "Stop now. Rowan has prepared food for us."

Game on.

"I'm not hungry." In reality she was starving, but she

couldn't show any desire to sit down and have dinner with her kidnapper and his jailbait girlfriend. Not yet.

He reached past her and shut off the monitor. "You have questions. We will answer them over the meal."

She swiveled around to face him. "Do you ever take 'no' for an answer?"

He smiled, and it transformed his features from austerely attractive to simply stunning. "Frequently."

"You've gone to great lengths to collect all this information on GenHance's illegal activities. I can't imagine it was easy or cheap." She gestured toward the computer. "Why not take it to the police? He can't own everyone."

"Jonah Genaro has such influence and wealth that it cannot be calculated," he said. "What he does not presently control or own, he can buy."

"In some countries I know that would give him unlimited immunity from prosecution, but this is America," she reminded him. "We have a free press, and they love nothing more than the opportunity to tear down omnipotent moguls like Genaro."

"He would never allow it."

Jessa wondered what country he had come from that he would believe one man could have so much power. Or was his conviction just another part of the ruse? "Whether or not he could, by keeping this secret, in effect you are helping Genaro protect GenHance."

He studied her expression. "What do you think the authorities in this country would do if they discovered the true nature of the Kyndred?"

He sounded like a conspiracy-theory nutcase. That would explain why he'd brought her to an underground bunker. "They'd detain ... these people. Test them to see just how powerful they are. Then they'd lock them up or try to use them." She glanced down and let her voice tremble a little. "All right, they'd probably do the same thing Genaro is doing—harvest cells so they could make their own superhumans."

"We do not protect Genaro," Matthias told her. "We protect ourselves."

She hadn't expected him to admit that much. "You're telling me that you're one of them. One of these Kyndred."

He nodded.

"But you're not American." Real dread washed over her now. "Are there others in Europe?"

"That I know of? Only me." He turned around. "Come. I am hungry, and Rowan does not like waiting."

"From what I've seen, Rowan doesn't like much," she told him as she followed him out of the room. "Does she have some problem with your bringing me here?"

"Ask her."

Jessa recalled the open hostility on the girl's face. "I don't think she wants to talk to me."

Matthias stopped her. "Rowan is very young and unsure of her place in the world. You are not. This makes her angry. She envies you."

She almost laughed. "I'm not that old, and according to you, I just lost everything I had in the world."

"No, you did not." He opened a door, from which came the scent of tomatoes, garlic, and herbs. "You have us."

Jessa walked into a large, well-appointed kitchen fitted with the latest appliances and two long granite-topped counters. Four leather-topped stools sat around a center island, where three place settings of Asian china had been placed. A long basket lined with a checked cloth held tiny, steaming rolls gleaming with drizzles of oil and grated garlic, and a colorful salad of field greens, sliced radishes, and shredded carrots filled a wide, shallow wooden bowl.

Rowan barely spared her a glance as she brought a steaming platter of linguine covered with a rich-looking red sauce to the table. "It's not getting any hotter," she told Matthias.

Jessa took the seat nearest to the door while Matthias sat on her right and Rowan hovered at her left. The young girl didn't actually sit down once over the next forty minutes, but stood and held her plate as she ate, as if she were afraid someone would take it from her.

Jessa waited until she saw both of them sample the food before she took a small portion for herself; she ate enough to quiet her rumbling stomach but no more. She considered asking questions during the meal, as Matthias had suggested, but when she noticed just how much Rowan ate she completely forgot about it. The skinny young girl demolished three heaping bowls of the salad and half the basket of rolls before digging into the linguine. Only after polishing off her fourth serving of the pasta did she sigh and bring her arm up as if to wipe her mouth on the sleeve.

She stopped herself, reached for a napkin, and then caught Jessa's fascinated gaze. "What's your problem?"

She offered a tentative smile. "You have quite an appetite." Before Rowan could snap her head off, she added, "This sauce is extraordinary—it's so fresh. You must have made it from scratch. Are you a chef?"

"Christ, no." She grabbed up the empty dishes and stalked over to the sink to rinse them.

When Jessa tried to finish clearing the table, Matthias caught her eye and shook his head. "Rowan," he said aloud. "The meal was excellent."

"Yeah, okay." The girl kept her back to them and scrubbed.

Jessa picked up the dishes and, before Matthias could stop her, brought them over to the sink. "If you're not a chef, you should be. I happen to love Italian food, and your sauce is one of the best I've ever tasted. Thank you for making it."

Rowan took the dishes from her, hesitated, and then muttered, "You're welcome." She turned to Matthias. "You want coffee in the library?"

"Please."

Jessa reluctantly followed him out of the kitchen. "I should stay and help her clean up."

"Rowan would not allow it. When she cooks, she is . . ." He paused as if unsure of the right words to use. "Master and servant."

"The kitchen is her territory." Jessa stopped outside the one door she recognized, the one that led to the library where she had awoken. "Does she have an eating disorder?"

"It is her body that is disordered," he corrected. "Food does not stay with her. If she does not eat like three men, she grows very thin."

As Jessa followed him into the library, she thought of Vulcan. He described having a similar problem with fluids; he was forced to drink an inordinate amount of water every day or he rapidly became dehydrated.

"So Rowan is also Kyndred." Thank God she wasn't one of the Takyn; Jessa couldn't imagine dealing with someone as surly and resentful as Rowan.

"You should know that she is," Matthias said as he went to crouch in front of the fire and add another split log. "We are sensitive to each other."

"I never said I was like you." She went to the love seat and shook out the crazy quilt before neatly folding it. "You've made a mistake, and so did Genaro."

"You still turn from the truth and hide behind this pretense." He came over to her, took the quilt from her hands, and tossed it aside. "Why?"

Chapter 10

Being so close to all of Matthias's muscle and intensity made Jessa want to run. She should have felt afraid or intimidated, and the fact that she didn't made her feet itch to get the hell out of there. Why was she responding to him like this, as if some unseen energy between them were growing and soon would explode? Common sense told her to first put some space between them; she couldn't maintain her charade of reluctant cooperation, not when she could feel his body heat melding with hers and smell the dark, compelling scent of his skin wrapping around her.

She'd move in a minute; there was something she had to know. Something that might explain all of it. "What do you want from me?"

"It is too soon for trust," he said, "and too late for doubt."

She couldn't tell if he was trying to reassure her or goad her. Maybe he meant to do both. "Tell me."

"I want many things." A faint groove appeared in his cheek. "For now, be with me. Talk with me. Come to know me. You will not regret it."

The timber of his voice was set to mesmerize, but she wasn't giving in to that. Not until she knew exactly what had motivated him to drag her out of her life and down into his. "Why did you save me, Matthias?"

"You are one of us. All we have is each other." He lifted his hand and skimmed his thumb beneath her right eye, tracing the crescent of thin skin beneath her lower lashes. "Have you never imagined being with your own kind?"

Her own kind. She would have laughed out loud had it not been so pathetic. There was no one like her, not even among the Takyn. Their unique abilities made them beautiful and strong and noble, and set them above other people. They were always doing amazing things with them, even in secret. Delilah had the ability to control and use animals, especially dogs, and had tracked and rescued countless people lost in the wilderness. Vulcan used his power over copper to create elaborate sculptures, which he donated to hospitals and museums, while Paracelsus kept an online site that constantly corrected the mistakes historians made about the past. Even Aphrodite, whose ability allowed her to instantly enslave any man she chose, had never used it to hurt anyone. She went out of her way not to.

Compared to the others, Jessa felt cursed by the shadowlight. It forced her to see the ugliness that existed in every heart, and had condemned her to spend the rest of her days alone.

His hand moved away from her face, and the cessation of the delicate abrasion made her flinch. This time the contact hadn't pushed her into the shadowlight—but why? She couldn't touch anyone without seeing.

"Jessa?"

Hearing him say her name enfolded her in a tangle of useless emotions and impossible longing. The man was built like a fortress, and he made the woman in her want nothing more than to collapse against him and hold on and feel his arms closing around her. Even as her logic argued against it, her body responded to the promise of his. He had gotten her away from Lawson; he had not harmed her; he would protect her.

All she had to do was give up everything that had kept her safe for the last ten years, and God only knew what else.

"I'm not like you and your friend. I live alone. I handle things on my own. I don't need anyone else in my life." She was laying it on a little too heavy; she sounded as sullen and defensive as Rowan. He would respond better to helpless but courageous. "Whatever abilities I may or may not have, they're my responsibility. Not yours."

"What if you could use them to help others like us?"

"What others like—" She stopped as Rowan came in carrying a tray with a stainless-steel thermal carafe and two colorful glazed mugs. Piled on a plate between the mugs were tiny triangular cakes studded with dried cranberries and walnuts.

"These are scones. I made them this morning. The coffee is decaf." She set down the tray and surveyed them both. "I'm going to bed. Just drop the tray in the kitchen when you're through." She left before either of them could reply.

"She bakes, too." Jessa went over and picked up one of the miniature tea cakes. "What does she do on her days off? Rescue people from burning buildings?"

"She feeds the homeless."

Of course she did. Rowan had that look of a true paragon about her. Matthias would sleep with no one less. "That's nice of her."

"Rowan will not admit it, but caring for others makes her happy." He prepared the coffee and handed her a mug. "You are the one who rescues the defenseless."

He had no right to talk to her like this. Not in the same breath he'd used to praise his girlfriend. She wanted to throw the hot brew in his face.

"You don't have your facts straight." She sat down and hunched forward to compose herself. "I don't rescue people from anything. I make a living at ruining their lives."

"Is that how you see your ability?" He sat down beside her. "The young men and women who work with you would not agree, I think."

"I've helped a few people in trouble who didn't deserve what happened to them," she conceded, forcing a note of shame into her voice. "That doesn't excuse the other things I've done. Ellen Farley is sitting in jail right now because of me."

His gaze turned shrewd. "Would it have been better to let her be killed by her partner?"

She absorbed the shock of his question, but only barely. "What are you, some sort of mind reader?"

"Like Genaro, we have friends among the authorities. Not as many, and they are not corrupt, but they help to protect us." He picked up a roll of paper from the table. "This was sent to us after the Farley woman was arrested."

Jessa took the fax and read it. It appeared authentic, but of course she had no way to tell if it was. It contained an interdepartmental memo from the Atlanta Police Department. According to the terse paragraphs, Ellen's partner, Max Grodan, had been identified as a fugitive and the primary suspect in a series of murders, and was being extradited to stand trial in Florida.

"She wasn't involved in the killings," she said quietly. "She was going to be his next victim."

"So you did not ruin her life," Matthias said. "You saved it."

He was very good, persuasive and sympathetic. She'd have to be the same. "You said you've found others whom GenHance was trying to kill." She handed the fax back to him. "Who are they, and where are they now?"

"Many places," he said. "Their names no longer exist. We arranged new identities for them before they were relocated."

Welcome to the Freak Protection Program, Rowan had said. "Is that the plan for me?"

He watched her face. "It was."

But not anymore, she silently amended. Maybe she had pushed enough for one night. "I'm a little tired. Am I supposed to sleep in here?"

"Rowan has prepared a chamber for you." He stood. "Follow me."

The room he showed her to was located a few doors down from the kitchen—probably so Rowan could keep an eye on her, Jessa thought—and contained a bed, a dresser, and a color television. There were also a variety of paperback novels on a three-tiered bookcase and one of the wrought-iron stands with a porcelain basin and jug. She walked around the room, looking for surveillance equipment, but discovered only a small spiderweb and a few patches of dust that Rowan had missed on the carved wooden headboard. She turned around to see Matthias standing in the doorway. Acutely aware of the bed behind her, she offered him a cool smile.

"This is fine," she said, and as he turned to leave she added, "You never told me what your ability is."

"No." He glanced back at her. "I did not."

With that he closed the door.

Matthias enabled the alarm sensor outside Jessa's chamber door, which, if she opened it, would send a silent alert through their security system. Wherever she went, the tiny transmitter he had planted in the heel of her shoe would track her movements.

Rowan was waiting for him in the communications center. "She scrubbed her cookies but I recovered them from the redundant drive." She pulled up on the screen the message board and the message Jessa had posted. "She warned her pals."

"We expected that she would." He read the message. "You can decipher the meaning of this?"

"It's not that complicated. Basically she's telling the others that she's alive, in trouble, and she's giving up control of the group until she's safe. She wants them to watch their backs and cover their tracks." She looked up at him. "You do realize, of course, that this whole nice-hostage act of hers is total bullshit."

He nodded. "She is afraid for her friends."

"I think her friends can take care of themselves just fine." Rowan used the keyboard and opened another window. "According to the late news, Queenie's just made the feds' top-ten most-wanted list, which I'd say totally blows the plan. You'd better make sure she doesn't find a way out of here. Genaro will have her on a cutting table so fast she'll think she's sushi."

"She does not wish to escape now."

Rowan uttered a sour laugh. "Matt, the only thing that girl wants is out of here. She's just trying to play us to find out how much we know. So quit thinking with the little head."

He ran a hand over his cropped hair. "My head is not little."

"Not around her, it isn't." Her mouth twisted. "And before you ask, no, I'm not explaining that one."

"Very well. Allow Jessa access to every room except the library and the armory." He stood. "I will relieve you in four hours."

She cleared the screen and brought up a game of mahjongg. "Pleasant dreams."

A lifetime of self-discipline and constant travel had taught Matthias to sleep where and when he could. He slept lightly and woke at whatever hour he wished. After Rowan had come to live with him, he discovered she could do the same, but for far different reasons. He also learned never to go near or touch her when she was sleeping, even when he knew she was in the throes of one of her nightmares. The one time he had tried to wake her, she had attacked him like a wounded animal before coming to her senses.

In his chamber he stripped to his skin, washed, and stretched out on the thin pallet that served as his bed. Jessa would not be sleeping, he guessed as he stared up at the ceiling. She would search the room, wait for some time, and then slip out to search the tunnels.

He closed his tired eyes and willed his body to relax. Being near her and refraining from touching her had required more effort than he cared to admit, but he was not accustomed to denying himself. When it was convenient, he sought out and used willing women at regular intervals to relieve his physical needs. Now it was decidedly not convenient.

Silencing his thoughts tonight proved as difficult as relinquishing his mind to the darkness. Sleep was like food: Having too much or too little could make one weak and muddled. He knew Rowan would not allow Jessa to escape, but the resentment and anger she felt toward their unwilling guest might influence her judgment.

He understood in part why his young friend disliked Jessa—she had enjoyed most of the advantages that life had denied Rowan—but there was more to it than he was sensing. Rowan had a good and generous heart, but she had already closed it against Jessa. It could not be merely out of envy.

Matthias drifted into the light, dreamless sleep from which he could easily wake, but the sound of footsteps roused him an hour before he was to take over the watch. He knew it was Jessa the moment she slipped into his chamber. Confronting her would serve no purpose but to frighten her, so he lay still and kept his breathing slow, and tracked her by the sound of her movements and the intensity of her scent.

She moved around the room, searching it methodically before she crouched down to look under his pallet. At first he imagined his chamber appeared odd to her, lacking as it was in most of the modern amenities, but then he remembered how her bedchamber had looked from the skylight. For a woman her needs and tastes were as Spartan as his own. She stood, and his skin prickled as she came around and moved to stand over him. He did not mind her looking down at his nakedness; he knew he was made well and that most women responded to his body with natural desire. He had looked upon her in her bed, too; it seemed fitting that she see him in his. The only sound he could hear was the gentle rush of her breathing, but she remained there looking down at him for some time. Then, so lightly that he barely felt it, her fingertips brushed over the insides of his wrists, first the left and then the right.

She was checking him for the marks, and touching him as little as possible so she would not use her ability.

He pretended to stir and turned onto his side, giving her his back. That allowed her to see the left side of his neck, and as he expected, she touched the twining black snake etched into his flesh.

Slowly her hand moved away, and he fought the impulse to turn over and pull her down atop him. If he did, he would have had her under him before she could gasp, and accepting him into her body before she could speak. His shaft, already stiff and thick, swelled and lengthened at the thought. In another time and place he would have ignored convention and done just that, for among his people no woman would touch a sleeping man unless she wanted his attention.

Perhaps on some level she did. *Touch me again and I will give you what you truly seek.*

To his great disappointment Jessa moved away, and left his chamber as silently as she had entered it. He turned over slowly and listened as her steps retreated before he opened his eyes. He could still smell her in the air, feel the silk of her touch on his skin. He sat up and looked down at his cock, the head of which had emerged, fully engorged and ready to stroke and pleasure.

Finally he understood what Rowan had meant, and in spite of his discomfort, he smiled. "Quit thinking, little head. The woman is not ready for us."

Not yet.

Samantha walked the streets of Atlanta for several hours until most of the euphoria she felt from the girl's blood faded away. A few times she considered calling Lucan on her mobile to let him know where she was—he didn't like not knowing—but she wasn't ready to listen to the inevitable lecture.

Yes, she was Darkyn. No, she had no choice but to live on human blood. Yes, she could make a little more effort in the assimilation department. But what was hammering inside her skull, what was really going to dig in and do a lot of damage, were the residual echoes of Abby's thoughts. She could still feel the girl's pleasure, still hear everything that had flashed through her head. Whether it would fade like the physical afterglow of feeding or remain imprinted was yet to be seen, but whatever happened she'd have to live with what she'd done to that girl. She'd taken her blood and in the process had brainwashed her.

Maybe the same way Lucan had done to her the first time he'd fed on her blood.

Her phone rang in her pocket. Lucan had a habit of reprogramming her ringtone without telling her; tonight it played the theme to the movie *Twilight*. She considered chucking the device down the sewer, but that would only make him come looking for her.

She flipped open the phone. "Leave me alone."

"I'd love to, sweetie," Alexandra Keller said, "but the pain currently drilling a hole in my skull won't go away, and morphine no longer works on me."

"You're the doctor," Sam snapped. "I can't do anything about it. I'm just a cop."

"You're also the only Kyn who was changed by my blood," Alex reminded her. "That means whenever you're in trouble, I feel it. As for what that feels like, ever stick an ice pick in your ear?"

"Please don't give me ideas." Sam stopped and looked around. She was standing at the back of the Armstrong building. She'd come back to him like some sort of goddamn homing pigeon. "Everything is fine, Alex. I'm just not having a great night."

"Same here. If everything is fine, why do you sound so pissed off?"

Sam looked up at the lights on the fourth floor. "Lucan took me out to hunt. My first time. I did it, but I had no idea.... I've been using him or bagged blood since I changed. You know what it's like when you use a human."

"Can't say I do," Alex admitted. "I have yet to sink fangs into anyone other than Michael. Was it that bad?"

"Before, when I was human, I thought I felt all those things because I loved him." She walked slowly down toward the loading platform. "It happened again with the girl I used for blood tonight. You feel the exact same thing. When you bite them, it's like an aphrodisiac on ricochet. They go crazy for you, and you feel that, and then you want them just as much. I can't explain it better than that."

"I've done something similar." Her tone remained neutral. "What's your problem with this, Sam? Would you rather have the girl feel pain and horror, like in the movies?"

"Jesus, no, of course not." Sam stopped at the front entrance to the building and sat down on the bottom steps. "It just makes me wonder, you know? I never fell in love until I met Lucan, and then it happened so fast ... but I didn't fall in love until after he used me for blood."

"Honey, I got to spend a little time with Luc after he grabbed me in Fort Lauderdale, and he would never—"

"No, Alex." She didn't want to hear about Lucan and what he'd never do. "It was bad enough finding out I look just like the chick he had a crush on in the seventeen hundreds or whatever. Maybe that's the whole deal for him: that I look like her."

"I know you're upset, Sam, but honest to God—"

"And what if I do that to someone else?" she demanded. "What if I bite them and make them think they love me and then somehow infect them?"

"You can't do that—"

"You infected me when Lucan gave me your blood, and you weren't even in the room—"

"Will you shut up and let me finish one fucking sentence, please?" Alex waited until she heard silence, and then added, "Thank you. Okay. Let's get a few things straight. You can't infect anyone unless they're already carrying Darkyn DNA, they're dying, and you give them your blood. That's the only way it happens without killing them. Got it?"

"Yeah," Sam muttered.

"I don't know what the deal is between you and Lucan right now," Alex continued, "but you are not now nor have you ever been a stand-in for Frances. He loves you, kiddo. He told me, and I saw his face and his eyes when he said it. He wasn't lying."

"He told you that when I was human," she reminded her, "and he was feeding on me. Not a lot, but enough to influence his feelings. You should have heard how he talked about humans. He called us ..." She trailed off as she tried to remember the exact phrase. "He called us a movable feast."

"If all you were to Lucan was a Happy Meal, then why did he give you my blood after Dwyer shot you? Why was he so desperate to save your life?" When Sam didn't reply, she said, "You're a beautiful girl, and I'm sure you're great in the sack, but really, sweetie. Look at the guy."

Samantha felt the hair on the back of her neck prickle, and turned around to see Lucan standing a few steps above her. She didn't know how long he had been listening, but his face had no expression and he didn't move.

"He's big, he's blond, and he's a badass," Alex was saying on the phone. "He can have—correction, probably has had—any woman he wants."

She stood up slowly. "They're all like that. Maybe that's all there is."

"I can't tell you why I fell in love with Michael, but I know it's not just the bond of blood," she said, all the humor vanishing from her tone. "You remember the high lord, Richard Tremayne. Richard's seneschal, Korvel, bonded me to him when I was separated from Michael. We spent a lot of time together, and then Richard hurt me and Korvel took care of me. That was all it took. Even after I left Ireland, Korvel came to me in my dreams. Worse, when I was asleep I called him to me. That's how powerful these bonds are."

Sam began walking up the steps. "So it took you over, too."

"Not all of me," Alex said. "I wanted to have sex with Korvel, sure, but I didn't. I couldn't, not even when I was dreaming. The love I felt for Michael kept pulling me back. When I finally realized what was happening, I knew what I had to do."

She stopped one step below Lucan. "What?"

"I told Michael everything." She sighed. "And do you know what that stupid bastard did? He offered to let me go back to Ireland. He said if I wanted Korvel more than him, he'd just have to accept it."

"Kyn males usually go insane when they're separated from their life companions." Sam saw her lover's eyes turn from misty gray to glittering chrome.

"Yeah, well, I don't think Mike would have waited around for the straitjacket," Alex said. "Sam, you know this works both ways. If you two split up, whatever happens to him probably will happen to you, too."

She reached up and skimmed her fingertips across the grim lines of his mouth. "I can't ever leave him, can I?"

"Do you want to?"

"The truth?" She could face it as well as him. "I wake up and I want him. I go to work and I think about him. I come home and I can't wait to touch him." She dropped her hand to his shoulder and took the last step so that she stood only an inch from him. "I don't think I can live without him anymore, Alex. Even if there were a way to get over this thing between us, I don't want to."

"Then there's only one more question I have for you," Alex said.

She closed her eyes as Lucan curled his hand around the back of her neck. "Okay."

"Why are you still on the phone with me?"

Sam laughed helplessly as Lucan took the phone from her and spoke into it. "Good evening, Alexandra. My *sygkenis* bids you good-night and farewell." He listened for a moment. "Yes, I will tell her." He switched off the phone and tossed it over his shoulder before he scooped Sam up in his arms.

"How much trouble am I in?" Sam asked as he carried her inside, mainly so she wouldn't break down and cry all over him.

"None, unless you were lying to Alexandra."

Lucan carried her into the elevator and from it to their suite. Only when they were inside and he had kicked the door shut did he set her down on her feet.

"I thought you weren't pissed off at me," she said carefully.

"Oh, I am that." He tilted her face up to his. "You should know that if you ever try to leave me, I will hunt you down and drag you back to my stronghold."

She shook her head. "You won't have to."

"So you say now. But understand what that means, my *sygkenis*." His fingers tightened on her jaw. "Alex's blood may run in your veins, but you belong to me, and I am not Michael Cyprien. I will not play the noble lover and sacrifice my love for you. You cannot bring someone like me out of the darkness and then change your mind about it. I am yours, Samantha. You have all of me. The beautiful mask and the monster beneath it. And make no mistake: I am a monster. One who will happily, *joyfully* tear apart anything that comes between us. As you yourself have already witnessed."

"Nothing like threatening the one you love to keep a relationship together." She rested her forehead against his chest. "I'm in love with a monster, and tonight when I fed on that girl, I felt like a monster, so that kind of works out." She looked up at him. "I'm afraid of what happened at the club. What happened between us when I was human. Alex said I need to talk to you about it. Can we do that without you reducing this place to a pile of smoking rubble?"

The phone rang.

"The building is safe," Lucan said, "but I cannot guarantee the telephone will survive the night." He strode over, snatched up the receiver, and said, "What now?"

Sam watched as he listened. Lucan muttered something in a form of English that hadn't been spoken in seven centuries and slammed down the phone.

"Is something wrong at home?"

"No, it was Kendrick." He looked at her. "Someone has gone on a killing spree here in the city."

Sam frowned. "Why is that our problem?"

"Witnesses say the attacker uses his hands to tear apart the bodies of the victims," Lucan said, and regarded his own velvet gloves. "It would seem that I am not the only monster in town."

PART THREE
Gaven

1 October 2008

Ancient Plot to Murder Emperor?

**Students Unearth Two-Thousand-Year-Old
Statue, Potential Assassination Conspiracy at
Ostia Antica**

A group of American archaeology students participating in a teaching excavation at the ancient Roman port colony of Ostia Arcana have unearthed evidence of a historical whodunit in the form of an eight-foot-tall marble statue of the goddess Minerva. The statue, believed to be deliberately concealed at the ancient port site, was discovered to contain an inscription referring to a conspiracy to assassinate Roman emperor Octavian Augustus.

"We're very excited," the team's chief archaeologist, Professor Jeffrey Williams, said during the international press conference held in Rome on Saturday. "This is the largest and most well-preserved statue of Minerva Victoria ever found, and the early evidence indicates that it was deliberately buried very early in the first century. As soon as the kids translated the inscription on the inside of the base, we understood why it was concealed in such an unorthodox manner." When asked how the team located the statue, the professor became somewhat chagrined. "I wish I could say we found it because of our meticulous research, but the area where we were working was not considered of any particular value, and has been used for years as an outdoor laboratory to demonstrate proper procedures on a dig. To be honest, it was simply dumb luck that all of the archaeologists who surveyed the site before our team never explored the interior tunnel where the digging equipment is stored, or they would have found the vault a long time ago."

The enormous marble statue, reported to be over eight feet tall and more than three feet wide, depicts the ancient Roman goddess Minerva (known to the Greeks as Athena) as winged and poised in a classic victorious stance. While the majority of statues from the era were sculpted with solid bases to provide better stability, a fitted marble slab concealed the Minerva statue's hollow base interior. The statue, encased in many layers of protective wools and linens, was found sealed inside a stone vault inside the service tunnel, which was originally excavated in 1911.

Professor Williams believes the Latin inscription found inside of the base provides the first solid evidence of a conspiracy to murder the emperor Augustus, long believed to have been poisoned in 14 CE by his ambitious wife, Livia, so that her son, Tiberius, could assume the throne.

"We're not releasing the translation of the inscription until the statue has been dated and authenticated," Professor Williams told reporters. "It would be irresponsible to do otherwise. What I can tell you is that once we prove this new evidence is legitimate, the historians are going to be busy rewriting a lot of their books."

2 October 2008

Tragedy Strikes Student Archaeological Dig at Ostia Antica

Sixteen American archaeology students and their instructor, Jeffrey Williams, have been killed in a tunnel collapse at the archaeological site where yesterday they had evidently discovered an intact statue of the goddess Minerva.

Maria Salza at the Center for Archaeological Studies in Rome issued this statement: "We extend our heartfelt sympathies to the families of the young Americans who lost their lives in this terrible tragedy."

According to witnesses, the students and their instructor had just entered the tunnel to retrieve some equipment when the collapse occurred. Although in the first hours after the collapse rescue workers held out hope of finding survivors, subsequent inspection of the site with specialized equipment revealed all of those who were caught in the collapse were killed instantly.

Workers have now begun the grim task of digging out the tunnel to recover the bodies and determine the cause of the tragic accident. An international search-and-rescue team provided by American biotech corporation GenHance, Inc., will be arriving this afternoon to provide their assistance.

"Our people will do whatever it takes to help with the recovery efforts," GenHance CEO Jonah Genaro told reporters. "We will also be bringing home the victims of this terrible tragedy. It's the least we can do for their families and loved ones."

Police are still interviewing witnesses, many of whom claim they heard an explosion just before the tunnel collapsed.

Chapter 11

Jessa spent most of her first night in Matthias's underground labyrinth searching through the tunnels and rooms. He and Rowan seemed to be the only occupants, and neither of them tried to stop her from moving about freely. She discovered why when she retraced her steps and found her way back to the communications center, the kitchen, and the library, only to find that she had been locked out of those rooms.

She guessed Matthias didn't want her helping herself to Rowan's knives or the computer system, but she didn't understand why the library had been made off-limits. Antique furniture and old books weren't much of a threat—unless they were concealing something else.

If I had to protect sensitive information, Jessa thought, *I certainly wouldn't hide it in a filing cabinet.*

Nothing told her where she was, except that she was obviously underground. She had to move carefully to prevent her footsteps from echoing, and the thick concrete sides of the tunnels and the absence of windows gave the place a cavelike feel. She was glad she'd never developed any form of claustrophobia, or she would have been climbing the walls by now.

None of what she saw looked new; from the stains, cracks, and condition of the concrete she guessed it was at least thirty or forty years old. She'd heard stories from her father about nuclear attack shelters that many paranoid American citizens had built during the Cold War era; for a time it had been quite a trend to have a bomb shelter in the backyard.

Was this place one of them? If it were, why would Matthias have installed a fireplace? The smoke had to be channeled up to the surface through a chimney or ventilation system, or he and Rowan would have suffocated. How was he dispersing the smoke without revealing the presence of his secret bunker?

She stopped in her tracks as she remembered something Matthias had said: *GenHance wants your ability. To have it, they must harvest it from your body.*

Was this some sort of research laboratory, like the underground facilities Paracelsus had discovered during his searches for evidence about their past? Had she been brought here to be experimented on again?

Jessa went to the next door, tried it, and found it unlocked. When she looked inside, however, she didn't see test beakers, Bunsen burners, or medical equipment. She saw big, comfortable-looking pillows scattered on the floor and three tiers of wall-to-wall shelving. Thin, brightly colored books stood in neat rows, arranged by height, and stretched the length of each shelf. She moved into the room, went to the nearest shelf, and took down one of the books.

The colorful front cover read *DK Eyewitness Books* and *Space Exploration* and featured a bird's-eye view of an astronaut in a space suit standing in the open cargo bay of the space shuttle with Earth looming like a giant behind him.

What was Matthias doing with a book that was published for children?

She replaced the book, which was one of more than a hundred DK books on the shelf. Beside them were more picture books, ranging from *Old Penn Station* by William Low to *The Story of Negro League Baseball* by Kadir Nelson. All of the books featured exceptionally vivid illustrations paired with simple text, and all seemed to be about every subject under the sun, from travel to history to biographies of famous people. All had been read many times, judging by the dings to the covers and the faint cracks on the spines.

As harmless as they seemed, the books didn't comfort

her. If Matthias and Rowan had brought children down here . . .

She backed out of the room and closed the door. She couldn't bring herself to believe they were involved with the doctors who had experimented on her and the other Takyn when they were children, or that the experiments were still ongoing. Paracelsus and Vulcan would have found some evidence of it.

She checked several other rooms, bracing herself each time as she expected the worst, only to find the most innocuous of discoveries: closets packed with collections of old radios, calculators, small electric motors, and lamps. In the next room she found a collection of fifty different folding chairs neatly arranged in concentric circles, and in another she wandered through a maze of stereo equipment. None of what she saw made sense to her; if Matthias were collecting these things, he didn't seem to care what they were worth. He displayed rare antiques next to yard-sale finds.

Her search also made her realize that Matthias was fond of very old weaponry, which he displayed in several locked collectors' cases hung throughout the tunnels. Most were some form of dagger or short sword, but there were two cases of antique pistols and one large collection of spiked hammers and maces. Each weapon had the marks of age and care; most had been carefully polished to a weathered gleam. The pristine condition of the blades reminded her of the old bronze sword in the glass case over the library fireplace. He had never cleaned that one, she guessed, not with the dark bloodstains streaking the ancient metal.

She wanted to ask Matthias why he was collecting things in such odd ways, and then she turned a corner and picked up a trace of his scent on the air. Everything seemed slightly magnified in this place; the smells seemed to be much sharper and more pervasive. But by following Matthias's scent she was able to locate his room, and after listening at the door for some time she decided to look inside.

As soon as she saw his bare body stretched out on the camp bed she should have backed out and left, but he didn't wake, and she couldn't pass up the opportunity to search his room. He kept almost nothing in the small chamber, which made it obvious he came here only to sleep. After moving quietly around the interior, she stooped to glance under the thin and uncomfortable-looking mattress upon which he slept, but found nothing, not even dust bunnies.

She stood and looked down at him. Asleep he should have looked younger or vulnerable, but his strong, handsome features appeared unchanged. Only when he smiled, she decided, did he change into someone less godlike.

For the first time she wondered whether he were one of the Takyn, and didn't yet realize who she was. They had been so adept and thorough at concealing their exact abilities as well as their identities that she had no way of recognizing one of her friends in the flesh, unless . . .

At some point during the experiments that had been performed on them, each of the Takyn had been tattooed with the image of an animal. After searching one of the abandoned facilities, Paracelsus had told the group that the doctors had used the tattoos to name them as well as classify their abilities. Aphrodite had suggested it might be better for all of them if they kept their tats under wraps, but Jessa had taken the extra step of having her own removed, which had taken several months and many painful treatments.

She reached down, bracing herself before she ran her fingertips quickly across the inside of his wrist, feeling it for the telltale texture left behind by laser treatments. Fortunately the shadowlight didn't take her, and all she felt was smooth skin over dense muscle. His other wrist proved to be just as unmarked.

Jessa straightened and bit at her bottom lip. Some of the others hadn't been marked on the wrists or arms; Delilah said her tattoo had been placed in an unmentionable area, while Paracelsus complained of always having to keep his shirt buttoned to the collar to cover the ink on his collarbones.

Matthias moved, making her catch her breath and freeze in place, but he only turned over onto his side and settled back into sleep.

He *was* marked.

Jessa stared down at the snake tattoo, wound in the shape of a sideways figure eight, that had been inked into the side of his throat. The only color used had been black, but the work was particularly detailed; she could count the tiny individual scales along the entire body, and counted three mock lights reflected in the reptile's single eye. The snake was depicted as biting—no, devouring—its own tail.

She knew enough about symbolism to recall that the snake eating itself represented infinity. *What do you think should last forever?*

She didn't meant to touch the tattoo, but something about it drew her fingers like a magnet. Only after a minute had passed did she realize something else—sometimes she could get away with a quick touch, but extended or repeated contact with anyone always triggered her ability. Yet touching Matthias like this was not sending her into the shadowlight.

Surviving a blizzard and an avalanche isn't a sin, she thought, shivering a little as she remembered the brutal cold he had endured. *Why would such a terrifying experience make you feel guilty or ashamed?*

Curious as she was to discover the reason he felt guilt and shame over his ordeal, Jessa had to be practical. The snake didn't prove anything except that Matthias had been tattooed sometime in the past. If she were going to believe his story about the Kyndred and being part of some rescue operation, she'd need more to go on than a mark on his neck.

Although she tried several times to find it, Jessa couldn't locate the security hatch Matthias had shown her. She felt sure she was moving through the correct tunnels, but found herself reaching only one dead end after another. Exhaustion began to tug at her feet, and reluctantly she returned to the room he had given her.

The door didn't have a lock on the inside or outside, so she took the straight-backed chair sitting beside the washbasin and propped it under the knob. It was too flimsy to keep the door shut for long, but if someone came in, the sound of it falling would wake her.

Normally she slept nude—another habit she and Matthias shared—but she kept her clothes and shoes on as she curled up on the bed. When the opportunity to escape came, she thought as she closed her eyes, she had to be ready.

Jessa fell asleep almost as soon as her head touched the pillow, and she was so tired she didn't expect to dream. Yet when oblivion overtook her, she felt herself drawn through the darkness back to more familiar surroundings: her bedroom in her apartment.

She stood beside her bed and saw someone in it, covered by her sheets. On one level she knew she was seeing herself in the past, but the shape under the linens seemed wrong. It was bigger and wider than it should have been.

Carefully she reached out to draw back the sheet, and went still as a large, hard hand caught her wrist and pulled her down on top of the body. Another male hand pushed aside the linen to reveal Matthias's face.

"This isn't real." She rolled off him onto her side. "This never happened."

"I watched you." His gilded jade eyes shifted as he looked at her skylight. "From there."

Jessa glanced up. "From the roof?" He nodded. "Why?"

"I wanted to see you." His fingers smoothed a piece of hair back from her face. "You were restless that night."

"I have trouble falling asleep," she admitted, placing her hand on his hip as if it were perfectly natural. She remembered what she usually did when she was restless and groaned a little. "You saw what I did?"

"I did. You were beautiful." He brushed a fingertip against the fringe of her lower lashes. "I wanted so much to come inside." His fingertips moved down to rub across her lower lip. "You brought me pleasure that night. Watching you, I shared yours."

"This is a dream." She ran her palm up to his waist, and then over the corded, unyielding muscles of his abdomen. "None of this is really happening."

He seemed amused now. "And if some of it did?"

Jessa buried her face against his chest and laughed. "I think I just got even." As she spoke, her mouth brushed against his skin, and she felt his body tighten. "God, this feels so real."

"It can be." His hand cradled the back of her head as his other arm curled around her, urging her closer. "Between us, it can be everything you've imagined and more."

"I can't even bump into a stranger without seeing the ugliness that they hide inside. Now I'm touching you, and all I see is you." Jessa lifted her face. "Who are you, and why are you in my dream?"

"The gods brought us together," he murmured as he bent his head. "Nothing will keep us apart."

Before Matthias's mouth touched hers, Jessa woke to the feel of something prodding her in the shoulder. She opened her eyes, expecting to see him, but only Rowan's scowling face hovered above her.

"Let's go, Queenie," the girl said. She was nudging her with a wooden spoon. "Come on, wake up. I haven't got all day."

Jessa sat up and blinked. "What time is it?"

"Breakfast time." Rowan thumped a tray filled with food onto the end of the bed. "French toast with almond butter, sliced peaches, and black coffee." She took a neatly folded pile of garments from under her arm and dropped them next to the tray. "Clean underwear and clothes, brand-new and in your sizes. Before you ask, I was the one who checked your labels while you were napping yesterday."

"Thank you," Jessa said.

"Bring the tray back to the kitchen when you're done. If you want a shower, your bathroom is at the end of the hall on the right. The hot water lasts about five minutes, so I'd make it fast."

Jessa eyed the chair, which was back in its original place by the basin. How had Rowan dislodged it and put it back without waking her? Or had Matthias come in and . . . She wanted to crawl under the bed now. "Did he come in here to check on me?"

Rowan arched her brows. "I cook for him, Queenie; I don't keep a GPS on him."

It must have been only a dream, Jessa decided. One

she'd think about later, when she was alone. "Last night the kitchen was locked."

"It's open when the rest of us are awake and harder to stab with the kitchen knives." She turned to go.

"I didn't need to go into the kitchen for that," Jessa pointed out. "I could have pried open one of those weapons cases."

Rowan looked back at her. "With what? Your teeth?"

Good point. "Why do you have all those old weapons down here?"

"Matt just likes to collect them. It's a guy thing." She hesitated, and then said in a gruff tone, "I serve three meals a day, but you can use the kitchen when I'm not working in there. Whatever you mess up, you clean up, or you and I are going to have a problem. Matthias is a vegetarian, and I cook for him, so don't go looking for anything that had legs."

Jessa eyed the wooden spoon in Rowan's hand. Obviously the girl knew about her ability or she wouldn't have used it—but there was something more to this ongoing hostility of hers. "If you like, I can help out with the cooking."

"Ah, the tentative hand of friendship is extended, right on schedule." Rowan's upper lip curled. "Be still, my fucking heart." She walked out.

Jessa made a trip to the bathroom before she ate. Rowan's breakfast tasted as delicious as dinner the night before, and she didn't have difficulty finishing it. She carried the tray back to the kitchen, where she found a fresh pot of coffee but no Rowan. She poured herself a second cup to sip as she hand-washed her dishes and put them in the rack beside the sink to air-dry.

"How did you sleep?"

Jessa turned quickly and almost bumped into Matthias's chest. It reminded her so much of the dream that she jumped backward to avoid the contact. "God, you're like a cat. What did you do, teleport in here?"

"What is teleport?" He said the word slowly, as if for the first time.

"It means . . . Never mind." He was just very quiet, and

she needed to stop thinking about her ridiculous dreams and pay more attention to her surroundings. "I'd sleep better if there were a lock on my door." She wouldn't be worried about dreaming anymore, either.

"You do not need one." He gave her his flash of a smile. "You are safe, Jessa."

"As you keep telling me." She made the mistake of gazing into his eyes and once more fell into that golden jade trap. She'd seen men with prettier eyes, but none with the intensity of his. Whenever he was around her, he gave her his full attention. It should have made her feel self-conscious, not gratified. "What time is it?"

"Morning." He retrieved a mug from the cabinet and poured a cup of coffee for himself.

She looked around the kitchen. "Don't you have any clocks down here?"

"We do not need them." He looked at her clothes. "I asked Rowan to fetch fresh garments for you."

"She gave me some." Now she felt self-conscious—and grubby. "I was going to change after I take a shower."

He sipped his coffee. "Tell her if you need any potions or paint."

"I beg your pardon?"

He frowned. "The unguents and colors women use." He made a vague sweeping gesture. "To put on the face and skin after you bathe."

"Do you mean lotion and makeup?" she suggested. When he nodded, she asked, "Your English is good, but I can tell it's not your native language. Where do you call home?"

"No place." Something—anger, regret—darkened his expression before he turned away from her. "When you are finished bathing, come to the library. We have much to discuss."

The rising sun irritated Lucan's eyes even after he put on the dark glasses his *sygkenis* had purchased for him, but Samantha seemed unbothered by the light. More annoying than his discomfort was the fact that they were being made to wait at the entrance to the property. "Why are we standing here when we could be inside?"

"We need a search warrant to enter the building without an invitation," Samantha told him in an absent tone. She was watching the mortal standing inside the small shack that served as a guard post. "Open your window, please."

Lucan pressed the button and held it until the glass slid down into the door. He understood her request as he breathed in a particularly sharp scent. "The sentry is afraid."

"He is, and not of us. Wait here." Samantha got out of the car.

While his *sygkenis* questioned the guard, Lucan sat back and closed his burning eyes. He had not tried to dissuade her from joining him on the hunt for this rogue Kyn; he knew from past experience that even if he ordered her to stay behind, she would simply follow him. Even when she had been human she had been utterly fearless.

Except when it came to her nature, he silently amended. Samantha could hunt vicious killers day and night, but when it came to feeding herself, she balked at the necessity as if she were a nun being asked to join an orgy.

He understood her aversion to their need for human blood. She was a child of the twenty-first century, and had grown up in a land of affluence and compassion. In America, it was said, no one needed to go hungry or die of starvation. She had also been brainwashed by dozens of ridiculous movies about vampires, all of which portrayed their natures as evil and their dependency on blood as uncontrollable and murderous.

The truth was far more complicated. After returning to their homelands from the Crusades, Lucan and many of his brother warrior-priests known as the Knights Templar had been stricken with the plague and had died. Three days after their deaths, they came back to life, clawing their way out of their graves and rising to walk the night. The warriors discovered they were no longer human, but vampiric creatures who could feed only on human blood. They were also incredibly strong, fast, and, with a miraculous ability to spontaneously heal, nearly impossible to kill. Each transformed warrior discovered he possessed a unique psychic talent along with a beautiful, powerful scent, and that the combination of both allowed them to bespell humans as well as control their minds. They became known by many as the "dark Kyn" of humanity.

The Darkyn soon discovered that they had to protect themselves and their kind, and formed secret communities known as jardins with their own ruling lords, territories, and strongholds. They also discovered that they didn't have to kill humans in order to survive, and began the work of learning how to coexist with them while hiding among their societies. They transformed some humans into their own kind, and used other, trusted mortals as their servants and guards.

A century passed, after which two things happened: The Darkyn lost the ability to change mortals, and every attempt they made proved fatal to the human. At the same time, a group of religious zealots became aware of the existence of the Darkyn, and vowed to hunt down and kill the former Templars. The zealots formed an order known as the Brethren, and while impersonating Catholic priests pursued the Darkyn all across Europe. As they hunted, captured, tortured, and killed the former Templars, the Brethren also realized they would not outlive their enemy. So they began breeding, raising, and training their own replacements, and the secret war between the Brethren and the Darkyn had endured for the last six hundred years.

It wasn't until early in the twenty-first century that Michael Cyprien, the seigneur who ruled over all of the jardins located in America, had accidentally changed a human into a Darkyn. Dr. Alexandra Keller, whom he had abducted and forced to perform reconstructive surgery to restore his ruined face, had become the first human in six centuries to survive the process of transition—this, according to Alex, only because she had first been genetically altered by the Brethren to become a vampire hunter. It was Alexandra's blood that Lucan had used on Samantha as she lay dying from a fatal gunshot wound, and that had transformed her into Darkyn.

Lucan had never regretted taking away Samantha's humanity in order to snatch her back from the cold clutch of death. By that time he'd known that he loved her more than any woman he had ever known, even the one he had once thought to be the great love of his life. Losing her would have been the same as committing suicide. Yet despite her transition, his *sygkenis* had not yet accepted what she had become. Sometimes Lucan wondered if she ever would.

Samantha was not using *l'attrait* on the guard; that much was obvious by the mortal's tight-lipped responses to her questions. She still insisted on relying on human methods, a practice he found charmingly naive but highly inefficient. Tired and rapidly losing patience, he climbed out of the Ferrari and went to deal with the guard himself.

"I thought you were going to wait in the car," she said when he joined her. Her eyes narrowed as his scent flooded the air around them. "Wait a minute."

"I have waited twenty. This is faster," he told her, and turned to the shack's small window. "You, there. Sentry. Attend me."

"Sir, as I told the detective . . ." The mortal breathed in, blinked, and gave him a foolish smile. "What can I do for you?"

"Where was this man of yours murdered last night?" Lucan asked.

"Right over here." The guard pointed to the other side of the shack.

Samantha gave Lucan an impatient glance as she walked around and then stopped. The strong odor of disinfectant cleaner did not entirely mask the smell of blood and gunpowder.

Lucan examined the wall. "There." He pointed to traces of pink staining the concrete.

Samantha crouched by the stain and examined the ground. "No shell casings, but . . ." She reached down with her scarred hand and pressed it over a spot in the grass, and then closed her eyes.

Her scent, as dark and seductive as midnight in the Amazon, grew strong and hot.

"His name was Theodore," she murmured in a faraway voice. "No. Ted. He's working on a crossword puzzle. He needs a five-letter word for 'temptation's fruit.'"

"Apple," Lucan told her. To the guard who was coming out of the shack, he said, "Stay there and do nothing."

The man beamed. "Whatever you say, sir."

Samantha opened her eyes, but her gaze had a blind quality to it as she looked toward the drive leading to the building. "Del calls down. He says I have to stop him if I can. Some kind of trouble. Someone hurt." She slowly rose to her feet and walked to the edge of the drive. "Fuck me, he's been working out. How did he get so big so fast? Right, have to do this the way Del wants. He'll listen to me." She stopped speaking but her lips moved as she shaped more words. Her whole body jerked violently, and then she wheeled backward as if she'd been thrown.

Lucan caught her from behind to keep her from hitting the wall in the same spot where the blood traces were. "Samantha."

She shook her head wildly. "No, oh, Jesus—no." She clapped her hands to her head, stiffened, and then sagged against him, turning and burying her face in his chest.

Lucan knew Samantha's ability allowed her to read the blood of the dead and through it see their last minutes of life, which often identified their killer for her. As much as it helped her with her detective work, it exacted a terrible price: She also experienced firsthand the victim's death.

"Lucan, oh, my God." She panted out the words, shuddering uncontrollably as she tried to collect herself. "The victim knew him. They were friends. And he tore his head off. With his hands. With his bare hands."

"Shhhh." He cradled her head and pressed her cheek to his heart. "It's done." Over her shoulder he saw a stocky man driving a golf cart toward them. "Was the killer one of our kind?"

She rubbed a hand over her damp face. "No. At least, I don't think so. But there was something wrong with him. He smelled like . . ." She shook her head as she straightened her shoulders and seemed to regain control over herself. "I don't know. Not like us. Not human. He smelled *wrong*."

The man in the cart stopped a short distance away and got out. He had a self-important stride, one that faltered as soon as Lucan's scent washed over him.

"Flowers?" the man muttered, looking confused.

Lucan beckoned to him as he put a supportive arm around Samantha's waist. She had recovered from the vision, but he could still feel how shocked she felt. "Do you know the man who killed your guard last night?"

"I do." The portly man's face twisted. "Bradford Lawson. He's out of control." He gave Samantha a stiff smile. "Sorry, ma'am. My name is Delaporte, but everyone calls me Del."

"Okay, Del." Samantha looked into his eyes. "Tell me, why did Lawson kill Ted Evans?"

He shrugged. "Ted tried to stop him. Bradford didn't want to be stopped."

"What was he driving when he left here?" she asked.

"He stole Dr. Kirchner's car." Del gave her a description of the vehicle and the license number.

Samantha copied the information into her electronic notepad. "Does anyone know what set this man off on this killing spree?"

"He's trying to find out where Jessa Bellamy is," he replied. "He really wants to kill her."

Lucan frowned. "For what reason? Were they lovers?"

"No. Bellamy humiliated him in front of our boss. Her boyfriend used a blade on him. Cut his hamstrings and crippled him." Delaporte sighed. "Can't blame them. Bradford's always been a real asshole with women."

Samantha glanced at the bloodstained ground. "The man I saw kill the guard wasn't a cripple."

"He's doing fine now," Delaporte agreed. "Except that maybe he's lost his mind."

"See, this is why I don't use *l'attrait*," Samantha said to Lucan. "Half the time their answers don't make any sense."

"Regardless, we should locate this Jessa Bellamy and

her boyfriend immediately," Lucan suggested. "Kendrick will have men available who can initiate a search while we rest." He turned to the mortals. "Both of you will forget what we have asked you and go about your business."

The two men nodded; the guard returned to the shack and the heavyset man walked back to his golf cart.

Lucan guided his *sygkenis* back to the Ferrari and helped her inside. The pale set of her face compelled him to lean over and place a gentle kiss on her lips.

"What was that for?" she asked, surprised.

"An apology, in advance of the offense." He pressed his gloved hand to her cheek. "You asked me last night why I would not let you die. I am a selfish man, Samantha, and I wager I will be until the end of time. But even before Dwyer shot you, living without you had already become unbearable. So you see, it was as much to save my life as yours, sweetheart."

She didn't speak, but her eyes glowed as she rubbed her face against his palm.

Chapter 12

"Nine dead, and four eyewitnesses who can positively identify Bradford Lawson as the killer." Genaro looked at the sweating faces around the conference table. "In addition to addressing the catastrophic failure of our security measures, we must now deal with the media exposure and the unwanted attention from the federal authorities. I would like an explanation, gentlemen."

Only Dr. Kirchner dared to meet his gaze. "The technician who allowed Lawson access to the storage area is dead. Once Lawson had injected himself with the transerum, there was no stopping him."

"Ted Evans tried, the poor bastard," Delaporte said. He touched the wireless receiver clipped to his right ear and stood. "Excuse me, sir." He left the room.

"We can deal with the eyewitnesses," Genaro's attorney said. "The FBI will be more difficult, but we have some influence there as well. Under no circumstance should we turn over Lawson to the police."

"You're assuming we can capture and contain him." Genaro tossed the file of hastily prepared reports onto the table. "So where is he and who is he killing now?"

"He's evidently targeted Jessa Bellamy," Kirchner said. "After he attacked her neighbors, he ransacked her apartment. But he's not completely mindless; he retrieved her computer equipment and took it with him."

Genaro looked at Riordan. "I assume you obtained access to her personal computer files."

"We hacked in and copied the contents of the hard drive yesterday, sir," his senior tech said. "We didn't recover anything useful on the first pass, but I'll have my people take it apart and search for encrypted data. However, under the current circumstances I doubt Lawson will find anything to help him locate Bellamy."

"Lawson had complete access to all the information we have on Bellamy," Genaro said. "He knows who she was, and what she can do. He'll use it to track her."

"He has more than data," Kirchner put in. "We know that the Kyndred are sensitive to one another, and have the ability to both broadcast their locations and track one another. The transerum Lawson injected was earmarked for our latest acquisition, and was designed to boost the latter effect." He saw Genaro's face and quickly added, "It will still take him some time to pick up her trail."

"Riordan, access Bellamy's credit accounts for traveling expenses. I want to see complete reports on where she does business outside Atlanta, where she takes her vacations, and any other movements she's made in the last ten years. Create a list of family, friends, and associates and any properties or time-shares they own." Genaro looked over at Delaporte as he reentered the room. "What now?"

"There's a homicide detective involved in the Farley case who is asking to speak to you, sir," his security chief said. "She's extraditing Farley's partner to Florida on murder charges. Evidently she knows about Lawson and Bellamy, and made the connection between Bellamy and Farley."

"Where is she?"

"We're holding her at the front gate, sir."

A cop from Florida wouldn't be able to get a warrant to search GenHance—not in Atlanta. "Give her the usual speech. We're at a loss to why this terrible tragedy happened, we're making arrangements for the families of the victims, and then get her the hell out of here." He turned to address the rest of his staff. "I want Lawson found. Have him followed closely, but do not interfere with his activities."

Kirchner cleared his throat. "Under the circumstances,

sir, permitting Lawson to roam freely would prove extremely hazardous to the general population."

"The public is not our concern, Doctor," he told him. "At this moment Lawson represents the best opportunity we have to locate and retrieve Bellamy. He won't stop tracking her until he finds her. He'll also save us the trouble of terminating her."

Genaro left the conference room and went to the security center, where he reviewed the archived surveillance videos of Lawson entering and leaving the building. The two men his director had murdered were of little consequence; what he was most interested in was the change the transerum had made to Lawson's physical condition. The man had arrived in a wheelchair, his face damp and pale, his voice tight with pain. The fresh bloodstains on his patient's gown and wrist bandage bore mute testimony to the condition of his wounds. Forty minutes later he had emerged from the lab in the dead technician's clothing, his movements easy and his pace brisk.

More remarkable to see were the alterations to Lawson's musculature. Genaro knew the man had been a dedicated bodybuilder, but even the steroids he had abused couldn't give him the power or the bulk that the transerum had. He appeared to have gained forty or fifty pounds of unilateral muscle mass, causing his enhanced physique to strain the seams of his clothing. Kirchner had projected a slight increase in body size and condition, but this went far beyond Genaro's expectations.

His only regret was that Lawson had availed himself of the transerum without being implanted first; the behavioral inhibitor Kirchner had designed to manage their test subjects would have given Genaro more options on how best to use and control him.

On the way to his office Genaro stopped by Kirchner's lab to have a word with the geneticist.

"I'm pleased with the progress you've made preparing the new acquisition," he told him, "but I want you to delay injecting it with the transerum until we bring in Lawson and perform a thorough screening."

"That would be prudent." Kirchner closed the door between his office and the lab before he added, "I'd also recommend we recover Lawson alive if possible."

Genaro's brows rose. "Given his current mental condition, that's unlikely."

"The transerum is designed to augment and enhance physical and mental abilities," the doctor said. "We've recommended that the buyers use it only on brain-dead specimens. As a result, we've never really considered what effect it might have on an active mind—or an unstable one."

"It will reverse any brain damage Lawson has," Genaro pointed out.

"It will repair the cellular damage," Kirchner agreed. "It's the psychotropic effects that concern me. Lawson was borderline psychotic to begin with; the transerum may enhance his delusions or even push him into a full and permanent break with reality."

"Is this sympathy for Lawson?" Genaro had never known his chief geneticist to be overly concerned with the welfare of their test subjects. This and the comment he had made during the meeting indicated otherwise. "Or are you experiencing some sort of crisis of conscience, Doctor?"

"I was thinking more of the market impact, sir," Kirchner said. "The buyers are expecting very specific results. I've worked with a number of these governments and coalitions in the past; if the transerum has an inherent flaw, they will not be understanding or politely ask for a refund."

A technician interrupted them to hand Kirchner a list.

"We've inventoried the storage unit." The doctor peered at the paper in his hand. "Lawson stole more than the transerum. The original sample is missing."

"He wouldn't have injected it," Genaro said.

"If he had, he never would have gotten out of the building." Kirchner crumpled the list in his hand. "We can't synthesize more transerum without the progenote, so if it's destroyed, the program is finished." He gave Genaro a guarded look. "Unless you can obtain another sample."

"The source no longer exists." It wasn't the truth, but he had no intention of allowing the doctor or anyone on his staff to know from where he had obtained the sample. "Don't worry about it. Lawson isn't a complete idiot; he knows how valuable it is. He'll either try to sell it or use it as a bargaining chip. Put the acquisition in stasis for now, and we'll do what we can to keep Lawson alive." He glanced out at the technicians working at various stations. "I'll send the engineers up to modify the testing chamber. One more thing—has anyone not assigned to the lab been coming here or talking to you about the acquisition lately?"

Kirchner's expression became shuttered. "As I told Chief Delaporte, unauthorized personnel are not permitted entry to the lab. As for me, I don't discuss the work with my staff; I wouldn't answer questions from an outsider." His cold eyes shifted. "If internal security has been compromised, it didn't originate here."

Genaro nodded. "Thank you, Doctor."

Genaro spent the next hour in his office studying Lawson's medical tests and the projection reports on the transerum.

Delaporte knocked once and ducked his head inside. "I'm sorry to interrupt you, sir, but I need to speak with you."

Genaro gestured for him to come in and set aside the chart. "Is it the detective?"

"No, sir, I handled that and went about my business. We have another situation." His security chief took out a handkerchief, unwrapped it, and placed it on Genaro's desk. In the center of the linen was a high-capacity USB memory stick. "Housekeeping found this in one of the men's rooms. It was taped to the back of a commode. I copied the contents onto a duplicate stick and swapped them out."

Genaro didn't touch it. "What's on it?"

"Internal memos, acquisition reports, accounting information, and transportation schedules, all dated within the last five weeks," Delaporte told him. "There's also a copy of every document we have on Bellamy. That may explain how she anticipated our retrieval. Someone working on the inside here could have warned her."

"Perhaps." Genaro regarded the memory stick. "Did you find any prints or DNA on it or the toilet?"

Delaporte shook his head. "No one has tried to retrieve the duplicate yet, but we'll continue to monitor the traffic in and out. The public has access to this restroom; it could be a handoff from the thief to an outside courier."

Genaro grew thoughtful. "This thief doesn't bother to encrypt the files he's stealing, but he takes great care not to leave any trace evidence. What does that tell you?"

"He knows we keep prints on file for everyone who works here," Delaporte said.

"If he has an ounce of intelligence, he's already switched out the prints in his personnel files." Genaro used the handkerchief to pick up the memory stick and sniffed it. "No, this man was concerned with only one thing: not leaving behind a single trace of his DNA. Can you guess why, Del?"

His security chief frowned. "He knows we can use it to figure out who he is."

"I would say our thief can't afford for us to obtain a sample of his DNA," Genaro said as he gently wrapped up the stick. "And there is only one reason for that."

Rowan paid a visit to the library before Jessa, flopping down in a chair and watching in silence as Matthias collected the books he needed from the shelves.

At length she spoke. "First we trust her with the run of the place, and now we're going to tell her about the superfreaks of the Dark Ages. Dragging your feet a little, don't you think, boss?"

He lifted one of his feet. "I walk as I always do."

"I'm being sarcastic again," she told him. "What I mean is, you're rushing into this too fast."

"Jessa is one of us." He turned to look for Brother Ennis's journal. "She should know all of it."

"I guess that means you're going to tell her about you and your adventures. Too bad we don't have a lab like GenHance's." She glanced up at the glass-encased sword over the fireplace. "A microscopic examination of the blade would definitely sweeten things up between you two. Unless she decides it's all too much and flips out, like I almost did."

She never needled him unless she had a purpose. "Is there something you want, Rowan?"

"Besides her out of here?" She spread her hands. "Not a damn thing, boss." She removed a folded paper from her back pocket and showed the front page to him. "Genaro has upped the stakes again."

He took the paper and read the front page quickly. "He must have killed him to arrange this." He noted her mulish expression. "You know that she cannot leave us now. Or is it that you want her dead?"

Outraged, she jumped to her feet and tore the paper from his hands. "You have the fucking nerve to say that to me? After everything I did for you?"

He knew she used her surliness and anger as a form of self-defense, but he imagined guilt was fueling her fury at present. "Was it so terrible, what you did? What you do now?"

The rigidness left her shoulders. "No. I bought into all this. I'm a good little soldier for the cause." She sounded as if she hated herself. "I did a lot worse before I met you and Andrew." She regarded the paper. "You want me to put this in her room?"

"Yes. You could also talk to Jessa and tell her the truth," he suggested. "There is no need to conceal it from her now, and it would ease your conscience. It might help sway her opinion of us as well."

"I'd rather be the nasty housekeeper, thanks." She folded and stuffed the paper back into her pocket before she abruptly changed the subject. "By the way, Drew didn't check in when he was supposed to this morning. He's three hours overdue."

He shrugged. "The demands on him will be many now. He will contact us when he is able."

"What if he doesn't?" she demanded. "What if he's been caught or compromised? He's all by himself down there."

"Drew knows the dangers. He has planned for them." Matthias found the last of the books and took it down, turning pages until he found the passage he wanted. "If he has been found out, he will take measures to protect himself."

"From Genaro and his happy little army of Mengeles."

She kicked the chair she had been sitting in. "We can't lose him, Matt. I should go down there and make sure."

Matthias looked up, surprised by the suggestion. "I need you here."

"Really. Why?" A faint sneer distorted her mouth. "You and Queenie seem to be bumping along fine. I'm just getting in the way now."

He put down the book. "I do not understand you. Say what you mean to me."

"You want her," she said flatly, "and if she gave you the green light, you'd be all over her. Shit, you had the perfect opportunity the other night when she sneaked in to search your room. Why didn't you jump her then?"

He thought of the brief dream he'd had before he'd woken and felt almost amused. "How do you know I didn't?"

"She came out of there too fast." She realized what she had said and quickly stared at the toes of her boots. "Which I shouldn't have been timing and I know it. Look, I know when I'm not necessary. Let me go down and see what's happening in Atlanta."

"No. For now, you will stay." He went to her and took her cold hand in his. "Much of what you have said is true, Rowan, but whatever I want from Jessa, keeping her here and keeping her alive are the two most important tasks I have. We need her ability to continue the search. I cannot do this without you."

"Yeah, okay. I'll stick around for the duration." She drew her hand from his and looked up at him with hurt in her eyes. "Just don't expect me to kiss her ass, all right?"

"You do not have to kiss any of her parts," he promised.

Rowan left, and by the time Jessa joined Matthias in the library he had finished arranging the books in the proper order. She had bathed and changed, and had woven her damp hair into a long braid; she smelled of Rowan's shampoo and his own soap.

"Sit." He gestured to a chair by the fire. "Was there enough hot water?"

"Yes, thank you." She looked around as if deliberately trying to avoid his gaze. "You have a nice library. How long did it take for you to collect so many books?"

"Ten years." He picked up a split length of oak from the wood basket and placed it on the fire. "Rowan found many of them for me from booksellers who use the Internet for their shops. They send books in packages now." He still found that rather disconcerting.

"People don't always have time to shop in the brick-and-mortar stores." Her gaze darted from the books to his face to the floor. "You know, I would never have guessed you to be the bookish type."

"I had no time for reading when I was a boy. There was always something more interesting to do outside." And how much trouble he would have saved himself and perhaps the world if he had become a scholar, as his father had wanted. "Do you read any books about history?"

"I did when I was in school. I rarely have time, but when I do read I like fiction." She seemed to forget her discomfort as her brows drew together. "Is this what you wanted to discuss? What books I read?"

"It would make things easier if I show you." He had to go carefully now. "I have been collecting these since I came to know there were more in the world like me. When I came to America ten years ago, I brought them." He carried the oldest manuscripts over to the table and set them in front of her. "I knew I would have to show the others proof of what we are."

She shifted a fraction to avoid touching him. "Others like you and Rowan."

He had expected she would continue to deny what she was, and still he felt impatient. "Yes."

"How do some old books prove what you are?"

"They do not," he said. "They prove what we were." He rested his hand on the topmost book. "No matter when they have lived, people have always kept accounts of what they know. They may lie to everyone around them, but most feel a need to tell the truth with their words. Sometimes in journals, like this one." He picked up the first book. "This belonged to an English priest named Ennis of Aubury. He questioned nonbelievers, and wrote down what they confessed to him under torture."

She drew back a little. "Why would you want to read something so awful as that?"

"For his truth." He opened it to the page he had marked with a piece of cord. "Read."

Jessa glanced at the page. "I'm sorry, I can't. It's not written in English."

As natural as reading Latin was to him, he often forgot that most Americans could not read the root of their own language. "I will translate for you. Ennis writes: 'Another peasant was found murdered in the fields. As the others before him, his throat was torn out but there was no blood in the wound. I questioned the outlaw heretic and he told me of the renegade and his companion, the ones who could not be killed. It is clear to me that the dark Kyn have infested the county.' "

She leaned over to examine the slanted, dense handwriting. "The 'dark Kyn'?"

"That is what they were called in this time." He turned to another page farther along in the book. "Here he writes: 'This morning I will go into the forest. The smith's wife swears she saw her dead son walking along the stream. I believe these creatures can take on the appearance of their victims so that they might lure more to their death. May the Heavenly Father help me bring this evil being into the light.' "

Jessa didn't say anything, but she pressed her lips together, and her fingernails dug into the armrests beneath her hands.

"I think Ennis did find him." He flipped through the rest of the pages to show her that they had been left blank before he closed the cover. "This is the oldest story I have found about them thus far."

She stared at the page. "Them?"

"Those the monk called 'the dark Kyn,' " he said carefully. "Creatures like us, who may have created us."

Her expression immediately changed, became guarded. "You believe that we were created by evil beings?"

"This one Ennis speaks of could change his shape," Matthias said. "So can some of our kind. There are more stories about them, how they came to be and why they were hunted." He gestured toward the stack of books. "The dark Kyn were human once, and then they were killed or died of sickness. They came out of their graves changed, very strong and very fast. They hunted at night, and lived on human blood. They had great power—abilities—like us."

She shook her head. "What you're describing sounds like the myths about vampires."

"They are never called that in these books," he pointed out. "Sometimes the writers call them '*maledicti*' or 'the cursed ones.' Rowan thinks the vampire stories began from tales of what they did during their wars."

Her wide-eyed gaze shifted to his face. "There were vampire *wars*?"

"At least three, and one in which they fought one another." He took out another book. "In this one a traveling French merchant returning from the East reported seeing terrible battles at night, in the countryside. He swore he saw men being slain and then rising up to fight again." He could feel her disbelief now, as if it were filling up the space between them with bricks and mortar. "I do not lie to you, Jessa. The words are here. Written by the hand of those who lived in these times. The old ones like us have been living in hiding for centuries."

"Of course they have. Vampires are supposed to be immortal." She folded her hands under her chin and rested her elbows on her knees, staring at the books. "When I was a girl, I used to love to read stories about the Loch Ness monster, and UFOs, and Bigfoot. I think when we're young we need that hope to hold on to. To think that there are still mysteries and wonders out there waiting for us to discover."

She tried to be kind even when she was shutting him out. "You do not believe me."

"I don't believe in vampires, Matthias. I can't." She dropped her hands. "If they were real, and you and Rowan were like them, or were created by them, then why don't you drink blood?"

"We are not the same. We are still mostly human." Frustration rose inside him. "You do not see."

"I would have to meet one of these dark Kyn before I could put any faith in these accounts of them." She sighed. "If they are still living among us, then they're very good at hiding. Rather like the Loch Ness monster."

She would never believe him now if he told her he had tracked some of them. "How do you explain what you can do with your touch?"

"I can't do anything." She exhaled slowly. "Do you think we're going to turn into vampires? Is that why you and Rowan live underground? Why you brought me here? Are you afraid of the sunlight?"

"When you took my hand in the car, you saw me in the snow and the mountains. You saw the worst of me." He offered her his hand. "Look again. I am not afraid of you seeing what is inside me."

She didn't move. "I think we should talk about how long you plan to keep me down here." Before he could reply, she held up her hand. "Please don't tell me that it's for my safety. I can't stay here forever, Matthias. I have to do something about GenHance. I have to go back—and take back my life."

"What life do you have up there?" he demanded. "You live alone. You have no lover or friends. The only time you willingly touch someone is to look into the darkness in their soul. If it were not for me and my bringing you here, you would be dead now. Butchered by GenHance for the ability you keep saying you do not have."

"You've tried very hard to convince me that you're my friend, and that I'm safe here." Jessa gestured toward the books. "This, and what you're saying, they don't make me feel safe, Matthias. They make me think you and Rowan are in trouble. That you need the kind of help that I can't give you."

He drew back. "You insult me now?"

"I didn't intend to," she said. "There's really only one way to prove you're right and I'm wrong. Show me everything you have. Tell me who the Kyndred are, where they're living, and what you've been doing to protect them. Let me talk to some of them."

For an instant he was tempted to seize her and shake some sense into her stubborn head. But perhaps he expected too much from her. "Rowan left the morning newspaper in your room," he told her. "Read it." He strode toward the door.

"What's in the paper?"

He glanced back at her. "You are, Jessa. You are wanted by the authorities for killing Lawson."

Chapter 13

The enhancements bestowed on Bradford Lawson by the transerum turned out to be even more spectacular than Kirchner had predicted. His injuries had healed almost instantaneously and completely, and his newfound strength seemed unlimited. Even his mind had been augmented, allowing him to think as fast as a computer and solve problems almost before they happened.

Only one minor problem had spoiled what should have been the ultimate state of perfection: He was starving.

Almost from the moment he had killed Ted Evans and left GenHance, a voracious hunger, unlike anything he'd ever felt, began to gnaw at his insides. Logic told him that his increased physical abilities would require more calories, but by the time he reached Jessa Bellamy's apartment complex he felt as if he hadn't eaten for a week. He'd ignored the grinding hollowness inside him as he snapped the neck of the complex security guard and went to her building, but after questioning and dismembering two of Bellamy's neighbors he'd been unable to stop himself from seizing what food he could find in the second's kitchen and eating until his jaw ached.

The hunger quieted enough for him to finish his interrogations and search Bellamy's apartment, but once he'd gone back on the road it had started in on him again. Stopping at a convenience store, he strangled the clerk before loading up the passenger seat of Kirchner's SUV with boxes of candy bars, racks of chips, and liter bottles of soda.

He hated eating all that sugar and junk as he drove out of the city—his new body deserved better—but if he didn't meet the demands of his altered metabolism, he suspected it would start eating him from the inside out.

A pity Genaro's transerum had such a serious flaw— one Jonah would have to address if he were to sell the stuff overseas. As soon as Lawson tracked down Bellamy and took care of that unfinished business, he would return to GenHance and have the old man do whatever it took to eliminate the unwanted painful side effect.

Fortunately his enhanced mental abilities were working with impressive efficiency. It had taken him only minutes to pick up Bellamy's trail; she had left Atlanta and traveled east. He wasn't entirely sure how he knew that she had; he only felt her drawing him to her. His sense of her remained bright and steady, as if she were a beacon only he could detect. There were others with her as well, at least two, but he felt only the vaguest sense of them. It didn't matter to Lawson who had given her refuge; they would die just as quickly as all the others.

Then he would have her to himself.

Jessa Bellamy wouldn't have to die right away, he decided, sorting through the many enjoyable fantasies about hurting women that he had dreamed up over the years. If her body proved to be even half as resilient as his own, he could keep her alive and hurt her for a very long time.

Flashing red and blue lights glared in his eyes, and in the rearview mirror he saw a highway patrol car speeding up behind him. Quickly he groped through the pile of empty wrappers beside him, found and stuffed two king-size Snickers bars into his mouth as he pulled over onto the shoulder, and put the SUV in park. He ate another four while waiting for the trooper to walk up to the driver's-side window, which he rolled down.

"What's the problem, Officer?" he asked.

The trooper's silly hat tilted down as he peered inside. "Have you been drinking tonight, sir?"

"Only some Pepsi." Enjoying himself a little, Lawson

held up one of the empty liter bottles. "I might be on a sugar high, but I don't believe that I was speeding."

"Can you tell me your name?"

Now that he had been transformed into the first true superhuman, he could never answer to the name Bradford Lawson again. He needed a new title, one that would tell this ignorant mortal and the rest of the mortal world what he had become.

"Apollo," he said. "I've become the god of the sun and light."

The trooper put a hand on the hilt of his service weapon and shuffled back. "Step out of the vehicle, please, Mr. Apollo."

Lawson opened the door, releasing a small flood of candy wrappers and chip bags onto the ground. They crackled as he stepped on top of them.

"I have the worst case of the munchies in history," he explained. "Not because I've been smoking pot, of course. A god doesn't need that sort of thing."

The trooper nodded and pointed to the front of the car. "Place your hands on the hood, Mr. Apollo, and spread your feet apart."

Cops these days simply didn't have a sense of humor, Lawson thought as he assumed the position. When the trooper moved to stand directly behind him, he threw his head back, smashing it into the man's face. By the time the trooper uttered his first howl of pain Lawson had picked him up and tossed him over the hood of the SUV. He sailed fifty feet and landed with a thud, rolling until his body lost momentum and flopped over onto his back.

Lawson picked up the flashlight the trooper had dropped, and switched it on, focusing the beam toward the spot where the mortal had landed. As he moved past the shoulder, his left foot plunged down into a hole in the ground. An angry buzzing exploded all around him, and a swarm of furious bees engulfed him.

Not bees, he thought as they zipped past his eyes, and he saw their distinctive colors. *Yellow jackets.*

"Get off," he shouted, swatting and whirling as he tried

to get away from the stinging insects. Their tiny bodies bounced off his face, neck, and arms; they burrowed into the openings of his shirt and trousers to attack the rest of his body.

Lawson hated being stung, and began to sob as he fell to his knees. He toppled over and lay there for some time, his entire body ablaze with hot, needling pain. Things grew fuzzy, and then dark.

Sometime later he came to and sat up. Dead yellow jackets fell from his shoulders onto the ground, and he smashed them with his fist. There didn't seem to be any more of them flying around him, but there were countless tiny, still bodies covering the ground.

He struggled to his feet. The transerum had protected him again, and he breathed in deeply as he felt no pain from the thousands of stings he had sustained. He kicked at the dead insects, grinding some of them to mush under his heel before he staggered over to see to the trooper.

He looked down at the cop's ruined face. "I wasn't . . ." His blood pounded in his ears, hot and heavy, and he couldn't seem to catch his breath. "Why did . . . you . . . pull me over?"

The trooper turned his head and coughed out more blood.

Humans could be more annoying than yellow jackets, he thought as he lifted his leg and rammed it down on the man's right knee. The resulting scream didn't entirely drown out the satisfying crunch of bone. "I can break . . . the rest of your bones . . . easy." Why was it so hard to remember words? "Why . . . did you . . . stop me?"

"Weaving," the cop choked out. "Weaving all over the road. Can't drive like that. Hurt someone."

Hurt someone? The words buzzed around his head like the yellow jackets, tiny and mindless and stupid. But they also cleared his thoughts and calmed his labored breathing as they reminded him of who he was now.

Why would he care if he hurt anyone? A god did not have to concern himself with the inherent weaknesses of mortals. He was stronger than them, ten times more intelligent, a new and vastly superior life-form. No one would ever again cause him pain or humiliation the way Jessa Bellamy had.

He could see her in his head so clearly now. Every detail of her treacherous, beautiful face, every arrogant look she had given him. She would never be satisfied with her attempt to cripple him, he knew, especially not now that he had ascended to a new level of existence. No, in her jealousy and ugliness she would want to harm him again—even try to kill him—as soon as she could.

"She sent you after me, didn't she?" Lawson bent down, seized the man by the throat, and lifted him off the ground with one hand. He bit the side of his neck, digging his teeth in deep before he ripped out of a chunk of flesh and spit it out. "The lying bitch swore out a complaint against me." He shook him a few times. "You were going to serve me with another restraining order? Was that it?"

The trooper didn't answer, his head lolling back and forth over his left shoulder.

"I never touched her." Lawson licked his lips and tasted the man's blood on them, and felt a new sensation surging through him. "I wanted to, but I couldn't. She'd have seen. All my secrets." The sound of his own voice crooning comforted him as he put the limp body on the ground and straddled it. "Couldn't have that." He ripped open the front of the trooper's uniform shirt and tore away the front panel of the protective vest beneath it. "The old man hates me for being young and strong. She'd go to him. Make him fire me."

Sometime later Lawson rose and walked over to pick up the flashlight he had dropped by the yellow jacket nest. He switched it on, but the bright beam of light hurt his eyes. He tossed it away, and then felt pain in his hand. Two bone shards were embedded in his palm, and he plucked them out before he walked back up to the road and got in the SUV.

Things had changed again, but he felt at peace with himself. Without saying a word, the trooper had explained everything that had gone wrong.

Now it was right. So right that it filled him with an indescribable emotion. All the work he had done at GenHance had been noble, and his heart had been in the right place, but ultimately the scientists had failed. All of their theories and conjectures had been wrong. Lawson wondered what Genaro would make of it when he told him.

The transerum contained no flaw, but rather a new imperative, one that had caused the final transformation of the mortal who had been Bradford Lawson, and the sacrifices that would have to be made to his glory.

Now he was truly Apollo, the god reborn to walk among men.

By the third day of her captivity, Jessa had determined three things: She apparently wasn't in any immediate danger, it would take weeks to completely search her prison, and Matthias and Rowan weren't going to be as easy to dupe as she'd hoped. As much as she wanted to escape and find some way to disprove the murder charge, she also knew she couldn't escape without first discovering what Matthias did or didn't know about the Takyn. If she didn't, he might try this again with Aphrodite, Vulcan, Delilah, or one of her other friends.

For his part, Matthias generally treated her like a guest instead of a prisoner, seeing to her needs and comfort without complaint and talking to her courteously. He watched her closely, however, and always seemed to be waiting around the corner whenever she walked through the tunnels.

Rowan's attitude toward Jessa gradually became less hostile, although she remained mostly distant or sarcastic, depending on her mood. Jessa quickly learned to avoid the girl when she was working in the communications room or cooking in the kitchen, the times when her temper was prone to flare fastest. She also refrained from asking questions or becoming too personal with the young housekeeper. She did refuse to let Rowan continue to wait on her, something she thought at first might provoke a confrontation. Yet when she told Rowan she didn't want breakfast brought to her room, all Rowan did was produce an old battery-operated clock radio and tell her to be in the kitchen at six a.m. or make her own meal. Jessa immediately tried to listen to the radio—a local broadcast would tell her where she was—but the small speaker produced only crackling static.

Matthias didn't bring up the subject of vampires again, which was a relief, as Jessa didn't know how to respond to his wild conjectures without further insulting him. Instead he allowed her to use his computer equipment whenever she asked, delivered a stack of paperback novels (none of which was newer than six months, she noted) to her room, and otherwise left her alone. When she asked whether she should return the books to him, he told her they belonged to Rowan. Later she saw him reading one of the books from the collection in the children's library room, and caught the faint movements of his lips as he silently sounded out some of the words.

Why would a grown man, even one who couldn't speak English perfectly, collect and read children's books when he owned one of the finest private libraries she'd ever seen?

Although he knew about her ability, Matthias didn't try to avoid having physical contact with her as Rowan did. Each day he seemed to find some excuse to touch her casually, whether it was passing a dish to her at the table or taking her arm to guide her in a different direction while walking with her in the tunnels. For the first couple of days Jessa stiffened each time, anticipating a return into the shadowlight, but no matter how prolonged the contact was between them it never took over her consciousness. Instead, something else invaded: an unfamiliar but pervasive blend of warmth and comfort that danced along her skin and brought all of her senses to an acute state of awareness.

Jessa had enough experience to know what was happening. Her physical attraction to Matthias grew stronger every day; her body responded to him more often on a purely feminine level. The fact that he could touch her without triggering the shadowlight removed the primary obstacle that had kept her celibate since her ability had changed, and the needs that had remained sullenly dormant for so long were now wide-awake and demanding more.

Every touch, no matter how brief or casual, had always been an ordeal for her. Now Matthias had changed all that, turning any physical contact into a kind of furtive aphrodisiac.

She didn't understand why she was so strongly attracted to a man about whom she knew so little. She still couldn't place his accent, or the strange formality of his English. He didn't speak like someone who had trouble understanding the meaning or the grammar; he spoke as if he came from a completely different world. His habits—eating with his fingers, rolling paper instead of folding it, and the way he sometimes watched with full concentration as Rowan used the food processor or the can opener—also made him seem out of step with the real world. And why would a grown man read, much less enjoy, children's books?

Then there was his relationship with Rowan, who was certainly more than his housekeeper. Jessa had first suspected the girl might be his lover, but Matthias showed her nothing more than a decidedly paternal brand of affection. She never caught them in an intimate moment, and while they might have been sneaking into each other's rooms every night, why would they hide it?

To keep herself occupied with something other than these perplexing observations and Matthias, Jessa spent hours on the computer checking through the contents of the hard drive for any files on the Takyn. To her disappointment she found nothing stored on the system but the files Matthias had shown her on GenHance, some Asian card games, and the service provider program they were using to gain access to the Internet.

She didn't want to rely on what Matthias had shown her, so Jessa began checking news sites and researching Gen-Hance's business activities since the corporation had been founded in the late eighties. While GenHance had a sterling reputation, very little real information existed about Jonah Genaro and his company. Most of what was published by the media was taken mainly from press releases issued by Genaro's own public relations department. Part of this was due to the fact that Genaro owned GenHance outright and, despite its size and diversity, had never offered up shares to be publicly traded. That made the corporation one of the largest privately held businesses in the world.

An old profile written by Forbes about Genaro, whom they identified as one of the most successful entrepreneurs in the world, filled in a few blanks.

"Genaro inherited ninety billion dollars from his Italian grandparents," she told Matthias one night over dinner. "Originally it was left to his parents, but they died in a car wreck in New York when he was sixteen. Their will specified that the family money was to be divided equally among their brothers and sisters and their children, but every other member of the Genaro family died in a boating accident three years later. They took the family yacht to sail over to one of their homes in Greece, but the engines exploded on the way there. No one radioed for help, so the boat burned and sank before anyone could get to them."

"He probably had them killed," Rowan put in as she finished clearing her plate.

The girl ate twice as fast as she and Matthias did, Jessa had noticed, and would sit with her hand or sometimes her arm curled around her plate, as if she expected it to be taken away from her. Rowan seemed to have some sort of love-hate relationship with food that bewildered Jessa, yet the girl was never stingy with the meals she prepared, and in fact often nagged her to eat more. Rowan looked up, caught Jessa watching her, and scowled.

"The article said he was in his first year at Oxford when the yacht accident happened," Jessa said quickly.

"He would not have bloodied his own hands," Matthias said. "He would have hired someone to do it."

"How would a nineteen-year-old kid even know how to arrange having his entire family killed?" Jessa asked him. "Never mind trying to do it long-distance from England."

"He had ninety billion damn good reasons to try," Rowan replied. "I bet he practiced with his parents first."

"But he was an only child." Jessa didn't want to defend the man who had probably framed her for murder, but she couldn't accept that Genaro could be so cold-blooded—not with his own family. "He must have loved them."

"The only things Genaro loves are wealth and power," Matthias advised her. "He will never have enough to redeem his name."

"What does his name have to do with it?" Jessa asked, but he merely gave her one of his enigmatic looks before he rose and left the kitchen. Irritated, she turned to Rowan. "I don't suppose you can tell me what he means."

"Don't believe everything you read in Forbes," was all the girl would tell her.

Rather than sneaking out of her room and searching the tunnels again, Jessa continued looking for evidence under the guise of constantly getting lost. She knew Rowan and Matthias were taking turns watching her through some sort of security system at night, but neither of them seemed to notice how often she took a wrong turn during the day. Her pretense allowed her to discover a great deal about her surroundings. What she thought were dead ends to the tunnels were actually old steel doors that extended into recesses in the concrete walls. From the look of them, Jessa guessed they were fire doors. She noted them as she explored, drawing a mental map of the tunnels, until she found the one she was sure concealed the tunnel that had led to the hatch that led to the surface and freedom.

The discoveries she made during her waking hours kept her quiet and watchful, but each night her caution seemed to evaporate as soon as she fell asleep.

Since the first night, Jessa had been dreaming vividly, always finding herself with Matthias in some familiar place: her apartment, her office, her favorite restaurant. Once, she was whisked off to the pool at her apartment complex, where she dreamed she was making laps with Matthias beside her, keeping pace.

In the dreams his presence never disturbed her; in fact, she behaved as if she had invited him into them. During the pool dream they swam together in sync from one end to the other, and when she suspected he was holding back she kicked off the last wall with all her energy and raced him to the deep end.

He surfaced at the same time she did, but rather than touch the wall he pulled her into his arms. "You cheat."

"I won." She twined her arms around his neck. "How did you learn to be such a strong swimmer?"

"When I was a boy I fell off my horse into a river, and I did not wish to drown." He treaded the water easily as he maneuvered her into a corner. "You are like a fish."

She grinned. "You'd better be referring to my ability to swim."

"You are all sleek and shining when you are wet." He parted his legs to bring her closer, and their bodies pressed together. "You move like the river. Like the rain."

Jessa felt his hands on her waist and curled her hands over his broad shoulders. "Why do I keep dreaming of you like this? As if you were always with me."

"Perhaps part of me was." He glanced down. "I want to kiss your mouth."

He often told her of his desire for her, but he never did more than touch her or hold her in his arms. It made her heart ache as much as her body.

"None of this is real," she whispered. "You can do anything you want."

"I will wait," he told her, pressing his forehead to hers, "until you want me when you wake."

"Don't wait." Jessa closed her eyes. "Please don't."

And then she woke, and Rowan was there, standing over her, not looking angry or indignant.

"Queenie." The girl tugged on her sleeve. "Come on, it's just a dream."

Disoriented from being wrenched from the intimate moment with Matthias, Jessa blindly pushed at her, making contact with only her denim-covered hip, and then snatched her hand away. "I'm sorry." She knew the girl disliked being touched, and suspected it had to do with something other than Jessa's ability.

"No problem." Rowan looked shaken as she backed away. "We all get bad dreams, right?" Before Jessa could reply, she hurried out of the room.

What happened to you? Jessa thought as she stared after her, and then covered her face with her hands. *What is happening to me?*

Jessa's first real opportunity to escape came after she had been with them for a week. After breakfast she washed dishes and then went to take her morning shower, but turned around and went back to the kitchen to ask Rowan if she had any facial moisturizer she could use. As she drew close to the open door, she heard Matthias and Rowan talking, and stayed out of sight.

"Tomorrow go topside and get the supplies we need," Matthias was saying. "I will stay with her. She does not have to be watched every moment now. She has stayed in her room every night this week."

"Yeah, we're all such good pals now, aren't we?" Rowan sounded disgusted. "Did it ever occur to you that she's been staying in her room only so we'd stop watching her at night? Which we have, so it worked great."

"Jessa could not know that."

"Okay, maybe she doesn't now," the girl said, "but she will the first time she sneaks out after hours. She wants you to trust her and confide in her, and she'll keep up the nice act until you do. For Christ's sake, Matt, I like her, too, but remember who you're dealing with. The woman made her living informing on people."

"We need Jessa's ability to see the truth," he told her. "Unless we convince her to work with us, share information, and help us to find the others, we will never get to the Kyndred before GenHance does."

Rowan made a rude sound. "You're living in a dreamworld, boss. That girl's never going to tell us a damn thing."

"Then let me dream. I enjoy it." He walked across the kitchen and opened something. "Here is the money. Go early, before she wakes. See your friend William while you are out."

Aware she could be discovered eavesdropping, Jessa silently retreated back to the bathroom, where she showered and considered what she would do.

Rowan would have to leave through the hatch door Jessa hadn't yet found, and since she believed that was the only way out it was imperative that she shadow Rowan in the morning. Rowan had been waking at six a.m., so if she left early, she'd go at five a.m. Jessa would have to get up earlier than that—four a.m. would probably be best—and then find a vantage point near Rowan's bedroom where she could stand watch and then follow the girl as she left in the morning. Since Matthias was no longer watching her, she might even have a chance if she were careful to see how to open the fire doors, and possibly follow Rowan up to the surface.

The sole drawback was the fact that she hadn't yet been able to search the library, where she was convinced Matthias was keeping whatever records he had on the Kyndred. She needed to do that today so that she could leave in the morning with a clear conscience. That meant coming up with an excuse that would allow her to spend at least an hour alone in the room.

Being in the shower reminded her of the pool dream, and she thought about every moment of it. Jessa couldn't understand why she kept dreaming of being with Matthias, but it was starting to get under her skin now. Somehow she was becoming obsessed with him—and she was never more aware of it as when she pulled herself out of her thoughts and discovered she hadn't noticed that the water of the shower was now running ice-cold.

She dried off, dressed, and went in search of Matthias. She found him in his exercise room, where he was working out with the stone disks she had seen during her first night of captivity. As before, he didn't stop lifting the heavy stones as he spoke to her.

"You were a long time bathing," he said, balancing two of the heaviest stones on the palms of his hands before he extended his arms forward and out. "Do you prefer cold water to hot?"

"No, I just got a little lost in my thoughts," she lied. There was no way in hell she was telling him about the dream, ever, so she focused on the excuse she'd invented. "I've been trying to keep an open mind and make sense of all this at the same time. I was wondering, would you let me look through all the books you have about the dark Kyn?"

"You cannot read Latin," he reminded her.

She covered her dismay with a rueful smile. "True, but you said some of them were written in other languages. I went to school in Europe, and I can read French, German, and Spanish."

He put down the stones, straightened, and turned to her. "You also said you do not believe in vampires."

"I don't," she agreed. "What I'd like to do is look through the books and see if there are any other clues as to what these people might have really been." His expression seemed doubtful, and she added, "I know they mean a lot to you. I'll be very careful with them, I promise."

He studied her expression. "Very well. I will meet you in the library in an hour."

She eyed the stones. "You lift those things for an hour? No wonder you're so . . ." Embarrassed now, she stopped.

"Ripped," he said. "That is what Rowan calls it, even though I never tear anything." He put his hand to the center of his chest. "It is good for the body and the heart." He picked up the smallest of the stone disks and offered it to her. "Try."

"No, I've never lifted weights. I'd probably tear something. I prefer to swim to keep in shape." Jessa turned to hide her embarrassment and headed to the tunnel. "I'll see you in the library."

"Jessa."

She stopped.

"If I could give you back your life," he said softly, "I would. Even if there were no place for me in it."

She closed her eyes, enduring the rush of emotion his voice tugged from her heart. He sounded so lonely she almost turned around and ran to him.

"You can't," she said, her voice breaking on the last word as she left him. *I can't.*

Chapter 14

Sam woke up near twilight to find herself alone in the bed. Usually she was the first to rise at night, but since Bradford Lawson's killing spree Lucan had been waking early and going out with the jardin trackers every afternoon. They were hunting for the killer's trail, sometimes until dawn, but so far they had been unsuccessful.

Something went wrong during the first night they went out, but Lucan wouldn't tell her what it was.

Sam didn't like it, but she had her own priorities when it came to homicide suspects, and she began building a case against Lawson. It might have been difficult to obtain the information she needed, but Kendrick had proved invaluable in that department. That evening he delivered to her copies of police reports, witness statements, and preliminary autopsy results on all of Lawson's victims.

"This is amazing," Sam told him. "It's everything I need. How did you do this so fast?"

"We have made very good friends among the local authorities as well as the FBI," he said. "They will help us as much as they can."

Even Lucan's *tresora*, Herbert Burke, would have been hard-pressed to assemble such a complete file. "Could I bribe you to move down to Fort Lauderdale and go to work for us?"

"I'm quite flattered, but I'm afraid I must refuse." The *tresora* smiled. "Once we pledge ourselves to our lords, the oath we take to serve is for life."

She grinned. "I hope Scarlet knows how lucky he is."

After seeing through her ability just what Bradford Lawson could do to a human being, she had called down to Fort Lauderdale to notify Garcia and her partner of a change in plans, and asked them to send up another officer to transport Grodan so she could focus on finding Lawson.

"He's escalating very fast," she told Rafael. "Each murder is more brutal than the last."

"Lawson might be one of these Kyndred Lady Alexandra is searching for," Rafael suggested.

"We won't know until we find him. And I know we're supposed to make nice with them and bring them over to our side, but that's not going to happen with this guy. He's turned into a killing machine, and I don't think he's going to stop until he finds this Jessa Bellamy."

"I find that unlikely," Rafael said. "Jessa Bellamy is wanted for murdering Bradford Lawson."

Sam went still. "What?"

"Ask Kendrick for a paper," he suggested. "It is front-page news across the country."

After she ended the call, she obtained a newspaper from the *tresora* and read the headline story. According to the reporter covering the story, second-degree murder charges had been filed against Bellamy after she attacked Lawson at a popular downtown restaurant. Hospital officials claimed Lawson died of his injuries several hours before he murdered Ted Evans.

"This is utter garbage," Sam told Kendrick. "Lawson was alive when he went to GenHance that night. He was alive when he left."

"It may be that the authorities are trying to locate Ms. Bellamy in order to secure her as a material witness, or place her in protective custody," the *tresora* suggested.

"When we do that, we generally don't first charge them with murder." She thought for a moment. "See what you can find out about this Bellamy woman, and where she might have run to."

Unfortunately Lucan was not as forthcoming with what he learned while out hunting for Lawson. Every morning her lover returned, grim and withdrawn, and placed several calls to some of the other American Kyn lords. He always spoke to them in one of the old languages that she didn't understand, and when she asked he told her only that they were discussing territorial matters. Then he would go down to the training room for an hour and return to drop, exhausted, into bed.

Sam didn't like it, but she held back from confronting Lucan about the situation. Whatever it was, he was taking it very personally.

Instead, she did what she could by spending her time at the various crime scenes and collecting all the information she could on Bradford Lawson. So far she'd uncovered several complaints of battery filed by former girlfriends, all of whom later dropped the charges, and a violent attack on a personal trainer who turned out to be a dealer specializing in performance-enhancing drugs. She had reached a couple of the girlfriends by telephone, but the moment she said Lawson's name they hung up on her. The personal trainer had dropped out of sight after being discharged from the hospital. Three of Lawson's former victims had abruptly moved out of the state and then disappeared as well, although there were no indications of foul play or missing-persons reports filed. It was as if they didn't want to be found again.

Tonight she was hoping that Kendrick had discovered some new information on Jessa Bellamy, the woman accused of murdering Lawson the day before he began his killing spree.

She went down to Kendrick's office on the first floor and found the *tresora* speaking in low tones to one of his staff. Both men abruptly ended the conversation as soon as they saw her, and the *tresora* invited her in as the other man left.

She eyed the thick folder on Kendrick's desk. "Has there been some new development in the case?"

"A body was just discovered near the interstate," he said, taking the folder and opening a drawer to put it away. "It may or may not be connected to the other murders."

She nodded toward the folder. "Shouldn't I have a look at it?"

Kendrick's expression turned troubled. "I don't think that would be a good idea, my lady. The crime scene photos are quite graphic."

"I'm a homicide detective, Ken," she reminded him. "I've seen it all and then some."

He still didn't give her the file. "It would be better if you first discussed this with Suzerain Lucan."

"He gave you orders not to show it to me, didn't he?" She didn't wait for a reply, but held out her hand. "I know you're immune to *l'attrait*, but I'm still a lot stronger and faster than you. Come on, hand it over."

"You will tell your lord that I did not do so willingly?" he asked as he gave her the file.

"Sure. I'll even give you a black eye, if you want." She opened the folder to a horrific image of human body parts. The next was another angle of the same scene, as were the other pictures. She looked up. "Where's the rest of the body?"

"That is all our people were able to recover, my lady."

She sat down as she studied the photos. "If a dead body stays outside long enough, it attracts the usual scavengers." She noticed some black mounds of feathers around the body parts. "Are these buzzards?"

"Yes, my lady."

She went to the next photo, which showed a close-up of one of the birds. "They look dead."

"They are, my lady. The police also recovered some other dead animals near the body."

"Even if the victim had been poisoned, it would have taken a couple of hours to do the same to anything that fed on the remains. These birds look like they dropped as soon as they touched it." She looked up. "Is that what happened?"

"We're not certain yet, my lady." He looked miserable. "One of the policemen on the scene observed some rats crawling near the body. They died a few moments after coming in contact with the remains." He paused, and then added, "So did one of the forensic technicians working at the scene. Evidently one of his gloves tore during the removal process."

She dropped the pictures in her lap. "Are you telling me this dead body is so toxic that no one can even touch it?"

"It would seem so, my lady." He took out a handkerchief and blotted the sweat from his forehead.

She thought of the photos she had seen of Bradford Lawson's other victims. He had dismembered some of them, but not as badly as had been done to this body. "Do we know who the victim was?"

"He was a Georgia state trooper." Kendrick stood. "We have sent tissue samples over to England for Lady Alexandra to analyze. Please, my lady, you should leave this unpleasant business to Suzerain Lucan and the other Kyn lords."

"Why?" she demanded. When he didn't answer, she said, "Kendrick, I'm the only real cop on the premises. I have to know what the hell is going on."

"We were able to recover the video from the trooper's vehicle dashboard camera," he said slowly. "The final images on the tape show him stopping the SUV Bradford Lawson stole from GenHance. It also shows Lawson attacking him."

"Lawson killed this man."

The *tresora* looked uneasy. "We believe the killer has to be a Darkyn using Lawson's mortal identity. A human could not do what he did to this man."

She curled her scarred hand into a fist as she remembered the bizarre, repulsive smell Lawson had been radiating when he had killed Ted Evans, and the sense of wrongness about it. "What did he do?"

"From the teeth marks on the remains," Kendrick said unhappily, "it would seem that he not only killed this man, but he ate parts of him."

Matthias met Jessa in the library as he had promised, and placed a short stack of books on his desk.

"These you should be able to read," he told her, and

showed her how he had marked the passages in each with a piece of cord. "Rowan translated the ones written in French for me, but she cannot read German or Spanish."

That surprised her. "Rowan speaks French?"

"She taught herself to read it from books, for cooking." He placed a writing tablet and pen beside the books. "Will you translate into English what you read?"

"I can." She glanced up at him. "I thought you read all these yourself."

"Those in Latin and English I can read myself," he said. "The stories in the other languages were read to me by a translator, but I did not write then."

She didn't understand what he meant. "You didn't know how to write in English?"

"Ten years ago I did not know how to read or write," he admitted. "Rowan has been teaching me, but I am a poor scholar."

She felt appalled now. "It's wonderful that you're trying. Weren't you able to go to school when you were young?"

"Yes, but not for reading or writing." He started to say something else, and then seemed to change his mind. "I will leave you now."

After he had gone Jessa took the first book and skimmed through it. Written in modern Spanish, the text detailed a number of religious trials that were held in Madrid in the late fourteenth century. The author of the book, a noted historian, had translated some of the medieval documents he had found while researching the legal proceedings. Jessa found one startling passage about the conviction of a Templar knight who had escaped persecution in France only to be apprehended in Spain.

The fugitive refused to give his name to the court, or identify his accomplices, or speak at all, even under the duress of torture. The chief interrogator noted that although he could tolerate neither food nor drink, he remained unnaturally strong and impervious to pain for some months. This was first attributed to the evil that had seized his soul and through it taken control of his mortal form, until a special investigator was sent by Rome to question the prisoner. The Italian priest used copper implements, which proved to be the only metal that could penetrate the knight's skin, and holy water, which caused it to burn. Before a confession could be taken, the prisoner took his own life by thrusting one of the investigator's copper daggers into his heart. His last words were reported to be: "Death could not hold me in my grave, nor will you keep me to rot here."

Jessa read over the translation she had written and then slowly closed the book. The text was compelling, and certainly fit in with Matthias's theory, but the historian had likely made some broad interpretations of the medieval records. She was tempted to keep reading and see what was in the other books, but that would waste the time she needed to search the library.

She began with the desk, which she found unlocked, but the contents of each drawer proved to be ordinary: a collection of pens and pencils, blank paper, and some newspaper clippings stuffed into a folder. She went through the articles, which were all stories about people in America and Europe who had gone missing. The last clipping was the front-page story about her being wanted for killing Bradford Lawson, the same article Matthias had shown her. None of the other people in the articles had been accused of murder, but the one common denominator was that they had all vanished abruptly and without leaving any clues as to their whereabouts—exactly, she thought, as she had.

Were these the other Kyndred Matthias had spoken of? Had he abducted all of these people before her? She counted the articles; there were more than twenty of them.

She got up from the desk and slowly walked around the room, inspecting each bookcase and looking behind the books. Other than some dust and a few spiderwebs, she found nothing.

She stopped in front of the fireplace and looked up at the old bronze blade mounted in the glass case. The dark stains on it still repelled her, but there was something about the way it reflected the light that made her reach up and touch the glass.

"It's hermetically sealed," Rowan said from behind her, making her jump and spin around. The girl gave her a chilly smile. "The only way you can get it out is to break the glass. For which you'll need a sledgehammer."

"I was just curious." Jessa kept her expression bland. "I've never seen such an old sword."

"They were all the rage around two thousand years ago." Rowan set a steaming mug on the desk. "Matt thought you might like some tea."

She was a little thirsty. "Thank you, that was very kind."

The girl ignored her and picked up the notebook with her translation. "Lovely handwriting. You dot all your Is and cross all your Ts. Do you starch your underwear, too?"

She decided to counter Rowan's sarcasm by giving her a compliment. "Matthias said you've been teaching him to read and write. I think that's really nice of you."

The girl scowled as if Jessa had insulted her. "He's not dumb, you know. It's not his fault he never had the chance to learn."

"I don't think he's stupid at all," Jessa said. "But he must be from a very poor country."

"Stop fishing, Queenie, and drink your tea." Rowan sauntered out.

Jessa returned to the desk and picked up the notebook, turning it over in her hands as she gazed around the room, and then stared at the fireplace. The brick mantel surrounding the hearth stood out a good foot from the wall, and appeared to have been built in different sections. She got up and went over, checking both sides, and then noticed something about the brick.

As a child she had walked hundreds of paths through the city squares, and most of them had been made from bricks formed by slaves who used clay from the river. The distinctive, old-blood color of the bricks had been unique, a color referred to ever after as Savannah grey.

The fireplace had been built with the same kinds of bricks. Jessa sat down on the floor and touched the warm, rough surface of the hearth. The archaic bricks, so coveted by builders and restoration experts, were very rare, and almost never seen outside the city. Either she was back in Savannah or close to it.

Tears stung her eyes. She'd sworn never to return to her childhood home; it would have been too dangerous. She'd bitterly regretted everything she'd had to sacrifice in order to create a new identity for herself, but after waking up in the intensive care unit and discovering that the fatal gunshot wound in her chest had completely healed in less than twelve hours, she'd panicked and run. And had been running ever since.

Jessa braced a hand against the brick to stand, and felt something move under her palm. She looked carefully at the mortar between the bricks and found a seam, and traced it before she tugged at the stones. A large section of the hearth shifted, but it was too heavy for her to slide out.

This was where he was hiding everything, she thought, and tried pulling at the section of brick again. It didn't budge, and there seemed to be something holding it in place. She spent the next thirty minutes trying everything she could think of to dislodge it, including wedging the tip of her pen into the seam, but under pressure the pen merely snapped in half and the section remained in place.

She muttered something rude under her breath as she stood and brushed the traces of brick dust from her hands before giving in to her temper and kicking the brick. That simply hurt her toes, and she hopped for a moment before she limped over to the desk and sat down to rub her sore foot. At least she knew where his hiding place was, and possibly where *she* was.

Now all she had to do was break into his cache, and break out of her prison.

Chapter 15

Riordan called together his techs for a short meeting, during which he reviewed the latest list of demands from the chairman. "We need the data collected and all reports finished by close of business today. Until further notice, everyone is also on twelve-hour shifts."

No one complained, but a few eyes rolled.

He turned to his senior tech, a whiz kid Genaro had recruited straight out of MIT. "Bill, I'll need all the files we recovered from Bellamy's hard drive."

"I was hoping to work on them this morning," Bill said. "Yesterday I noticed some gaps in the ROM that didn't look right. They could be hidden file markers or something like that."

"I'll follow up on that for you," Riordan promised.

Once his techs returned to their cubicles, Riordan went into his office. Lori, his assistant, had gone down to collect the mail, but had left his morning drink—a chilled bottle of vitamin water—on his desk next to a pile of messages. He drank half the bottle while sorting through the slips and waiting for his terminal to boot up.

The morning conference had derailed his schedule, something he couldn't afford with Genaro on the warpath, but he had a dedicated crew and they'd work quickly to pull the necessary data. Everything else would have to wait.

Bill came in with a CD containing Bellamy's files and closed the door. "What's going on, Andy? Everyone's been so jumpy today you'd think the floor was hot-wired."

Riordan had kept his staff loyal by keeping an open-door policy and working alongside them rather than over them. At times, like now, he regretted that he couldn't be more honest with them. "You want me to give you the need-to-know speech again?" he asked as he took the CD.

"No, I get it," the tech admitted. "But it's hard to work in the dark. The newspapers are saying this girl killed the director. We know she didn't."

"If and when I can tell you anything more, I will. Damn it." The pen he was holding had snapped, and was now leaking blue ink onto his fingers. "Lori's downstairs. Cover the phones for me for a minute, will you?"

Riordan went to the men's room closest to his office and tried to scrub the ink from his hands. As he did, one of the guys from accounting came in with a newspaper under his arm.

"Morning." The man nodded and stepped into a stall.

Riordan dried his hands, studied them, and reached again for the soap dispenser. As he did, Delaporte came in to use one of the urinals. As the heavyset man passed him, he caught a whiff of something.

"That a new cologne?" Riordan asked him.

Delaporte glanced at him as he stood in front of the urinal and unzipped. "What?"

Riordan grinned. "You smell like perfume and coffee, Del. Been chasing one of the girls around the typing pool?"

"No, I ..." He frowned. "I was just going about my business."

"That feels better," the accountant said as he stepped out of the stall and came to the sinks. "Hey, Andy, who do you like for the Super Bowl this year?"

"Cardinals are looking pretty good. So are the Steelers." Riordan soaped his hands. "But the Bucs still have a shot, I think."

As the other man expressed his opinions of all three teams, Riordan saw Delaporte glance at the stall the accountant had used before joining them. Now he understood why the security chief had come here when he had his own office and private restroom five floors down.

Move.

"You won't get that off with regular soap," the security chief advised him. "Go over to the lab; they have a solvent hand cleaner that removes everything."

"Thanks, Del." Riordan dried his hands a second time, nodded to the accountant, and walked out and down the hall to the elevator. As he did, he checked his watch. He had rehearsed and timed everything he needed to do, and he knew it would take him precisely four minutes and nineteen seconds to either get out alive or kill himself.

Andrew Riordan had no intention of committing suicide.

He pressed his fingertip into a recess hidden on the underside of the rail at the back of the elevator, triggering the unit he'd installed in the ceiling of his office. He then set his watch to countdown as he heard muffled shouts coming from the data center. He stepped through the doors into the elevator and pressed the button for the lobby level.

Four minutes, ten seconds to live.

Footsteps thudded in the corridor, and someone called, "Hold those doors, please."

Riordan pressed the Close Doors button and held it until the panels slid shut and the cab began to descend. He didn't glance up at the security camera hidden in one of the lights, and kept his stance and expression casual.

Three minutes, forty-one seconds.

Forty.

Thirty-nine.

At the lobby level he stepped out of the elevator and walked through the back hall to the secured exit to the delivery platform. He took a key card from his wallet, swiped it, and pushed the heavy door open. Once outside the building, he jogged away from the senior employee parking lot, where his car was waiting, and went to the back lot where the platform workers kept their vehicles. There he took a duplicate key he'd made to Bill's compact car, unlocked it, and got in.

Two minutes, ten seconds.

He saw the first of the security guards emerge from the

building as he was pulling out, and made a one-eighty turn to head toward the eight-foot-tall fence running across the back of the property. Bill's tiny car bumped and bounced as it left the paved lot and traveled over the uneven ground, but it had a lot of pep and picked up speed nicely. Riordan had it up to eighty mph by the time he reached the fence and rammed the car through it.

One minute, thirty-eight seconds.

Metal shrieked and sparks exploded as Riordan flew over the deep ditch beyond the fencing and landed with a hard jolt. The little car's back wheels spun for a few seconds as they hung on the opposite edge of the ditch; then the tires dug in and the car shot forward with a high-pitched roar of its small engine. Riordan drove expertly through the back property, following a trail winding around the trees and the brush until he came to a utility road and made a sharp left turn.

Seven seconds.

Riordan opened the driver's-side door, braking enough to reduce the car's speed to a safe level before he jumped out and hit the ground rolling. Bill's car continued down the straight road for another quarter mile before it ran off into the trees and crashed.

His watch beeped, indicating his time was up. Drew switched off the countdown function as he retreated behind a ficus tree and watched the road until he spotted several dark vehicles driving at high speed toward Bill's wrecked compact.

Time to live.

Riordan ran every morning before he came into work, and covered the mile of uneven ground to his next destination in less than five minutes. Under the camouflage tarp covering the four-wheeler he'd stashed in the woods were also two tanks of gas and a backpack containing ten thousand dollars in cash, clothes, a disposable cell phone, and his new identity. The ATV started up at once, but the cell phone's battery was drained and needed recharging.

"Shit." He had forgotten to pack a charger, and would have to buy another phone before he could call in to

Rowan and let her and Matthias know he'd been exposed. That wouldn't happen for at least four or five hours, after he'd put some distance between him and GenHance and picked up the rest of what he needed, but it couldn't be helped.

He climbed on, started the engine, and took off.

Jessa spent the rest of the day in the library writing out translations in English of the passages she read concerning Matthias's supposed vampires. She no longer had any interest in the books, but the task allowed her to calm down and think more clearly. Her life had been completely disrupted, and her isolation here had led her to feel some reluctant sympathy for Matthias and Rowan. She'd almost forgotten that they were, in fact, keeping her prisoner here.

It had to be the dreams. Something about them was affecting her, was making her feel trust for a man who had abducted her. Who had imprisoned her.

I want to kiss your mouth.

What else did he want from her? What else would he take?

Once she finished the translations, she left the notebook beside the books and returned to her room, where she sat and mentally reviewed everything she had seen in the tunnels and rooms. It would be next to impossible to steal a knife from the kitchen; Rowan immediately noticed anything that was out of place. She'd never seen any hand tools around that might help her pry loose the bricks. Some of the daggers in the display cases looked strong enough, but the cases were always kept locked.

The dinner hour came and went, but Jessa didn't bother to join Rowan and Matthias in the kitchen. She couldn't bring herself to keep up the pretense anymore.

She tried to nap, but her thoughts refused to let her sleep. She took one of the paperbacks Matthias had given her, but the beautifully written words of Val McDermid's historical mystery danced before her eyes. Finally she gave up trying to entertain herself and went to get something to snack on from the kitchen.

When she saw Matthias working at the counter, she almost turned around and went back to her room.

"You did not come for the evening meal," he said without looking at her.

"I forgot the time." She smelled something sweet. "I'm not very hungry anyway." At the same time, her stomach growled.

"Sit down," he said, taking some strawberries from the bowl Rowan kept on the kitchen table. "I will share my fruit with you."

Jessa watched Matthias sort through and pile the strawberries into a crystal bowl before he began adding other things to them. After seeing him work out with his odd stone weights she expected him to be clumsy or heavy-handed, but instead he worked with a chef's confident skill.

"Do you always cook for your prisoners?" She winced as she saw him pour balsamic vinegar over the fruit. "Or is this your way of getting rid of them?"

"You do not eat as you should. That is why you are so quick to anger." He added sugar and cream to the bowl before bringing it to the table. "An empty belly only feeds the temper." He reached for the pepper grinder and twisted it over the fruit.

Jessa muffled a laugh. "Just out of curiosity, have you ever heard of using a cookbook?"

"No." He swirled the bowl a few times before he reached in and plucked out one of the cream-coated strawberries, holding it by its green top as he offered it to her.

"Thanks, but I'm not crazy about—"

"Taste." He rubbed the tip of the strawberry across her bottom lip, smearing some of the cream mixture along the curve when she didn't cooperate. "Are you afraid you will like it?"

She bit the strawberry in half, intending to spit the vile thing back into his face. Then the warm berry's tart juice, made silky and sweet by the sugar and smooth cream, filled her mouth. The vinegar and pepper only amplified the tastes, giving it a very subtle edge and touch of heat.

"Oh." Jessa didn't realize she had closed her eyes until she opened them. "That's . . . different."

Matthias's faint smile didn't reach the translucent jade of his eyes as he brought the rest of the strawberry to his mouth, his teeth neatly separating the berry from the top. His jaw muscles flexed as he slowly chewed and swallowed, but his eyes never left hers.

"Okay, so I was wrong." Feeling a little self-conscious, she licked the cream from her lips. "It's good." She tried to take another.

One big hand pushed the bowl out of her reach. "Only good?"

He had to rub it in, of course. "It's great."

"Do you want another?" He took a second berry from the bowl, but when she tried to take it from him, he moved his hand away. "Open your mouth."

Jessa didn't like the way he was looking at her—as if *she* were something he wanted to bite. "I can feed myself, you know."

"Not very well." He held the strawberry under her nose. "Open."

With a sigh she imitated a guppy.

Matthias didn't let her have it this time. Instead he teased her, placing the berry between her lips and then taking it away before she could take a bite, rubbing it here and there until she grabbed his wrist.

Shadowlight.

Jessa stood at the edge of a winter forest. Thick, icy air wrapped around her, and snow was everywhere, under her feet, weighing down the tree branches, and slowly swirling above her head, spinning and floating as it fell from the sky. The setting sun polished each flake until they glinted like tiny bits of glass. Ahead of her a clearing funneled its thick white drifts between two enormous, frost-covered stones.

Sunlight.

Her heart beat once, twice, and then she was back in the kitchen, still trying to arm-wrestle a strawberry away from Matthias.

Disoriented as she was by the unexpected touch-sight, she couldn't seem to let go of his wrist. "Is this really necessary?"

"When you want something, it is." He didn't seem to notice anything was wrong with her. With a deliberate show of strength, he brought the strawberry to his mouth, biting it so that streams of juice and cream ran down his palm and onto her fingers.

Jessa released him, but now he took hold of her wrist and guided her hand to his mouth. The shock of returning to herself so quickly faded as he put his tongue to her skin and slowly licked one finger and then another clean. Her breath rasped in her throat as he took the tip of her smallest finger into his mouth and sucked lightly.

"What are you doing?" she heard herself ask, her voice so low and distant it seemed to come from that faraway winter forest.

"Tasting." His free hand spanned the front of her throat before he slid it under her hair and curled it over the back of her neck. "Do you want more?"

He didn't mean the strawberries, which was fine, because she couldn't think about them. As she tried to form the word "no," his tongue found the center of her palm and stroked it before his teeth tested the sensitive mound of flesh beneath her thumb.

That love bite set something loose inside her, a hot, heavy, feline ache that climbed over her breasts and inched down to curl in her lap, sinking sharp little claws into the tense muscles of her thighs and drawing a thick, silky tail of sensation between them.

His hand on her nape tugged, urging her forward. He was going to kiss her.

In her mind she saw herself crossing the now unbearable distance between them, pressing his mouth to the tight peak throbbing over her heart. She saw her own hands tearing open her blouse so he could get at it, so he could suck her properly, while she took his gilded hair in small, tight fists—

His face blurred before her eyes as he came closer, and the warmth of his breath touched her lips. "Jezebel . . ."

The name and all its secrets hit her like a slap, and she jerked, finding her feet and almost knocking over the chair as she backed away. A stumble later she had put three feet and a fortress of sanity between them.

If Jessa understood anything, it was the shadowlight. It never lied to her, never showed her anything but cold, hard truth. Matthias had walked through that winter forest; he had left something terrible in it. He might have killed and buried someone there; that might explain what she had seen and felt the first time she'd touched him.

"I think I've had enough." A quick turn allowed her to hide most of the shaking and the stupid look she felt sure was plastered on her face. "Good night."

Jessa didn't hear him following her, but halfway to her room she felt him loom up behind her. Confronting him interested her about as much as encouraging him, so she kept moving. She reached her room and turned the pretty porcelain knob when his hand shot past her cheek and flattened against the edge to hold the door in place.

A wall of hard chest muscle brushed her shoulders before he bent his head to murmur beside her ear, "You're afraid of me. Why?"

Afraid of him? If he didn't soon get away from her, she was going to climb up him and the wall and dig her way out of here with her bare hands.

Or worse, she wouldn't.

"I'm tired of you." She pulled on the knob and managed to get the door to open an inch before he shoved it closed again.

Jessa ducked under his arm to get out from under him, but he turned her and had her up against the wall before she could blink. This close she could see every detail of the mark on his throat. What sort of man believed that forever was a black snake biting its own tail? She forced herself to look up into his face, but light from behind him effectively masked his features.

"You are still empty." His fingers spread over her abdomen, the edges of his fingernails scratching the fabric of her skirt as he pressed them in and out in a kneading motion. "Do you feel it here?" His hand shifted lower, stopping just short of sliding between her legs. "Or here?"

"I said I would stay here and let you protect me from Genaro," Jessa said, keeping her tone reasonable. "You never said that I'd have to sleep with you for it."

"Sleep with me?" He sounded amused. "That is not what I want."

"Good." Now she was lying, too. "Just so we're clear."

"Just so we're clear," he repeated, almost thoughtfully. "It means so that we understand each other, yes?"

"That's it. No sleeping together. No dreams." She glanced down meaningfully, but he didn't step back. "Now you say good-night and go away."

"But you do not yet understand me. When I have you"—he clamped his hands around her waist—"you will not dream. You will not sleep."

Jessa grabbed his shoulders as he lifted her off her feet and pinned her to the wall. His head bent, but instead of forcing a kiss on her lips he put his mouth to her ear.

"When I have you," he said again, "there will be nothing between us. No clothes. No fear. No words."

The smell of him, all summer heat, clouded her thoughts. "It doesn't work like that."

"You will give yourself to me. I will take you." He pushed the hem of her skirt up with his knee and nudged her thighs apart. "I will put myself inside you here, where you need me. Where I need to be." He bit her earlobe, the side of her jaw, and the spot where her neck curved into her shoulder before he lifted his head. "That is how it will work. Am I clear to you?"

Jessa closed her arms around his neck and held on as the unyielding iron of his thigh rubbed against her. Sweat traced the line of her back as her struggle turned inside out and she fought the wild heat rising inside her. If she didn't put a stop to this now she would do anything he wanted, right here against the wall.

"That's enough." She pushed at his shoulders. "Put me down. I can't do this. Not with you."

"You will," he said, his mouth as cool and hard as his words against her lips.

PART FOUR
Takyn

April 29, 1998

Dear Mom,

Hi from Italy! I'll probably get home before this letter arrives, but Donnie's on the phone trying to confirm our flight back and I have to write all this stuff down before I forget something. You would not believe what's happened in the last three days. Seriously!

I really love Italy, and Donnie is the best fiancé a girl could have. But honestly, Mom, I hate climbing mountains. It's cold, it's wet, and there's nothing but rocks and trees and more rocks and trees. When we get back from this trip, and you ever hear me or Donnie say the words "mountain climbing" again, I want you to slap some sense into both of us.

Saturday Donnie and I drove to the Alps and stopped at that inn I told you about, the really pretty one at the base of the mountain in that pretty town. We were just planning to stay there for the night and make a one-day trip to Berlin to get some chocolate and that cuckoo clock Grandma wanted. Well, you know how Donnie gets the minute he's near anything taller than a hill, and then he met this group of German rock climbers. They got to talking and next thing I know this chick Gerta is lending me some of her gear so we can go climbing with them.

I didn't want to go. Seriously! Our tour guide back in Rome told us it was the wrong time of year to climb. But you know Donnie. Show him a rock hammer and he's strapping on his boots. Anyway, the Germans were pretty nice for climbers, and that girl Gerta helped me keep up. Still, it took five hours to climb up from the inn to this stupid pass, and by the time we got to the top I was ready to ralph up my breakfast in Donnie's lap. Everything was all slushy and dripping, and then this huge slab of snow and ice just collapsed and rolled down the mountain. I swear, if we hadn't stopped under this big boulder overhang thing, your little girl wouldn't be writing this letter. Seriously.

I wanted to go down right then, but one of the Germans spotted another climber in the snow and yelled, and of course we had to slog through all this crap that came off the top of the mountain to dig the poor guy out. At first I thought he was dead for sure, and then he opened his eyes and sat up and—oh, God, this is, like, the most embarrassing thing—he was totally naked. The only thing on his bod was this wicked tat of a snake.

Fritz, one of the German guys, said people do that sometimes when they get hypothermia—they get a little weird in the head, think it's hot instead of cold and then start stripping. Seriously! Thank heavens Donnie had a change of clothes in his pack or the poor guy would have finished freezing to death.

The amazing thing was that even though he was buck naked and got hit by an avalanche and everything, he wasn't hurt, not really. I mean, he had a bad cut on his head, and he was kind of out of it, but no broken bones or anything like that. Gerta thought he might have some kind of, like, brain injury, because he couldn't talk or tell us his name or anything. He didn't seem to understand us, either, no matter what language we used. I said some stuff I remembered from high school French class, and

Donnie tried Italian and Spanish, but no luck. Did you know Germans speak, like, twenty different languages? They tried everything they knew, until Gerta said he was probably, like, really traumatized from getting caught in the avalanche and we should take him down to the inn and get a doctor to take a look at him.

I thought it would take forever to climb back down with this guy being hurt and all, but he kept up with us and even showed Fritz this faster way down, so he must have been a really experienced climber. He didn't seem upset until we got to the inn, and then he got a little freaked out. He kept looking around like he didn't know where he was. Donnie said it was a delayed reaction or something. First the guy looked like he was going to pass out right there in the parking lot, and the Germans had to grab him to keep him from running out into the middle of the street.

The people at the inn didn't know who he was, but since he was hurt and kind of starved-looking they were really nice and gave him a room and a huge free meal and stuff. They also called this doctor from the village who checked him out. Later he came by to talk to me and Donnie, and said the man had some sort of amnesia that usually happens to people after they go through wars and stuff. The name of it had letters, like PMS, but I can't remember exactly what they are now.

I almost freaked out the next morning when we went to check on him, and the innkeeper said he borrowed some gear from the Germans and went back up the mountain. Seriously! You'd think after what he'd been through he'd be scared to climb, but no, the guy jumped right back on the horse. He didn't come back until just before we were going to leave, and he looked better, but I think he was really upset. He still couldn't talk to us, but he used his hands to, like, say thank-you, and gave Donnie and Fritz each an old, nasty-looking coin.

I wanted Donnie to throw that thing away, it was so covered with crud, but he said he thought it was really old and we should have it appraised. So while we were in Berlin Donnie took it to this coin dealer, and the dealer washed off the crud and got all quiet and then he told Donnie that it was pure gold and in mint condition and stuff. Get this, Mom: It's, like, two thousand years old and worth a huge pile of money. Seriously!

The dealer said we could get a lot more money for it from a collector in the States. Donnie's worried we could get in trouble for taking it out of Italy, but I'm just going to stick it in my bra. Like customs is going to look there, right? So when we get home we're going to sell it and use the money to pay for a really nice wedding. Donnie said if we sell it to the right person there might even be enough left over for us to put a down payment on a town house. Tell Daddy, since I know that will make him happy, ha ha ha.

Oh, I almost forgot—I don't know what happened to the man with amnesia, but he was gone when we stopped at the inn on our way back to Rome. The innkeeper said he just walked down the road the day we left and disappeared. Donnie thought about calling the newspapers, you know? But I told him that they would for sure want to know where that guy found the coin and if there were more, etc. So we're not going to tell anyone. I know—you and Daddy would say we should go to the police, but we really did save that man's life. So we're looking at this like a little reward for being Good Samaritans, that's all.

We're going on to Venice like we planned, and I'll call you from there to make sure you have the right flight number and gate and stuff and when we'll be arriving at LAX. Give Daddy and Jimmy and Sarah a hug for me, and see you next week!

Love,

Becky

Chapter 16

The many wars Matthias had fought had not all taken place on blood-soaked battlefields. Some, like the one Jessa was fighting, happened in the endless expanse of the soul, where the combatants could not be seen or heard, only felt.

In that golden place within, where the truth of her shone bright and hot as the summer sun, she fought herself.

Her body trembled and her fingers dug into his arms, and she was so rigid that she felt like a bundle of dry twigs ready to snap. But her soft, lush mouth welcomed his, and she tasted as sweet and hot as her hidden self, the woman he met every night in his dreams, all woman, all eager desire now.

The dampness of her skin and the change in her scent told him that she would soon lose this battle, and if she did so in his arms she would never forgive herself. That alone gave him enough will to fight back his own need and ease away from her.

"There is no reason to fear this," he said, keeping their hands linked. "It has been between us since the first moment."

"When you kidnapped me," she snapped.

"When I looked into your eyes." He ran his hand over her hair, moving it back from her brow. "I knew then that you were made for me. That you were meant for me."

"I'm not afraid of you," she said again, with less conviction. "And I'm certainly not *meant* for you."

He wanted to pick her up, carry her into her room, and show her with his mouth and hands and body what he could say only with words now. But that was what she was expecting: to be overpowered, to be taken. That would allow her to continue the battle inside her soul, for she could then hold both sides of herself blameless.

As much as he wanted her, he would not force her. "I will wait for you to come to me."

"I don't know what is more insulting," she said, her face becoming a mask of calm. "You thinking that I'm afraid, or that I'd want you."

"I do not think. I know." He pressed his mouth to her brow before she could move away. "You cannot command fate, Jezebel."

"That's not my name," she said through clenched teeth.

"Neither is Jessa." He released her and left her there.

Matthias spent the rest of the evening working the stones until his muscles ached and he dripped with sweat. After he bathed, he went to his room and slept for an hour before rising and going to the communications room. There he read through his e-mails, and found one sent from a mobile phone with an unfamiliar number.

From: D.
To: Rainman
Subject: Moving
Hey, everything looking peachy? Not so much here. I'm okay but my apartment caught fire so I'm out looking for a new place. I have what's left of the furniture, but I could use some help with moving it or I'll have to borrow a truck. I'll be hanging at Tag's place until noon. Give my regards to the ladies.
Later, D

"D" identified the sender as Drew Riordan, as did the beginning words, the first letters of each spelling "help." Rowan was the only one who could interpret the meaning of the rest of the message, but Matthias could guess the gravity of his situation. The only reason Drew would have sent a coded message was if somehow his presence at

GenHance had been discovered, and he had been forced to leave to avoid being taken.

Matthias went to wake Rowan, who blinked sleepily until he told her about Drew's message. She sat up and read the copy he had printed.

"They didn't catch him in the act, but they found out what he's been doing," she said as she decoded the message. "He had time to dupe his files and then fry all the computers in his department before he took off."

"His absence will confirm that he was the one passing information to us."

"So will all the crap they find when they search his office." She threw off her covers and bounced out of the bed. "He needs transportation. He says he's going to wait for a pickup in Price Park until noon. If we don't show by then, he'll steal something and go to ground."

Matthias caught her arm as she went to the closet. "You cannot go alone to retrieve Drew."

"You can't leave Queenie here by herself," she said. "She's already noticed the fire doors sealing the tunnels. How long do you think it will take her to figure out that the dome lights open them?"

"GenHance will be searching for Drew," he told her. "I will send for one of the others to accompany you."

"They're all too far away to get to Atlanta by noon." She heaved out a breath. "Matt, we knew this might happen, and now it has. I'll be fine." She eyed the door. "Now would you get out of here so I can change?"

"Come to the library before you go," he said.

Rowan met him there a few minutes later. She had dressed in her leather garments, and carried her spare helmet and a hard-sided case that fastened to the back of her motorcycle.

Matthias handed her an envelope filled with currency, a disposable mobile phone, and a pair of sheathed blades.

"I don't like weapons," she reminded him, but clipped the sheaths to her belt above each hip.

"Neither does Drew. Here is his photo." He handed her the snapshot Drew had given him when they had first met.

"Wow." She studied it. "He *does* have red hair. But he doesn't look geeky." She glanced up and saw his expression. "He described himself to me once on the phone."

"I will send him a photo of you as well, so that he will know you on sight," he told her. "You will be careful and return as soon as you may."

"No, I'll be reckless and probably stop for dinner on the way back." She grinned. "Don't worry, boss. I can't think of anyone I'd rather have watching my back than Drew." Her mouth twisted. "Except you."

Matthias pulled her into his arms and held her for a moment, and then let her go.

"See you soon," she promised, and slipped out.

He went to the fireplace to retrieve the blank documents he would need to use to create a new identity for Drew, and saw faint marks on the edges of the false bricks. Jessa had found his cache, and had tried unsuccessfully to open it. Her offer to translate the stories about the dark Kyn had been a lie.

He went out and down the tunnel toward her room, which he found empty. The lingering trace of her scent led him to Rowan's room. She must have been outside listening to them. She would have heard Rowan speak of the dome lights that opened the fire doors. That meant there was now nothing to stop her from going topside—except him.

Jessa watched as Matthias came out of the library, and as soon as he went around the corner toward Rowan's room she moved, hurrying inside. She went immediately to the fireplace cache, which he'd left open, and reached into the steel-lined box, taking out a stack of files.

The topmost was labeled with her adopted name, Minerva Jessamine Starret, and contained a complete dossier on her dating back to the year her father had adopted her. Matthias had found copies of the old newspaper articles on Darien's funeral, the massacre at Oglethorpe Consolidated, and her own disappearance from the hospital. There were also dozens of photographs, all candid shots of her in Atlanta. He must have followed her for days to take the shots; he had photographed her standing by her car, entering her office building, driving downtown, walking through parking lots . . . and sitting by the fountain in the park.

He *had* been there that night, watching her. Listening to her.

Jessa tore the photographs out of the file and flung them into the flames, and then threw the entire folder in on top of them before she opened the next one in the pile.

The rest of the files contained the same type of information on dozens of men and women all over the country. Some of the profiles were comprehensive, but four contained only bits and pieces on four people who had not been identified by name: a professor, a zoologist, a cop, and a midwife. Jessa recognized the description of the zoologist—she had to be Delilah. Then she saw that someone had written the name Delilah in the margin of one of the pages.

He knew as much—if not more—about the Takyn as she did.

Jessa's anger swelled as she focused on the masthead at the top of one of the forms. She couldn't believe her eyes at first, and flipped through the others to find the masthead the same on each one. Every report had been written on company stationery by one Andrew Riordan, chief technical supervisor at GenHance, Inc.

Matthias had lied to her all along. He wasn't saving her from GenHance. He was working for them. He'd taken her for them.

She pitched all of the files into the flames, and when they didn't burn at once she scanned the room. She spotted and seized a small oil lamp sitting to one side, removed the wick holder, and dumped the contents on top of the smoldering heap of folders. The oil caused the fire to roar, scorching the stones around the edge of the hearth before it died down. By the time it did, all of Matthias's dossiers had been reduced to curls of ash.

She checked the cache again for more information, but found only several stacks of bills and an envelope filled with blank passports, driver's license forms, and Social

Security cards. She emptied the cache, grimacing as she pocketed several thousand dollars. She didn't want to steal his money, but she'd need it once she escaped. She took the rest and fed it to the fire, taking considerable, savage delight in watching his money and means of changing his identity burn as well.

She knew Matthias might have discovered her ruse by now, so she left the library and followed the route she had planned. Now that she knew they'd been using the fire doors to seal off the tunnels, and how to open them, she made her way to the one that concealed the surface hatch. Rowan had left it open, but as she passed over the threshold a shadow separated from the wall and strong arms grabbed her from behind.

"You did not say good-bye," Matthias said against her ear.

Jessa kicked and writhed, frantic to free herself, but he kept her locked against him and lifted her off her feet, hauling her back into the tunnels and using his elbow to press the dome light and seal the fire door.

"Stop fighting and I will put you down," he said.

"Go to hell," she shouted, thrashing against his arms.

Matthias carried Jessa back to his room, where he placed her facedown on his pallet, straddled her waist, and reached for one of the belts hanging on the wall.

She jerked her head up. "You are not beating me with that."

"I do not beat women." Quickly he looped the pliant leather around her wrists, cinching them together before he tied them to the top of his pallet frame. Her heels drummed against his back as she arched and pulled but found she could not free herself.

"Be still," he told her, putting one hand on her neck and the other flat against her right shoulder. "It will be easier if you are."

She jerked. "I'm not lying here and letting you rape me."

His own anger flared; how could she think he would do such a thing to her? He bent over and put his mouth next to her ear. "If I wanted to fuck you, woman, I would have tied you down on your back."

Her movements stilled, and she dragged in some air. "What are you going to do to me?"

When he did this in the past he found speaking in a soft, persuasive voice helped greatly, but there was no point in speaking to her, not when she was in this agitated state. He would gentle her first, and then they would talk.

Matthias felt the taut muscles in her neck and back, and worked the flat of his fingers against them, rocking his hand as he rubbed until he felt some of the tenseness ease. She was all fight and fire, but one could not battle forever, and even the fiercest flames eventually burned low.

He wished he kept a brush in his room so he could draw it through the blue-black mass of her hair, now spilling all around her face in wild abandon, but he kept his own too short to need grooming. Once he had rubbed both sides of her neck and both shoulders, he went to work on her spine, pressing his fists on either side and moving his knuckles in gentle, circular motions.

"You're giving me a massage?" he heard her say. "Are you crazy?"

"Shhh." He made his way down as far as her waist, and then lifted his weight and shifted back onto her thighs. The curves of her flanks tempted him to part her legs and rub her where she most needed the relief, but that he would do later, when she opened herself to his touch willingly. He merely allowed himself to run his hands over her buttocks once before he shifted back again, stroking his thumbs across the bunched muscles of her thighs.

She had beautiful hips and strong legs. Once he reasoned with her, he would use his hands on them again.

Matthias turned completely around so that he straddled her thighs but faced her feet, and lifted the right calf by the ankle. She tried to back-kick him again, but he held her fast and tugged down the trouser to expose her leg.

"Let go," she snarled, straining against his grip.

"Lie still." When she didn't, he added, "I can do this with your legs bound."

That quieted her at once.

Returning to his task, he wrapped his hand around her leg, beginning just below the knee. With firm, drawing strokes, he worked her calf from knee to ankle, going down a little farther each time, pumping the heel of his hand against the rigid extension of her muscles until that, too, softened. He attended her other leg, and when she had gone limp beneath him he took hold of her left foot.

She groaned something, and he heard the leather of his belt creak.

A woman's foot was a tender, delicate thing, and Jessa's narrow, gracefully arched sole was the same color as her lips. It proved to be almost as sensitive, he discovered as he found the first of her pleasure points just beneath the center of her toes. Using his fingertips, he caught and squeezed the nerve endings there with just enough pressure to make her twitch, and then brought his thumb up beneath to smooth over the spot.

"Please." Her words came out in a low plea. "Please don't do that."

Matthias found a second point, and then a third, and attended to them with equal care. He had never known a woman to have more than that, but his ministrations revealed another two along the arched inside. The skin was so delicate he feared he might bruise her with his hands, so he lowered his head and put his mouth to her so that he might use his tongue.

She bucked under him, crying out as he drew the edge of his teeth over one spot and then the other to see just how responsive they were. "Matthias."

From her shivering and moving under him she was close, so he used his mouth on her other foot, nipping and licking with deliberate pressure, his fingers playing over the other bundles of nerves in tandem, until he felt her body stiffen and the sound of pleasure and release come from her throat.

Matthias lifted himself from the pallet and reached for his belt, releasing it and removing it from her wrists. Both were slightly reddened, chafed not from the loops but from her struggles against the leather. He massaged both wrists gently before he rolled her over and sat down beside her.

She stared up at him, her rain-colored eyes drowsy. "Why did you do that to me?"

"You needed it." He brushed a trickle of sweat from her temple. "It has been a long time for you."

"I don't need . . ." She bit down on her lip and looked away from him.

He caught her cheek and turned her face back to see his. "Your pleasure is enough. When you come to me, when we join our bodies, I will make you feel much more than that."

"You'll kill me," she whispered.

He smiled. "Never."

Jessa tried to sit up, but her arms trembled too much, and she slumped back. "I can hardly move. Is this your ability? Massaging someone into a vegetative state?"

"It is not an ability," he said. "Mostly it is what I did to my horse whenever he became unhappy."

Her eyes widened, her lips quivered, and then she began to laugh. "You rubbed me down like a *horse*?"

He shrugged. "I did not do the same to his hooves. He would not have felt it. Or liked it as much." He took her hand in his. "We must speak the truth to each other now, Jessa."

She stiffened. "You could start by telling me why you lied about working for GenHance."

"I did not lie—"

"I found the files in the library," she said. "Every report you have came from GenHance. Did they hire you to abduct me? Is this some sort of brainwashing by isolation?"

"The reports are from GenHance. Until today, my friend Drew worked there. He sent us copies of all the reports on those Genaro has identified as Kyndred. We have been trying to reach them before they are taken. You were the latest." He saw that she didn't believe him. "You heard me speaking to Rowan about this."

"Maybe you both knew I was listening." Doubt filled her eyes. "It doesn't matter anyway. I burned all the files. And your money, and your fake IDs."

Now it was his turn to chuckle. "You are very loyal to your friends, Minerva."

She shook her head. "Don't call me that. Minerva Starret died in that hospital ten years ago. I just inherited the body." With a groan she sat up, using his hand as leverage, and then rubbed her damp face. "I need to use your washbasin."

He put an arm around her, helping her over and holding her upright as she picked up the water jug and tipped it to fill the basin.

"Matthias?" she murmured.

He bent over. "Do you need a towel?"

"No."

The last thing he saw was the swing of the jug before it smashed into his face.

Chapter 17

Lucan accompanied the hunters back to the interstate and the scene of the last man known to be killed by Lawson. Eight days had passed since the senseless murder, but their nightly searches had turned up nothing of use. It was as if the man had existed for only a space of forty-eight ghastly hours, and had been snatched up by the hand of God from this desolate place.

"The ground still reeks of him," Devon, the lead tracker, said. A falconer in his human life, he had acquired as a Kyn warrior the ability to see through the eyes of his hunting birds. After discovering the animals that had died after exposure to the body, however, Devon had left his peregrines behind. "'Twill have to be burned over and strewn with copper." He crossed himself. "Perhaps even blessed."

"The Heavenly Father and fallen angels had nothing to do with this." Lucan crouched, removed his glove, and touched the ground. Where the body parts had lain, the soil felt wrong, but he could not define how. He scanned the area before he stood. "Gabriel Seran is yet in Europe chasing after lost Kyn, is he not?"

"So it is said, my lord," Devon said.

"Damn me. If anyone could track this thing, it would be him." His mobile rang, and he checked the display before he flipped it open. "What is it, Alex?"

"Hello to you, too, big guy," she replied. "Kendrick said you were out hunting, but this can't wait until morning. I analyzed the tissue samples he sent over from the last victim. The good news is, we can break out the champagne. Bradford Lawson is definitely not Darkyn."

He would celebrate later. "What else can you tell me?"

"The victim's tissues are saturated with a powerful neurotoxin."

"A what?"

"A poison produced by the body and lethal to pretty much anything that breathes," she explained. "I can't identify it, but the components share similar characteristics to flying-insect venom."

He took the phone away from his ear, stared at it, and then spoke again to her. "Alex, while I am quite certain that you have more knowledge in your smallest finger than the sum of what resides between my ears, I can assure you that a bee or a wasp did not kill this man."

"Not unless there were a couple million of them involved," she agreed. "Whoever or whatever this killer is, he probably can produce this venom in large quantities. My guess is he uses it like our abilities, and with it he can stun or kill anything he bites or touches."

Lucan gazed at the men around him. "Does this venom affect us?"

"Fortunately, no," she said. "I tested it on several Kyn blood samples, and our pathogen ate it for breakfast. But, Lucan, that makes us the only living things who are immune to it."

"This is all very well and good," he told her, "but we cannot pick up a scent trail, and there have been no more bodies."

"If he's begun eating them, there won't be." She sighed. "The tissue samples sent to me gave off an extremely strong odor that blocked out everything else I could smell in the lab, even Michael. It's probably a hundred times worse there. You need to move away from where the body was found." She hesitated. "Has Sam tried to read the victim's blood?"

"No. Seeing what Lawson did to the first victim caused her to collapse." He stared at the blood-soaked ground. "I will not allow her to know what was done here."

"I understand." And the tone of her voice told her that she did. "Call me if you need anything else."

Some of the knot in his gut loosened. "Thank you, my lady."

Lucan switched off the phone and breathed in. He had hunted hundreds of killers during his lengthy existence. Not one of them, no matter how mad, had given off such a stench.

"My lord?" Devon asked.

"Lady Alexandra has determined that this one is not Kyn," he told the men. "Nor is he human."

"A changeling, perhaps?" one of the other hunters suggested. "There are creatures who feed on the dead. If he has been using their blood . . ."

"She vows he is not one of us. And changeling or not, no Kyn can consume flesh." Lucan paced around the marked perimeter as he inhaled over and over. As before, there was no scent trail leading away from the crime scene, but the farther he moved from the rotten odor left behind by the body, the easier it was to breathe. Then he picked up the faintest trace of something else—a different scent, one of sweat and chemicals—emanating from another source.

He found the flashlight sitting in a clump of weeds, and removed it. The batteries were dead, but as soon as he picked it up the sour, unpleasant smell intensified.

"I think he must have handled this," he said to Devon when the tracker joined him, and indicated two dark stains on the handle. "Blood." He sniffed them. "Not polluted as the dead man's was."

"Give it to me," a familiar voice said.

Lucan looked up to see his *sygkenis* walking down from the road. He handed the flashlight to Devon before he strode up to meet her. "You were not to come to this place."

"Yet here I am." She planted her hands on her hips. "Ordering Kendrick to keep me away was a nice move. Too bad it didn't work."

When she tried to walk past him, he seized her by the arm. "This is my work, not yours. You will return to the city."

She smiled up at him. "You want me to accept what I am, and be Darkyn, and handle all the shit that comes along with it, but only when it's convenient for you and I won't get in the way? Is that how you think this is going to work?"

"Samantha, you cannot see this. Not after what was done to this man. Lawson—"

"Ate parts of him. I know. I made Kendrick tell me. That's why we have to find him, tonight, before he does this again." She tried to shrug off his hold. "I'll be all right."

"No."

"You can't stop me—"

"I can." He picked her up to toss her over his broad shoulder, but she wound her arms around his neck and kissed him. That sent all the fear and anger out of his head, and slowly he lowered her down onto her feet.

"Bloody hell," he muttered against her mouth. "You are not fighting fair."

"No one says I have to. Listen to me." She put her cool hands to his cheeks. "I can do this. I'm stronger than you think. Let me help you."

He lifted his head. "Devon," he called out, not looking away from her beautiful eyes.

"My lord." The tracker joined them.

"Give my *sygkenis* the flashlight." To her, he said, "There is some blood on the handle. I think it came from Lawson." When she opened her mouth to argue, he added, "I know he is still alive. But you were able to read my blood that night at your apartment."

"You died a human death and came back to life as something else," she reminded him. "That was the only reason I could."

He nodded. "Until last week, this man was mortal. Alexandra says he is not Darkyn, but perhaps he underwent a transition like ours."

"Maybe." She took the flashlight from Devon. "The blood is a week old anyway, I probably won't." Abruptly she stopped speaking and gripped the handle, denting the aluminum surface beneath her fingers as her eyes closed.

She shuddered once, and then froze. The flashlight fell to the ground.

"Samantha." He rested his hands on her shoulders. When she didn't respond, he shook her. "Wake up. Damn it, you will not do this to me again. *Samantha*."

"No," she said softly as she looked up at him, her eyes huge. "I won't. Yellow jackets."

"What? He is wearing a yellow jacket?"

"They killed him." She moved past him and went to a spot some yards away. He followed her, and there saw the mounds of dead insects on the ground around a broken nest. "Here." She pointed to a depression in the ground. "You were right. He did die. Right here."

"Where is the body?"

"He rose again, the way we did. But he's not like us. He's like the insects. On the inside, where you can't see it." Her expression twisted as she pressed her hands to the sides of her head. "I can feel him now. He's in my head. He can feel them, too. Jesus, he's almost there."

"Where?" When she didn't answer, he caught her chin. "Samantha, look at me. Where has Lawson gone?"

"He's gone to where Jessa Bellamy is," she said simply. "He's gone to Savannah."

Jessa dropped the handle that had broken off the porcelain pitcher, bent, and pressed her fingers to the side of Matthias's neck. His pulse beat steadily under her fingertips, and the cut on his forehead wasn't bleeding too much.

"I'm sorry," she said before she stepped over his motionless form and ran out of the room.

She'd never struck another person in her life, and she felt horribly ashamed of herself. She didn't want to leave him like this, helpless and alone. But this was her only chance to escape, and whether he was telling the truth or just another elaborate series of lies, she had to get away from him.

She opened the fire door leading to the surface hatch, and went through it to a narrow stairwell. She climbed up two levels, and saw a landing with two different doors. She discovered that neither was locked, and the first one she tried opened to a small, neat garden with a stone path leading out to a street.

Jessa knew the moment she walked outside that she was in Savannah. As cool and damp as the air was, she could smell the river, and the lush scent of growing things. As she made her way to the street, she noticed the flower beds and the neat rows of small green plants laid out in the tiny yard. Then she glanced back and stumbled as she saw the tall, stately house with its elegant lines and the faded but still sparkling outer coat of dark blue paint.

Sapphire House. She'd been kept prisoner under her own home. She was standing in her own backyard.

Jessa shook her head, backing away from the sight before she turned and ran. It was a bad dream—it had to be—but then she saw the square where Darien had died, and the imposing spires of St. John's, and even the much-hated coffee shop across the street.

Matthias had brought her home.

Pain lanced through her head as she fled down the street, away from the square and toward the river. She didn't know where she was running, only that she had to run; she had to escape this. And still the questions screeched inside her head: How had he known? Why hadn't he told her? How could he have built that place under her own house?

She had to stop and catch her breath at the entrance to the riverfront walk, and as she gulped in air she remembered something: Darien had never permitted her to go down into the cellar. He'd frightened her with tales of rats and spiders lurking down in the dark corners, and kept the door latch padlocked.

But more than once during her holiday visits from school Darien had disappeared from the house, only to reappear hours later. None of the servants ever saw him leave. Once, when she asked him about it, he told her he'd found his own little hiding place in the house, and he went there when he wanted some peace. Jessa also recalled some odd references to masons coming to the house to talk to her father in the sporadic letters Geraldine had written to her.

The age of the walls, the odd sizes of the rooms, and the

library and the fireplace now made sense. Her father had loved sitting by the fire and reading. Matthias hadn't built the underground shelter. Darien had, probably using the same tunnels his ancestor had for storing the goods he'd smuggled into the city.

I've spent more on Old Blue than likely I should have, Darien had told her when they'd discussed her legacy. Yet Jessa could never remember her father making any major alterations to the house, or buying any high-priced items. They'd lived quietly and modestly, and Darien hadn't cared to throw parties or waste money on keeping up with Savannah society. The only thing she could remember him purchasing regularly, in fact, were the books he loved.

Jessa climbed down the stairs to the side street leading around to the riverfront. All of the shops, bars, and restaurants were closed, so she had the walkways to herself. As she looked out across the river to the new hotel that had been built on Hutchinson Island, she folded her arms around her waist. Everything she knew had changed now, and everyone she had loved was gone. Darien and Tag couldn't help her with this; there was no one she could rely on, no one to tell her what to do or where to go.

She was thinking like Minerva. She couldn't do that. She had to get away from the memories as well as Matthias.

A clock in the window of one of the shops told her it was close to three a.m. In a few hours businesses would begin to open; she'd have to find an Internet café and contact Aphrodite. She could trust Di, and knew that if she asked, her friend would take her in, at least until she could figure out what to do next.

"Jessa," someone whispered.

She turned around, expecting to see Matthias, but found only the empty stretch of walkway. Quickly she hurried toward the next alley that led up to street level, and when she heard the whisper a second time she broke into a flat run.

Clouds rushed in from the sea, covering the moon and blocking out the starlight. Jessa flinched as lightning flashed over the bridge and thunder boomed, exactly as it had the day Matthias had abducted her from the restaurant.

He was coming for her again. He'd take her back to Sapphire House, back to the ruins of her life, and then she would go crazy.

"Jessa." A tall, broad shadow appeared in front of her, blocking her only avenue of escape. "I've been looking for you."

She didn't recognize the voice, but it wasn't Matthias. Something crawled over her skin, a sense of wrongness, as if the shadow were some sort of nightmare she'd woken to. The man moved closer, and the smell of him struck her like a fist to the belly.

"I knew you'd get away from them," the voice said. "I could feel you thinking about and planning every little detail. Just the way you did with me."

Now she knew the voice. "Mr. Lawson?" She backed up a step. "What are you doing here?"

"Waiting for you." The shadow moved into the light, and it was Lawson, or a man who looked like him, except much bigger, with bulging limbs encased in skintight clothing. Some of his garments had begun tearing in the middle of the seams, as if his body had somehow swelled after he had dressed. He had been very well developed, she remembered from meeting him in the restaurant, but he hadn't been like this. She would have thought he was wearing some sort of padding under his clothes, except for when she looked into his eyes.

After one glance she couldn't bear to look at his face again. His eyes had turned as shiny and black as an insect's, with no visible corneas, irises, or pupils. When he smiled, she saw something long, sharp, and pointed flash.

Fangs, she thought. *He has fangs.*

"You look surprised," he said. "Did you think I wouldn't find you?"

Jessa couldn't move. "What happened to you? What did that to your eyes?"

"You did," he said. "You attacked me. You had me crippled."

"I didn't do anything—" She stopped as she remembered the attack in the restaurant. "Matthias couldn't have done this to you. I was there. I saw—"

"It was the transerum," he told her. "I went to Gen-Hance and stole it. Injecting myself with it was the only way I could repair the damage you did to my body. But I'm not angry with you anymore. You made me very strong." He lashed out, slamming his fist into the wall beside him, and left a deep crater in it as bits of smashed brick fell to the ground. "You see? I couldn't do that when I was human. You made me into a god."

Suddenly she knew everything Matthias had said was the truth. GenHance was experimenting on human beings. Somehow they'd done this. And seeing that Lawson now had fangs, she realized that maybe even the stories about the dark Kyn were true, too.

What could she say to him, now that he was like this? Was there any way to change him back to the way he had been? Her stomach rolled as she sensed that there wasn't. "Mr. Lawson—Bradford—you should be in the hospital. The doctors can help you."

"I don't need help. I'm right where I need to be, with you. I came to thank you in person." He stretched out his arms in an affectionate gesture. "Come here and I will."

Chapter 18

Matthias woke up with a throbbing head, blood in his eye, and drenched clothes. He saw the fragments of his water jug on the floor around him, checked the gash on his brow, and pushed himself slowly to his feet. The pain receded as he used his sleeve to clear his eye.

He remembered now. Jessa had pretended to be weak-kneed after the rubdown. He'd helped her to the basin. And she'd bashed him in the head so hard she'd knocked him out. Now she'd fled, and as she knew how to get to the surface, she was probably out on the streets, looking for help.

He had to find her before she was seen.

When Matthias emerged topside, he calmed himself, cleared his mind, and breathed in. Jessa had left a trail of her scent through the little kitchen garden Rowan had planted that led out to the street. He followed it, but once outside the property the scent thinned, telling him that she had broken into a run to the east.

He should have told her where she was before this. How frightened and confused she must have felt to step out into the night and see Sapphire House. To know that she had been held beneath the home in which she had been raised all this time.

He walked east, grateful only that it was still some hours until dawn. He still had a chance to track her and catch her before she exposed her presence in the city. He would explain how he had come to purchase Sapphire House at auction solely for the purpose of using its vast underground labyrinth of old smuggler's tunnels as a safe haven for Kyndred on the run.

He stopped in every place that she had, and with each step felt his skin tingle and his chest tighten. Emotion roiled inside him, snarling need mingling with fear, empathy with anger. He had become so attuned to her that he imagined he could feel her, body and soul. From the sensations he felt he guessed she was nearer to him, and she was afraid.

He lost the scent for a moment, and looked around before he realized that she had descended the stairwell leading to the riverfront. He took the steps three at a time as he hurried down and ran out onto the river walk.

Concentrating on the frighteningly acute sense of her, Matthias turned north and moved silently along the storefronts, keeping to the shadows as he looked ahead. He would not charge at her or grab her. He would call her to him. He would find the words to regain her trust. He had to.

Clouds thickened across the sky, and then he heard her scream. His muscles bunched and he broke into a flat run.

Jessa stumbled backward out of an alleyway, almost into his arms. She turned and shoved at him, but not to thrust him away.

"He's coming," she said, her eyes filled with terror. "Run. We have to run."

"Don't go, Jessa," Matthias heard a man's voice croon. "We have so much to do tonight. And tomorrow. And next week. And next month."

He saw a man coming toward them, and while he seemed normal enough, something about him made Matthias thrust Jessa behind him. "She is not for you."

"I know you." The man shuffled forward and then straightened as he studied Matthias. "You're the man she hired to cut me."

He peered at Lawson's face. "She did not hire me. I came to her aid."

"I know what she had you do. She told you to cripple me." The thing cocked its head. "Do you know they were going to put me down? Kill me, just because I'd been injured on the job. That wasn't covered in the employee benefits package. I never saw a single paragraph on reasons employees will be terminated permanently."

Matthias knew then that Lawson was crazy. His training also told him he was no match for him, not unarmed and trying to protect his woman.

"Stay close to me," he said to Jessa before he looked up to the sky and drew on the power inside him.

Lightning flashed, illuminating for a few seconds the face of the thing. Matthias recognized the features as Lawson's, but when he looked into its solid black eyes, all he saw were the depths of hell.

The clouds swelled full and ugly, and tiny drops of water and larger pellets of ice began to fall all around them. Lawson skewed his head to one side and yowled as a chunk of hail bounced off his head. Nothing touched Matthias or Jessa.

"Why isn't it hitting you?" Lawson demanded, covering his head with his hands.

"The rain belongs to me. So does the woman." Matthias lifted his eyes once more and sent out his power. An instant later a torrential flood of water came crashing down around them.

Matthias seized Jessa's hand and pulled her with him as he ran from the thing in the alley and into the blinding rain. Only his sense of the ground beneath his feet led him back to the stairwell to the upper street level. He could feel the thing coming up fast behind them, and stopped only long enough to scoop Jessa into his arms before he mounted the stairs.

She slung an arm around his neck and curled her other hand into his sleeve before she looked back over his shoulder. "He's coming up the stairs."

Matthias thought quickly, and when he reached the top of the stairs he abruptly changed direction, across the narrow street and into the long park. He headed for the small, roped-off area where the city was repairing damage done to one of the old statues in front of the Cotton Exchange.

The old lion statue, which had been struck by a driver

who had lost control of her car, had been demolished in the accident, leaving behind only a paw. Debate had raged back and forth for some time, but eventually the people of the various historical societies had agreed to replace the lion with a more modern work of art that embraced both the history of Savannah as well as its future.

Matthias had seen the replacement installed over a series of months. The ten-foot-high sculpture, made entirely of old wrought iron recovered from the factory down by the river, formed an enormous, open sphere. The long rods of iron had been stretched out into elongated strips and twisted into shapes representing the different continents of the world. On the shape representing America, the artist had welded a brass replica of a magnolia bloom.

The vanity of the past, the artist claimed, had been shaped by his hammers into a vision of Savannah as part of the global community of cities leading the way into the future.

Matthias was simply glad the sculptor had weakened the wrought-iron rods by stretching them, and had made the interior large enough for two people to stand inside. He stopped beside it and put Jessa down on her feet. Gripping two of the rods, he strained, pulling them apart.

Once he had made a space large enough for both of them to pass through, he turned to her. "Get inside."

She shook her head. "He's too strong. It won't protect us."

"It won't." He looked into her eyes. "I will."

She hesitated a moment longer, and then squeezed through the gap to step inside the sculpture. Matthias followed, turning to press the bars back in place. By the time he moved Jessa to the very center of the sphere, Lawson had reached them.

"I don't want to die again," she whispered, staring at the madman on the other side of the bars. "But you heard him. He isn't planning to kill me right away." She brought his hand up to her neck. "If it looks like he's going to take me . . . can you?"

"If I must, I will." He watched Lawson as the other man circled around the sculpture. "Only wait, Jessa."

"This is very helpful of you." Lawson bared his fangs as Matthias wrapped his arms around her. "Like monkeys in a barrel. Or was it turkeys, or fish?"

"Did you tell Genaro where we are?" Matthias asked him.

"I tell Jonah all sorts of things," the madman said. "Her name, for example—it's Minerva, not Jessa. Did you know that? Funny that she's named after a Roman goddess. When I made the final transition, I became a god myself." He stopped and peered in at them. "I don't like the way you male mortals taste. Come out of there, give her to me, and I'll let you run away again. Maybe I'll be so busy with her I even won't bother to look for you right away."

"You will have to kill me," Matthias told him, "to take her."

"I can do that." Lawson wrapped his huge fists around the iron bars and began to pull.

"Matthias."

"Close your eyes," he said softly, and waited until she did. He held her close as he did the same and lifted his face.

He sent every ounce of his power flying up into the sky directly above them, making himself the conduit and the storm the vessel. The air crackled and all the hair on his body and Jessa's rose up, drawn along with the power. A low, deep sound reverberated overhead as the storm gathered in on itself, and small white lines sizzled through the dark mass.

Power filled the sphere as a thick bolt of lightning struck the sculpture, electrifying it. Matthias looked as Bradford Lawson screamed, and millions of volts of power streamed from the iron through his hands and into his body.

Jessa kept her eyes closed, at one point burying her face against Matthias's chest, but he watched Lawson as the primeval power rammed through Lawson's limbs and arched between him and the sculpture. The jittery shaking of Lawson's body made it seem as if he were performing some grotesque sort of dance. The bolt lasted another three seconds before it vanished, and Lawson fell against the smoldering iron bars, his face a blackened, smoking ruin.

Matthias released Jessa only long enough to pry apart the bars again, and put his arm around her shoulders as he eased her out. As the pounding rain tapered to a softer shower, he glanced back at the dead man clinging to the sculpture.

"This is your ability," she said, the rain streaming down her face like a thousand tears. "You created the storm. You controlled the lightning. The same way you did the day we met, at the restaurant."

"I can bring the rain." He smoothed the drenched hair back away from her face. "Lightning is drawn to me wherever I am in the storm. If I think very hard, I can summon it."

She looked over her shoulder, stared at Lawson's body, and then turned back to him. "We can't leave him here like that."

"The authorities will find him in the morning and take him away. Whatever was done to him will be discovered. Then GenHance will come for him." He put his hand to her cheek. "We cannot know how much he told them. We must leave the city before they arrive."

"Where can we go?" she asked.

"Rowan and Drew are coming back from Atlanta. I will contact them and have them meet us at a safe place in the country. Then we will decide together where we will go." He stroked his thumb beneath her eye, catching the tear that spilled from it to mingle with the rain on her face. "There is no more time for me to chase you or talk to you. You have seen for yourself what GenHance can do. We must fight this battle together, or what was done to Lawson will be only the first of countless horrors." He put his hand on her shoulder. "Will you give your trust now? Will you stay with me?"

Jessa closed her eyes on the last of her tears before she put her hand over his. "Yes."

Rowan violated every speed limit on the highway, but she rolled into Atlanta just after dawn. Since she'd arrived too early to hit a Starbucks, she stopped at a combination gas station and food mart to top off her tank and grab something to eat.

The muddy-looking carafe of coffee at the hot-beverage station made her wrinkle her nose, but they had bottled springwater and bags of powdered sugar–covered mini-doughnuts, one of her guilty pleasures. She sat on the curb outside the store and dialed home to let Matthias know she'd made it, but he didn't pick up the line.

"How much you want to bet that he and Queenie are sharing a shower this morning?" she asked one of the doughnuts before she popped it into her mouth.

Polishing off the rest of the bag took her less than two minutes, and she washed them down with half the bottle of water before splashing her hands with the remainder. Once she'd wiped her fingers dry with her bandanna, she took out the photo of Drew Riordan and studied it.

He had pale skin like Queenie, but the glorious blaze of his spiky red hair washed out everything else in the shot. He had very dark eyes, but they didn't look black or brown. Navy blue or hunter green, she decided. He wasn't smiling, but the faint bracketed lines on either side of his very decent mouth made it obvious he did, and often. The hump from a broken nose—probably from a schoolyard brawl with some kid who'd called him Bozo—didn't spoil his face. Neither did the beard he wore trimmed close to the square angles of his jaw.

"Irish," she murmured. With a name like Riordan, that was a given, although he'd been adopted out like the rest of them. "Your parents probably picked you because you had the right color hair."

She tucked away the photo and stood, brushing the light dusting of crumbs and powdered sugar from the front of her jacket. On impulse she tried dialing Matthias's mobile number, but that went almost immediately to voice mail.

"This is Ro," she said after the tone. "It's morning, and I'm here. I'll call in later when I hook up with Drew. And I'm worried, so answer one of the phones next time, okay?"

She pocketed her phone and blew out a frustrated breath. Queenie might be a champion conniver, but she wouldn't do anything to Matt. For one thing, she couldn't—the boss had serious muscle and skill, and he could take her down with one hand tied behind his back. She also didn't think Queenie would try to screw with him, at least not physically. She watched him the same way he watched her, and while her expression never gave away anything, the eyes said it all.

"Face it: They're about to become a couple, and you have to deal with it," she said to herself as she walked to her bike. "She's classy, and he deserves her. But she'll never feed him as well as you have."

Nor would she ever deserve him. None of them did.

She nodded to an older man at the next pump who was filling up his Lexus, and had just straddled her bike when her phone rang.

She answered it without checking the display. "About time, boss."

"I'm sorry, but I'm not your boss," a soft, feminine voice said. "This isn't even my phone. It belongs to my boyfriend, Andy."

Rowan checked the display, which showed Drew's mobile number. "What's up, Andy's girlfriend?"

"I hate to bother you," she said, "but his family has been calling here all night trying to reach him. There's some kind of emergency back at home, and they need to speak to him right away, but this is the only phone he carried with him, and honestly, I have no idea where he is today. I thought I'd try some of his friends and see if they could get a message to him for me."

"Good try, bitch," Rowan said, checking her watch. It would take the people monitoring the call another two minutes to track her signal.

"Excuse me?" the girl said faintly.

"Come on, you people are supposed to be better than this," she taunted. "That's not the only phone he has. He has no family and, oops, his name isn't even Andy."

The sweet tone became crisp. "Mr. Riordan is in a great deal of legal trouble. We know he's responsible for destroying company property as well as flagrantly violating the confidentiality clause in his employment contract."

"Flagrantly." Rowan was sorry to see she had only forty seconds left; she was really beginning to enjoy herself. "That's a beautiful word. They send you to corporate pretty-speak school or something, babe?"

"We assume Mr. Riordan is your friend," the woman continued, her tone tight and unfriendly now. "If he wants to avoid a lengthy prison term, he must return to Gen-Hance at once. Perhaps you could—"

Rowan made a dinging sound. "Whoops, time's up. Give Jonah this message: Andy says he can go fuck himself." With five seconds to spare Rowan switched off her phone, pulled off the back, and popped out the battery, heaving it into the road. The phone she wiped clean before dropping it into the courtesy container of window cleaner beside the pump.

The old man at the Lexus gave her a cautious look. "Everything okay there, miss?"

Rowan bared her teeth. "Just found out my boyfriend's cheating on me."

"Then he's an idiot, honey." He gave her an admiring look, and for a moment she could see the handsome young man he had been. "I'd dump him. I'd make him pay for the phone, too."

She gave him a genuine smile this time. "Oh, yes, sir. He's going to pay. He surely is."

Chapter 19

Genaro listened to the recording of the girl's voice for a third time, switching it off just before she uttered her obscene message meant for him.

"She must have destroyed the phone immediately after she ended the call, sir," Delaporte said. "It's the only way she could have terminated the signal before we located her. We know she was somewhere downtown, so she's in the city."

He suspected Riordan wasn't working alone, but the girl's speedy arrival meant that his cohorts were well organized. "What were you able to glean from the background noise?"

"The beeps are from a gas pump being used," Bill, the technician who had assumed Riordan's position, said. "There're also two repeating tones from an audible walk signal used exclusively in the business district. The station was on a corner at an intersection with a pedestrian crossing, and there are only two of those in that area."

"Obtain the security videos from both stations, and interview the clerks," he told Delaporte. "I want to know what she looks like and what she's driving." He turned to Bill. "What other numbers were you able to salvage from Riordan's SIM card?"

"Just that one, sir. The rest of the data was too badly corrupted by the virus he triggered." He shuffled his weight from one foot to the other. "Sir, I know it's not my place, but I can't believe Andy had anything to do with this. Maybe someone blackmailed him, or . . ." He saw Genaro's expression and paled. "Right. Well, I think I'll get back and try to run the SIM card again."

Delaporte watched the younger man flee from the office. "I recommend we put someone else in Riordan's position."

"He'll do for now." Genaro saw his private-line light flash and picked up the phone. "What is it?" He listened as one of the police captains, a man with a predilection for very young girls, related two reports that had come in from the authorities in the eastern section of the state. "Fax all of the witness statements to us at once, and keep me updated." He hung up the receiver. "Lawson was seen in Savannah last night. He confronted Jessa Bellamy and the man who took her from the restaurant, and shortly after was struck by lightning."

"Lightning?" Delaporte's brows rose. "He's dead, then."

"He was for several hours," Genaro said, and templed his fingers. "Lawson revived this morning and killed three people working in the county morgue. Shortly thereafter he was seen down at the docks, where he hijacked a truck."

"What interests me is the man with Bellamy. There was a lightning storm the day Lawson tried to retrieve her at the restaurant."

"If he's one of them, and he has control over weather . . ." His security chief sighed. "We've never encountered one with that kind of ability, sir."

"He could be a progenitor." Genaro stood. "We will need to contain Lawson now. Tell your men to use whatever force is necessary, but get him out of the truck first."

"It would be simpler to shoot him while he's driving, sir."

"The truck is a tanker used to fuel ships," he told him. "It's filled with enough high-grade marine fuel to take out a city block."

"We'll get him out of the truck first, sir," Delaporte promised.

Genaro went to the lab, where Kirchner was working

with one of the engineers on the new containment unit. "We're bringing Lawson in today," he told him after sending the engineer out of the cell. "You'll need to be ready to process him."

"We will, sir." The doctor picked up a chart and took out his pen to make some notes. "I'd like to do a full workup on him if there's time."

"He survived a lightning strike," Genaro told him.

Kirchner stopped writing and glanced up. "A direct hit?"

"Apparently so. He was pronounced dead and transported to the morgue, where he revived a few hours later. I'll send over the reports as soon as they arrive. You'll need to investigate this further."

"Sir, the transerum does have its limitations," the doctor said. "The resurrection factor is directly related to pathogen stimulation. The death of the host effectively ends the dormant stage. We've never known a host to survive a second death experience." His cold eyes grew dreamy. "Unless a new mutation has occurred that revives the host indefinitely."

"I am not in the business of selling eternity, Doctor," Genaro said. "There's no profit in immortality. Whatever is responsible for Lawson's third rebirth, I want it identified and eradicated from the transerum. You will report on this only to me; is that understood?"

Kirchner looked as if he wanted to argue with him, but in the end he nodded and went back to his work.

Genaro stopped by the isolation room, where the acquisition lay in a chemically induced coma. He came several times during the week to inspect the condition of the body, which was being kept in peak condition by the physical therapists on staff. That and the complex network of equipment surrounding the bed would keep the body alive and healthy indefinitely.

He'd ordered Kirchner to remove the bandages from the lower half of the battered face, and the bruises and cuts around the nose and mouth were slowly healing. Extensive cosmetic work still had to be performed, but that could wait until they were prepared to bring the body back to consciousness.

Because the acquisition had no mind, it wasn't a person anymore, and was referred to only in terms used for laboratory specimens. It allowed his people to work without unnecessary sentiment or attachment, but the day would soon come when the body would again become a person, and would need a new name.

It was like being God, Genaro thought, and creating the first man.

"Adam," he said to the body. "That is what we'll call you."

He turned and left the room, unaware that under the bandages, the eyes of the body moved beneath their lids, as if watching something no one else could see.

The place in the country Matthias drove to was a bed-and-breakfast located in a farming district near the border of Tennessee. He didn't stop along the way, but she was glad he didn't. Watching Savannah disappear in the rearview mirror was like waking up from a sad dream. They didn't talk during the drive, either, but after the encounter with Lawson and the revelation of Matthias's ability, Jessa felt almost numb. Discussing anything would have been beyond her, and he must have sensed that.

Matthias came around the car to help her out, and kept an arm around her waist as he walked with her to meet the older couple who had emerged from the inn.

"Jessa, these are my friends, Sarah and Paul Clark." He turned to the couple. "I am sorry we woke you so early."

"Nonsense, Gaven," the woman said, reaching for him with open arms. She had black hair streaked with silver and features that reminded Jessa of her favorite language teacher in school. Her smile turned wry as she turned to Jessa. "Welcome to Clarks' Bed-and-Breakfast."

"It's nice to meet you." Jessa kept her hands in her pockets.

The tall, stoop-shouldered man nodded to Jessa. His expression was more reserved, but he had kind eyes and shook hands with Matthias with enthusiasm. "Good to see you, Matt." He looked past them. "No one on the road for twenty miles."

Jessa looked back. She could see almost a mile down the road, but then the asphalt disappeared over a sloping hill.

"My husband was an eagle in his past life," Sarah joked.

Jessa glanced at Matthias. "They're like us." He nodded, and she eyed Sarah's hair a second time. The couple appeared too old to be Kyndred, and yet their voices sounded very young.

"She's very intuitive, Gaven," Sarah said. "I guess this isn't necessary." The air around her seemed to split in half, sweeping away the image of the older couple, leaving two strangers in its place: a plain-faced, skinny woman with strawberry blond hair, and a dark-skinned, wide-bodied man with a shaved skull and eyes that were the color of ripe cantaloupe. For a moment she thought he was blind, until she saw the pinpoints of his pupils, which were tightly constricted. Both appeared to be in their late twenties.

"My wife likes to play dress-up." Paul's oddly colored eyes shifted as he studied Jessa's face. "Sarah is also very tactile, so you should tell her."

She drew back a little. "You can see what I'm thinking?"

"I can see the tension in your facial muscles increase whenever ability is mentioned." He smiled. "You've also discreetly avoided touching us."

She'd never admitted her ability to anyone but the Takyn. For a moment she struggled with the words. "When I touch someone, I have a vision and see the things they've done that were wrong, or made them feel guilty. Whether they want me to or not. Exactly when, where, and how it happened."

Rather than look repelled, Paul smiled. "I'd better tell you the story about that car I boosted when I was sixteen, and the time Sarah dressed up as Cindy Crawford for our anniversary."

"It's all right, Jessa." Sarah chuckled at her expression. "We don't keep secrets from each other, and now that you're here, we can't. Come inside now so I can feed you two."

Inside the large, well-equipped kitchen Sarah expertly prepared a hot breakfast of pecan-studded pancakes, sliced peaches, and fragrant chamomile tea. She happily accepted Jessa's offer to set the table while Matthias told Paul about Drew Riordan being exposed, Rowan's trip to Atlanta, and the terrifying encounter with Lawson.

"You'll need to go to the farm, Matt," Jessa heard Paul say. "Sarah and I will drive you all out tomorrow."

"Where is the farm?" she asked Sarah.

"It's a place Gaven owns in central Tennessee. He spends time there every spring and summer, grows organic produce, and gets away from all that." She made a vague gesture toward the north. "When Paul and I met him, we'd just lost everything—GenHance seized our costume business, called in the note on our house, cleaned out our accounts, and had us both charged with income tax evasion. If Paul hadn't seen them coming, they probably would have gotten us, too."

"How did you end up here?"

"Matthias didn't tell you? He owns this place." Her eyes twinkled. "He has about two hundred different properties all over the country. He asked us if we'd like to run an inn, and since Paul and I like people, and we've always dreamed of having a little country house, it seemed perfect."

"I'm not the first one he's brought here," Jessa guessed.

"He brings us others from time to time. The ones who are almost ready to relocate and take up new identities. It gives them a little break before they have to become someone else." Sarah handed her a platter with three tall stacks of pancakes. "Serve yourself first, or the guys won't leave you a crumb."

Over pancakes Sarah told them some funny stories about some of their guests. Jessa winced as she heard about the newlyweds who had gone for a nature walk, succumbed to a moment of passion, and ended up with a case of poison ivy in the worst possible places. Paul contributed his tale of the New York executive who had been grimly determined to ride one of their horses and have photos taken to show his friends back in the city, at least until he slid off the back of the horse and sprained his tailbone.

Matthias excused himself from the table so that he could use the Clarks' phone to contact Rowan, leaving Jessa alone with the couple.

Jessa wanted to ask Sarah more details about her life and her ability, but didn't quite know how. She'd spent so many years hiding her own that she had no idea how to even initiate such a conversation.

Once more Paul saw her anxiety. "I think Jessa would like to hear about something other than our fun with the guests."

She gave him a grateful look. "Other than Matthias and Rowan, I've never met others like me in person. I have so many questions. Do you mind?"

"Not at all," Paul told her. "Ask away."

"How did you two meet each other?"

Sarah grimaced. "It was pretty typical of how people like us usually hook up. Paul and I met through a social group for single adults searching for their biological parents. We hit it off, compared notes, and found out we had a lot in common."

"Sarah and I were probably born in Chicago," Paul put in. "That's where we were both adopted as infants. Most of the records were lost, but we know the Catholic Church was involved in placing us. We also made sure we weren't related before we got romantically involved."

"Thank heavens for mail-away DNA tests," Sarah said.

"We both went to good families and had normal childhoods, at least until I was hit by a car when I was twelve, and Sarah contracted meningitis when she was sixteen. We both should have died, but instead we came back, better than new." He gestured toward his face. "My eyes used to be brown. The doctors thought the brain hemorrhaging caused the change in the color of my irises." He glanced at his wife. "Sarah did better. She kept her ability a secret from everyone."

"It wasn't hard," she said, and the air wavered around

her as her image blurred and changed into that of a wide-eyed, stocky man in a white lab coat. "This doctor was the only one who ever caught me dressing up," he said in Sarah's voice, "and he quit drinking the same day." The air parted, restoring her to her normal appearance.

Jessa had watched the transformation more closely this time. "You don't actually change shape."

"I wish I could. I'd definitely do something about this mug of mine." She patted her angular cheek. "What we think I do is alter the light around me so what you see is how I want to appear to you. I can also cast an illusion that changes the appearance of anyone within five feet of me, which is how I can do this." The air around the table wavered, and suddenly Jessa saw two Sarahs sitting at the table. She laughed as she looked down at herself and saw that she had been changed into a Sarah clone as well.

"That is amazing," she said.

"It's just a brain trick," Sarah said, dispelling the illusion. "It doesn't fool Paul, because he can see the shifts in light intensity whenever I dress up. I need the light, too; I can't use my ability in complete darkness. Also, my body stays the same. So while you may see Paris Hilton"—she changed into an exact twin of the famous socialite—"what you get is still plain old Sarah Clark." She dropped the illusion.

Jessa's head started to whirl from watching all the rapid changes. "Using your ability doesn't make you tired?"

"Just the opposite. I always feel terrific afterward. Hungry sometimes." She nodded toward her husband. "Orangesicle Eyes here, on the other hand, can give himself a three-day migraine when he overdoes it."

"My retinas sometimes take in more information than my brain can handle," Paul explained. "That's what triggers the headaches. Fortunately I've learned how to control the dilation of my pupils. I look with my ability only when I really need to see."

"Can you see through things? Is that how you could tell no one was on the road this morning?" Jessa asked.

"No, my vision functions on line of sight, just like everyone else's." He pointed up. "But I can detect thermal disruption in the air from engine exhaust, body temperature, or any heat-producing source up to fifty miles away."

"You both seem so normal," Jessa said before she thought. "What I mean is, you seem to have accepted this so well."

"I had some problems when I was younger," Sarah said, her smile fading a little. "Every girl wants to be prettier, and God knows I'm not a beauty. I used an illusion to get the cutest guy on campus. I almost married him, until I decided a week before the wedding to have him meet the real Sarah to see if he really loved me or the illusion. He freaked out and accused me of giving him drugs. Then he spit in my face and left me." She met Jessa's gaze. "That's the worst thing I've ever done, in case you're worried about bumping into me."

"It was the best, too." Paul reached over and took her hand in his. "You could have kept up the illusion for the rest of your lives. He would have never known."

"Everything happens for a reason." She smiled at her husband. "You'd think a guy with eagle eyes would take one look at me and run the other way, but this one didn't."

"I saw what was really beautiful." He lifted her hand and kissed the back of it. "First time you smiled at me, baby."

Matthias rejoined them. When Jessa asked after Rowan, he said he had been unable to reach her, but left a message on her voice mail telling her about their new location.

"We're not expecting anyone to come in for a week," Sarah told Matthias as the men cleared the table. "Paul and I are going to make a run to town for supplies and maybe see a movie, so you'll have the place to yourselves most of the day."

"We're going to see a movie?" Jessa heard Paul murmur to his wife as she joined him at the sink.

"Of course we are. That double feature sounds good." She nudged him with her elbow, and in a lower, scolding tone added, "Some people need some alone time."

Paul smiled at her. "Will you make out with me in the back row?"

"Keep it up, smart guy, and I'll go as your grandmother," Sarah warned.

The couple showed them to two adjoining rooms, and after setting out fresh linens and clean clothes, and telling them what they could find in the kitchen for lunch and dinner, the Clarks left for town in their old pickup.

Jessa retreated to the bathroom, where she showered and tried not to imagine Matthias doing the same in his. She should have been ready to drop, but now that they were alone she felt as if she'd arrived at some new and slightly terrifying place. The feeling didn't go away when she wrapped herself in a big towel, came out into her bedroom, and looked at the adjoining door to his. It was locked on her side, so the choice was hers.

Just as he'd told her it would be.

He'd saved her life twice now. He'd protected her, first from GenHance and then from the monster that Bradford Lawson had become. He had brought her here, and wherever they were going next, she knew she'd be safe with him.

Gratitude didn't make her release the dead bolt.

She'd loved Tag. He'd made everything fun, even the first time they'd made love, when he'd joked about letting her kick him in the groin afterward to make things even. A few years after losing him, she'd tried with other men, the ones she could bear to touch. She'd even considered taking Caleb as a lover until she'd discovered his guilty crush on Angela. Jessa knew what it was to wish, and to want, and to have, but she'd never known it with the intensity that Matthias brought out in her.

It wasn't lust or loneliness that made her open the door. He'd come to her in her dreams, where she had fallen in love with him, and now she was awake, and she wanted him.

Jessa wasn't surprised to see him standing just on the other side, wearing a towel around his hips.

"You should sleep." His eyes never left her face.

He hadn't dried off but dripped with water, as if he'd felt her there and walked out of the shower to meet her.

"I'm not tired."

He didn't move. "You have not truly looked inside me. There is more to me than what you have seen."

"I know who you are." She stepped over the threshold. "You're a stranger, and a friend, and a protector. You've come to me in the night, in my dreams. Matthias, you're the man I'm going to love for the rest of my life."

He couldn't seem to speak. His chest expanded as he inhaled, held the breath, and slowly released it. Then he knelt on one knee before her, and pressed his face into her abdomen, and wrapped his arms around her legs. She looked down at the sunlight gilding the wet, gleaming strands of his hair and put her hand to the back of his head, stroking it as the wonder of the moment shimmered over her.

No shadowlight. Only sunlight. Only love.

When he rose he lifted her, shifting his arms so that he supported her shoulders, and held her as he crossed the room. Placing her gently on the edge of the bed, he knelt again, smoothing his hands down her arms before he tugged free the fold that held the big towel around her.

Jessa kept her hands at her sides and hoped he liked what he saw.

He unwrapped her like a gift, lifting her a little to pull the towel free before he dropped it to the floor. A big hand splayed over her spine, and as he came up he eased her back, bracing himself over her on his elbows.

Jessa reached between them to pull away the last thing keeping their skin apart, and brushed the shaft of his stiff, thick penis with her knuckles as she pushed the towel over his buttocks until it slipped away. Matthias's tense body shook as he bent his head, tasting her mouth with his.

The kiss was slow and soft and made lights dance inside her head.

She felt his hand stroke down the side of her body before he caught the back of her thigh and brought it up to cradle his hip. She did the same with the other, and forgot to breathe as she felt him nestling against her, the hot, straining knob of his cock pressing into the wet silk of her folds. She could feel her labia flowering open to him, caressing and enveloping him, and in reflex she tightened, holding him there a moment longer so she could savor, so she could remember.

Jessa didn't realize her eyes were closed until he kissed one lid and then the other. She looked up at him, saw herself in his eyes, and lifted her face so she could give him her mouth as he gathered her up with his arm. She opened for his tongue, soothing the hard thrust of it with sweet strokes of her own, and then he drove inside her, wide and hard, deep and unstoppable.

That first, astonishing stroke seemed endless; he kept pressing in, taking and filling until some primal sound rose from her throat and he touched the heart of her sex. Celibacy had kept her almost as narrow and tight as she had been the first time, and the tender, vulnerable flesh inside her body contracted around him, trying to accommodate the ruthless penetration as well as hold him in place. The stretching, burning sensations within brought on a rush of simple, feminine fear. Could he feel how tightly they fit? Would he know how easily he could hurt her?

"You are as tender as a maiden." He rolled onto his side, bringing her over onto hers and relieving some of the internal pressure. "Put your hands on my shoulders."

Jessa slid her hands up and looked down as he put his hands over her breasts. The dark gold of his skin against the whiteness of hers made her arch against his palms, but when he worked his fingers over her, rubbing and squeezing and fondling with the same strange technique he had used on her feet, something unraveled inside her.

"You have very fine breasts," he told her. "It will give me pleasure to watch our son suckle them."

Strangely that thought aroused her as much as his touch. "I'm not pregnant."

His mouth curved. "I will fuck you and give you my seed until you are."

That outrageous statement dumbfounded Jessa. It also filled her with wild delight.

He moved his thumbs against the tight beads of her nipples, abrading them lightly before he lowered his head and took the left peak into his mouth. He dampened it with his tongue before he sucked, tugging with a firm rhythm that made her forget about the slight discomfort between her thighs and the slight motion of his shaft inside her.

The movement of his cock into the ellipse of her sex made the sound of a gentle kiss, and then a passionate one.

He eased his mouth away and draped her thigh over his hip, holding it there as he braced her. His other hand he wedged between them, pressing the tip of his middle finger into the split at the top of her mound. He quickly found the small ridge of her hood and pressed again, this time to expose her clit.

"Oh, God." She jerked as he massaged her there, and drove herself down on his penis, working it deeper into her drenched sex.

"Do you hurt anymore?" he asked her, his jaw set.

Trembling on the brink of an orgasm, she shook her head and clutched at him. "Gaven, please."

He rolled her onto her back, rocked his hips to spread her thighs wider, and stroked in deep. This time her sex accepted every hard inch he gave her, and pulled at him, eager and needy. He kept his thrusts slow but deep, the bed shaking under them from the heavy, powerful pistoning of his body into hers. He reached between them again to finger her clit, and that shoved her over the edge.

If pleasure were an abyss, it didn't have a bottom. Not with Matthias. Jessa tumbled through the dark heat and dancing light, lost to herself, found again in his arms.

Matthias kept at her, fucking her through the climax as she rode it out, and then through the tremors to the building of the next. She writhed, trying to free her hands so she could touch him, but he had her wrists pinned and held her there, at the mercy of his relentless cock. Jessa wrapped her legs around his hips and thrust back at him, rubbing as much of her body against him as she could.

The second time she came, she tightened around him, forcing him to feel every ripple, and, before he could resist, taking him with her into that beautiful darkness.

Into the shadowlight.

Chapter 20

Matthias knew the greatest pleasure of his life in Jessa's arms. Her body accepted his, although at first it took some coaxing, and permitted him to worship her with all the passion he felt. As soon as he spilled his seed into her, he felt the glow of life beginning. This day, this very first time together, he had given her his son.

He opened his eyes to look upon her face, and instead saw the wilderness around him. Immense old trees, their bare, blackened limbs made glassy with ice, stood as sentries and witnesses to what a few months ago had been a field of grain. Snow drifted down, gently shrouding dozens of bodies where they had fallen. Barbarians cut to pieces by blows from expert hands wielding the finest blades in the world. Romans impaled on sharpened stakes and pierced by hundreds of hastily made arrows.

Matthias didn't have to count the dead. He knew the name of every Roman whose body littered the ancient battlefield. But he could not be here. The gods would not be so cruel as to tear him from his lover's arms and send him to this place. He did not believe his eyes, not until he saw the lone, hunched figure of one of the fallen rise, stumbling over the bodies as he went from man to man, reaching for the throat of every Roman.

Looking for life in the kingdom of the dead.

Tanicus peered at him from across the field, but Matthias knew he didn't see him. Still he tried to call out to him, to warn him before the arrows began to fly out of the forest. But Tanicus kept moving, performing his grim task, his breath leaving white clouds in the still air, the blood from his side wound streaming down to paint his legs with thin red streaks.

Once more Matthias stood frozen in time, unable to move or do more than watch as the arrows came and struck the Roman. Then came the barbarians from the trees, slinking out of their hiding places, and one who stood taller and strode with a different pace.

The courier from Judea, the one who had been a centurion, now dressed in the furs and wools of Rome's enemy.

The courier went to Tanicus, who had been driven to his knees. He lifted his fur-wrapped sandal and kicked the Roman over.

"You should have remained in camp, Prefect." He gestured, and his creatures surrounded the Roman, stripping him of his cuirass and braces while the courier drew his sword. "Have no fear. I will give you a proper burning, and send you with your men to Elysium."

Matthias roared in silent rage as the traitor braced his foot against the strong neck of the fallen Roman and drove his sword into Tanicus's chest. Then he saw what the dying soldier could not: a border patrol charging toward the battlefield from the south. The traitor looked up, his face twisting with fear, and tried to pull his sword from the Roman's body.

With the last of his strength, Tanicus reached up, grasping the blade with both hands, holding it in place.

Out of time, the traitor barked orders to his men, and they fled back into the trees. Only when they had gone did Tanicus release the blade, his gashed hands falling on either side of his body, the bloody palms open to the sun.

Matthias tried to close his eyes, but something would not permit it. The patrol went into the woods after the barbarians, and the field became still and lifeless again. The sun raced across the sky, following them as twilight settled over the battlefield. Then two hands twitched, curled, and reached up to grasp the traitor's blade a second time.

Tanicus wrenched the sword out of his chest, using it as

a brace to push himself up. He tore at his under tunic, and watched with wide eyes as the wound in the center of his chest stopped bleeding and began to seal itself. Still holding the blade, the Roman staggered to his feet.

Tanicus knelt by the body of one large Roman, rested his hand on the man's chest, and murmured a prayer, and then carefully removed the cloak tangled under his body. He did the same to other men, wrapping himself in their cloaks before he used a saddle blanket that had fallen to the ground to wrap up the sword. He had to take it with him, for it was the only real proof he had that the courier from Judea was betraying his people to their enemy.

Tanicus turned around and changed direction, trudging toward the trail leading up into the mountains. Matthias knew, as the Roman did, that the border patrol's camp lay on the other side of the ridge, and the high pass through the mountains was the quickest route to it.

Snow began to fall as Tanicus walked up the trail. He pulled the cloaks tighter around himself and covered his head, but the storm came fast, as they often did in the high places. Soon the Roman was battling his way through roaring wind and pelting ice, his head down, his arm clamped around the bundle that held the sword.

He never heard the snow above him break loose, and stopped only as the first edge of it engulfed his legs. The massive drift knocked him off his feet and pushed him into the boulders on the opposite side of the pass, where he disappeared under tons of ice and rock.

Time passed. The pass remained buried in snow, which never completely melted away. Romans marched through the pass, and then barbarians came from the other direction, leading their army. The sky brightened and darkened, the light coming and going faster and faster. Blurs of bodies moved through the pass. Sometimes Matthias could catch glimpses of them and their strange dress, while the snow sloping on both sides of the pass gradually grew steeper.

The second avalanche came, pouring through the pass and scouring it clean. On a slope beyond, a group of young people huddled to one side, watching with fearful eyes as the tumbling ice streamed past them, leaving behind the still form of a man. The snow took with it the remnants of ancient woolen clothing, which had long ago rotted away from his body.

They babbled in their strange tongues as they hurried over to the man and pulled him from the snow. He opened his eyes and looked upon the faces of these children, whose speech he could not understand, and whose clothing and gear were unlike anything he had ever known. One of the young men offered him a hand and an encouraging smile.

Tanicus, the Roman who had been betrayed, who died twice, first at the hand of the traitor, and then on the whim of the gods, lifted his arm and took his hand.

You were the Roman buried in the snow.

Matthias looked at the woman standing beside him, watching the rescue. It was Jessa, and it was she, not the gods, who had brought him here.

Yes. I am Gaius Maelius Tanicus.

Jessa came out of the shadowlight into the sunlight, her body wrapped around Matthias's. She didn't know how she had taken him with her into the vision of what had been, but he had been there with her and watched everything that had happened to him in the distant past. Fate had brought the man she loved to her through time.

"I'm sorry." And she was, for putting him through that. "I didn't mean to take you there with me."

He was watching her, his eyes dark with the shadows of that past. "I wish that I had told you first. I knew you would not believe me."

"Some things have to be seen to be believed." She stroked his face with wondering fingertips. "You were buried for so long. It must have terrified you to wake up in our world."

"I thought at first I was in some other place. Elysium, perhaps." He smiled a little. "The children who found me were so young and kind. But they had so many strange things, and their language—I could not fathom more than a few words. From there they took me down to the village and I saw the land beyond the strange dwellings and roads. Land does not change so much over time. I knew when I saw the ridge behind me that I stood where the border patrol's camp had once been. But it was gone. Everything I knew had vanished."

Matthias told her how he had kept silent and accepted the help of the people who had taken him in, although it had been most difficult when the doctor had come to examine him, and he got his first look at modern medical instruments.

"The wounds in my chest and on my hands and side were no longer there, and had left no scars. It was as if they had never happened," he said. "I had grown thin, and my limbs were weak, but after the people gave me a meal I felt strong again. I borrowed some clothing and ropes and went back up on the mountain. I found the traitor's sword in the snow, and what was left of the purse I had carried. I came down and gave the young men some coins in return for their kindness. Then I left and followed the road south, to Rome."

Jessa learned it had taken him several weeks to make the journey, and along the way he picked up enough of the modern version of Italian to make himself understood. He found an antiquities dealer and traded one more of his coins for the odd paper money everyone used, and traded that for food, rooms, and better clothing.

"I knew what had happened to me only when I came to the city," Matthias said. "The Rome I knew no longer existed. What buildings I remembered had become crumbling ruins. The ancient statues of the city bore the likeness of many of the noblemen I had known and served. The first numbers I learned were to tell the year: 1998. I had slept on the mountain, in the ice, dreaming of rain for almost two thousand years."

"Why did you dream of rain?"

"I cannot say. But that is all I remember from my sleep." His gaze grew distant. "Endless dreams of rain."

"You must have known on some level that you were buried alive," Jessa said. "Perhaps you simply wanted the snow to melt away, so that you could be free again." She

propped herself on one elbow. "You were Kyndred before
the avalanche. That must be what allowed you to survive all
those centuries buried in the snow."

"I had no power over the storms when I served the emperor," he said, shaking his head. "I was an ordinary man.
A soldier. I did not discover my ability until sometime after
I woke to this world, when a man tried to rob me. Then it
seemed to come out of me on its own. The thief was struck
down by hail that never touched me. The rain came down
for hours after he fell."

Jessa realized something. "You must be the very first
Kyndred."

"I have never found another from my time," he said. "Even
the old ones, the dark Kyn, they came into this world centuries after my first life." He rolled onto his back and stared at
the ceiling. "The courier who tried to slay me on the battlefield . . . he escaped that day. In time I found accounts of him
in the history books. They say he was elevated through the
ranks of the army, and later was named a senator of Rome.
He grew wealthy and powerful, until he was struck down by
a plague, but his sons carried on his cursed name, and passed
it through all their generations to this time."

Jessa frowned as she felt a peculiar twinge inside her
head, like the beginning of a bad headache. "What was his
name?"

"Septus Janus Genarius," he told her. "Jonah Genaro is
his last living descendant." He glanced at her and sat up.
"Jessa?"

She pressed the heels of her hands to her temples.
"Something's wrong. I can feel . . ." She trailed off as her
stomach surged and she fought against the alien sensation.
"It's Lawson."

"Lawson is dead."

"No. He survived." She looked at him. "He can feel me,
the same way I can feel him. He's coming here, Matthias.
He's coming to kill both of us."

Rowan left her bike under a tree by the pretty fountain in
Price Park and scanned the area. A couple of people with

dogs were walking on the other side of the grounds, but she saw no one else. She checked her watch, and saw it was two minutes to noon.

"You'd better show, Drew," she muttered, "or I'm going to be pissed at you forever."

"What else is new?" a voice said from above.

Rowan tilted her head back and saw a man standing in the tree over her bike. "What are you doing up there, you idiot?"

"Maintaining cover, smart-ass." He jumped, dropping down twelve feet before landing neatly beside her. "Were you followed?"

"Am I six years old?" she countered.

"No." He looked her over. "Sixteen, maybe."

"Twenty-one and legal, thank you very much." She shoved her spare helmet into his hands. "Hop on. We've got a lot of road to cover."

Something whizzed past her cheek and thunked against the tree. Two more things zipped past her nose before Drew knocked her to the ground.

Drew seized the back of her collar. "Keep your head down and crawl," he said. "Behind the fountain. Move it."

Rowan crawled, ducking again as more bullets hit the tree where she'd just been standing.

"I wasn't followed," she insisted as she got behind the fountain and huddled next to Drew. "They must have been tailing you."

"If they'd spotted me," he said, "I'd already be lying on a slab at GenHance." He looked up as something pinged against the metal sculpture, and grinned. "Oh. We're okay."

Rowan stared at him. "We're being shot at. We're unarmed. We're about to be killed or taken, or both. Probably both. We're *screwed*, is what we are, Andrew."

"Have faith, baby girl." He lifted his head and looked toward the source of the shots before ducking down. "Do you have any pennies?"

"A couple thousand in a jar back home," she snapped. "Tossing one in the fountain and making a wish will not make the bad guys go away. Just FYI."

Drew shoved his hand into her hip pocket and pulled out a handful of change. He sorted out the silver and dropped it, curling his fingers over the remaining pennies.

"So your bike, is it pretty good on gas?" he asked in a conversational tone. "I've been thinking about getting one for years, but with gas prices the way they are, it seems like the right time."

"You're crazy. That's it. I'm going to die with a crazy man." She folded her arms over her waist. "Well, at least I never slept with you."

"You're going to live long and prosper, baby girl. And you never know." Drew made a V sign with his fingers, winked, and stood. "Hold your fire," he shouted at the men crossing the park. He held up his arms. "We're not armed. We surrender."

Rowan grabbed the leg of his jeans. "Hey. I'm not surrendering, you nitwit."

"Get up and raise your hands," he said out of the side of his mouth. "So the nice shooters *think* that you are."

Rowan realized something, rose, and stood beside him, holding her hands in view. "The fucking fountain is made of copper."

"Uh-huh." He lowered the fist holding the pennies and pretended to rub his nose, while the fountain began to shake.

She sniffed. "You could have mentioned it before."

"And spoil the fun?" Drew glanced at her, his eyes glittering like two new pennies. "I thought you'd be more of a wild biker chick. You sound just like my mother."

Rowan watched the men advancing on them. "Four of them."

"Yep."

"What are you going to do about the guns?"

He opened his palm and the pennies in it began to float around his fingers. "Put a cork in them."

The fountain stopped shaking and produced an eerie whine as the copper basin began undulating.

The shooters stopped a few feet away from the fountain and aimed for their heads.

"Guys." Drew smiled. "Put down the guns, turn around, and walk away."

One of the men laughed. None of them moved.

Drew sighed. "It never works in the movies, either."

The pennies streaked away from his hand, moving so fast Rowan couldn't follow them. One man's gun exploded in his hand, and as the blast knocked him backward the others dropped their guns and shouted, seizing their bloody hands, in which Rowan saw penny-size wounds.

"Shit, Drew, you only hit one out of four."

"I got their hands, didn't I?" He scowled at her. "You try ramming a penny down the barrel of a weapon from thirty yards away; *then* you can complain about my aim."

She chuckled. "Okay, it was pretty cool."

"And everyone says pennies are worthless." Drew touched the basin of the fountain and slowly raised his hands like a magician trying to conjure. The copper screamed as it flared up as if molten, shedding flakes of green rust as the water it contained poured out and flooded the ground.

The uneven wall of copper split in two, then four, then eight sections before they lifted into the air and stretched out over the four men. Each of the copper strips wove through the others before the ends drove themselves into the ground. Drew sent more copper from the fountain to reinforce the strips, until he had fashioned a crude but effective cage around the shooters.

Rowan heard a shout, and looked over at a white-faced man who had stopped at the curb and was peering through the open window of his car. "Call nine-one-one," she yelled to him. "These terrible men have vandalized the park."

The man gunned his car and sped off.

"No one wants to do the right damn thing anymore." Rowan walked over to the cage, reached in, and grabbed the uninjured hand of the man closest to her. The image of a voluptuous, Marilyn Monroe–type blonde in a tight sequined dress filled her head, and her body went into shift. A moment later she pouted her red lips and looked into the man's wide eyes.

"Honeybunch, how could you shoot at me?" she said.

"Rosie, I swear I didn't see you." Caught up in the vision of the woman he loved, the shooter smiled. "I thought you were back in LA."

"I was too lonely for you, sweetie pie." Rowan leaned close. "How did you find us? Who else is going to try to hurt me?"

The man's eyes glazed over. "We tracked the bike. Teams all over the city." He grunted as one of the other men slammed a fist into the side of his head, and he slumped back.

"You can't get away," the second man told her. "You're dead."

Rowan stood, shifting back into herself as she turned to Drew. "What?"

The side of his mouth curled. "Can you do the blonde again? Maybe for the rest of the day?"

"Shut up." She walked past him. "And come on. We need to steal a car."

Chapter 21

Bradford Lawson felt like a new man. He didn't look like one, not yet, as the transerum was still healing the damage from the lightning strike. But large patches of burned flesh were sloughing from his face, falling like black dandruff into his lap. He could feel the same itch all over his body as his skin slowly regenerated.

The truck he'd stolen as a present for Jessa Bellamy handled beautifully, even when he drove it over a hundred miles an hour. And he had to, now that she was moving again. He'd hit the accelerator as soon as he'd felt the connection between them becoming weaker and thinner, and it was growing stronger. He was close enough now to taste the brightness of her fear.

She knew he couldn't stay away.

Jessa felt a little different now, too. Lawson wasn't sure if it was because he'd come back from the dead in a different phase of his transformation, or if she had changed from being in his presence. She had given him so much delight with her cringing and pleading in Savannah; he was sure that seeing him now would have her crawling to him to kiss his feet and beg for his forgiveness.

He'd make her kill her boyfriend first, he decided. Then he'd take her back to GenHance and have Genaro transform her into a suitable mate. One he could beat as much as he liked, and who would always heal, just as he did.

The goddess to his god.

A roadblock ahead made him press the air brakes and

coast to a stop behind a long line of cars. The unmarked cars and the big men in the dark suits looked like feds, Lawson thought, but they might be working for Genaro. Then he saw the silver BMW at the very front of the line and smiled.

There she is.

Lawson put the truck in reverse, smashing into the car behind him, before he shifted gears and plowed into the one ahead. The force of the truck hitting the station wagon sent it skittering into the next. He crashed through both and turned the wheel, going around the others and hitting two oncoming cars, flipping one and rolling the other into the shoulder.

He saw Jessa and her boyfriend climb out of the car and run, and stopped the truck just before it hit the barricade of unmarked cars. A cloud of black dust wafted from him as he jumped down.

"Sir." One of the big men came toward him and distracted him. "You'll have to move—"

Lawson took hold of the man's left arm, ripped it from his body, and used it to knock the head off his shoulders. He took a bite out of the arm before he dropped it and started after Jessa.

He had missed lunch and breakfast. Maybe he'd have Jessa feed her boyfriend to him instead.

The sky clouded overhead as Lucan's driver came to a stop.

"The roadblock is in place, my lord," the driver said. The sound of vehicles smashing together made him remove his shades and peer through the windshield. "There is a truck trying to drive through the stopped cars."

Sam felt Lawson before he climbed out of the tanker truck, and grabbed Lucan's arm. "That's him on the other side of the roadblock. The one in the truck." Her hand shook as she reached for her weapon.

"No, sweetheart," he told her, tugging her hand away. "This is my work." He took off his gloves and opened the door before he looked back at her. "If I fail, summon Richard. He will be the only one strong enough to stop him."

"Wait." She climbed out after him.

Lucan turned to thrust her back into the car; then they both heard the Kyn warrior cry out. Sam watched in disbelief as Lawson pulled off the Kyn's arm as if it were an insect wing and used it to decapitate him.

Lucan's eyes turned to chrome. "Stay here, Samantha." He strode past a man and a woman fleeing from Lawson.

Sam called to the two mortals to take cover, but a blue sedan screeched to a stop between them and the couple jumped into the backseat. The sedan spun around and sped away from the roadblock.

She turned at the sound of smashing glass and saw the windows of every car Lucan passed explode outward. Lawson, who was covered in some kind of black soot, stopped a few feet away from her lover.

"You're one of the old ones," she heard Lawson say. "I'm your new god."

"There is only one God," Lucan informed him pleasantly. "You are not Him."

Lawson lifted one of his hands, and a bolt of electricity shot out, hitting Lucan in the chest and sending him soaring backward to land on top of one of the cars, crushing the hood inward with the impact.

Sam pulled out her weapon and started to run.

Rowan looked back at them. "Are you okay?"

"Yes." Matthias put his arm around Jessa. "How did you know we would be on this road?"

"Sarah called Drew. My cell phone's history." Rowan turned her attention back to the road, but glanced in her rearview. "Who the hell was the guy shooting lightning out of his hands?"

"Lawson," Jessa said, her voice bleak. "He's coming after me again. GenHance did something to him, made him like us, and like the dark Kyn. And something else. Something worse."

"We passed a truck stop about two miles down the road," Drew said. "We should change cars there." He smiled at

Jessa. "Nice to meet you at last, Ms. Bellamy. You're even prettier in person."

Rowan made a rude sound. "Save it, Andrew. She's taken."

"Yes." Matthias turned to Jessa, who held his hand between hers. "She is."

Rowan eyed him in the mirror. "Was that GenHance with the roadblock back there?"

"No," Jessa said before he could reply. "They weren't GenHance or the police. That woman who got out of the car was wearing a gun in a holster, but she didn't dress like a cop. And that big man with the fair hair . . ." She gripped Matthias's hand. "This is going to sound a little strange, but when I passed him, I smelled flowers."

"Could be he was a florist," Drew suggested.

Rowan chuckled. "Or he likes wearing perfume."

Matthias knew the man and the woman had been dark Kyn, but he didn't want to frighten his friends or disturb Jessa. There would be time later, when they were safe, to speak of such matters. "Drew, what happened to Lawson to make him as he is now?"

"Evidently he broke into the lab at GenHance and injected himself with the transerum," the younger man told him. "He's pumped full of it now, and if it works the way Kirchner predicted, he'll be next to impossible to kill."

"He had fangs," Jessa said. "He also survived being electrocuted."

"That would mean he's mutated." Drew rubbed his eyes. "They haven't perfected the transerum yet. They were letting Lawson run around to see what effect it had on him."

"It turned him into a monster," Jessa said, shuddering. "He doesn't even look human anymore."

"What can kill him?" Matthias asked as Rowan pulled off into the truck stop.

"You have to separate the brain from the body to kill both," Drew said. "My guess is by decapitation, dismemberment, or ripping out his spine. Burning might work, too, but he'd have to be incinerated to ash."

Jessa stiffened. "He's getting closer, Gaven," she said in a low voice. "They weren't able to stop him."

Matthias scanned the parking lot. He spotted a welder's flatbed truck, which was stacked with pipes, and an old fueling station that had been boarded up and appeared unoccupied. He measured the distance from the fueling station to the diner.

"Rowan." He pointed. "Park the car over there."

Lucan heard Samantha screaming his name, and the sound of a truck engine. He rolled off the ruined hood of the vehicle just before the tanker smashed into it, shearing off the front end. From the ground he leaped up onto the side of the truck, wrenching open the passenger door.

Lawson turned, kicking at his face, and screamed as Lucan seized his leg. Before Lucan could do more than shatter the bones in it, the wounded man hit him with another burst of power, which knocked Lucan out of the cab and onto the road.

Lucan rolled to avoid the back wheels of the truck and staggered to his feet. The burns to his face and chest throbbed painfully as he watched the truck knock aside the cars his men had positioned to block the road, and heard the roar of the engine as Lawson accelerated.

"Lucan." Samantha reached him and grabbed his arms. "Your face."

He could feel the wounds healing. "It will pass." He turned to her. "Help the mortals who have been injured."

"You can't go after him."

"My talent shattered his leg. I can kill him." He bent and kissed her with his scorched lips. "Take care of the people here."

He took one of the cars Lawson had not destroyed, and followed after the tanker, trying to gain on it before Lawson reached a populated area. Fortunately the only dwellings Lucan saw ahead of them were a gas station and a restaurant, which he was sure Lawson would pass.

Sure until the tanker slowed, and then turned.

*   *   *

"It has to be me," Jessa said to Matthias after he told them about his plan. "I'm the one he wants."

He shook his head. "Sarah and Paul will be here soon. She will cast an illusion over me—"

"He'll reach us before they do." She looked at Drew. "Are you as fast as Rowan says? Can you pull me out in time?"

As he nodded, Rowan walked over to Matthias and held out her hand.

"It's my turn." When he didn't touch her, she wrapped her fingers around his wrist. "Queenie, in case you were wondering." Her body blurred, and when she turned around she was a mirror image of Jessa. "He really loves you."

"Rowan, I can't let you—" Jessa began, but the younger girl waved her hand.

"You don't get a vote. No one does. Like I said, my turn." Her gaze shifted as the sound of a truck braking drew their attention. "No more time to discuss it. He's here. Matthias, you've got the car. Drew, you'd better not miss this time."

"I won't." He sprinted off toward the welder's truck.

Matthias caught the keys Rowan tossed to him. "You will be careful."

"No." She grinned. "But I'll get him." She jogged off toward the fueling station before either of them could say another word.

Jessa stared after her. "She's one of the shape-shifters. I had no idea."

He tugged her arm. "Come. We must go to the car before he sees both of you."

The tanker slowly entered the drive into the truck stop, and coasted to a stop. Jessa crouched behind Rowan's car with Matthias and watched as the tanker slowly turned toward the fueling station, where Rowan, still in Jessa's form, stood between the pumps. The truck carrying the pipes backed in behind her, and Matthias opened the door to the car and started the engine.

Rowan walked forward until Lawson could see her

standing in the sunlight. With a grand sweep of her arm, she lifted her hand and flipped him her middle finger.

The tanker's engine gunned, and Lawson barreled toward her.

Lucan drove into the parking lot and saw Lawson driving the tanker toward a lone mortal female standing at the other end of the complex. He was too far behind to stop Lawson from running her down, and could only watch the woman die.

Before Lawson reached her, long copper pipes shot past her on either side, ramming through the windshield of the tanker and wrapping around the tires. If that were not unlikely enough, the pipes began to writhe like snakes and slither over the sides and roof of the tanker as it came to an abrupt stop.

Electricity crackled over the tanker's cab as Lawson forced open the driver's-side door and fell out of the truck. One of the pipes, embedded in his chest, came with him, and then wrapped around him like a boa, tightening until he threw out his arms and shrugged it off as if it were no more than paper ribbons.

Lucan got out of the car and started toward them, but stopped in his tracks as a sedan flashed past him. No one was driving it, but it was headed directly for the tanker, Lawson, and the woman.

"You have to stop running away from me, Jessa," Lawson said as he limped toward the girl, dragging his shattered leg along. "It's time for us to be together."

"Not in this lifetime, pal," Jessa said, taking a short pipe out of her jacket and holding the ends in her hands. She was jerked up into the air a moment before Lawson reached her, and flew over the fueling station just as the sedan hit the back of the tanker and burst into flames. The fire spread to the tanker, which was leaking fuel now on all sides.

White bolts of electricity flared all around Lawson, who shouted the girl's name as he turned, watching her float down next to the diner. Copper pipes crept up and wrapped themselves around his legs, holding him in place. "Come here, you bitch."

Lucan would never be sure what ignited the contents of the tanker—Lawson's power or the fire spreading from the sedan—but the truck exploded into a fireball that engulfed the fueling station and most of the lot around it, and blew out the windows of the diner and every vehicle in the lot by the diner. As burning fuel and parts of the tanker rained down, several cars parked on the far end of the lot caught fire as well.

A vague form struggled in the midst of the flames, and then fell to the ground, its lower limbs encased in melting copper.

Lucan saw no sign of the mortal female who had flown in the air, or what had caused the pipes to impale and imprison Lawson. What he felt was indefinable, unfamiliar. He would have said he sensed another Kyn nearby, but they were not Kyn. They were something else—and they were already gone.

He made sure none of the mortals was injured before he climbed back into the car and returned to the roadblock. Samantha ran to him before he could stop the car, and flung herself at him.

"Is he dead?"

He held her close. "This time, I believe he is." He saw an old pickup truck, driven by an older mortal with stooped shoulders, approaching the roadblock. His men glanced at the four dark-skinned farmhands sitting in the back and then waved them through. As the truck passed, the mortal's companion, a kind-faced woman, caught Lucan's gaze and did something that astonished him.

"What is it?" he heard Samantha ask.

"That mortal who just passed us," he told her. "She winked at me."

Epilogue

Lucan squinted as Alexandra Keller blinded him with her penlight. "That is beyond annoying."

"So are you," she said as she checked his other eye, "but somehow I manage not to stab you repeatedly in the heart with a copper dagger, no matter how often I am tempted." She stepped back and showed him three fingers. "How many do you see?"

He folded his arms. "Nine."

"Do you *want* me to check your retinas again?" she demanded. "I'll get the drops this time. I swear to God."

"Three."

"Thank you." She scribbled something on her notepad. "Well, suzerain, it looks like you're going to live. I'll break the news to the jardin gently."

"You have an evil heart. I have always loved that about you." Lucan pulled on his shirt and began buttoning it. "Was Michael able to learn more about the woman and her friends?"

"Not a lot," Alex said. "But Lawson's former employer, GenHance, was very interested in the remains we didn't recover from the wrecked sedan. They were expecting four bodies. They even gave us names."

"All adopted orphans, I imagine."

She nodded. "Looks like we missed meeting some Kyndred by the skin of your corneas. But our human friends in the FBI planted some cremated ash in the wreck and falsified a few documents, and that got the biotech corporation to back off. They think we recovered four bodies, all dead, with no viable DNA. That should give Michael some time to find out exactly who the bad guys are, what they're up to, and how much they were involved in what happened to Lawson."

"You did survey his remains?"

She nodded. "Nothing remarkable. Human, normal DNA, extra crispy. Not a trace of pathogen or augmented genes. Whatever was in him, whatever made him so lethal, was burned out by the fire. I'll continue studying the tissue samples from the remains of his victims. Maybe I'll find something to explain what he was, and how he got that way."

Samantha came into the office. "What's the verdict?"

"I did my best," Alex said as she closed her medical case, "but sorry; you're still stuck with him, honey."

"Could have been worse, I suppose. No, Lawson's dead." She laughed as Lucan nipped one of her fingers. "Cut it out. Alex, I can't find anything on Jessa Bellamy. She simply doesn't exist anymore; it's like she's been erased. If she and these other people involved in killing Lawson were Kyndred, they're very good at covering their tracks. As good as we are, I think."

"After what I saw them do," Lucan said, "I am not convinced we should be looking for them."

"I was Kyndred," Alex reminded him. "So was Samantha. We—they—may have been created by the Brethren for other reasons, but they are the only beings in this world like us. And if the Darkyn are going to survive, we have to find them."

Jonah Genaro stood outside the window to the lab as the latest acquisition was rolled in. Kirchner and two techs were busy hooking up monitors and adjusting the restraining straps, although the pitiful condition of the body in the glass coffin hardly merited either.

Beside him, Delaporte read from the crime scene report. "The remains of the four bodies in the sedan that hit the tanker were recovered. The consulting physician determined that they were too badly burned to offer any viable DNA."

"Why was a consultant brought in?"

His security chief flipped through the forms. "A Dr. Alexandra Keller. She's a reconstructive surgeon out of Chicago, doing a study on third-degree-burn patients. The FBI brought her in as a special consultant on the Lawson case. We barely had time to switch out Lawson's remains before Dr. Keller arrived."

Genaro nodded. "Riordan?"

"Still at large, but he should surface sometime in the near future. We weren't able to recover anything from his apartment, but along with the criminal charges we've filed, we've emptied his accounts and destroyed his credit. After what he did to our men in the park, I've issued orders to shoot him on sight." Delaporte gave him an uneasy look. "I hope you agree that's the best approach to take with this one."

"Agreed. File the reports and keep me updated." After Delaporte left, Genaro switched on the intercom. "Have you performed the microcellular tests?"

"As soon as it was delivered from the morgue." Kirchner's iron gray hair badly needed a trim, as it flopped over his glasses. "Cellular regeneration has begun on a limited level, as you can see from the eyes, but there isn't enough body mass to sustain it. If you want to keep it alive, we'll have to augment."

"No, that will not be necessary." Genaro studied his greatest failure. The black, twisted form appeared to be little more than a mound of charcoal sticks with eyes, which were open and staring up at Genaro's face. "Will it take much longer for his tissue to begin regenerating?"

"I doubt it, sir." The geneticist checked the preservation unit's LED display. "BP and heart rate are beginning to rise. Brain activity indicates consciousness as well. Once I've completed the physical and neurological exams, we can begin harvesting."

Genaro watched as the thing in the coffin opened the hole that remained of its mouth in a soundless scream. It was evident that what remained of Bradford Lawson could not only see, but could hear as well. "Excellent. Be sure when you've recovered the cells to dismember the remains before you incinerate them."

He turned his back on the window and walked away.

Rowan shut off the lights in the bare kitchen and came out into the tunnel in time to bump into Drew, who was hauling out the last of the computer equipment.

"You're really going to take all that crap with you to California?" she asked as she followed him out. "Why not buy new stuff when you get there?"

"If you're looking for a fugitive computer genius who just lost all his tech," he told her, "one way to find him is to monitor specific equipment purchases." He stepped aside so she could open the hatch to the stairs. "Plus I installed a duplicate setup over at the farm. The boss doesn't need it anymore."

Rowan remembered something Matthias did need, and turned around. "I've gotta grab something. I'll meet you at the car."

When Rowan caught up with Drew, she pushed a book into his hands. "Here. Put this in with your stuff."

"I didn't get you anything." Drew held it up so he could read the cover in the streetlight. "Gourmet Cooking for Two. Hell, Rowan, why don't you just go with me?"

She grinned. "You couldn't pay me to move to California, pal. I'm heading north, back to egg creams and civilization."

Drew tucked the book in the back of his car. "Oh, wait. I do have something for you." He turned around and caught her in a clinch so fast Rowan had time only to take the kiss that came with it.

"There. We're even." He set her back on her feet and dodged her swat. "Take care of yourself, baby girl."

"Bastard." She gave him a hard hug before she stalked off.

Matt had insisted on buying her a new bike to replace the one she'd ditched in Atlanta, and she hadn't refused. She was never going to be a car chick, and she needed to be on the move again. The boss had already set up a guest room for her, and Jessa had practically begged her to stay with them, but while Rowan could be a good sport, she wasn't a masochist.

Somewhere out there is someone for me, she thought as she straddled her bike. *Someone who doesn't want a goddess. Someone who will never, ever eat a Filet-O-Fish in front of me.*

"Yeah, right," she answered herself. "But how will I know for sure?"

Drew pulled to a stop by her bike in time to hear her. "Know what?"

"How does someone like me know if any guy really cares?" she said without thinking.

"That's easy." He smiled. "When he holds your hand, you won't change into Angelina Jolie." He waved and took off.

She watched his taillights disappear, and laughed all the way to the interstate.

Rowan rode through the night, and arrived in Tennessee just after dawn. She made her way across fields and down dirt roads that didn't exist on any map except the one in her head. Another hour passed before she arrived at the gates to the sprawling grounds of the farm.

Matthias had planted so many trees around the house she could hardly see it from the road. A small intercom next to the locked gates invited her to press its buttons, but as she looked out over the acres of good, rich soil waiting to be planted, she dropped her kickstand and got off the bike.

Before leaving Savannah, she had gathered a few things for them and bundled everything up in her favorite tablecloth. Now she tucked in a hastily written note and left it at the foot of the gates. With one last, long look at her friends' home, she strapped her bundle to the back of her bike, got on, pressed the call button at the gate, and took off, heading north toward her future.

Jessa woke to the sound of Matthias getting dressed. She stretched with the pleasure of a cat before she pulled off the covers and joined him.

"Someone is at the gate," he said before he kissed her. "It is probably Rowan. Go back to bed."

"I spend too much time in this bed already," she teased as she went to the closet they shared and took out a pair of faded jeans and a suede blouse. "You are going to talk her into staying with us, I hope. She won't listen to me."

He nodded. "I will bribe her. She cannot resist organic plums."

When they walked down to the gate, Jessa saw no Rowan, only an oddly shaped red-and-white-checked bundle sitting outside the gates. Matthias opened the doors and then picked up the heavy bundle, untying the knot to reveal a blue teddy bear, the bronze sword from his library, and a folded piece of paper.

He read the note and then looked out at the road. "She said she could not bring herself to tell you."

"Tell me what?"

He handed her the note.

Matt and Jessa,

The bear is for the baby, not the blade. I wish I could stay, but I have to find someone. Drew told me how to look for him. I'll be in touch.

Jessa, I have a bigger surprise for you. And we'll talk about it the next time I call. Just remember, whatever names we use, we're still friends. No matter what.

Love,
Aphrodite

Jessa felt shocked and confused and elated, all at the same time. "Rowan is my best friend," she said helplessly.

"And mine." He kissed her brow.

"We have to find her. I mean . . ." She made a frustrated gesture. "How could she write this and then just leave?"

"She will return someday, when she has found what she is looking for." He looked out at the road again, and put his arm around her. "Now come. *I* have not spent enough time in that bed with you."

Read on for an excerpt from
Lynn Viehl's next Novel of the Kyndred,

Dreamveil

"So I do not salt the eggplant or the zucchini," Bernard said, "or cook in separate pots. Chef, this is America, not Nice. Everything here . . . it is quick. No one could tell a difference."

Jean-Marc Dansant turned away from his sous-chef, mainly to keep from throttling him. "I could tell."

"The fat woman no complain or send it back. She no care." Bernard threw out his hands in his favorite gesture, a combination of frustration and helplessness. "It was fine. The best . . ." He paused as he groped for the correct English, but failed. "The best *courgettes á la Niçoise* I make."

"*Naturellement.*" He removed his white jacket and tossed it in the laundry bin. "The problem, Bernard, is that she ordered ratatouille."

"*Je m'en fiche.*" His sous-chef stalked out of the back door. A few moments later the sound of squealing brakes and crashing metal came from the alley.

Dansant didn't feel alarmed by the noise. No doubt his sous-chef had knocked over the garbage bins again with his car. Bernard in a temper was nothing if not predictable. After inspecting the immaculate kitchen for the last time, Dansant shut off the lights and went out into the alley to survey the mess.

He expected the smell of garbage and the sight of it spread from one side of the alley to the other. He did not expect to see a motorcycle lying on the ground in front of Bernard's Volvo, or his sous-chef standing over a tall, skinny boy whose leather garments were badly scuffed. The biker removed his helmet, and from under a mop of disheveled dark curls revealed the thin, furious face of a dark-eyed, pale ... young woman.

In profile she was all angular bone and creamy white skin, the stately line of her nose at odds with the decadent contours of her mouth and the stubborn set of her jaw.

"Bernard," Dansant spoke sharply to cut off the sous-chef's stream of obscenities in their native language.

His voice drew the girl's attention for a moment, and he saw that her lashes were like her hair—black, thick, and curly. They framed eyes that seemed too dark to be so bright. She stiffened, as if bracing herself for more trouble, and then saw his face. Whatever she saw made her body change, and she shifted, moving as if she meant to come to him.

Dansant understood; the feelings rising inside him made nothing in that moment more important than going to her. "Did you knock her down?" he asked Bernard without looking at him.

"*Non.* She crash into my car." He stabbed a finger at the motorcycle. "Look at the bumper, the grille. They are ruin." He turned his finger on the girl. "You pay for this."

Bernard had to repeat his demand for payment twice more before the girl heard him and turned to face him. "The hell I will. You shouldn't be parked out here in the dark. It's illegal and dangerous."

Hearing her speak made Dansant's situation worse. The girl's low voice had a faint rasp to it, and brushed against his ears like a silk cord. Silk—yes, that would suit her more than her boyish leather. He imagined wrapping her in yards of scarlet and gold, weaving it around the length of her torso, coiling it along her long limbs, knotting it so that her hands were bound to his, so everywhere he touched her she would feel it twice, on her body and against her slim fingers. ...

Never had he thought such things about a woman, Dansant reflected, appalled. Not even with Gisele.

How could she do this to him, this girl? She'd barely glanced at him, and he was ready to grab her and drag her inside and lay her out on the closest flat surface.

He breathed in deeply, hoping the stench of the alley would clear his head, but smelled a familiar coppery scent. At last he saw more than her eyes, her face. Her gloves were in shreds, and both of her knees showed, scratched and bloodied, through tears in her trousers.

Here she was hurt, in pain, and all he'd thought of was having her for his pleasure. He was no better than the idiot berating her.

"I work here," Bernard was telling her. "I park here every night. Bah." He pulled out his wallet and offered her an insurance card. "You give me yours."

"I'm not responsible. Someone hit me from behind." The girl ignored the card, hobbled slowly to where the motorcycle lay beside the car, and crouched down. She ran her hand over one misshapen tire, then the other. "Damn it, they're both blown."

"Miss. *Miss.*" When she didn't respond, Bernard stalked over to her. "We call the insurance; let them say who pay."

She bent over to look under the car. "I don't have any."

His sous-chef did the same. "What do you say?"

"Insurance." She stood, bracing one hand against the hood of the Volvo to steady herself. "I don't carry any on my bike."

"So now *I* must pay for everything. Such convenience for you." Bernard straightened and took out his mobile. "I call police now."

"Wait a minute." She gave Bernard her full attention. "There's no need to get the police involved. We can work this out between the two of us."

She tried to sound more amicable, but for the first time Dansant caught a glimpse of fear in her eyes, and moved quickly over to stand beside her.

"I am French," Bernard informed her before Dansant could say a word, "no stupid. I know your game. You crash into my car on purpose, force me to give you money."

"No, Bernard," Dansant told him. "Clearly it was an accident." And if the man didn't soon shut up, Dansant was almost certain he was going to beat him senseless.

His sous-chef folded his arms. "She is scumming me."

"Scamming," she corrected. "And no, I'm not doing that. Look, this was an accident; that's all. Why don't we just call it even and walk away?"

"You ruin my car. You have no insurance. You are no walking away." Bernard began to dial his phone.

"Ta gueule." Dansant took out his wallet, eyed the car, and removed a handful of hundreds, which he put in the sous-chef's soft hand. "This will pay for the damages, plus two weeks' pay."

"Chef." Bernard frowned at the money. "I do not need my pay tonight."

"Yes, you do. You're fired. Good-bye, Bernard." Dansant turned to the girl, who stared at him with visible disbelief. Over Bernard's sputtering, he said, "You are hurt, but I can help you. Come with me."

"I'll be fine, thanks." She seemed genuinely unconcerned about her injuries. "Who are you?"

"Jean-Marc Dansant. I own this restaurant. Come, mademoiselle." He took her arm, and when she pulled back, he gestured at her knees. "Look there; you are bleeding. I have a first-aid kit inside."

"My name is Rowan." She turned her head. "My bike—"

"It cannot be taken, not as it is now," he assured her.

Rowan stared at the hand on her arm, and then into his eyes. "Why are you doing this? You don't know me."

She is afraid—of me?

"Oui." He didn't have the words to tell her, not yet. Not when he didn't understand what was pulling him to her. Whatever it was, he could not let it vanish into the night. He released her as he tried to think of something to say. "It is the kindness of a stranger, yes?"

"Not something I usually depend on." Rowan looked down at herself and sighed. "But I do need to clean up."

He clenched his teeth as images of his hands undressing her and washing her filled his mind. "Then come inside with me, please." He offered her his hand this time, and, after a long, silent moment, she took it.

"Jamais dans ma vie," Bernard called after them as

Dansant guided her through the kitchen door and into the restaurant. "You be sorry you fire me. I am best sous-chef in—"

Fortunately the heavy steel door cut off the rest of what he shouted.

"Wait, please." Dansant left her by the long prep table and retrieved the first-aid kit from the dry-storage room. When he returned she had stripped off her jacket and the shreds of her gloves, and was washing her hands at the rinsing sink beside the industrial dishwasher. Under a black T-shirt she wore a long-sleeved white thermal, the cuffs of which were stained red with blood.

For the first time he realized how very tall she was—only an inch or two shorter than he was—and how perfectly her long body would fit to his. He'd never made love to a woman who matched him physically. Nor would he if he left her standing and bleeding in his kitchen while he indulged in such fantasies.

"Let me see," he said as he put the kit on the sideboard.

"They're not too bad. My gloves took the worst of it." She showed him her grazed, reddened palms before looking down. "My knees are a mess, though."

Dansant pulled an empty crate over to the table. "Sit here."

She didn't move. "Thanks, but I think I can do this by myself."

Dansant removed some gauze pads and a small bottle of peroxide from the kit. "You are still shaken, *ma mûre*."

She limped over to the crate and perched on it. "So, are you usually this kind to strangers?" Before he could answer, she added, "I'm not going to sue, if that's what you're worried about."

That she thought of herself as a stranger to him was perplexing. From the moment he'd seen her face, he'd known her. Not who she was or why she had come to him now, but everything that mattered between a man and a woman. All he had to do was be patient and wait for her to give herself over to him. Then he would show her they were meant to be together.

Doesn't she feel it?

"I do not worry about this." He knelt before her to inspect the damage to her knees. "There is debris in the wounds. From the ground." He would need scissors to cut away her trousers legs. "I must remove it."

As soon as he put his hand on her leg, Rowan stiffened. "I don't think so."

He glanced up. "You do not like to be touched."

"Oh, sometimes I like it fine." She stared at his mouth before lifting her eyes to his, and he saw a glimmer of heat and longing. "It's the stranger part I have trouble with."

"So do I." More than he could ever tell her. "Perhaps just for tonight, we should think we are friends."

"Friends." She seemed amused by this, but leaned back on her elbows. "All right, Dansant. Do whatever you want."